J. M. COETZEE

and the Idea of the Public Intellectual

J. M. COETZEE

and the Idea of the Public Intellectual

edited by Jane Poyner

OHIO UNIVERSITY PRESS

ATHENS

Ohio University Press, Athens, Ohio 45701
www.ohio.edu/oupress
© 2006 by Ohio University Press

The following chapters have been revised from previously published material:

Chapter 2, by Peter D. McDonald, in *Book History* 7 (2004): 285–302. Reprinted by permission of Penn State Press and the Society for the History of Authorship, Reading and Publishing.

Chapter 3, by Derek Attridge, in *J. M. Coetzee and the Ethics of Reading: Literature in the Event* (Chicago: University of Chicago Press; Scottsville: University of KwaZulu-Natal Press, 2004). © 2004 by The University of Chicago. All rights reserved.

Chapter 7, by Elleke Boehmer, in "J. M. Coetzee's *Disgrace*," ed. Derek Attridge and Peter D. McDonald, special issue, *Interventions* 4, no. 3 (2002): 342–51.

Chapter 10, by Laura Wright, in *Writing "Out of All the Camps": J. M. Coetzee's Narratives of Displacement,* by Laura Wright, 109–19 (New York: Routledge, 2006).

Ohio University Press books are printed on acid-free paper ∞ ™

12 11 10 09 08 07 06 05   5 4 3 2 1

Library of Congress Cataloging-in-Publication Data

J.M. Coetzee and the idea of the public intellectual / edited by Jane Poyner.
   p. cm.
Includes bibliographical references and index.
ISBN-13: 978-0-8214-1686-0 (alk. paper)
ISBN-10: 0-8214-1686-3 (alk. paper)
ISBN-13: 978-0-8214-1687-7 (pbk. : alk. paper)
ISBN-10: 0-8214-1687-1 (pbk. : alk. paper)
   1. Coetzee, J. M., 1940—Criticism and interpretation. 2. Politics and literature—South Africa—History—20th century. 3. South Africa—In literature. 4. Animal rights. I. Poyner, Jane.
   PR9369.3.C58Z54 2006
   823'.914—dc22

CONTENTS

ACKNOWLEDGMENTS

I wish to thank Benita Parry for her tireless support during the preparation of this volume, for her intellectual input into the work, and for her inspiration. Michael Bell, Neil Lazarus, and Rashmi Varma generously offered themselves as readers and advisers, for which I am very grateful.

I would like to thank each of the contributors for their hard work and enthusiasm for the project. Many thanks to J. M. Coetzee for agreeing to be interviewed. I would like to acknowledge Gillian Berchowitz and John Morris at Ohio University Press for advocating this project, and Carolyn Sherayko for preparing the index.

The Humanities Research Centre and the Centre for Research in Philosophy and Literature at the University of Warwick, as well as the British Academy, made possible the conference at which the ideas for the volume began to take shape.

I wish to thank my wonderful—and very significant—family: Liz, John, Cliff, Jill, Cathy, John, Teresa, Sarah, Chris, Rachel, Kerry, Ewan, Grace, Esmé, Rory, Anna, Isobel, Joe, Mark, Jack, Oliver, Ella, and George. Above all, special thanks go to my mother and to Mehdi, for everything.

J. M. COETZEE

and the Idea of the Public Intellectual

INTRODUCTION

Jane Poyner

[A]ll men are intellectuals, all men do not have the function of intellectuals in society.

—Antonio Gramsci, *Prison Notebooks*

I

It would not be an overstatement to say that J. M. Coetzee is one of the most influential novelists of the twentieth and twenty-first centuries, as evidenced by the burgeoning scholarship generated by his writing both in South Africa and internationally, as well as by his growing lay readership and the intense interest in his private persona (ironic, in part, because he resists this attention, for he is a writer who is known to be doggedly reserved). His work has been lavished with literary awards, including South Africa's prestigious CNA Prize. He was the first novelist to win the Booker Prize twice, and in 2003 he was made the Nobel Laureate in Literature.

By engaging self-consciously with the ethics of writing in his critical essays and all his works of fiction, often through the portrayal of the conscience-stricken white writer, Coetzee has chosen to enter the long-running and expansive debate about the ethics of intellectualism and the authority of the writer. By so doing, he deliberately places himself in the public domain, if one understands writing as necessarily a public activity. This concern for intellectualism reaches its apogee in Coetzee's uncanny performance of his fictional alter ego Elizabeth Costello in a series of lectures he gave in the United States on ethical issues such as animal rights and the nature of evil (published subsequently in *The Lives of Animals* [1999] and then *Elizabeth Costello* [2003]), which have left critics bewildered in their attempts to untangle Coetzee's and Costello's points of view. Each of Coetzee's novels portrays a (troubled) writer-figure or intellectual, albeit, in a number of the texts, only on the most minimal, symbolic level.[1] Similarly, Coetzee's nonfiction is marked by its concern for intellectual practice.[2] In *Giving Offense: Essays on Censorship* (1996), for instance, in the chapter titled "Taking Offense," he outlines a model of the ideal intellectual, with whom he finds himself identifying:

> Complacent and yet not complacent, intellectuals[,] pointing to the Apollonian "Know yourself," criticize and encourage criticism of the foundations of their own belief systems. Such is their confidence that they may even welcome attacks on themselves, smiling when they are caricatured and insulted, responding with the keenest appreciation to the most probing, most perceptive thrusts. They particularly welcome accounts of their enterprise that attempt to relativize it, read it within a cultural and historical framework. They welcome such accounts and at once set about framing them in turn within the project of rationality, that is, set about recuperating them. (4)

The intellectual, as Coetzee suggests, in supporting his or her own position with reasoned and rationed argument, is ready to accept the reasoned and rationed criticism of fellow intellectuals (and others), indeed, sees this as his or her social function: to criticize and be criticized while, importantly, imparting expertise or knowledge with the purpose of effecting change. In light of the above comments, it surely must be deemed ironic that it was criticism of Coetzee's novel *Disgrace* (1999), which depicts black-on-white rape at a time when rape is endemic in South Africa, that may have precipitated his departure from Cape Town to Adelaide, Australia, in 2002, where he now lives.

The "purpose of effecting change" is the concern of the essays contained in the present volume, since the ethical responsibilities of the writer are what preoccupies Coetzee in all of his novels. By taking stock of the contribution made by Coetzee to literature and to postcolonial and sociocultural theory, this is the first collection of essays on the author to address a specific theme, the ethics of intellectual practice, in recognition of Coetzee's continued concern for the debates around writing and intellectual history. Until recently, such concerns were generated in the oeuvre from postcolonial or South African paradigms. Moving in general chronologically through the novels, the essays variously take account of the impact Coetzee has had on South African literature and postcolonial and cultural studies, as well as his sustained interest in European modernism and philosophical thinking.

II

Coetzee's sociocultural heritage, his positioning on the peripheries of the Afrikaner community and, despite his sympathies with the Left, his profound suspicion of political rhetoric per se, have led to his sense of marginalization within South Africa and have, in turn, informed his ethics of intellectualism.[3] Born in 1940 in Cape Town, English was the language he spoke at home—signifying his linguistic dislocation from Afrikaner society —and he spent part of his childhood in Worcester, South Africa (1948–51). The family returned to Cape Town when Coetzee was in his teens, where as a Protestant he attended a Catholic high school—again compounding his sense of alienation from the community in which he found himself.[4]

Peculiar for what might loosely be termed a "progressive" South African novelist and intellectual writing during, and post-, apartheid, and jarring with his carefully staged public intellectualism, is Coetzee's well-known aversion to political discourse at a time when key political organizations like the ANC were advocating the use of politically committed literature as a "weapon of the struggle."[5] In Coetzee's reading of Nadine Gordimer's intellectual work in *The Essential Gesture* (the title alludes to engaged writing), he aligns himself with Gordimer's suspicion of an "orthodoxy of opposition."[6] Gordimer is of course a very different kind of intellectual and novelist from Coetzee: always more outspoken in her political commentary and engaged in her art, she has explicitly aligned herself with the Left and with the ANC, though her position on the use of violence in South Africa's resistance movement has shifted during the course of her career.

The essays in this volume will show that there is a tension in Coetzee's writing—both his fiction and essays—between the private and public spheres, a tension that is fervently contested amongst his readers and critics. Known to be a fiercely private individual who spurns media attention, Coetzee rarely gives interviews, and those he does give are characterized by his evasiveness and circumspection. Take, for instance, the interview that opens this volume, or consider the notorious correspondence between Philip R. Wood and Coetzee, published in a special issue of *South Atlantic Quarterly* (1994), in which Coetzee's taciturn responses make the lengthy questions of his interviewer look vaguely ridiculous.[7]

Indeed, Coetzee is criticized frequently for his elusiveness or silence on matters of politics and, similarly, for the opacity of his fiction. His memoirs, *Boyhood* (1997) and *Youth* (2002), are remarkable for their presentation of their protagonist "Coetzee" in the third person, a device that allows author to distance himself from character in his story and, in some senses, allows Coetzee to abnegate responsibility for his actions. (In fiction, of course, we are required not to equate the author with the characters he or she creates.) In *Youth,* for example, the Dostoevskian antihero "Coetzee" engages in a tawdry love affair, in part, he tells us candidly, to furnish his fiction more colorfully. While showing a deep lack of humanity for the woman "Coetzee" encounters, at the same time he (Coetzee/"Coetzee"?) identifies the silencing effects on the political climate in South Africa of what Gordimer calls "responsibility as orthodoxy": "There is more to the sorry business, however, than just the shame of it. He has come to London *to do what is impossible in South Africa: to explore the depths.* Without descending into the depths one cannot be an artist" (131) (italics mine).[8] In this respect, however, living out his ethics of intellectualism, Coetzee resembles many of the fictional characters he portrays, who maintain their silence as a means of symbolically eluding interpretation or being read, and thereby resisting domination. Both in life and in his fiction, for Coetzee silence represents the freedom and autonomy of the intellectual and points up his or her integrity as a purveyor of truths (in *Doubling the Point* he claims expansively that "[t]he only truth is silence" [286]). In other words, as the essays that follow will demonstrate, the apparently paradoxical nature of Coetzee's work—his insistence on fleshing out debates about the role of the intellectual while at the same time refusing to make his politics explicitly or publicly known—constitutes his scrupulously orchestrated ethical position. In the opening chapters of this book, David Attwell argues that Coetzee successfully occupies this seemingly paradoxical position, while Peter McDonald suggests that, though Coetzee clearly objected to the censorship laws governing fiction during the apartheid era, his writing sometimes inadvertently reinforces the polarity between aesthetics and politics that he wanted to undo.[9]

At the same time, and somewhat problematically, Coetzee, as a reviewer in venues such as the *New York Review of Books,* is less than circumspect in his opinions and in making his dispositions and opinions known. Indeed, one could map his stances on matters political and ethical from these reviews. Here, for example, we see a characteristic disdain for the public role expected of writers by society:

> The Nobel Prize for literature, awarded for 1949, presented in 1950, made Faulkner famous, even in America. Tourists came from far and wide to gawk at his house in Oxford, to his vast irritation. Reluctantly he emerged from the shadows and began to behave like a public figure. From the State Department came invitations to go abroad as a cultural ambassador, which he dubiously accepted. Nervous before the microphone, even more nervous fielding "literary" questions, he prepared for sessions by drinking heavily. But once he had developed a patter to cope with journalists, he grew more comfortable with the role. ("Making of William Faulkner")

That he makes controversial public interventions on the one hand yet shirks publicity on the other—moreover, that he seemingly holds his critics in contempt—begs the question: is Coetzee guilty of wanting to have his cake and eat it?

III

To what extent, we might ask, can a highly private writer like Coetzee be said to be an intellectual? Antonio Gramsci's distinction between the traditional and the organic intellectual is called to mind: while the traditional intellectual is free-floating and, perhaps, construed as remote and confined to the ivory tower, the organic intellectual responds to specific conditions in a role akin to political activism. In chapter 1 Attwell identifies the typical association made between the traditional intellectual and the private sphere, and the organic and the political. He goes on to examine the tension between the positions of public and private that Coetzee would seem to occupy, and asks whether there is a conflict of interests here. Attwell proposes that if the public sphere can only admit the political intellectual and therefore only the political should seek entry, "then Coetzee is surely at liberty to suggest that if the conventions of the public sphere are to be treated as sacrosanct, then it should not make demands on those writers who might expose their arbitrariness."

The term "intellectual" was popularized by the Dreyfus affair in late-nineteenth-century France.[10] The Jewish Captain Albert Dreyfus, accused of treason, expelled from the French army, and incarcerated in the notorious Devil's Island penal colony, was famously defended by Émile Zola in "J'accuse," his open letter to the French president.[11] Zola and a number of fellow writers, by speaking out publicly in support of Dreyfus against the anti-Semitic railings of the Right, standing for universal notions of truth and justice, undaunted by the opposition this would unleash, took upon themselves the duties of the public intellectual. Coetzee explicitly invokes the affair in *Age of Iron* through Mrs. Curren's condemnation of the apartheid state (127), and again in *Disgrace* when Professor David Lurie, after being disciplined by his university for an affair with a young student, implicitly aligns himself (with a pretense to martyrdom) with the persecuted Dreyfus (40). Initially an advocate of Dreyfus, Julien Benda reentered the fray in the 1920s with his well-known *La trahison des clercs* (1927), a polemic, informed by the affair, in which Benda argues that the intellectual must maintain independence from all organized social bodies, especially political ones, in order to speak the truth to power.

The literary critic and public intellectual Edward Said reinvigorated the debate in his 1993 Reith Lectures *Representations of the Intellectual* (the point at which Attwell opens his discussion of Coetzee by situating him within the question "What is the public intellectual?"). Said, while rightly identifying an underlying conservatism in Benda's study, in part adopts his position: the intellectual should ideally remain amateur rather than expert since the expert is necessarily partial—itself a kind of untruth since partiality and expertise require the manipulation of truths into particular agendas (7).[12] For Said, the role of the intellectual is public critic, which can only be achieved effectively through such distancing. He considers

> whether there is or can be anything like an independent, autonomously functioning intellectual, one who is not beholden to, and therefore constrained, by [*sic*] his or her affiliations with universities that pay salaries, political parties that demand loyalty to a party line, think tanks that while they offer freedom to do research perhaps more subtly compromise judgement and restrain the critical voice. As [Régis] Debray suggests, once an intellectual's circle is widened beyond a like group of intellectuals—in other words, when worry about pleasing an audience or an employer replaces dependence on other intellectuals for debate and judgement—something in the intellectual's vocation is, if not abrogated, then certainly inhibited. (*Representations*, 51)

Attwell, in chapter 1, is particularly concerned with the notion of publicity: by entering the public domain, making public interventions, does an author have a responsibility to that public? For Attwell, Coetzee's fiction portrays the very ethical writing and reading practices which the author himself resists, thereby making complex the tensions between his private and public personae.

In chapter 2 Peter McDonald turns to "The Novel Today" (1988), one of Coetzee's major public interventions on the ethics of intellectual practice, in which Coetzee champions the novel as a rival rather than a supplement to the discourse of history. While McDonald recognizes that in this talk Coetzee is not advocating literature that is abstracted from the political, he suggests that Coetzee inadvertently reinforces the polarity of the discourses of politics and art, and thus to some degree plays into the hands of the censors, to whom, he makes clear, he is opposed. Canonical works, McDonald argues, were viewed by the censors in apartheid South Africa as being of a higher order than political discourse—which would account for Coetzee's fiction evading the censor.

IV

The debate over the social role of the intellectual has a long history, from Aristotle and Socrates to Edward Said, Ngugi, Arundhati Roy, and Wole Soyinka. In South Africa, under the conditions of colonialism and then apartheid, it is particularly urgent. Writing and intellectualism in these contexts have been profoundly politicized; indeed, punitive and prohibitive measures were written into the apartheid constitution. The Afrikaner National Party, which displaced the Smuts regime in 1948, outlawed oppositional groups such as the ANC; banned, exiled, and murdered numbers of those opposed to the regime; instituted widespread and draconian censorship; and prohibited sexual relations across the "colour line." All these measures were overseen by a violently oppressive secret police who were implicated in a number of murders of prominent political activists, most notably Steve Biko in 1977.[13]

Black writing, in the politically inclusive sense,[14] suffered particularly under colonialism and apartheid. As Coetzee has shown in *White Writing* (1988), oral narratives in the nineteenth and early twentieth centuries were suppressed or misrepresented by white colonials. Black writers, until recently, were largely denied access to higher education and were thus excluded from current literary debates, while their writing, which was often censored, has been dismissed by some recent critics as rudimentary in style and essentialist in content.[15] These factors made the responsibility and accountability of the white intellectual and writer more pressing and complex: how were white intellectuals and authors to represent others' stories without exercising an ethically dubious authority over them? Writers like Coetzee, André Brink, Breyten Breytenbach, Athol Fugard, and Nadine Gordimer—all of whom are white—have been attentive to the privileges their racial identity necessarily accorded them,[16] and their work has circled around the experience and concerns of writing under an oppressive regime and of representing racial alterity.

The egregious oppression of South Africa's black peoples and the responsibilities felt by oppositional South African writers, black and white, were the driving force behind the movement for committed literature, a site of contest that in large part Coetzee has shirked. In order to achieve "relevance and commitment"—the criteria in Gordimer's model outlined in *The Essential Gesture*—resistance literature typically embraced a social realist mode, engaging in Gordimer's case with a sophisticated Lukacsian model. Other "committed'" novelists have been more experimental. The creative writer and cultural critic Njabulo Ndebele, for instance, calls for a "rediscovery of the ordinary" in what constitutes for some commentators a hybrid, postmodern style: black South African writers, he insists, should reappropriate the folk and pop art of the townships as a means of resisting the commonplace opposition of people and state, in other words, bypassing dominant grand narratives. In another vein, critics such as Neil Lazarus have recognised the ethical content—and thus the *usefulness*—of modernist writing. "Contemporary white South African literature," Lazarus argues, "must now be defined not only by its negativity, but also by its marginality and acute self-consciousness." Commenting on recent white South African writing, including Coetzee's modernist aesthetic, and dismissing the appropriateness of a postmodern critical model, he goes on:

And one is tempted to ask whether a literature displaying these characteristics, and written after—and frequently even in the idiom of—Kafka and Beckett and, for that matter, Kundera, could be anything other than modernist; especially when it is borne in mind that as a discourse it is so *ethically* saturated, so *humanistic* in its critique of the established order, so concerned to represent *reality*, and so *rationalistic* that it would be quite inappropriate to describe it as postmodernist. ("Modernism and Modernity," 148)

Attwell, in his monograph on Coetzee's early work up to *Age of Iron*, takes Lazarus to task over his rejection of postmodernist critiques of white South African writing, suggesting that, in Coetzee's case, the "problem . . . is to understand [Coetzee's] postmodernism in the light of his postcoloniality."'[17]

Drawing upon the work of Linda Hutcheon on the "politics of postmodernism,"[18] Attwell continues, "I share Lazarus's appreciation of the ethical value of this writing, but what is puzzling is his insistence that it would be impossible for postmodernism *in any form* to achieve an ethical stance" (21).

In *Doubling the Point* Coetzee distances himself from the trend in writing he refers to as "radical metafiction," which, he says, is in danger of "swallowing its own tail" (204, 86). This comment is curious given Coetzee's own acutely metafictional style, exemplified in novels like *Foe, The Master of Petersburg,* and, most recently, *Elizabeth Costello,* yet its sentiment—its disavowal of navel gazing in art and criticism—is indicative of the ethical motivations evident throughout his oeuvre.

Because Coetzee returns repeatedly to the metafictional trope of the conscience-stricken author-figure or intellectual, and because his fiction is so theoretically informed, literary critics have often engaged in highly textual, often poststructuralist, readings of the work.[19] It is noteworthy, therefore, that Derek Attridge, who is known for his engagement with deconstruction, especially of a Derridian mode, questions (in chapter 3 of this volume) the reliability of these highly textual readings of Coetzee. Addressing the very private activity of fiction reading (in contrast to Attwell and McDonald, whose concern is primarily with the public domain), his essay reveals his discomfort in particular with reading Coetzee allegorically—a mode that has become the signature of Coetzee criticism. Attridge suggests that reading in this way can often divert attention from what is significant about a literary work *as a literary work:* a literal reading is a reading that resists the various temptations to move away from the experience of the work to meanings of a fixed kind, whether historical, moral, or political. Coetzee's work, Attridge suggests, is particularly valuable in considering this issue, since it states the process of allegorizing without becoming allegory—or if it is allegory, it is a type that has escaped the fixity characteristic of traditional uses of the mode. According to Attridge, the event of the reading—in which meanings are performed, or better, the process of meaning is performed, but not solidified—is more complex than any meanings that can be derived from it. Ultimately, the peculiar inventiveness and singularity of Coetzee's fiction, for Attridge, lies in its resistance to such nonliterary uses and in its invitation to the reader to experience an alterity that cannot be domesticated. (It is this mode of reading that Dominic Head takes up in chapter 5.)

Michael Marais, in chapter 4, suggests that there is an ethical process ongoing in Coetzee's fiction that intentionally distances the texts from history, in what constitutes effectively a break from the public. Marais argues that any ethical claim about literary writing rests on a range of assumptions about the way in which texts relate to history. Referring to the novel *The Master of Petersburg* and through it the trope of death, Marais examines Coetzee's questioning of standard assumptions on the nature of this relation, and goes on to argue that Coetzee's fiction self-consciously prioritizes the literary text's relation to an otherness beyond history.

Literary critics have tried to anticipate the shifts in form and content of the literature of South Africa now that apartheid is over. To what extent do novelists engage with the ethical writing practices advocated by the movement for committed literature? Has the end of apartheid opened new paths in fiction and signaled more experimental forms in which to present them? Negotiating the realms of the private and public spheres, as we might say Coetzee does, Dominic Head considers such questions in his essay. He argues that complicity often links the writer, the text, and the world or political discourse. Comparing the works of the apartheid years up to *The Master of Petersburg* with the more recent ones, Head questions whether postapartheid such associations are made less compelling. Drawing on a notion similar to Attridge's reading event, Head suggests that Coetzee's fiction always incorporates a double bind: while the texts, particularly the earlier ones, encourage allegorical readings, at the same time the reductiveness of this practice might even, chillingly, strike a literal chord, but might also be self-defeating on the part of Coetzee. Understanding Coetzee as writing his own peculiar brand of "resistance" literature that is suspicious of all forms of orthodoxy, including that of resistance, Head then asks where Coetzee's writing might lead him, now that with *Disgrace,* according to Head, Coetzee is lessening the emphasis on allegorical writing and reading.

V

Throughout his career Coetzee has attracted, and perhaps even courted, controversy. *Disgrace* received damning criticism from sections of its South African (and world) readership for its stark portrayal of the rape of a white woman at the hands of three black intruders. Choosing to address the subject of rape, particularly that of a white woman by black men, is deeply troubling for many readers and critics at this moment in South African history, when the incidence of rape, particularly of *black* women, is endemic and when a traumatized society is still coming to terms with its brutal past in a country where racist stereotypes of the black man as the natural rapist still prevail. In an ANC-commissioned report on racism in the media, the novel has been held up as illustrative of white racism in South Africa today. Rosemary Jolly makes reference to this report in her reading of *Disgrace*.[20]

Highlighting Coetzee's ethically nuanced public/political domain, Sam Durrant, Elleke Boehmer, and Rosemary Jolly all argue that *Disgrace* makes an implicit critique of South Africa's Truth and Reconciliation Commission. Drawing parallels with *Waiting for the Barbarians,* Durrant argues that, in Professor David Lurie, *Disgrace* offers the story of a man who rejects the language of public confession and instead finds a way of "living it out from day to day, trying to accept disgrace as my state of being." "Living through" or "living out," Durrant suggests, would seem to involve an oblique recognition of one's ethical responsibility for the other: both Lurie and the Magistrate in *Waiting for the Barbarians* must live through the consequences of their attempt to ignore or block out the suffering of the other. In forcing his protagonists to become more alive to the reality of other people's lives, in urging his readers to overcome a certain state of ignorance or even stupor, Coetzee presents fiction that is in accord with the basic ethics of humanism. Yet, Durrant proposes, Coetzee also departs from this model in his engagement with the lives of animals, with that which lies beyond the realm of the human.

Elleke Boehmer unravels the calibration of scapegoating in *Disgrace*. As epitomized by Lucy's refusal to speak of her experience of rape, the narrative offers graduated instances of traditionally subjected bodies carrying— literally bearing—the effects or manifestations of wrong which others have inflicted: the diseased goat, the killed dogs, the pregnant Lucy. Boehmer considers the implications for a gender politics of these different states of sorriness—in the sense both of bearing a burden of apology and of pitifulness. Drawing on both the post-Enlightenment discourses generated by the novel and the South African contexts from which it speaks, Boehmer tacitly questions the efficacy of South Africa's Truth and Reconciliation Commission in bearing witness to the horrors of apartheid, and in laying its ghosts to rest in the (troubled) present.

Concerned with Coetzee's critique of a proliferation of distinctively southern African hypermasculinities, reading it as a crucial, ethical contribution to an analysis of the epidemic of violence against women and children in the region, Rosemary Jolly focuses on *Disgrace* but refers to the masculinities depicted in Coetzee's texts of the apartheid and transition eras and argues that the issue of violence against women and children can only be understood in terms of hypermasculine formulations within the southern African context. She utilizes women's stories of egregious abuse told at the TRC hearings as empirical evidence of such a climate of violence. She argues that Coetzee, from *Dusklands* through to *Disgrace,* has consistently portrayed the role of discourses of racialized and engendered hegemony as key factors in a systemic, sexualized brutality that is seen by the perpetrators of this brutality to manifest their dominance. From an ecofeminist position, Jolly then attempts to show that Coetzee's fiction finds a way out of these damaging categories beyond the human, through animals.

VI

The ethical writer's and intellectual's task is, in part, to address the oppression of any marginalized group as well as to challenge its perpetrators, even if only through (the act of) writing. Writers *and* intellectuals like Chinua Achebe, Arundhati Roy, and Wole Soyinka, for instance, have questioned whether the secluded sphere of writing can be considered a sufficient form of contest. Roy has chosen ultimately to write a single novel only and thereafter to devote herself to her activism, whilst Achebe and Soyinka have both taken breaks from writing fiction in order to focus on their political work.

On the ethical question of being "merely a writer," Coetzee's fellow South African Nadine Gordimer contends that "art is on the side of the oppressed" since art by definition is "freedom of the spirit" and can therefore only represent (support) those seeking freedom. The act of writing, she quotes Roland Barthes, is ultimately his or her "essential gesture as a social being," and she adds that "creative self-absorption and conscionable awareness" are the "foetuses in a twinship of fecundity" (see *Essential Gesture,* 291, 286, 299–300). Michael Bell argues in chapter 9 that "[i]n Coetzee, the literary as such proves over and over again to be a radically discomforting, albeit indispensable, category for a certain kind of truth telling."

Bell, Lucy Graham, and Laura Wright all show, from different theoretical perspectives, that these boundaries between public and private are unsettled and clouded in Coetzee's performance of his protagonist Elizabeth Costello (*The Lives of Animals* and *Elizabeth Costello*)—what Graham calls "textual transvestism." According to Bell, *The Lives of Animals* expresses dramatically why Coetzee finds it difficult to believe, as Coetzee puts it elsewhere, in "believes in," and it reveals the relationship between the ethical positioning of the speaker, Costello, her audience, and, indeed, herself. Bell reads Costello as a device put into play by the author to convey those feelings or sentiments that Coetzee himself finds difficult to express; that she allows him, as a deeply private and elusive figure, in some senses to hold his silence while testing the limits of acceptable discourse. Bell suggests that these "clues" embedded in *The Lives of Animals* radically rework our conception of normality by shifting the ground on which common assumptions are made, such as "Whom do we mean by 'one of us'"? Bell's essay at the same time offers new readings of Coetzee through the work of D. H. Lawrence.

Laura Wright, drawing on animal rights and feminist debates, finds that Costello is enacting a "rant": a highly personal and at times angry philosophical exploration, which allows Coetzee to create a place of signification from which to voice an ethics that potentially undermines all binary modes of thought. Controversially, Wright enacts her own rant on the ethics of intellectualism, thereby reproducing the methodology of Coetzee in his performance of Costello.

Lucy Graham argues that critics who have acknowledged Coetzee's "elusiveness" and the distance between Coetzee and Costello have often interpreted Coetzee's scripting of Costello as mere evasiveness, a distancing device, and have expressed impatience with his apparent reluctance to take a stand himself. The "lessons" that make up the *Elizabeth Costello* collection, Graham argues, should be seen in the context of a tradition of female articulation in Coetzee's oeuvre. Like Costello, Magda in Coetzee's *In the*

Heart of the Country (1977), Susan Barton in *Foe* (1986), and Elizabeth Curren in *Age of Iron* (1990) are women who write and reflect on the processes of writing. Graham shows that the women in Coetzee's fiction play an important role in interrogating authorship and discourses of origin. As I believe the essays collected here will show, the Coetzee oeuvre is ever in a state of flux, and with the figure of Elizabeth Costello (who even makes an appearance in the most recent novel, *Slow Man* [2005]), readers and cultural commentators of Coetzee are left wondering where his writing will lead next. These essays go some way in answering such questions by identifying the shift from "Third World" locations and locutions to the more privately realized presentation, in *The Lives of Animals* and *Elizabeth Costello,* of the idiosyncratic and outspoken Costello figure. (Indeed, one might ask whether the end of apartheid has allowed such a shift, from public to private, to take place.) I believe, however, that the essays will leave the reader in no doubt that interest in Coetzee's writing and in what comes next will persist beyond his apparent withdrawal, both literally and literarily, from the so-called Third World.

Notes

1. *Dusklands* (1974) parallels and thereby correlates two very distinct narratives: the story of a colonial explorer Jacobus Coetzee who records unselfconsciously the violent history of his journey into Namaqualand, and that of Eugene Dawn, a twentieth-century propagandist writing in the service of the U.S. government in its war in Vietnam. Colonialism and U.S. imperialism are thereby identified as violently oppressive ideologies. In *In the Heart of the Country* (1978) the isolated and psychotic Afrikaner spinster Magda symbolically resists the (patriarchal) drive to be narrativized into a story, while at the end of *Waiting for the Barbarians* (1980) the Magistrate prepares to document the last days of the settler community. Like the colonizers in the poem by Constantine Cavafy to which Coetzee's title refers, this community is "waiting for the barbarians." (In Cavafy's text the barbarian is always an imagined other.) The elusive Michael K in *Life & Times of Michael K* (1983) takes symbolic authority over the twinned metaphors of writing the land and writing the body as a gesture of resistance to (textual) oppression. In *Foe* (1986) Susan Barton resists the patriarchal attempts of the author-figure Foe to misrepresent the story of her shipwreck on a Robinsonian island while simultaneously Barton inadvertently "colonizes" Friday's story. The protagonist Mrs. Curren in *Age of Iron* (1990) is writing a letter to her self-exiled daughter in America. Set during the

waning years of the apartheid regime, the novel pits ethics, or the private sphere, against politics, or the public sphere, when Mrs. Curren is confronted by what she perceives as the political dogma of both the state and the political activists she encounters. Dostoevsky in *The Master of Petersburg* (1994) struggles with the demons of a guilty conscience just as he struggles with the idea of his writing when he abuses his dead son's memory in pursuit of a good story. In *Disgrace* (1999), published shortly after the closing of South Africa's Truth and Reconciliation Commission hearings, during which stories of egregious oppression were brought into the public realm, Professor David Lurie seeks personal reconciliation with himself and with the "new South Africa," while at the same time struggling to find inspiration for his opera. Here, Lurie's ethical consciousness operates interdependently with his artistry: as his private life falls into disarray, so he loses control of his muse. In *The Lives of Animals* (1999) and *Elizabeth Costello* (2003) Coetzee's alter ego Elizabeth Costello delivers her impassioned, heartfelt "lessons" on emotive issues such as animal rights and the nature of evil.

2. *White Writing* (1988), for example, is a sociohistorical study of early white South African literary and artistic genres in which "white," according to Coetzee, is politicized, meaning "no longer European, not yet African" (11). Such writing—*écriture blanche,* as Roland Barthes would have it—is characterized by its erasures and evasions about black people and their cultures. *Doubling the Point* (1992), a collection of interviews and essays on literature and culture edited by David Attwell, is premised upon a modernist notion of "doubling back" and autocritique where the modern writer is hyperaware of the limits of his or her own authority. In the central essay in the book, "Confession and Double Thoughts," Coetzee analyzes the confessional writing of Tolstoy, Rousseau, and Dostoevsky, identifying the problems that encumber confession: finding the truth about the self, which, in turn, is imbued with problems of deception and self-deception, and closure: how to end the unending cycle of truth-telling and self-abnegation into which the confessant might fall. Elsewhere, Coetzee links the bold assertion that "[a]ll autobiography is storytelling, all writing is autobiography" with the problem of "how to tell the truth in autobiography" (391–92). Writing becomes an act of self-disclosure that is plagued by the problems inherent in confession. *Giving Offense: Essays on Censorship* (1996), as Coetzee remarks in his introduction, addresses "the passion that plays itself out in acts of silencing and censoring" (vii), from the trial of *Lady Chatterley's Lover* to rooting "apartheid thinking" in "demon possession." Coetzee invokes the Romantics' preference for sentiment over reason: "passion" here is the operative term since political debates about censorship per se hold no interest for him, as he remarks elsewhere (*Doubling,* 299).

3. In *Doubling the Point* Coetzee tells David Attwell, "Sympathetic to the human concerns of the left, he is alienated, when the crunch comes, by its language—by all political language, in fact" (394).

4. At twenty-one Coetzee left South Africa for London, where he worked as a computer analyst for a number of years, at the same time taking a Masters in Literature by correspondence at the University of Cape Town. Awarded his degree in 1963, he wrote his dissertation on the novelist Ford Madox Ford, a writer in whom, as he comments

in *Youth*, he would come to lose interest. In the mid-1960s he moved to the United States and studied for a PhD in literary linguistics at the University of Texas, Austin, on the Irish novelist and playwright Samuel Beckett—an acknowledged influence, among many, on his own fiction. He embarked upon his career as a lecturer at the State University of New York, Buffalo (1968–71), where he also began work on his first novel, *Dusklands*, informed by his experiences in America. Coetzee then returned to South Africa to take up a teaching position at the University of Cape Town, where in 1984 he was made Professor of General Literature. In subsequent years he divided his time between the universities of Cape Town and Chicago, and in 2002 moved to Adelaide, Australia, to work as an honorary research fellow.

5. For a discussion of this issue see ANC activist Albie Sachs's well-documented speech, "Preparing Ourselves for Freedom," in which Sachs highlights the limitations of engaged art.

6. See Gordimer, *Essential Gesture*, 106.

7. See Wood, "Aporias."

8. See also Gordimer, *Essential Gesture*, 293.

9. In *Doubling the Point* Coetzee, in conversation with Attwell, comments, "I regard it as a badge of honour to have had a book banned in South Africa, and even more of an honor to have been acted against punitively, as Fugard and others were officially, and Brink and others unofficially. This honor I have never achieved nor, to be frank, merited. Besides coming too late in the era, my books have been too indirect in their approach, too rarefied, to be considered a threat to the order" (298). Peter D. McDonald makes reference to these remarks in "'Not Undesirable.'"

10. See, for instance, Kramer, "Habermas, Foucault," 30.

11. The letter was published in the literary newspaper *L'Aurore* (The dawn), on January 13, 1898.

12. Jeremy Jennings and Tony Kemp-Welch make this point in "Century of the Intellectual," 10.

13. Biko was instrumental in forming the Black Consciousness Movement in South Africa in the 1970s, inspired by the earlier movement in the United States. Apartheid legislation included Prohibition of Mixed Marriages Act, Act No. 55, 1949; Immorality Amendment Act, Act No. 21, 1950; amended 1957 (Act 23); Suppression of Communism Act, Act No. 44, 1950 ("communism" was defined in broad terms as radical politics); Bantu Building Workers Act, Act No. 27, 1951; Separate Representation of Voters Act, Act No. 46, 1951, amended 1956 (disenfranchisement of "Coloureds" from common voters' roll); Native Labour (Settlement of Disputes) Act, 1953; Bantu Education Act, Act No. 47, 1953; Natives (Prohibition of Interdicts) Act, Act No. 64, 1956 (prevented blacks from appealing to the courts against forced removals); Extension of University Education Act, Act No. 45, 1959 (ended black students attending white universities); Terrorism Act, 1967; Bantu Homelands Citizens Act, 1970 (removed black people's right to South African citizenship). See Boddy-Evans, "Apartheid Legislation."

14. Under apartheid law racial identity was categorized into the hierarchy of White, Coloured, Asian, and African.

15. For an early account of the emergence of black English, including a discussion of the (mis)representation of indigenous oral narratives, see Gray, *Southern African Literature,* chapter 7. In "Postmodernism and Black Writing in South Africa," Lewis Nkosi refers to the "formal insufficiencies, . . . disappointing breadline asceticism and prim disapproval of irony, and its well-known predilection for what Lukacs called 'petty realism, the trivially detailed painting of local colour,' [in sum, the] naively uncouth disfigurements" typifying black South African writing (77). He speculates that black South African literature has tended to resist a postmodern mode, in part because of the isolation of black creative writers from South African universities, where current theories were being disseminated.

16. All except Coetzee have been censored, and Breytenbach spent some years in prison.

17. Attwell, *J. M. Coetzee,* 20.

18. See Hutcheon, *Politics of Postmodernism.*

19. See, for instance, Maes-Jelinek, "Ambivalent Clio." Teresa Dovey makes extensive psychoanalytic readings of Coetzee using the theories of Lacan and Freud. See, for instance, *Novels* and "Waiting for the Barbarians."

20. See Rosemary Jolly in this volume. In a special issue of *Interventions* David Attwell and Peter McDonald debate the discussion of the representation of race in *Disgrace* in the ANC report, giving markedly different accounts. See SAHRC, *Inquiry;* Attwell, "Race in *Disgrace*"; McDonald, "*Disgrace* Effects."

Bibliography

Adorno, Theodor W., "Commitment," *New Left Review* 87–88 (1974): 75–89.

Attridge, Derek, and Rosemary Jolly (eds.). *Writing South Africa: Literature, Apartheid, and Democracy, 1970–1995.* Cambridge: Cambridge University Press, 1998.

Attwell, David. *J. M. Coetzee: South Africa and the Politics of Writing.* Berkeley: University of California Press, 1993.

———. "Race in *Disgrace.*" In "J. M. Coetzee's *Disgrace,*" edited by Derek Attridge and Peter D. McDonald. Special issue, *Interventions* 4, no. 3 (2002): 331–41.

Bellamy, Richard. "The Intellectual as Social Critic: Antonio Gramsci and Michael Walzer." In Jennings and Kemp-Welch, *Intellectuals in Politics,* 25–44.

Boddy-Evans, Alistair. "Apartheid Legislation in South Africa," http://africanhistory. about.com/library/bl/blsalaws.htm (accessed January 26, 2005).

Coetzee, J. M. *Age of Iron.* 1990. London: Penguin, 1991.

———. *Boyhood: A Memoir.* 1997. London: Vintage, 1998.

———. "Critic and Citizen: A Response." *Pretexts* 9, no. 1 (2000): 109–11.

———. *Disgrace.* London: Secker and Warburg, 1999.

———. *Doubling the Point: Essays and Interviews.* Edited by David Attwell. Cambridge, MA: Harvard University Press, 1992.

———. *Dusklands.* 1974. London: Vintage, 1998.

———. *Elizabeth Costello.* London: Secker and Warburg, 2003.

———. *Foe.* 1986. Middlesex: Penguin, 1987.

———. *Giving Offense: Essays on Censorship.* Chicago: University of Chicago Press, 1996.

———. *In the Heart of the Country.* 1976. London: Vintage, 1999.

———. *Life & Times of Michael K.* 1983. Middlesex: Penguin, 1985.

———. *The Lives of Animals.* Edited by Amy Gutmann. Princeton: Princeton University Press, 1999.

———. "The Making of William Faulkner." *New York Review of Books,* April 7, 2005, 4–9.

———. *The Master of Petersburg.* 1994. London: Minerva, 1995.

———. "The Novel Today." *Upstream* 6 (1988): 1–5.

———. *Waiting for the Barbarians.* 1980. London: Minerva, 1997.

———. *White Writing: On the Culture of Letters in South Africa.* New Haven: Yale University Press, 1988.

———. *Youth.* London: Secker and Warburg, 2002.

de Kok, Ingrid, and Karen Press (eds.). *Spring Is Rebellious: Albie Sachs and Respondents on Cultural Freedom.* Cape Town: Buchu Press, 1990.

Dovey, Teresa. *The Novels of J. M. Coetzee: Lacanian Allegories.* Craighall, South Africa: Ad. Donker, 1988.

———. "Waiting for the Barbarians: Allegory of Allegories." In *Critical Perspectives on J. M. Coetzee,* edited by Graham Huggan and Stephen Watson, 138–51. London: MacMillan, 1996.

Du Toit, André. "Critic and Citizen: The Intellectual, Transformation and Academic Freedom." *Pretexts* 9, no. 1 (2000): 91–104.

Gordimer, Nadine. *The Essential Gesture: Writing, Politics and Places.* Edited by Stephen Clingman. London: Jonathan Cape, 1988.

Gramsci, Antonio. *Selections from The Prison Notebooks of Antonio Gramsci.* Edited and translated by Quintin Hoare and Geoffrey Nowell-Smith. New York: International, 1971.

Gray, Stephen. *Southern African Literature: An Introduction.* Cape Town: David Philip, 1979.

Hutcheon, Linda. *The Politics of Postmodernism.* London: Routledge, 1989.

Jennings, Jeremy, and Anthony Kemp-Welch. "The Century of the Intellectual: From the Dreyfus Affair to Salman Rushdie." In Jennings and Kemp-Welch, *Intellectuals in Politics,* 1–24.

——— (eds.). *Intellectuals in Politics: From the Dreyfus Affair to Salman Rushdie.* London: Routledge, 1997.

Kramer, Lloyd. "Habermas, Foucault, and the Legacy of Enlightenment Intellectuals." In *Intellectuals and Public Life: Between Radicalism and Reform,* edited by Leon Fink, Stephen T. Leonard, and Donald M. Reid, 29–50. Ithaca: Cornell University Press, 1996.

Lazarus, Neil. "Modernism and Modernity: T. W. Adorno and Contemporary White South African Literature." In "Modernity and Modernism, Postmodernity and Postmodernism." Special issue, *Cultural Critique* 5 (1986–87): 131–56.

Maes-Jelinek, Hena. "Ambivalent Clio: J. M. Coetzee's *In the Heart of the Country* and Wilson Harris's *Carnival.*" *Journal of Commonwealth Literature* 22, vol. 1 (1987): 87–98.

McDonald, Peter D. "*Disgrace* Effects." In "J. M. Coetzee's *Disgrace,*" edited by Derek Attridge and Peter D. McDonald. Special issue, *Interventions* 4, no. 3 (2002): 321–30.

———. "'Not Undesirable': How J. M. Coetzee Escaped the Censor." *Times Literary Supplement,* May 19, 2000, 14–15.

Nkosi, Lewis. "Postmodernism and Black Writing in South Africa." In Attridge and Jolly, *Writing South Africa,* 75–90.

Parry, Benita. "Speech and Silence in the Fictions of J. M. Coetzee." In Attridge and Jolly, *Writing South Africa,* 149–65.

Sachs, Albie. "Preparing Ourselves for Freedom." In de Kok and Press, *Spring Is Rebellious,* 19–29.

Said, Edward W. *Representations of the Intellectual: The 1993 Reith Lectures.* London: Vintage, 1994.

South African Human Rights Commission (SAHRC). *Faultlines: An Inquiry into Racism in the Media,* http://www.gov.za/reports/2000/racism.pdf, 2000.

———. *Inquiry into Racism in the Media: Hearings Transcripts* XIV.3/3 (April 5): 121–42.

———. *Investigation into Racism in the Media: Interim Report,* http://www.sahrc.org.za/sahrc_introduction_to_interim_report.pdf, 1999.

Wood, Philip R. "Aporias of the Postcolonial Subject: Correspondence with J. M. Coetzee." In "The Writings of J. M. Coetzee," edited by Michael Valdez Moses. Special issue, *South Atlantic Quarterly* 93, no. 1 (1994): 181–96.

J. M. COETZEE IN CONVERSATION
WITH JANE POYNER

JP: In *The Essential Gesture,* Nadine Gordimer warns of the dangers of conformity to an "orthodoxy of opposition" to the apartheid government. How difficult do you think it now is, as an intellectual-academic, to criticize the ANC government? Does fiction have an important part to play in maintaining a critical opposition?

JMC: (1) I interpret the first part of the question to mean: How difficult do I think it is for someone who is either an intellectual or an academic to criticize the ANC government? Answer: Not difficult at all. (2) It is hard for fiction to be good fiction while it is in the service of something else.

JP: Could you comment on South Africa's Truth and Reconciliation Commission: to what extent has it fulfilled its objectives, and is the conception of confession misplaced in the public sphere? In other words, does such a mode of confession suggest a performance without any judicial authority?

JMC: In a state with no official religion, the TRC was somewhat anomalous: a court of a certain kind based to a large degree on Christian teaching and on a strand of Christian teaching accepted in their hearts by only a tiny proportion of the citizenry. Only the future will tell what the TRC managed to achieve.

JP: How important do you think it is for artists and writers to memorialize catastrophe and atrocity, such as the Holocaust or apartheid?

JMC: For artists and writers individually? Surely artists and writers will decide for themselves what is important to them.

JP: Your fiction attracts a lot of attention from postcolonial critics. As a discourse (or set of discourses), does postcolonialism interest you? And if so, what problems does it raise or are implicit in it?

JMC: I don't read much academic criticism.

JP: In *Doubling the Point* you state that "sympathetic to the human concerns of the left, [you are] alienated, when the crunch comes, by its language—by all political language, in fact" (394). To what degree is this a sentiment that you continue to experience?

JMC: There is no longer a left worth speaking of, and a language of the left. The language of politics, with its new economistic bent, is even more repellent than it was fifteen years ago.

JP: Edward Said describes the intellectual as "an individual endowed with a faculty for representing, embodying, articulating a message, a view, an attitude, philosophy or opinion to, as well as for, a public. And this role has an edge to it, and cannot be played without a sense of being someone whose place it is publicly to raise embarrassing questions, to confront orthodoxy and dogma (rather than to produce them), to be someone who cannot easily be co-opted by governments or corporations, and whose raison d'être is to represent all those people and issues that are routinely forgotten or swept under the rug."[1] Said assumes a public role for the intellectual; how far would you agree with his comments?

JMC: What Said writes here constitutes a definition, not a comment. The resurrection of the term *public intellectual,* which for years was not part of public discourse, is an interesting phenomenon. What is the explanation? Perhaps it has something to do with people in the humanities, more or less ignored nowadays, trying to carve out a niche for themselves in the body politic.

JP: Said has also suggested that the intellectual should always occupy a position of marginality ("the whole point is to be embarrassing, contrary, even unpleasant" [Reith, 9]) in order to remain objective in their critique of political/public discourse. As a novelist, an academic, and an intellectual, do you find yourself occupying, or wishing to occupy, such a position?

JMC: It is difficult to be a so-called successful writer and to occupy a marginal position at the same time, even in our day and age.

JP: Are there points at which you see the role of the novelist conflicting with that of the public intellectual? I am thinking, for instance, of writers like Rushdie, Arundhati Roy, and, of course, yourself. How does one negotiate one's roles as intellectual, academic, and novelist? Is the novelist's conception of truth necessarily different from that of the intellectual?

JMC: I try to avoid the term *role,* which implies that one is giving oneself to a part that is already written. Of course there is a larger scheme in which we may all be said to be playing roles. But that scheme is invisible to us.

JP: In recent times in the United States and Britain there has been a great deal of discussion about professionalism within the institution of the university, where academics are put under greater pressure to publish and to be accountable to more rigorous assessment of their research and teaching. What is your view of the state of the academic world today? Do you see these shifts as a threat to the intellectual's freedom of speech?

JMC: (1) I would question your assertion regarding accountability and rigor. What happened to universities, in my view, had little to do with creating higher standards and everything to do with imposing a business model on them. (2) Universities seem to be fairly miserable places nowadays. (3) The question is too general. Which intellectuals? When and where did (or do) such intellectuals have freedom of speech? What freedom of speech did (or do) they have?

JP: Has your move to Australia opened up new possibilities for your writing?

JMC: Yes.

JP: What do you think are the strengths and weaknesses of current South African writing?

JMC: I don't know the range of current South African writing well enough to comment.

Notes

1. Edward W. Said, *Representations of the Intellectual: The 1993 Reith Lectures* (London: Vintage, 1994), 9.

I

THE LIFE AND TIMES OF
ELIZABETH COSTELLO

J. M. Coetzee and the Public Sphere

David Attwell

ANY DISCUSSION of J. M. Coetzee's relationship with the public sphere will have to acknowledge certain sensitivities. The first is that despite his celebrity, especially since he won the Nobel Prize, Coetzee remains, in a particular sense, among the least known of South African writers. Notoriety has little bearing on public ownership in this case, an observation that should encourage us to ask what it means to know a writer—to know what Edward Said in the Reith Lectures calls "the image, the signature, the actual intervention and performance, all of which taken together constitute the very lifeblood of every real intellectual" (10).

Second, Coetzee resists fiction's being made to deliver usable ethical content: "a story is not a message with a covering . . . not a message plus a residue, the residue, the art with which the message is coated. . . . There is no addition in stories. . . . On the keyboard on which they are written, the plus key does not work" ("Novel Today," 4). Yet, partly *because* he demonstrates that in stories "the difference is everything" (4), Coetzee's fiction is proving especially resourceful in generating a discussion of ethics in fiction or of the relationships between ethical and fictional discourses.

Third, a point about the ethics of reading a resistant text: Coetzee's persona has been known to generate a certain impatience among readers who would prefer writers to be more amenable to public debate. The more curious and attentive reader, however, will want to work with and through the difficulties of the text and the enigmas of the public performance, knowing that some discomfort will persist. Coetzee has said of Erasmus and his followers that there can be no true "Erasmians"; similarly, there can be no Coetzeeans. To make a public case on his behalf is—for reasons I hope this essay will elucidate—to risk traducing the very qualities of his writing one most respects, including his uncanny combinations of power and instability, intensity and elusiveness.

But to begin: Coetzee is not a public intellectual in the most widely accepted sense of the term, a sense that Said's Reith Lectures have helped to define. He has not in any consistent or obvious way "spoken truth to power," nor has he discarded academia to speak as the gifted dilettante, nor has he abandoned what Said would have called his "darker gods" (in Coetzee's case, perhaps, an interest in desire and the unconscious) for a discourse of secular rationality—three principle criteria in Said for accreditation as a public intellectual. As we all know, Coetzee has resisted being drawn into the public sphere, for reasons he has made clear, namely, that a rule of entry into the public and especially the political arena is that one speak the discourses of power, and he feels that is too high a price to pay. Conducting even a limited foray to defend the discourse of fiction against what he pointedly called its "colonization" by the discourse of history, he once remarked, "I do not even speak my own language," and added, "Let me hasten to get through what I have to say before the flattening takes place" ("Novel Today," 3).

Occasionally, this vigilance lapses. To my knowledge, the most memorable public intervention Coetzee has ever made was over the proposed visit of Salman Rushdie to South Africa in 1988, in the last years of apartheid and shortly before the Iranian fatwa against Rushdie. By this stage, the cultural boycott of South Africa had been nuanced, with the exiled African National Congress agreeing that a democratic culture existed inside South Africa and that it should be supported. In terms of this view, Rushdie was invited to attend a book festival in Cape Town and appear as a fellow Booker prizewinner with Coetzee to discuss censorship. With the Baxter

Theatre packed with newly accredited democrats expecting Rushdie to appear, bringing with him the breezes of cosmopolitan freedom, onto the stage walked Coetzee, not with Rushdie but with Nadine Gordimer. She was there to explain Rushdie's absence—in fact, this became the cause célèbre. *The Satanic Verses* had appeared a week earlier; extracts had been faxed to Cape Town; the festival's organizers—the Congress of South African Writers and the *Weekly Mail*—had been asked by Islamic leaders to cancel Rushdie's visit under threats of violence. (With that revelation Capetonians, who had become familiar with the sound of bombs in the early hours of the morning, could imagine the auditorium imploding if Rushdie *had* been present.)

Into this electricity Coetzee spoke: as the only member of the company who seemed to have actually read *The Satanic Verses,* he said that Rushdie knew exactly what he was taking on in the novel; he should have been informed of the risks of such a visit, including that of an unreconstructed police force enjoying the spectacle of an attack on the Left by a black religious minority; it was wrong for the organizers to protect a united front at the price of acceding to the demands of fundamentalists; the organizers had, in fact, connived in censorship and had violated a key principle of *The Satanic Verses* itself, namely, the protean qualities of writing that could be taken as a model of freedom that the fundamentalists—in their insistence that after the one Book there were to be no more books—would do everything to suppress; instead of assembling to discuss censorship, we were all party to it, in an event that reinstitutionalized it in the name of an elusive democracy.

Unusually for Coetzee, he was saying exactly what his audience wanted to hear: they were on their feet applauding. A week later, the fatwa was declared; the seriousness of the threat was confirmed; Coetzee acknowledged he may have been mistaken. But if anything, the moment would have validated his skepticism about the role he found himself momentarily being celebrated for; because with a change in the political wind, his intervention and what it stood for were becalmed in an indifferent corner of history as the aftermath of the fatwa unfolded.[1]

Far more characteristic, then, of Coetzee's public presence is the group of statements I have alluded to in which he defends the specificity, traditions, and right to public recognition of fiction or, on the most frequently cited of these occasions, of storytelling.[2] A feature of these statements is that he interprets the demand for him to speak as a public intellectual as inimical to his work, indeed as hostile to the very identity as writer on which the demand for him to speak is predicated. But it is equally characteristic that he has declined to foreground these statements himself; it is the commentators and critics who have wanted to do so. Paradoxically, his address at the *Weekly Mail*'s book festival of 1987, published obscurely in a Cape Town poetry magazine as "The Novel Today" and never subsequently collected, is probably his most widely cited statement outside his fiction. Here he speaks of fiction as rival to the discourse of history, in opposition to the prevailing climate that treats it as supplementary to history, or as a subgenre of historical discourse, whose value is limited to the revelation of the "subjective experience" of history. In these statements, Coetzee's reading of the cultural landscape seems Foucauldian; though it would be Foucault registered not as theory so much as a turning of that whole landscape into an existential battleground. Coetzee has underplayed these statements himself, I suspect, because they are, of course, defensive, and he has no desire to take up a beleaguered position. The real battle for the authority of fictionality will, in any case, be fought in the fiction itself. What Coetzee has chosen to do, however, outside of the fiction, is to explore the tension between his practice and its times in certain essays, and it is possible to read these essays as exercises in intellectual autobiography. I will discuss two of them here, namely, "What Is a Classic?" and "Erasmus: Madness and Rivalry." Before I do so, however, let me collect certain threads from the literature on intellectuals.

MUCH of the literature on intellectuals explores the tension between abstraction and specificity, between speaking independently and speaking in terms of a particular mandate. Julien Benda's famous attack on intellectuals in *La trahison des clercs,* which is Said's benchmark, is the product of his dismay at the possibility that real intellectuals are a dying breed—"those whose activity is essentially not the pursuit of practical aims . . . [those who] in a certain manner say: 'My kingdom is not of this world'" (in Said, *Representations,* 4–5). Said points out that despite the apparent otherworldliness, however, Benda is indeed caught up in a historically urgent situation, namely the Dreyfus affair. Antonio Gramsci, to whom Said gives rather less attention than Benda, famously distinguishes "traditional" from "organic" intellectuals precisely in order to disaggregate the ways in which intellectuals speak from within particular interests, traditions, and sites of agency. In *Legislators and Interpreters,* Zygmunt Bauman suggests that whereas it was once possible for intellectuals to speak as legislators from an assumed totality of culture, they are now required to speak as interpreters, translating between particular communities and traditions (3–5). Coetzee is sensitive to this shift: Elizabeth Costello, his eponymous public intellectual, often speaks as a legislator, which makes her performance seem anachronistic, but Coetzee embeds her speech within fiction, thus playing the role of interpreter, mediating between Costello's world of hard-earned intuitions, opinions, and rights, and ours, which needs to know what game is being played.

In *Anxious Intellects,* John Michael argues that intellectuals are necessarily caught in a certain "schizophrenia" or "double bind": "On the one hand, history teaches again and again that appeals to universals and transcendence . . . tend to mask the impositions of self-interested elites and the victimization and silencing of troublesome or dissonant differences. . . . On the other hand, without an appeal to the transcendent . . . there can be no intellectuals, no politics, and no community at all" (12). Michael settles for a paradox that he insists is *constitutive* of current intellectual practice: the field of what he calls "local transcendentals and specific universals" (9). One speaks in the name of something putatively universal, but always in relation to the specific instance and context.

This is also Pierre Bourdieu's view. In the last essay he wrote before his death, he says, "we all have in mind the opposition between the pure intellectual and the engaged intellectual. And this opposition makes it difficult to understand the paradoxical reality that is the intellectual, as it is an 'autonomous' individual, a 'purist' who commits himself. . . . for intellectuals to engage even more efficiently, and even more seriously, they must, at the same time, be even more autonomous and even more committed" (3).

Coetzee's essay "What Is a Classic?" deals with this very tension, though in personal terms. At the heart of the essay is the question of whether being addressed, arrested, or moved by the classic—such as the experience he describes of hearing, as a fifteen-year-old, Bach's *Well-Tempered Clavier* drifting from a neighbor's house as he mooned around the back garden of his suburban home in Cape Town—is an experience of something timeless and ineffable or whether it is determined by material interest, in the particular example, that of a young colonial electing European high culture to escape a social and historical dead end (anyone who has lived in Plumstead, where this drama is played out, will know how complete that fate would be).

To sharpen the question, Coetzee relates his position to that of T. S. Eliot, who in October 1944, with the Second World War building to a climax in central Europe, gave a lecture with the same title to the Virgil Society in London. To summarize Coetzee on Eliot rather swiftly: Eliot's project was to subsume his own historical, part-American identity within an English identity, to subsume that Englishness within a pan-European identity, to attach Europe to Catholicism and ultimately to Rome as its rightful cultural capital, and to position Virgil's *Aeneid* as the founding epic of the entire tradition ("What Is a Classic?" 1–8). Coetzee proposes two possible readings of Eliot's project: on one hand, a sympathetic "transcendental-poetic" reading that takes seriously the call from Virgil and understands the elaboration of a European destiny as the expression of that vocation; on the other hand, a "socio-cultural reading" that reads it as the "essentially magical enterprise of a man trying to redefine the world around himself" (8). In taking over Eliot's title, "What Is a Classic?" Coetzee tantalizes us with the possibility that his relation to Eliot is itself Eliotic, because it takes tradition to be inescapable; however, in practice, Coetzee is far from Eliot because he implies that Eliot's magic is not available to himself. In other words, Coetzee acknowledges being caught in the contradiction mentioned earlier in relation to intellectuals, the contradiction that is dramatized in Eliot as that between the transcendental and the sociocultural, but Eliot's resolution is not available to Coetzee, because Eliot—as one of Bauman's legislators—was able simply to write himself out of it, though not without some difficulty.

Coetzee does attempt a resolution but it is not entirely conclusive. Following the example of J. S. Bach's legacy disappearing during the eighteenth century and then resurfacing in the hands of Mendelssohn and others in the nineteenth, Coetzee argues that the classic is defined not inherently but posthumously—that is, what defines it is a tradition of apprenticeship, of performance and testing by specialists who come after. On the basis of this analogy with music, which Coetzee admits is tenuous, the literary classic would survive through testing by continuous critique; in this sense, the classic *uses criticism* to ensure its survival (19). In emphasizing the role of the professional coterie in whose gift lies the survival of the classic, this resolution seems somewhat conservative—it is also contradictory, since a point of departure in the argument is the impression made by Baroque music on an *untutored* ear—but the logic of the essay is not to valorize tradition in any simple-minded sense; it is, indeed, to demystify the classic, even to find a material, though obviously not an economic, explanation for it. The idea of apprenticeship is precisely a way of drawing together the transcendent and the historical.

Perhaps we should ask, what sharpens this tension in Coetzee's particular intellectual biography? Since I cannot pretend to do justice to all the implications here, I shall settle for a few broad strokes. *Youth* confirms earlier confessions of particular aesthetic allegiances: Pound and Eliot, the beginnings of modernist prose in Ford Madox Ford, Beckett's fiction—these are obvious route markers. Then, the antecedents that Coetzee chooses from the history of the novel are those writers who have brought self-consciousness to the surface and writers in whose work one easily discerns a process of self-invention: Beckett, Joyce, Kafka, and Nabokov, but also Defoe, Dostoevsky, and Sterne. It is not only the history of the novel to which we must turn, however, it is also the history of stylistic criticism, and of structuralism, semiotics, and deconstruction. For Coetzee writes not only within Eliot's sense of tradition as a body of texts, but also with a sense of *language* as tradition, language as a field in which one takes up a position using found instruments. If we trace much of this history back to Russian formalism, which fed several of the streams I have mentioned, it is striking that formalism's own project to define literariness, like Coetzee's defense of fictionality, was taken up against a social background of a prevailing, millennial historical consciousness.

Turning more directly, however, to this question of historical consciousness: Coetzee is peculiarly sensitive to the sociology of culture, although it does not seem to interest him as a field of inquiry: he is sensitive to it in that it provides an inescapable horizon for his work. It is a sensitivity learned on the bone, in which the history of colonialism and its aftermath have been central and definitive. Where Coetzee has brought this consciousness to the surface of the nonfictional writing, it has often been, as I have suggested, through a Foucauldian reading of power.[3] As for its expression in the fiction and autobiography, it is everywhere, but it surfaces in an acute and even dangerous sense in the essay on the classic. Discussing Eliot once again but in unmistakable reference to himself, he says,

> To such young people [colonials], the high culture of the metropolis may arrive in the form of powerful experiences which cannot, however, be embedded in their lives in any obvious way, and which seem therefore to have their existence in some transcendent realm. In extreme cases, they are led to blame their environment for not living up to art and to take up residence in an art world. This is a provincial fate—Gustave Flaubert diagnosed it in Emma Bovary, subtitling his case study *Mœurs de province* —but particularly a colonial fate, for those colonials brought up in the culture of what is usually called the mother country but in this context deserves to be called the father country. ("What Is a Classic?" 7–8)

Boyhood and *Youth,* which take over Flaubert's subtitle, handle this matter with relentlessly self-deprecating irony, but the relevance of the diagnosis extends to recent fiction, where there is a different tone: David Lurie in *Disgrace* exemplifies the problem, and while his condition has a certain tragic potential, the novel brutally avoids dignifying it as such. Lurie's high cultural affiliations trap him in the past, sealing him off from meaningful relationships with almost everyone around him. Although he does his best to aestheticize it, his coercive treatment of Melanie is revisited on him and his daughter in terms of a return of the repressed. For as long as the prevailing culture cannot recognize the pathos of Lurie's situation, however, then what might otherwise have appeared as tragic self-destruction undergoes a bathetic reduction to disgrace. I am arguing that a hard-nosed historical self-consciousness is intrinsic to the concerns of *Disgrace,* that indeed, such self-consciousness is pushed to the limit in that novel, literally, in the sense that it defines a boundary, an unforgiving blankness that refuses consoling fictions.

In "Erasmus: Madness and Rivalry," we find the following observation by Pierre Bourdieu about the "bi-dimensional" quality of public intellectual life: "In order for the intellectual to exist there must exist an autonomous universe within which a writer, a Zola, a sociologist, or a philosopher, has accumulated capital specific to the historian, the philosopher, etc., and that person must choose to come out of this universe, enter into the political arena and perform a prophetic act aimed at imposing values which are acceptable within his universe" (3). For simplicity let us call these universes of which Bourdieu speaks sphere 1 (a particular discipline) and sphere 2 (the public sphere). Bourdieu argues that it is not only the *right*—one that has to be defended—of the intellectual to move from sphere 1 to sphere 2, it is also a *duty* (4). He recognizes too, however, that this movement is by no means a simple passage from the one to the other: intellectuals need to be self-critical and self-reflexive; they should keep their autonomy refurbished; they should resist the apparent authority of the media and "re-appropriate their own instruments of dissemination" (5). These caveats imply the presence of pitfalls governing the movement between spheres, so much so that it would be safe to assume that the more self-consciously an intellectual inhabits sphere 1, the more awkward and conflicted might be the entry into sphere 2. For example, if it is intrinsic to the activity of sphere 1 to question conventions and systems of agreement, then the movement into sphere 2 is likely to be clouded in self-doubt and possibly bad faith. From there it is only a short step into the condition of the Dostoevskian underground man, who envies and despises the state of rational self-possession that the movement between spheres necessitates—a rationality that Coetzee has called "the worm of complacency at the heart of sincerity" (*Giving Offense*, 5). Coetzee is especially sensitive to this problem: Eugene Dawn in *Dusklands* is an example of an intellectual whose passage from sphere 1 to sphere 2 spins out of control as he becomes mired in unproductive solipsism. Similarly, the Magistrate in *Waiting for the Barbarians*, Mrs. Curren in *Age of Iron*, and Dostoevsky in *The Master of Petersburg* are all in a sense intellectuals, who are challenged at critical moments to step out of their circumscribed roles and speak to the general malaise around them; each, in his or her own way, fails the test and then becomes painfully detached from the rules of discourse that he or she is being asked, or sometimes forced, to play.

Elizabeth Costello, however, is sui generis. She enables Coetzee to fictionalize the writer-as-public-intellectual more directly. One may see her as a compromise and a surrogate: a compromise because through her Coetzee goes some way toward meeting the demands placed on him to step into the public limelight, and a surrogate because she does, to some degree, speak for him—when called on to speak publicly, Coetzee ushers her into sphere 2 instead, enabling him to stand back and observe the ironies and the play of positions. There is more than "a version of the academic novel" here, as Marjorie Garber suggests (79); there is also a kind of hubris: the game is, in a sense, to absorb the public domain into the codes of fiction, as a form of *reprisal.* Those who heard Coetzee's Ben Belitt Lecture at Bennington College ("What Is Realism?"), the Tanner Lectures at Princeton (*The Lives of Animals*), the Una's Lecture at the Townsend Center for the Humanities at Berkeley (*The Novel in Africa*), or the Carl Friedrich von Siemens Foundation Lecture (*The Humanities in Africa*) would have found their expectations undergoing a certain disfiguration as Coetzee began to absorb them into his performance. The narrative contract Coetzee creates in these stories is simply the latest in a series of efforts to give to fictionality an authority to challenge the demand for public accountability. Said cites Jean Genet as saying that if intellectuals did not want to be political they should stay out of the public sphere (Said, 82); if this is so, then Coetzee is surely at liberty to suggest that if the conventions of the public sphere are to be treated as sacrosanct, then it should not make demands on those writers who might expose their arbitrariness.

But to focus on Coetzee's essay on Erasmus: it could be read as a meditation on these very issues, a meditation, that is, on the public face of the writer-intellectual who distrusts secular rationality—particularly in times of violence, when reason seems given over to madness, without necessarily being aware that the dementia has already set in. It reflects on the difficulties of crafting a position—or a nonposition—from this distrust, a position that resists falling into the dominant rivalries. It ends with an acknowledgment that the more successfully such a position is crafted, the more likely it is to suffer the fate of collecting acolytes and detractors who erect it as a new rational standard, so that its legacy traduces what it stands for. Coetzee turns to the figure of Moria in *The Praise of Folly* because in her he admires Erasmus's efforts to develop a mode of performance that falls outside the prevailing culture's conceptions of seriousness.[4]

Erasmus's Moria models this position in a number of ways. She sees through the madness of those who see themselves as reasonable and self-possessed while in reality giving themselves over to rivalry. She positions herself against this madness, speaking the truth but mixing it with comic delight. What is unique about Folly's mode of truth is its *positionality:* it comes "not from 'the wise man's mouth' but from the mouth of the subject assumed not to know and speak the truth" (*Giving Offense,* 94). Folly's truth entails "a kind of *ek-stasis,* a being outside oneself, being beside oneself, a state in which truth is known (and spoken) from a position that does not know itself to be the position of truth" (94). Coetzee's deeper admiration for this position and the kind of performance it implies is evident in a sentence such as this: "Such speech, in which the linear propulsive force of reason gives way to the unpredictable metamorphosis of figure into figure, yields a bliss that is the object of the desire of those most open to the promptings of desire; and the first manifestation of such bliss is of course laughter, an anarchic convulsion of the body that marks the defeat of the defenses of the censor" (95). Here we have Erasmus, in an early Renaissance text that draws on forms of medieval folk humor (mock oration and parody) leading modernist and postmodern fiction down the path of one of its own most desirable projects: the release of the unconscious.[5] Behind the rhythm of Coetzee's sentence, however, one can also just glimpse his admiration for the self-generating prose rhythms of Joyce, Musil, Beckett, and Faulkner.

Moria's performance is noteworthy in other ways. She is, by definition, unsocialized, rude, and comic. She associates herself in a general way with sexuality—the folly of which obviously undermines the most serious—but also, more specifically, with the phallus. This is not the "big phallus," "the pillar of the law behind which every reasonable man stands," but "a phallus of a second species, naked, ridiculous, without robes and crown and orb and sceptre, without grandeur, the 'little' phallus that speaks for/of Moria; not the transcendental signifier but a thing of sport, of free play, of carefree dissemination rather than patrilinearity" (96). This is also the phallus of Greek comedy, in other words, the original *slap-stick.* Like Moria herself, the little phallus can be feminine. As a representative of both the feminine and the parodic, Moria does not set out to expose or destroy social conventions: her wisdom lies in working with them, without being ruled by them. "All human affairs," says Coetzee (echoing Moria), "are played out in disguise. . . . Without social fictions there is no society" (96). What is the position of someone who sees behind the masks, but refuses to expose them violently? The position suggested by *The Praise of Folly* consists of questions rather than answers: "What is *to take a position?* Is there a position which is not a position, a position . . . in which one knows without knowing, sees without seeing? *The Praise of Folly* marks out such a 'position,' prudently disarming itself in advance, keeping its phallus the size of the woman's, steering clear of the play of power, clear of politics" (99–100; italics in original).

Elizabeth Costello, I suggest, is an Erasmian solution. Admittedly, she is not exactly a figure of fun: her son thinks of her not as a performing seal but as a cat, "one of those large cats that pause as they eviscerate their victim and, across the torn-open belly, give you a cold yellow stare" (*Costello,* 5). She may not convulse her hearers with laughter, but she distrusts rationality—delivering a sharp critique of it, in fact—and her voice is tinged with madness, as her pragmatic daughter-in-law, Norma, doesn't hesitate to point out (81). The point of this madness is that it enables things to be said that could not easily be articulated by a public intellectual in the real world; nevertheless, her voice *lingers* as a mark of ethical accountability.

The relationship between Costello and Coetzee is, of course, complex. To propose that he should step out of his fiction and take responsibility for her positions would be to short-circuit the game. In his reading of *The Lives of Animals,* Peter Singer is frustrated at being unable to distinguish Costello from Coetzee, and he responds inconclusively (*Lives,* 91). There is no doubt that Costello's general concerns are indeed Coetzee's: he is also a professed vegetarian and has elaborated this in an ethical critique of meat-eating cultures; theorizing realism is obviously a kind of second nature; equally obviously, he is interested in the fate of the novel, and of the humanities in Africa and so on. Not all the connections between the author and the stories are this self-evident: the debate between philosopher Thomas O'Hearne and Costello, on the accessibility of animal consciousness, elaborates a motif running through Coetzee's early fiction, in which the protagonists imagine themselves entering the being of crabs, snakes, and insects. The philosophical dramas of consciousness and its objects, and of being and becoming, which are striking features of *In the Heart of the Country,* prepare for Costello's advocacy of what she calls "the sympathetic imagination." In other words, Costello's surrogacy is genuine—she enables him to have his say on certain matters, even though "having a say" remains governed by self-reflexive questions about positionality.[6]

Against the grain of my argument, let me ask whether somewhere in *Elizabeth Costello* a position in the more common sense can be discerned, a position that could be said to undermine the artful provisionality of the nonposition described thus far. The place to look for it might be in the phrase I have just mentioned, the "the sympathetic imagination." One of its obvious manifestations is the following: "If I do not convince you, that is because my words, here, lack the power to bring home to you the wholeness, the unabstracted, unintellectual nature, of that animal being. That is why I urge you to read the poets who return the living, electric being to language; and if the poets do not move you, I urge you to walk, flank to flank, beside the beast that is prodded down the chute to his executioner" (*Costello*, 111). The statement comes toward the end of Costello's seminar on the poets and the animals, which ends in dissension. It leads to a cris de coeur in which she wonders how it is possible that so many decent people around her can participate daily in "a crime of stupefying proportions" in which they consume "fragments of corpses that they have bought for money." On their way to the airport, her son, John, stops the car, takes her in his arms, and dubiously comforts her with the words, "There, there. It will soon be over" (115). This moment and its context define the ethical parameters of Costello's sympathetic imagination: they include her regard for the living energy that is shared by the earth's creatures and her clear-eyed recognition of the otherness and strangeness, the sublimity, of death. Costello is, of course, "beside herself" when she speaks so passionately—a plight that is aggravated by her sense that no one takes her seriously—but Coetzee is suggesting that such desperate speech may have a primordial value: citing Lacan (who is citing Plato) on the potential power of such extrarational statement, he says, "We can only bow our heads before it" ("Erasmus," 89).

The Costello stories, then, associate speech or writing that is positioned outside, or perhaps alongside, rationality with a particular kind of ethical consciousness, a consciousness that does not belong to formal philosophy and that includes a recognition of one's participation in the precariousness of being. If one were asked to speculate about the relationship between this ethical consciousness and the "life and times" in which it is developed, one might say that the Costello stories do not go "beyond history" so much as get below it. What I mean is this: given history's failures (which are, substantially, the failures of reason) the conditions of possibility for the development of a more redemptive consciousness might well be ontological, before they are social; that is, they may be related to a new consciousness and valorization of being itself. Coetzee is suggesting that the conditions informing the need for a revitalized ethics may well include the radical discontinuities of experience and culture that are characteristic of colonial and postcolonial societies, Africa included, but the actual articulation of such an ethics need not be political in the first instance. Under certain conditions, it is possible for ontology to trump politics, even though political discourse remains—in the last instance—part of an inescapable historical reality.

Let me conclude by returning briefly to Edward Said. When he was invited to give a lecture in the Cape Town parliament at a conference entitled "Values, Education and Democracy" in February 2001, he spoke on the importance to national development of a book culture and of critical literacy. He concluded, however, by speaking about music: while musical performance requires interpretation in terms of an ideal, it is "always provisional, partial and incomplete, no matter how superb." By learning to use several *languages*—by which he meant different kinds of performance conventions, *play* not as jouissance but as social practice—we and our students would learn "to grasp and dissent from our fate as citizens in society, to make and unmake, to construct and deconstruct the forms of life into which we have been formed and from which mortality decrees that we must leave" ("Book," 18–19). The remark is made more poignant by Said's recent passing. It could have come, however, from Elizabeth Costello, and possibly even from Coetzee himself. Perhaps there is a sense in which Said's and Coetzee's modes as public intellectuals can be seen to converge.

Notes

1. My account of these events is constructed from memory. The Jerusalem Prize acceptance speech is regarded as a significant public intervention but it became widely known only long after its delivery when it appeared in *Doubling the Point*. It appeared originally in French in *Le Nouvel Observateur.*

2. "The Novel Today" is the most cited of these statements. Related positions can be found in interviews published ephemerally. See, for example, *Buffalo Arts Review, Speak,* and *Sjambok.*

3. This is apparent not only in the statements dealing with the rivalry between fiction and history but, as Coetzee points out in *Doubling the Point,* also in the governing conception of *White Writing.*

4. There is a theoretical lineage behind the argument which I will summarize briefly here, although its outlines will be known to readers who have followed Coetzee closely. It takes up the debate between Foucault and Derrida on the impossibility of reason and philosophy having access to the discourse of madness. It recalls the famous distinction in Lacan (and Shoshana Felman) between the knowing subject (le *sujet supposé savoir*) and the subject of writing which is constituted by the weave of signifiers (*le savoir supposé sujet*). From this distinction it develops the prospect of writing which escapes self-presence, writing freed, that is, from the constraints of rational self-possession, showing that it was only this writing which was banished from Plato's *Republic* (*Giving Offense,* 85–90). Coetzee also calls up René Girard's theory of mimetic violence, behind which lies a dialectical theory of desire which can be traced from Hegel through Kojève to Sartre. The theory argues that desire does not know itself; it proceeds from lack; consequently, it needs a model which refers the desiring subject to a desired object, the result being rivalry between model and subject. When the distance between model and subject becomes diminished, the rivalry increases and with it a propensity to violence.

5. Coetzee's Erasmian *ekstasis* bears comparison with Graham Pechey's notion of "the post-apartheid sublime," which Pechey defines as a plurivocal discourse freed from the necessity to reinvent absolutes (Pechey, "Post-apartheid Sublime," 73).

6. We should see this in the light of Coetzee's remark that he "does not respect his own being-offended," and finds "it hard to respect in the deepest sense other people's being-offended," though this does not mean breaking a tactful silence when necessary (*Giving Offense,* 5–6).

Bibliography

Bauman, Zygmunt. *Legislators and Interpreters: On Modernity, Post-Modernity, and Intellectuals.* Cambridge: Polity Press, 1987.

Bourdieu, Pierre. "The Role of Intellectuals Today." *Theoria,* June 2002, 1–6.

Clingman, Stephen. "The Public in the Private: Authorship and Authenticity in South African Writing: Gordimer and Coetzee." Unpublished.

Coetzee, J. M. *Age of Iron.* London: Secker and Warburg, 1990.

———. *Disgrace.* London: Secker and Warburg, 1999.

———. *Doubling the Point: Essays and Interviews.* Edited by David Attwell. Cambridge: Harvard University Press, 1992.

————. *Dusklands*. Johannesburg: Ravan Press, 1974.

————. *Elizabeth Costello*. New York: Viking, 2003.

————. "Erasmus: Madness and Rivalry." In Coetzee, *Giving Offense*, 83–103.

————. *Giving Offense: Essays on Censorship*. Chicago: University of Chicago Press, 1996.

————. "Grubbing for the Ideological Implications: A Clash (More or Less) with J. M. Coetzee." Interview by A. Thorold and R. Wicksteed. *Sjambok* (University of Cape Town), n.d.

————. *In the Heart of the Country*. Johannesburg: Ravan, 1978.

————. *The Humanities in Africa (Die Geisteswissenschaften in Afrika)*. Munich: Carl Friedrich von Siemens Stiftung, 2001.

————. *The Lives of Animals*. The Tanner Lectures. Edited by Amy Gutmann. Princeton, NJ: Princeton University Press, 1999.

————. *The Master of Petersburg*. London: Secker and Warburg, 1994.

————. *The Novel in Africa.*. Occasional Papers. Berkeley: Doreen B. Townsend Center for the Humanities, University of California, 1999.

————. "The Novel Today." *Upstream* 6, no. 1 (Summer 1988): 2–5.

————. "Speaking: J. M. Coetzee." Interview by Stephen Watson. *Speak* 1, no. 3 (1978): 23–24.

————. "Too Late for Politics?" Interview. *Buffalo Arts Review* 5, no. 1 (Spring 1987): 6.

————. *Waiting for the Barbarians*. Johannesburg: Ravan Press, 1981.

————. "What Is a Classic?" In *Stranger Shores*, 1–19. London: Secker and Warburg, 2001.

————. "What Is Realism?" Ben Belitt Lecture, Bennington College. *Salmagundi* 114–15 (Spring/Summer 1997): 60–81.

————. *White Writing: On the Culture of Letters in South Africa*. Johannesburg: Radix, 1988.

————. *Youth*. London: Secker and Warburg, 2002.

Erasmus, Desiderius. *The Praise of Folly and Other Writings*. Translated and edited by Robert M. Adams. New York: Norton, 1989.

Garber, Marjorie. "Reflections." In Coetzee, *Lives of Animals*, 73–84.

Gramsci, Antonio. *Selections from the Prison Notebooks*. Translated and edited by Quinton Hoare and Geoffrey Nowell Smith. New York: International, 1971.

Michael, John. *Anxious Intellects: Academic Professionals, Public Intellectuals, and Enlightenment Values*. Durham: Duke University Press, 2000.

Monday Paper. University of Cape Town. Online archive. www.uct.ac.za/general/monpaper 18, no. 33 (November 1–8, 1999).

Pechey, Graham. "The Post-apartheid Sublime: Rediscovering the Extraordinary." In *Writing South Africa: Literature, Apartheid, and Democracy, 1970–1995*, edited by Derek Attridge and Rosemary Jolly, 57–74. Cambridge: Cambridge University Press, 1998.

Robbins, Bruce. *Secular Vocations: Intellectuals, Professionalism, Culture*. London: Verso, 1993.

———, ed. *Intellectuals: Aesthetics, Politics, Academics.* Cultural Politics. Minneapolis: University of Minnesota Press, 1990.

Rushdie, Salman. *The Satanic Verses.* Dover, DE: Consortium, 1988.

Said, Edward W. "The Book, Critical Performance, and the Future of Education." *Pretexts* 10, no. 1 (July 2001): 9–19.

———. *Representations of the Intellectual: The 1993 Reith Lectures.* London: Vintage, 1994.

Singer, Peter. "Reflections." In Coetzee, *Lives of Animals,* 85–91.

2

THE WRITER, THE CRITIC, AND THE CENSOR

J. M. Coetzee and the Question of Literature

Peter D. McDonald

SEEN AGAINST the background of the vast scholarly and polemical literature on censorship, J. M. Coetzee's *Giving Offense* (1996) stands out as an
avowedly singular intervention. As Coetzee himself points out in the preface, the twelve essays that make up the volume, most of which originally
appeared between 1988 and 1993, constitute neither a history nor a "strong
theory" of censorship (vii). Rather they represent an attempt, first, "to understand a passion with which I have no intuitive sympathy, the passion
that plays itself out in acts of silencing and censoring" and, second, "to
understand, historically and sociologically, why it is that I have no sympathy with that passion" (vii). These prefatory remarks prepare the way for a
wide-ranging interdisciplinary study that is at once psychoanalytic, literary,
historical, sociological, and autobiographical. They also make plain the antirationalist spirit of Coetzee's enquiry, which centers not so much on leg-
islative history or the practice of censorship as on the passions revealed and
concealed in writings for or against it. One of the most important essays,
"Emerging from Censorship" (1993), seeks, for instance, to understand the

curiously "contagious power" of the censor's "paranoia" (37). Why is it, Coetzee asks, that writers—and here he includes himself—so often "record the feeling of being touched and contaminated by the sickness of the state" (35)?

The antirationalist spirit of this question is as evident in the essays on specific censors and dissident writers as it is in some of Coetzee's own general arguments against censorship. "[C]ensorship is not an occupation that attracts intelligent, subtle minds" (viii), he notes at one point, before adding that it "puts power in the hands of persons with a judgemental, bureaucratic cast of mind that is bad for the cultural and even the spiritual life of the community" (10). Characteristically, given the focus of his inquiry, he bases his objection not on matters of principle but on judgments about the censors' quality of mind and the pernicious public effects of their authority. A similar logic underlies his analysis of the censors' more immediate impact on writers. What concerns him most in this case is the psychological damage censorship inflicts irrespective of whether or not a writer's works have been banned, an effect he feels he can represent only in an arrestingly precarious series of gendered and highly sexualized figures. In ideal conditions, the "inner drama" of writing can, he suggests, be construed as a transaction between the writer and the "figure of the beloved," the internalized reader whom the writer "tries to please" but, as importantly, "surreptitiously to revise and recreate" as "the-one-who-will-be-pleased" (38). "Imagine what will happen," he then asks, "if into this transaction is introduced in a massive and undeniable way the dark-suited, bald-headed censor, with his pursed lips and his red pen and his irritability and his censoriousness—the censor, in fact, as a parodic version of the figure-of-the-father" (38). The logical consequence of this consciously Freudian chain of figures is inevitable: "Working under censorship is like being intimate with someone who does not love you, with whom you want no intimacy, but who presses himself in upon you. The censor is an intrusive reader, a reader who forces his way into the intimacy of the writing transaction, forces out the figure of the loved or courted reader, reads your words in a disapproving and *censorious* fashion" (38; italics in original).

Once again Coetzee conducts the argument not in terms of principle— he makes no appeal, say, to the language of rights—but through a "speculative" analysis of the censor's passion and the effects of his "contagious power"

(37). He also argues from personal testimony. Though never banned, he did have the misfortune to begin his publishing career in the 1970s, one of the worst decades in the history of censorship under apartheid, and so his striking image of the censor as an unwelcome, "intrusive reader" is all the more disconcerting because it comes, as he notes, partly from introspection (37).

Yet he did not intend this to be merely an autobiographical exercise. His purpose was to analyze the discourse he shared with other writers working under censorship, whether in South Africa or elsewhere, and to situate it historically. His image of the censor as a patriarchal monster or censorious bureaucrat was, he recognized, not particularly unique or new, nor was it untouched by the paranoia he detected in the censors themselves. It was part of his European cultural inheritance, reflecting his continuity with a tradition of increasingly "settled and institutional" hostility between artists and "governmental authority," which he dates from the late eighteenth century (9). Artists, he notes, have over the past two centuries assumed it as "their social role, and sometimes indeed as their vocation and destiny, to test the limits (that is, the weak points) of thought and feeling, of representation, of the law, and of opposition itself, in ways that those in power were bound to find uncomfortable and even offensive" (9). Though Coetzee himself is acutely sensitive to the potential pitfalls of this heroic authorial self-construction—he analyzes this powerfully in essays on Solzhenitsyn and André Brink (117–46, 204–14)—he is equally aware of the extent to which the countervailing idea of the censor as adversary has shaped the institution of literature in modernity. The censor, as hateful guardian of the Law, is an opponent the transgressive modern writer has somehow needed.

Just how these nightmarish censor figures, who have for so long haunted Western literary culture, relate to the all-too-human censors of history, particularly in the case of apartheid South Africa, is not always easy to predict. Indeed, what makes the once secret history of Coetzee's own fate at the hands of the apartheid censors so challenging and significant is the unexpected gulf the archives reveal between the reality of his felt experience under censorship—which was, of course, not just his—and the official response to his work. Though there were many censors in the system with a "judgemental, bureaucratic cast of mind," and no doubt many who could be cast as dramatis personae in Coetzee's version of the writer's "inner drama," those who read and reported on his own novels seem disturbingly miscast for their role. *In the Heart of the Country* (1977) and *Life & Times of Michael K* (1983) were, as I have reported ("'Not Undesirable'"), read and passed by an unusually sophisticated group, appointed in part for their literary expertise: Anna Louw, a respected writer in Afrikaans; H. van der Merwe Scholtz, a minor poet and professor of Afrikaans literature; F. C. Fensham, a professor of Semitic languages; and Rita Scholtz, an educated "ordinary" reader with special literary interests. Their reports echo the praise Coetzee received from many of his earliest critical champions, and at times they even read like fairly interesting literary criticism. Anna Louw, in fact, very quickly reworked her censorship report on *In the Heart of the Country* into two reviews in local Afrikaans newspapers, praising it as her choice for book of the year for 1977. A decade later she published a more elaborate English-language version in which she responded enthusiastically to the novel as an allegory of a Calvinist consciousness.

A report on a third novel, *Waiting for the Barbarians* (1980), that has only recently come to light, confirms this unexpected pattern. In this instance, the censor and chair of the relevant reading committee was Reginald Lighton, an elderly (he was born in 1903) retired professor of education at the University of Cape Town.[1] A former teacher and inspector of schools, Lighton was, like Merwe Scholtz, firmly part of the censorship establishment by 1980. He had served on the early Publications Control Board as a member and then vice-chairman from 1970, and when the new censorship system was set up in 1975 he was an assistant and then deputy director of the new Directorate of Publications. He was also something of a literary man. A minor novelist, a children's writer, and a literary anthologist, his modest success was not harmed by the fact that he was also a school inspector. His one novel, *Out of the Strong* (1957), an uplifting moral tale for teenage boys, went through two editions and four reprintings, no doubt partly because it was, like his anthology *Stories South African* (1969), prescribed for white secondary schools. Lighton did, it seems, have a bureaucratic cast of mind—he served on endless councils and committees and clearly enjoyed being an administrator—but, if his report on *Waiting for the Barbarians* is anything to go by, he was not especially judgmental or censorious. Like the others who read Coetzee's work, he was also not disapproving.

Waiting for the Barbarians, like the other two novels, reached the censors via customs in Cape Town, who intercepted the first consignment of the Secker and Warburg hardback edition and submitted a copy to the directorate on November 25, 1980. Following the usual practice, the copy was then passed on to the principal reader, in this case Lighton. Dated December 7 and written in English, his report begins with the required brief synopsis of the story, which he introduces with a series of quotations from the confrontational blurb that Coetzee had either written or authorized.

> "For decades [an]old Magistrate had [*sic*] run the affairs of a tiny frontier settlement, . . . occupying himself in philandering & antiquarianism, ignoring the confluence of forces . . . leading to war between the barbarians (frontier nomads) & the Empire he serves [*sic*]." The Magistrate's situation "is that of all men living in unbearable complicity with regimes which elevate their own survival above justice & decency."

Having set this out, Lighton immediately notes, "The locality is obscure; some oasis in an arid region north of the equator, where winters are icy." He stresses that "it is nowhere near Southern Africa, nor is there any white populace" and that "there are no apparent parallels," though he adds that "some symbols may be found." The rest of his summary comprises a sketchy account of the plot and a short character analysis of the Magistrate, whom he describes as "a compassionate, sincere man, a loner who has gone 'seminative,' to the extent that he antagonises the police & military authorities—for he reveals some sympathy with the barbarians." Coetzee's novel, in his view, is a "sombre, tragic book," that ends "with the bloody but always unbowed Magistrate heading the dispirited remnants of the populace 'waiting for the barbarians.'" No doubt the ironies of his use of the much-cited phrase from "Invictus," W. E. Henley's bombastic late-Victorian poem about manly heroism in the face of death, were not intended—his experience as a writer of stories for boys seems to have colored his interpretation of Coetzee's ending.

The passages Lighton thought "may possibly be regarded as undesirable" almost all fell under Section 47(2)(a) of the 1974 Publications Act, which dealt with what might be "indecent or obscene or offensive or harmful to public morals." Most center on the Magistrate's various real or imagined sexualized encounters with the young barbarian girl (Coetzee, *Waiting*, 30, 40, 44, 55, 63, 66, 149), a town girl (42), and an older woman (151), but he also highlights the scene in which the Magistrate voyeuristically witnesses sex between the town girl and a young boy (97). Though he underlines those pages containing scenes of full intercourse (63, 97), he remarks that all these "sex incidents" are "generally vague, implicit." Under clause (a), he also notes scenes of "brutality," especially Colonel Joll's public flogging of the captured barbarians (103–8) and Warrant Officer Mandel's torturing and mock hanging of the Magistrate (115–16, 119–21). For the rest, he simply counts up the words *fuck* ("8 times") and *shit* ("6 times")—he finds the soldier's abusive language on page 138 especially noteworthy. The only passage he feels might be undesirable in other ways is the scene in which Mandel first reads the charges, ranging from incompetence to treason, against the Magistrate (84). From the page number, it is most likely that he was concerned about the Magistrate's comments on the Bureau's cynical abuse of due process: "They will use the law against me as far as it serves them, then they will turn to other methods. That is the Bureau's way. To people who do not operate under statute, legal process is simply one instrument among many" (84). Lighton may also have been worried about his subsequent analysis of Mandel's character, however. The Magistrate goes on to describe Mandel as one of those "men who might as easily go into lives of crime as into the service of the Empire (but what better branch of service could they choose than the Bureau!)." In Lighton's view, these comments might be deemed "prejudicial to the safety of the State, the general welfare or the peace and good order" (47[2][e]).

Yet, despite these potential difficulties, he was in no doubt that the novel was "not undesirable." His reasoning, which, in effect, became the committee's recommendation, is worth citing in full.

> This is a somewhat Kafkaesque type of narrative, with the narrator an elderly somewhat Quixotic Magistrate, for long posted at a little frontier outpost, who has sought a modus vivendi if not operandi with the nomadic tribes (the barbarians). But the officiously overbearing Imperial police & military find in him an impediment to their plan to extend Imperial sway to subduing the barbarians. So there is tension between the ambitious authoritarians and the indulgent Magistrate. He loses position & authority,

& suffers severe battering. Doom, brutality and suffering suffuse this sombre book unrelieved by any lighter touches. The few across the line sex incidents are almost entirely inexplicit & in no case lust-provoking. The locale is as obscure as Erewhon, and any symbolism more so—apart from the arrogant tyranny of State [*sic*] senior ideologists—their blinkered ideological outlook & ruthlessness. [*Added as an afterthought:* Further symbolism could with diligence be extracted. All is of world-wide significance, not particularized.] Though the book has considerable literary merit, it quite lacks popular appeal. The likely readership will be limited largely to the intelligentsia, the discriminating minority. There are less than a dozen "offensive" words, and all are commonplace & functionally in context. We [*I* is crossed out] submit there is no convincing reason for declaring the book undesirable.

The other committee members, including Rita Scholtz, who would go on to chair the committee on *Michael K,* and F. C. Gonin, who had passed *In the Heart of the Country,* simply endorsed this conclusion, which the directorate subsequently agreed not to appeal.

Now that reports justifying the release of all three novels have been unearthed—*Dusklands* (1974) and *Foe* (1986) were not scrutinized—it is possible to make some general remarks about the official response to Coetzee's work. To begin with, it is clear that all the censors recognized that his novels tested the limits of the 1974 act, especially on matters of public morals and state security. They include sexually frank episodes, scenes of torture and brutality, and they are directly or indirectly critical of the apartheid state or its agents. Their political subversiveness is especially evident in *Michael K,* but, as Fensham notes, *In the Heart of the Country* also displays "traces of protest literature," and Lighton recognizes that the agents of the Bureau and the Empire, for all their lack of specificity as "symbols," had some local resonances (McDonald, "Not Undesirable," 15). His comments on torture, Joll, and Mandel are particularly noteworthy, given Coetzee's subsequent reflection on *Barbarians,* the torture chamber, and the ethics of writing. *Barbarians* is, Coetzee notes in "Into the Dark Chamber" (1986), "about the impact of the torture chamber on the life of a man of conscience," a subject that made it potentially complicit with the apartheid regime, since there was "something tawdry about *following* the state . . . making its vile mysteries the occasion of fantasy" (Coetzee, *Doubling*, 363–64; italics in original). Coetzee would later develop this line of argument more fully, not least in his challenging critique of Brink (*Giving Offense*, 204–14). Yet complicity was only one side of the "dilemma proposed by the state." Ignoring, as opposed to exposing, its "obscenities" was equally unacceptable (*Doubling*, 364). *Either* self-censorship *or* complicity—such was the grim alternative that writing under the censor's intrusive gaze seemed to impose. For all his candor about the "contagious power" of this gaze, Coetzee nonetheless felt the writer's "true challenge" was "how not to play the game by the rules of the state, how to establish one's own authority, how to imagine torture and death on one's own terms" (364). In the absence of the detailed information contained in the censors' reports it was not possible—though it was of course for some always tempting—to judge to what extent Coetzee managed to rise to his own challenge. It is worth recalling that while the censors' decision not to ban any of the three novels they scrutinized was a matter of public knowledge at the time—the fact that the books were embargoed and then released was noted in the press—it was not known which censors acted in his case or how they justified their recommendations. On the basis of this new evidence, we can now make a more informed retrospective assessment of the censors' response to Coetzee's own struggle to avoid the state's dilemma. Unexpectedly this turns on their openness to, and idea of, the literary, since, for all the readers, the committees, and ultimately for the directorate itself, his novels' *potential* undesirability was mitigated by their manifest literariness. They were not banned because they were *sufficiently* literary.

This of course begs a number of large questions, not least because it meant various things. The novels were literary first in the sense that they had, as Lighton puts it, no "popular appeal." Their readership was restricted to the "intelligentsia, the discriminating minority." This quasi-sociological conception of the literary did not simply mean that the novels could be passed because their impact in South Africa was expected to be slight. It also assumed that undesirability was relative. No content was inherently or absolutely undesirable, since its power to offend or threaten depended either on the number and kind of readers it was likely to reach or on the way in which those putative readers were likely to respond to it (or on both).

To this extent, the censors' conception of the literary depended in part on their construction of the "literary reader." As Rita Scholtz claims in her report on *Michael K,* its "sophisticated and discriminating" readership would "experience the novel as a work of art" (McDonald, "Not Undesirable," 15). This conviction was inseparable from the censors' second, more aesthetic understanding of literariness. The novels were also literary, and likely to be read as literature, they argued, because of their formal and rhetorical complexity, subtlety, or obscurity. This was particularly important in relation to public morals. The novels' aesthetic qualities functioned as a kind of protective covering rendering any potentially undesirable sexual or violent content innocuous. Anna Louw, for instance, felt that the disturbed first-person narrative mode of *In the Heart of the Country* made tolerable the rape scenes, which "might, *in a different context,* be questioned as undesirable" (15; italics mine).

This idea of literature as a privileged aesthetic space, set apart from more ordinary forms of discourse, including less literary novels, was not just based on assumptions about form, however. Aspects of the three novels' content and themes, in particular their temporal and spatial settings, were also important, not least in relation to their potential subversiveness. They did not pose a threat to the apartheid state, the censors argued, since, as literature, their settings were either universal or not simply, essentially, or directly reflective of the *contemporary* South African situation. On this issue their judgments were not always predictable. In the case of *Waiting for the Barbarians,* Coetzee's most antirealist novel, with its largely invented geography and nonspecific placing in a colonial past, it is hardly surprising that Lighton emphasized its redeeming universality, not only through his comments on its setting but through his various allusions to the canon of Western literature ("Kafkaesque," "quixotic," "Erewhon," etc.). Though it could be argued that the novel resists this kind of reading—for one thing, South Africa is covered by Lighton's term "world-wide"—it is of all Coetzee's fictions the one most amenable to those committed to the belief in canonical art's universality. (Elsewhere I have argued that his novels resist nation-centered readings and the equally reductive pieties of the particular [*"Disgrace* Effects"].)[2] It is also, for the same reasons, the novel that leaves Coetzee most vulnerable to the charge of self-censorship, not, as he thought, complicity.

Yet on this issue he clearly could not win. The dogma of universality—canonical literature is about everywhere and all times—was simply too entrenched in the censors' thinking. For Rita Scholtz *Michael K*'s universality—she privileged a reading of it as an allegory of the alienated human condition in the late twentieth century—enabled it to rise above its concretely realized setting and explicitly "derogatory" comments on the state—she did not mention that the novel is set in the future (McDonald, "Not Undesirable," 15). Like Lighton, she used the appeal to universality to downplay, if not erase, what she took to be the novel's relatively direct relevance to contemporary South Africa. Though Anna Louw echoed this wishful universalizing tendency in her individual comments on *In the Heart of the Country*, the committee, in their general report on that novel, took a different approach to its narrative displacements. They argued that its portrayal of interracial sex was "perfectly acceptable" because the story was set sometime in South Africa's colonial past (15). In each case, then, the novels were passed not only because they were not popular, or because their aesthetic qualities rendered them harmless, but because their real or imagined spatiotemporal displacements—into South Africa's past or future, into a universal contemporary situation, or into the realm of pure imagination—and their manifest canonicity de-emphasized or overwhelmed their relevance to contemporary South Africa. All these factors ensured that despite their potential undesirability they could be officially approved because they were not going to cause offense or threaten the state. They were *too literary* to warrant banning, or, to be more precise, they were, in the censors' view, too readily amenable to their idea of the literary and ways of reading to be proscribed.

That the apartheid state put a group of censors so committed to defending the literary in such a powerful position is startling enough. Things become more disconcerting, however, if we set these censors' relatively uncensorious judgments in the context of the critical reception of Coetzee's work in the late 1970s and 1980s. This is partly because some critics did not fit the censors' construction of the "literary reader." Indeed, while the censors secretly judged Coetzee's novels acceptable because they were too literary, some leading critics, particularly in South Africa but also elsewhere, openly considered them objectionable on the same grounds. If we take Coetzee's own much-cited essay "The Novel Today," which he originally delivered as a talk in Cape Town in November 1987, as a testament to the way he felt critics were responding to his work at that time, then the challenges posed by the censors' approval become all the more acute. On that occasion, and to that local audience, which he assumed was hostile, Coetzee portrayed himself as "member of a tribe threatened with colonisation," his provocative figure for the novelist whose own specifically literary discourse was in danger of being appropriated by the discourses of politics, ethics, and, most notably, history ("Novel Today," 3).[3] The main point of his talk was, as he put it, to oppose the "powerful tendency, perhaps even dominant tendency, to subsume the novel under history," where history was taken to be a fixed, self-evident reality to which the novel was supposed to bear witness (2). He also wanted to correct the misperception that novels, like his own, that were not "investigations of real historical forces" were somehow "lacking in seriousness" (2). This negative assessment, according to which his novels were at best irrelevant or at worst inimical to the struggle against apartheid, was of course only strengthened by the fact that they were never banned.

According to the dominant view, only those novels that in a realist mode put their literariness in the service of ethics, politics, and history deserved to be valued and taken seriously in the pressing circumstances of South Africa in the 1980s. This concerned Coetzee not just because it devalued his own work, but because it assumed that literary discourse has no public value or authority per se. That assumption could be articulated in two ways. Where proponents of the "dominant tendency" recognized literariness, they did so because it made possible especially effective ways of judging or bearing witness to history (e.g., "from the inside," as Stephen Clingman's Lukacsian study of Gordimer has it). This weaker formulation, which was the focus of Coetzee's critique, granted the literary some, albeit only instrumental, value. According to the stronger formulation, which Coetzee acknowledged only implicitly, the value of the literary was at best negligible, at worst nugatory. In this view, the literariness of a novel is irrelevant, or relevant only negatively as obfuscation, since its value is wholly dependent on its status as a social document dealing with issues of race, class, and gender. This view is implied in Coetzee's sardonic comment, "There is a game going on between the covers of the book, but it is not always the game you think it is. No matter what it may appear to be doing, the story is not really playing the game you call Class Conflict or the game called Male Domination or any of the other games in the games handbook" ("Novel Today," 3–4).

His answer to both the stronger and the weaker forms of instrumentalized reading was emphatic. Not content simply to defend his own novelistic practice, he insisted on literature as a specific kind of discourse, distinct from the discourses of history, politics, and ethics; or, as he put it, "storytelling as another, an other mode of thinking" (4). This appeal to distinctiveness did not simply mean that, contrary to the weaker version of the "dominant tendency," literature was an autonomous, rather than supplementary, discourse, since, for Coetzee, distinctiveness also entailed rivalry. Against the stronger version of the dominant view, the version that sought to efface literariness altogether, he insisted that the literary existed in a rivalrous relationship to the discourses of politics, ethics and history. Read as literature, in other words, his novels could be seen not simply to disturb but to displace the authority of the historical categories—including race, class, and gender—pervading, and often deforming, the wider public discourses in and about apartheid South Africa. This further move was not without risk, a point I shall develop later.

Coetzee's formalist appeal to the literary as a discourse with its own distinct, or, more strongly, rivalrous, mode of existence looks like a version of the censors' privileged aesthetic space, an affinity that would, of course, invite further suspicions of self-censorship and compound the historical ironies. Far from being patriarchal monsters determined to usurp the position of the beloved reader, it seems the unexpectedly literary censors, not the politicized critics, were Coetzee's closest allies in the 1980s. For Anna Louw that was not surprising. Coetzee, she felt, was on her side. She eagerly noted some reservations he had expressed about "politically committed literature" in a 1978 interview, before adding that such writing had, in her view, "reached a fever pitch in both English and Afrikaans literary circles" in South Africa ("Calvinist," 50).[4] Yet the bogus drama of this next unexpected turn—it is not difficult to imagine the headlines: "Great Writer Loved by Censors, Hated by Critics"—obscures a more testing set of reversals that reflect more profound theoretical and ultimately cultural anxieties about the literary. In the febrile political context of South Africa in the 1980s, Coetzee's novels did not just fall victim to the censorious critics or, perhaps more damningly, to the censors' approval. This was partly because the censors were not simply state functionaries who applied the law mechanically. It was also partly because the critics did not see themselves only as evaluators and interpreters of Coetzee's novels. The situation was made more challenging, and worse still for Coetzee, because both the censors and the critics took on the additional task of policing the category of the literary, of deciding what constituted literature, or more narrowly, what could count as serious literature, which they of course defined in opposite ways.

Their opposing definitions can briefly be summed up if we follow the cogent formula Stanley Fish proposed in a major theoretical essay of 1973.[5] To summarize two dominant attitudes to the literary in Western thinking, both of which relied on a purely linguistic analysis of the difference between literary language and a supposedly normative ordinary language, Fish outlines what he terms "message-plus" and "message-minus" approaches to the question. "A message-minus definition is one in which the separation of literature from the normative center of ordinary language is celebrated; while in a message-plus definition, literature is reunited with the center by declaring it to be a more effective conveyor of the messages ordinary language transmits" (103). One of the chief difficulties with these traditional formulations, Fish then points out, is that, while purporting to be universal in scope, and to define literature once and for all in purely linguistic terms, each entails a set of specific, and wholly opposed, aesthetic valuations. "Message-minus theorists are forced to deny literary status to works whose function is in part to convey information or offer propositions about the real world. . . . Message-plus theorists, on the other hand, are committed to downgrading works in which elements of style do not either reflect or support a propositional core" (104).

The relevance of this seemingly abstruse theoretical problem to the murky circumstances of Coetzee's reception in the 1980s is not difficult to see. The censors, who were adherents of the message-minus definition, passed Coetzee's novels because they were sufficiently literary on their terms. As literature they were far enough removed from more ordinary discourses, including less literary novels, that would, with the same content, be offensive or subversive. By contrast, the critics, who at best followed the message-plus view, downgraded Coetzee's novels because they were too literary according to their definition. They lacked seriousness because they did not engage effectively (that is, realistically) enough with the struggle against apartheid.

Fish's essay is worth invoking in this context not only because it clarifies the stakes involved in this strange, previously invisible contest between the censors and the critics in a usefully concise way. It is also especially pertinent because it influenced Coetzee's own thinking about the category of the literary, as evidenced in his 1987 talk. At one point, for instance, he updated Fish's arithmetic—all the pluses and minuses—bringing it into the age of the desktop computer: "There is no addition in stories. They are not made up of one thing plus another thing, message plus vehicle, substructure plus superstructure. On the keyboard on which they are written, the plus key does not work. There is always a difference; and the difference is not a part, the part left behind after the subtraction. The minus key does not work either: the difference is everything" ("Novel Today," 4).

This explicitly allusive passage, one of many in the talk as a whole, casts a different light on Coetzee's defense of the distinctiveness of the literary and on his relationship to the censors. Though his talk was quite clearly a defense of literature's autonomy, it was not in any way an endorsement of the censors' morally compromised faith in subtraction, where the literary becomes an aesthetic covering that sets canonical novels apart and renders them innocuous. Nor did it offer any backing for his critics' morally laudable faith in addition, where the literary becomes an effective supplement to more ordinary discursive modes. In his view, literary discourse was neither more nor less than the discourses of politics, ethics, and history. It was just different—though, as I have intimated, his further insistence on its status as a rival discourse goes beyond mere difference, problematically reinscribing the literary in a broader cultural struggle for power and privilege. To the extent that he insisted on difference, however, Coetzee was as far from the censors as he was from his more adversarial critics, who were, at least at the level of theory, rather more like each other than they would have liked to acknowledge. For one thing, both assumed that form and content are in principle separable; and, for another, both presupposed that the literary could be defined only relative to a putatively fixed norm of a message-bearing ordinary discourse. These were two assumptions Coetzee's appeal to distinctiveness

—"the difference is everything"—was intended to repudiate. As he argued in "The Novel Today," with reference to the critics, and a year earlier in "Into the Dark Chamber," with the censors in mind, literature's authority, and his claim to seriousness as a novelist, lay in its irreducible power to intervene in the public sphere on its own terms, since its effectiveness, including its political effectiveness, and its literariness were inseparable. The trouble was, despite Coetzee's efforts, surreptitious or otherwise, to court a beloved ideal reader, few actual readers appeared willing or able to recognize, let alone endorse, this idea of the literary in the 1970s and 1980s.

To Coetzee it looked at that time as if his particular literary project was imperiled by two very different and especially intrusive kinds of reader: the judgmental, wholly unliterary censor, on the one hand; and the appropriative, politicized literary critic, on the other. Yet, as I have tried to show, the situation was made all the more testing because the actual censors who read his novels behind the scenes were not quite the opponents they seemed. Now that their detailed reports have emerged from the shadows it is possible to offer a new retrospective reading of the situation, which links the censors and the critics in unexpected ways and puts the question of literature at the center of things. On the basis of this new evidence, Coetzee could still be figured as the embattled member of a marginal tribe threatened with colonization by two opposing but equally intrusive forces—censorship and literary criticism—though we would now have to acknowledge that both were directed toward a common goal: misrecognizing the distinctiveness of his novels by assimilating them into their contradictory conceptions of the literary. In this analysis, it could be argued that Coetzee emerges as a hero of the margins, as, say, a Kafkaesque hunger artist working in the tradition of a minor literature, always against the odds.

This is still a popular image of Coetzee-as-novelist, one that he, of course, partly authorized in his polemical 1987 talk, particularly when he shifted the locus of his argument from difference to rivalry. Yet championing him in this way only complicates matters further, in my view. For one thing, the move from difference to rivalry had the unhappy effect of implicating Coetzee in a troubled European high-cultural tradition of "metacultural discourse," as Francis Mulhern has usefully termed it, according to which the literary represents not only a distinct mode of discourse but also a genuine alternative, particularly when set alongside the political. "What speaks in metacultural discourse is the cultural principle itself," Mulhern notes, "as it strives to dissolve the political as locus of general arbitration in social relations" ("Beyond Metaculture," 86).[6] Coetzee's claims about rivalry echo this tradition in so far as they present the literary as a real choice, in the logic of an either/or, set against some abstractly conceived "political discourse." In so doing, I would argue, he threatened to undermine his powerful claims about difference by overstating his case and by mirroring the equally exaggerated distortions of his most outspoken opponents: where he tended toward a hyperinflation of the literary at the expense of the political, they did the opposite.[7] None of this rests easily with an idea of Coetzee as an embattled hero of the margins.

Championing him in this way can be limiting in other, more general respects as well, especially if it entails stabilizing his particular definition of the literary or turning it into yet another universal. Doing so would simply repeat the mistakes of the censors and critics and so risk ignoring the most significant lesson of Fish's essay: "All aesthetics . . . are local and conventional rather than universal, reflecting a collective decision as to what will count as literature, a decision that will be in force only so long as a community of readers or believers (it is very much an act of faith) continues to abide by it" (108).

In this respect it is important to remember that, for all his indebtedness to Fish in "The Novel Today," Coetzee spoke in 1987 as a novelist, not as a literary theorist. His object was not, following Fish, to expose the logical impossibility of ever establishing a stable, "objective" definition of the literary on purely linguistic grounds. It was to intervene in a collective debate about what counts as literature and to persuade a community of readers to change their ideas. As his own often hyperbolic language reveals—all that rhetoric of rivalry and colonization—he was defiantly defending his own heterodox literary faith against more powerful (because more widely shared), but no more solidly founded, orthodoxies. Though aimed at his more adversarial critics, this challenge could, as I have argued, equally have been directed at the approving censors.

If this less enchanted analysis does not exactly rally to Coetzee's cause, neither does it undermine the value or persuasiveness of his case. On the contrary, it makes it all the more compelling because it insists on the literary, not as a universally fixed or "natural" category, nor as a privileged discourse above the fray, but as the site of constant cultural, legal, political, and ethical struggle in which Coetzee, as novelist, is just one, relatively powerless, figure among many. Nor does this perspective preclude anyone from endorsing his particular literary faith. Though his conception of the literary as a rival to the discourses of history and politics, in my view, risks pushing the important argument about difference too far and closes down too many possibilities, especially considering the long tradition of satirical fiction, I, for one, would rather be a "Coetzeean" than anything else when it comes to literary matters. Difficulties would arise only if this commitment was seen as anything other than a corroborating act of faith in our time.

This admittedly rather dispassionate stance would not only have important consequences for literary criticism, however. It would also oblige us to open up more effective lines of communication between literary theory and cultural history. If the first stage in the argument is to move against the censors and the critics by shifting the locus of literariness from the text to the reader, the second is to historicize the resultant "interpretive communities" more radically, as Fish always insisted, and so make possible a "truly new literary history" (97–98).[8] Relocating the question of literature in larger and more richly realized sociopolitical contexts, encompassing numerous intersecting communities, including censors, critics, writers, publishers, teachers, and so-called ordinary readers, requires a parallactic style of cultural history, which privileges no single point of view. Written from neither the critic's nor the writer's perspective—the vantage points for most traditional literary histories—this kind of narrative would involve a particularly comprehensive, if never impossibly totalizing, account of how the overdetermined, often conflicting, and always volatile desires of various interest groups (*communities* perhaps presupposes too much) have shaped literary history, or, more accurately, shaped the category of the literary in history. Such an approach would necessarily pay particular attention to the fractious, and now also wholly globalized, public arena (*public sphere* implies an unwarranted degree of coherence) in which the sometimes costly effects of specific definitions of the literary are worked out and felt. It is here that books are banned or approved, writers praised or blamed, and seemingly innocent matters of taste linked to larger questions of social and political power—all in the name of what "we" (who exactly?) call literature. Moreover, it is in this arena that the apparently abstract question of literature confronts an unpredictable world in which censors are not just state functionaries serving oppressive regimes but also morally compromised devotees of the literary, where progressive critics can be self-appointed literature police, where writers constantly risk making it new, and where everyone dreams up their own versions of the ideal literary reader. Above all it is in this arena that the paradoxical authority of the literary—not as a privileged discourse above or outside the law, history, or politics but as the most fragile of categories—is revealed most acutely and poignantly.

Notes

1. The biographical details are all contained in the forms each censor was required to fill in when applying to be a reader. Publications Control Board Archive, reference IDP 1/5/3, vol. 1, National Archives of South Africa, Cape Town.

2. Derek Attridge's essay "Oppressive Silence," to which I am especially indebted, is an indispensable guide through the questions of particularity, universality, and canonicity in relation Coetzee's work.

3. Despite a number of opportunities, Coetzee has not permitted "The Novel Today" to be published outside South Africa in a more accessible form. It appeared in its entirety only in *Upstream,* a small, local scholarly journal. The *Weekly Mail,* a courageously critical antiapartheid newspaper launched in 1985, which organized the book week at which Coetzee spoke, also included an abridged version of the essay in the issue for November 13–19, 1987. Although Coetzee reasserted his commitment to some of its terms in an interview with Joanna Scott ten years later, the essay has remained a highly occasional piece, charged with the heat of a very particular moment, a point I hope my own reading of it respects. Coetzee's target was both general and specific. As his own formulation of the "colonising process" suggests, he had in mind a dominant, Lukacsian style of reading—antimodernist, broadly realist—popular among critics in South Africa at the time, to which, in Coetzee's view, the *Weekly Mail* was especially committed. In the talk he noted that the occasion was "arranged by an active and unashamed proponent of this colonising process" (3). Though Coetzee, who was already an internationally acclaimed Booker prizewinner, clearly felt the local pressures most acutely, it should be noted that South African critics were not the only ones skeptical about his work at the time. There is not enough space here to give an extended analysis of the history of his critical reception in the 1970s and 1980s, but the following pre-1987 pieces give a preliminary idea of some of the more notable critical responses: for *Barbarians,* see JanMohamed, "Manichean Allegory"; for *Michael K,* see Gordimer, "Idea of Gardening," and Z. N., "Much Ado about Nobody." Also worth mentioning

in this regard are Clingman, *Novels of Nadine Gordimer,* which praises Gordimer for engaging directly and critically with the historical realities of apartheid South Africa, and Attwell, *J. M. Coetzee,* which makes a powerful case for the reflexive historicity of Coetzee's fiction. I am extremely grateful to David Attwell for clarifying Coetzee's reference to the *Weekly Mail* in the talk.

4. Louw was interpreting circumspect comments Coetzee had made in an interview with Stephen Watson in 1978. She probably had in mind his remark that he doubted "that the political thinking of writers is of any more interest or value than anyone else's"; and perhaps his subsequent comments about some Black South African writers "working with models which I regard as very dubious" ("Speaking," 22–23). In the same interview, he also observed that the description of the "political situation" as an "inhibiting factor" (Watson's words) "could be belied at any moment by the emergence of one or two Black writers who can achieve—I know this is a dirty word nowadays, but let me use it—that necessary distance from their immediate situation" (23). Louw's rather loaded article is, in many ways, a rare example of apartheid thinking in a reasonably sophisticated literary-critical context. She takes it as axiomatic, for instance, that "indigenous black writing" was in its "infancy" (this in 1987), and focuses her attention on white writing and Coetzee's "mixed English and Afrikaans" background, praising him as an "authentic South African voice" ("Calvinist," 50). In her view, this background set him above other English writers, like the "competent Nadine Gordimer with her obsession with the urban African political scene"; and others, like Alan Paton, Jack Cope, and Guy Butler, who "often sound like the first generation Colonial writing letters home, sometimes over-romanticizing, at other times complaining rather impotently about the other white racial group, the Afrikaners" (50).

5. Though Fish made some slight changes to the essay when he republished it in 1980, he did not alter the passages I cite. For ease of reference I have keyed all the quotations to the more widely accessible 1980 version.

6. In a powerful and provocative study Mulhern identifies "metacultural" tendencies both in the well-established European tradition of "Kulturkritik," which he traces from Matthew Arnold to T. W. Adorno through Julien Benda and F. R. Leavis, among others, and in the younger, apparently antagonistic, tradition of British "cultural studies" from Raymond Williams to Stuart Hall. In my view, Coetzee's arguments about rivalry can be linked to the former tradition. For an extended discussion of this see Francis Mulhern, *Culture/Metaculture,* and, as important, the lengthy exchange with Stefan Collini in the *New Left Review* (see Collini, "Culture Talk"). See also Collini, "Defending Cultural Criticism"; Mulhern, "Beyond Mataculture" and "What Is Cultural Criticism?"

7. Coetzee's subsequent reflections on Erasmus's *In Praise of Folly*—first published in 1992—in particular his account of Erasmus's desire to define a nonposition outside the contests of ideological rivals, might suggest that he too came to have doubts about his earlier emphasis on the literary as a rival discourse. However, he restated his commitment to the term *rivalry* in a 1997 interview. This was in response to a question referring to Attwell's conception of the relationship between fiction and history as complementary. See Coetzee, *Giving Offense,* 83–103; "Voice and Trajectory," 100–1.

8. Derek Attridge makes a similarly compelling case for a new approach to literary history in his introduction to *Peculiar Language* (1988); see esp. 14–16.

Bibliography

Attridge, D. "Oppressive Silence: J. M. Coetzee's Foe and the Politics of the Canon." In *Decolonizing Tradition: New Views of Twentieth-Century "British" Literary Canons*, edited by Karen R. Lawrence, 212–38. Urbana: University of Illinois Press, 1992.

———. *Peculiar Language: Literature as Difference from the Renaissance to James Joyce*. London: Methuen, 1988.

Attwell, D. J. M. *Coetzee: South Africa and the Politics of Writing*. Cape Town: David Philip, 1993.

Clingman, Stephen. *The Novels of Nadine Gordimer: History from the Inside*. London: Allen and Unwin, 1986.

Coetzee, J. M. *Doubling the Point: Essays and Interviews*. Edited by David Attwell. Cambridge, MA: Harvard University Press, 1992.

———. *Giving Offense: Essays on Censorship*. Chicago: University of Chicago Press, 1996.

———. "The Novel Today." *Upstream* 6, no. 1 (1988): 2–5.

———. "Speaking: J. M. Coetzee" Interview by Stephen Watson. *Speak* 1, no. 3 (1978): 23–24.

———. "Voice and Trajectory." Interview by Joanna Scott. *Salmagundi* (Spring/Summer 1997): 82–102.

———. *Waiting for the Barbarians*. London: Secker and Warburg, 1980.

Collini, Stefan. "Culture Talk." *New Left Review* 7 (January–February 2001): 43–53.

———. "Defending Cultural Criticism." *New Left Review* 18 (November–December 2002): 73–97.

Davis, Gaye. "Coetzee and the Cockroach Which Can't Be Killed." *Weekly Mail*, November 13–19, 1987, 19.

Fish, Stanley. "How Ordinary Is Ordinary Language?" In *Is There a Text in This Class? The Authority of Interpretative Communities*, 97–111. Cambridge, MA: Harvard University Press, 1980. Reprint of *New Literary History* 5, no. 1 (1973): 41–54.

Gordimer, Nadine. "The Idea of Gardening." *New York Review of Books*, February 2, 1984, 3, 6.

JanMohamed, Abdul R. "The Economy of Manichean Allegory: The Function of Racial Difference in Colonialist Literature." *Critical Inquiry* 12, no. 1 (1985): 72–73.

Lawrence, Karen R., ed. *Decolonizing Tradition: New Views of Twentieth-Century "British" Literary Canons*. Urbana: University of Illinois Press, 1992.

Lighton, Reginald. Biographical pro-forma. Publications Control Board Archive, reference IDP 1/5/3, vol. 1, National Archives of South Africa, Cape Town.

———. "Censors' Report on *Waiting for the Barbarians*." Publications Control Board Archive, reference P80/11/205, National Archives of South Africa, Cape Town.

————. *Out of the Strong: A Bushveld Story.* London: Macmillan, 1957.

Louw, Anna M. "'n Fyn geslypte metafoor" [A fine, polished metaphor]. Review of *In the Heart of the Country. Beeld,* January 23, 1978, 10.

————. "*In the Heart of the Country:* A Calvinist Allegory?" *PN Review* 14, no. 2 (1987): 50–52.

————. "'n Onvergeetlike indruk" [An unforgettable impression]. Review of *In the Heart of the Country. Die Burger,* December 2, 1977, 2.

McDonald, Peter D. "*Disgrace* Effects." In "J. M. Coetzee's *Disgrace,*" edited by Derek Attridge and Peter D. McDonald. Special issue, *Interventions* 4, no. 3 (2002): 321–30.

————. "'Not Undesirable': How J. M. Coetzee Escaped the Censor." *Times Literary Supplement,* May 19, 2000, 14–15.

Mulhern, Francis. "Beyond Metaculture." *New Left Review* 16 (July–August 2002): 86–104.

————. *Culture/Metaculture.* London: Routledge, 2000.

————. "What Is Cultural Criticism?" *New Left Review* 23 (September–October 2003): 35–49.

N., Z. "Much Ado about Nobody." *African Communist* 97 (1984): 101–3.

Publications Act of 1974. *Government Gazette,* no. 4426 (October 9, 1974): 61–62.

Sanders, Mark. Review of *Giving Offense: Essays on Censorship,* by J. M. Coetzee. *Boston Review,* October–November 1996, 44–45.

Short, Alan Lennox, and Reginald Lighton. *Stories South African.* Johannesburg: APB, 1969.

3

AGAINST ALLEGORY

Waiting for the Barbarians, Life & Times of
Michael K, *and the Question of Literary Reading*

Derek Attridge

IT'S HARDLY surprising that one of the terms in the critical lexicon most
frequently applied to Coetzee's novels and novellas before *Disgrace* is *allegory*. Their distance—with the exception of *Age of Iron*—from the time
and place in which they were written, the often enigmatic characters (the
barbarian girl, Michael K, Friday, Vercueil, and many others), the scrupu-
lous avoidance of any sense of an authorial presence, the frequently exigu-
ous plots: all these encourage the reader to look for meanings beyond the
literal, in a realm of significance that the novels may be said to imply without ever directly naming.

These proposed allegorical meanings vary in their specificity. At one
extreme, manifested in many journalistic reviews, the novels are said to represent the truths—frequently the dark truths—of the human condition.
Somewhat more narrowly, they may be taken to allegorize the conflicts and
abuses that characterize the modern world or that have been fully acknowledged only in modern times. But there is a different and more specific type
of allegorization that Coetzee's fiction invites, deriving from the widespread

assumption that any responsible and principled South African writer, especially during the apartheid years, will have had as a primary concern the historical situation of the country and the suffering of the majority of its people. The consequence of this assumption is the impulse to translate apparently distant locales and periods into the South Africa of the time of writing and to treat fictional characters as representatives of South African types or individuals.

My purpose is not to deny the valuable insights that this mode of reading has produced and no doubt will continue to produce.[1] But we are dealing here with novels that, to a greater degree than most, concern themselves with the acts of writing and reading, including allegorical writing and reading. Before relying too heavily on allegorization as a primary mode of interpretation, therefore, we need to ask how allegory is thematized in Coetzee's fiction, and whether this staging of allegory as an *issue* provides any guidance in talking about his *use* of allegory (and about allegory more generally).

Although there is, to my knowledge, no generic rule that prohibits allegories from referring to allegory, these moments in the texts inevitably have the effect of puncturing any consistent experience of extraliteral correspondences, just as those moments when Shakespeare's characters talk about acting in a play suspend for an instant our suspension of disbelief. One well-known example occurs in *Life & Times of Michael K* when the medical officer imagines calling after K as he runs away: "Your stay in the camp was merely an allegory, if you know that word. It was an allegory—speaking at the highest level—of how scandalously, how outrageously a meaning can take up residence in a system without becoming a term in it" (166). This interpretation of K's mode of existence in the Kenilworth camp has frequently been extended by commentators to embrace the whole novel;[2] yet the fact that it is advanced by the well-meaning but uncomprehending medical officer must throw some doubt on it and on allegorical readings of the work more generally. Similarly, interpretations of Vercueil in *Age of Iron* that allegorize him as the angel of death must take account of Mrs. Curren's own tendency to do just that throughout the novel—as well as her readiness to reject the allegory at other times. At the very least, we have to say that an allegorical reading of Vercueil's part in the novel cannot be straightforward.[3]

With this encouragement from the fiction itself, I want to ask what happens if we *resist* the allegorical reading that the novels seem half to solicit, half to problematize, and take them, as it were, at their word. Is it possible to read or discuss them without looking for allegorical meanings, and if one were to succeed in that enterprise would one have emptied them of whatever political or ethical significance they might possess?[4] This is not an easy project, not least because, as Northrop Frye has observed, all commentary of a traditional kind is, in a sense, allegorical, in that it attaches ideas to the images and events it encounters in the text (*Anatomy*, 89). For Fredric Jameson, too, "Interpretation is . . . an essentially allegorical act" (*Political*, 10). To say what a fictional work is "about," or to find any kind of moral or political injunction in it, is to proceed, in an extended sense of the word, allegorically. If a wholly nonallegorical reading of a literary work were possible, it would refrain from any interpretation whatsoever and would seek rather to do justice to the work's singularity and inventiveness by the creation of a text of equal singularity and inventiveness. Coetzee's *Foe*, for instance, might be said to be an example of such a nonallegorical reading of Defoe's *Robinson Crusoe*.

My interest, however, is in the protocols and practices of literary commentary—whether those of the informal conversation, the newspaper review, the classroom lecture, or the academic essay or book—and therefore in the kinds of speaking and writing about the novels that *do* make claims, in discursive rather than literary language, about their importance and the pleasure and insight to be gained from them. What I mean by a *nonallegorical reading* in this context will, I hope, emerge from what follows, but I want to make it clear at the outset that I don't mean the avoidance of any interpretation whatsoever but rather the avoidance of certain *kinds* of interpretation.[5] Some of the impetus for this undertaking comes from two well-known essays that I first read a long time ago and that have lingered in my memory with the sense that their implications were somehow more far-reaching than I had allowed. The earlier is Susan Sontag's 1964 essay "Against Interpretation"[6] (the title of my essay is, of course, an echo of Sontag's). This famous piece is a protest against all commentary implying that the point of an artwork is to *say* something. As Sontag puts it, "The interpreter says, Look, don't you see that X is really—or, really means—A? That Y is really B? That Z is really C?" (654). Fourteen years later, Donald

Davidson issued an equally forthright challenge, this time to the idea that metaphors convey a special meaning over and above their literal meaning: for Davidson, "metaphors mean what their words, in their most literal interpretation, mean, and nothing more" ("Metaphors," 30).[7] I have never seen a connection made between these two essays, but it seems to me that —leaving aside the details of their arguments—they are motivated by the same impulse: for Sontag what is important about artworks, and for Davidson what is important about metaphors, is not what they *mean* but what they *do*.

OVER the centuries, the fortunes of allegory have had something of a roller-coaster ride. Preeminent as a medieval Christian technique of reading, allegory was downgraded by the Romantics—notably the Schlegels and Coleridge—as the bad mechanical, disjunctive twin of the organic, unifying symbol. Walter Benjamin's mid-1920s thesis *The Origin of German Tragic Drama* started the process of allegory's rehabilitation, though it did not have a considerable effect until the mid-1950s, when it became easily available for the first time. In the English-speaking world allegory was championed most influentially, though rather differently, by Paul de Man in *Allegories of Reading* and "The Rhetoric of Temporality" and by Fredric Jameson in *The Political Unconscious.*[8] More recently, some studies of postcolonial literatures have argued for a significant role for allegory, albeit allegory redefined in the light of both this recent theoretical revaluation and the literary practices of post-colonial writers themselves. Thus Jameson has somewhat notoriously proposed the "sweeping hypothesis" that all "third-world" works of literature are "national allegories," since in these cultures the private and the public are not opposed ("Third-World Literature"). Stephen Slemon, too, has argued that, whereas imperialism relies on old-fashioned allegory, many postcolonial novels use a revitalized version of the trope to reveal the discursive and revisable nature of colonial history ("Allegory").

It is certainly possible, and frequently rewarding, to read Coetzee's fiction through the lens of one of these modern or postmodern theories of allegory (*Waiting for the Barbarians,* in fact, is one of Slemon's examples).[9] But what the novels seem most powerfully to solicit from the bulk of their readers is a relatively straightforward process of allegorization, whereby characters and the events that befall them are taken to represent either wider (in some cases, as I've said, universal) or more specific meanings. The urge to allegorize Coetzee—and I am including here the urge to treat elements in the text as symbols or metaphors for broader ideas or entities—is, I believe, rooted in the formidable power of this traditional trope to make sense of texts that, for one reason or another, are puzzling when taken at face value. It is one form of the reading for meaning from which both Sontag and Davidson, in the essays mentioned above, try to escape.

What I am calling a nonallegorical reading—we might call it a *literal* reading—is one that is grounded in the experience of reading as an *event*. That is to say, in literary reading (which I perform at the same time as I perform many other kinds of reading) I do not treat the text as an object whose significance has to be divined; I treat it as something that comes into being only in the process of understanding and responding that I, as an individual reader in a specific time and place, conditioned by a specific history, go through. And this is to say that I do not treat it as "something" at all; rather, I have an *experience* that I call *Waiting for the Barbarians* or *Life & Times of Michael K.* It is an experience I can repeat, though each repetition turns out to be a different experience and therefore a nonrepetition, a new singularity, as well.[10]

Every time I read a fictional text, the meanings of the words solidify into the customary ingredients of such writing—characters, places, relationships, plot complications, and resolutions—that are derived from my familiarity with the genre, my participation in the shared meanings of my culture, and from my own personal history. In some reading events, however, there seems to be more to what happens: I register a strangeness, a newness, a singularity, an inventiveness, an alterity in what I read. When this happens, I have two choices (putting a complicated matter very crudely): I can deploy reading techniques that will lessen or annul the experience of singularity and alterity—and this will usually involve turning the event into an object of some kind (such as a structure of signification)—or I can seek to preserve the event as an event, to sustain and prolong the experience of otherness, to resist the temptation to close down the uncertain meanings and feelings that are being evoked. In both cases, I am concerned with *meaning*, but in the first case I understand it as a noun, in the second as a verb.

I can, one might say, *live* the text that I read.[11] This is what I mean by a literal reading. By the end of this chapter, in fact, I will be arguing that an equally apt term for literal reading, in this sense, is *literary* reading.

I'VE noted that allegorical interpretation is frequently spurred by a lack of specificity or some other peculiarity in a work's temporal and geographical locatedness, rendering the literal interpretation problematic and encouraging the reader to look for other kinds of meaning. The paradigm case of Coetzee's temporally and spatially unspecific fiction is *Waiting for the Barbarians.* This was the work that, on its publication in 1980, brought Coetzee to the world's attention, and it remains his best-known novel (though *Disgrace* may now be challenging that preeminence). Charting an undetermined year in the life of an unnamed outpost of an unidentified Empire, and centered on an act of torture, the novel was published at a time when memories of Steve Biko's murder in detention by the South African security police—and the subsequent cover-up—were still fresh in many minds. In a sense, the novel was able to have its cake and eat it: a powerful posing of the question of torture and of the responsibilities of those in power in the places where it is allowed to happen, it could be read both as an indictment of the atrocities that were keeping apartheid in place at the time of its publication and as a universally relevant, time- and place-transcending narrative of human suffering and moral choice.

Both these readings (which are not mutually exclusive) do justice to significant aspects of the novel: the sense of helpless anger the reader shares with the Magistrate is both strengthened and given a real-world focus when the connection with South Africa in the late 1970s is made, and the painful dilemma of the liberal conscience gains added resonance from the awareness that it has been, and will be, played out, if perhaps not on a universal scale, then at many times and in many places. In their different ways, these readings are both allegories: the events traced in the novel are understood as standing for other events, either historically specific events or generalized and endlessly repeated events.[12] The danger they both court is of moving too quickly beyond the novel to find its significance elsewhere, of treating it not as an inventive literary work drawing us into unfamiliar emotional and cognitive territory but as a reminder of what we already know only too well.

The most economical way to give some sense of a nonallegorical response is to describe a few moments in the continuous experience of reading, and—for the duration of the reading—living through this novel. Here is a characteristic passage, which occurs after the barbarian girl, partially blinded by her torturers, has been left behind in the town as a beggar, and the Magistrate has brought her into his apartment.

> The fire is lit. I draw the curtains, light the lamp. She refuses the stool, but yields up her sticks and kneels in the centre of the carpet.
> "This is not what you think it is," I say. The words come reluctantly. Can I really be about to excuse myself? Her lips are clenched shut, her ears too no doubt, she wants nothing of old men and their bleating consciences. I prowl around her, talking about our vagrancy ordinances, sick at myself. Her skin begins to glow in the warmth of the closed room. She tugs at her coat, opens her throat to the fire. The distance between myself and her torturers, I realize, is negligible; I shudder.
> "Show me your feet," I say in the new thick voice that seems to be mine. "Show me what they have done to your feet." (27–28)

A standard commentary on this passage, unhampered by the qualms about allegory I have been voicing, would focus on the fact that this is one of many passages that signal the novel's insistence on the self-deceptions of the liberal conscience, in the thinness of the dividing line between overt repression achieved by violent methods and the subtler forms of oppression produced by laissez-faire attitudes, the pursuit of personal gratifications, and an unwillingness to rock the boat. The fascination with the body that characterizes erotic attachment cannot, the novel tells us, be separated from the fascination of the body evident in the torture chamber.[13] The Magistrate's acknowledgment of this connection, however, is a moment of insight from which he appears not to profit.

The soundness of this analysis can't be doubted, and these are indeed important claims powerfully made and deserving of our attention. But how thin it is compared with the experience of reading the passage, especially in the context of the novel! How much it has to leave out! There exists no critical vocabulary that will do full justice to the multiple, simultaneous, constantly changing effects of a passage like this; all I can do here is present in somewhat prosaic terms a few of the events—intellectual, affective, and physical—that may occur in an engaged reading.

Encouraged by the present tense and first person, we undergo, along with the Magistrate, the complex unfolding of feelings and associations. We sense his own awareness that he is playing out the standard rituals of seduction—the fire, the drawn curtains, the lamp; the disappointment embodied in "refuses" followed by the promise of satisfaction in "yields" and "kneels." We are conscious—as he is—of a history of sexual exploitation (of women, of servants, of subordinate races) tending to make the scene little more than the repetition of a host of previous such scenes. But the denial that follows ("This is not what you think it is"): is this the standard seducer's lie? Yes and no, it appears: the reluctance with which the words come shows that it is not a straightforwardly transparent statement. It is the beginning of an excuse—but an excuse for what exactly? Neither the Magistrate nor the reader knows. Awareness that there is some deception involved leads to a moment of self-revulsion as the Magistrate imagines himself from the woman's point of view, an old man with a bleating conscience. Better to do what he wants to do, whatever it may be, than agonize about it and apologize for it, a ridiculous figure skulking around her, talking but not touching. Yet there is of course also a sense of the ethical rightness of this hesitation, this self-doubt: he is sick at himself both for his making of excuses and for his obscure and unnamed desires.

And all the while we are aware that the girl remains closed to him (and therefore to us), that his "This is not what you think it is" is premised on an access to her thoughts, which he does not in fact have and knows he does not have. How she reads this scene, with its lamplight and its circling, prattling old man, remains wholly inaccessible. Her clenched lips may not be a response to the Magistrate's self-exculpations; her ears, contrary to his assumption, may be wholly alert. And although the subsequent action is perceived by the Magistrate in highly erotic terms—"Her skin begins to glow"; "opens her throat to the fire"—his own thought processes help us to resist the temptation to ascribe erotic motives to the girl.

Nothing obvious leads to the Magistrate's grim realization that follows this action, and at one level it is an absurd statement: the distance between him and the girl's torturers is anything but negligible. The association is felt, not thought, however: the sudden vulnerability of the exposed throat, the surge of erotic attraction, the obscurity of the impulses that make themselves known—these are elements in the reader's experience as well as the Magistrate's. And that complex of feelings, that momentary complicity with something dark and destructive, is more significant testimony to the power and distinctiveness of literature, and to the brilliance of Coetzee's art, than any extracted moral about the errors of liberal humanism. The Magistrate is, to be sure, not some kind of floating, self-determining subject; he is the precipitate of a long history of oppression and exploitation, but that history is experienced as an individual composite of assumptions, proclivities, and fears. By the time we reach the "new thick voice that seems to be mine" we have ourselves tasted a little of that sensation of being taken over, of something foreign to us uttering itself through us.

What I have just presented is a description of part of my own experience of these sentences; the use of "we" is of course a rhetorical gesture rather than a genuine plural. There is no guarantee that it coincides with the way anyone else experiences the passage (and of course the next time I read it I will be a different reader and perhaps will want to say different things about it). But after many conversations about Coetzee's fiction, after reading many responses to it, I know there's a good chance that many others have experienced something like this—and, most important for my present argument, that they have valued the experience *for itself,* not because it pointed to some truths about the world in general or South Africa in the 1970s in particular. And if the highlighting of those truths is an important function of the novel—and it's certainly the case that we can never be reminded too often of them—this fact has to be qualified by an awareness that the experience of passages like this complicates any process of allegorical transfer by questioning the rational procedures on which this type of interpretation depends. Once we attend to the details of our encounter with the novel, these seem far in excess of the allegorizations we are tempted to produce—and more explanatory of our enjoying and prizing of the novel than the political, historical, or moral truths that we can apprehend perfectly well without Coetzee's aid.

And what of the many moments in the novel when the Magistrate finds interpretation simultaneously invited and baffled? The wooden slips and the ruins among which they are found, the marks of torture on the barbarian girl, the words of the old barbarian man on his horse, the moment in front of the waterbuck when "events are not themselves but stand for other things" (40), the many dreams? As we've seen, apart from problematizing the very idea of allegorical interpretation, they contribute to the novel a sense of realms of meaning inaccessible to the Magistrate's rational powers, yet perhaps all the more strongly effective because they cannot be translated into words. The point I wish to make is that allegorical reading of the traditional kind has no place for this uncertainty and open-endedness, this sense that the failure to interpret can be as important, and quite as emotionally powerful, as success would be. The dreams in the novel evoke a yearning for the normality of life in which children play in the snow, a normality that seems achieved in the final, waking encounter; yet their very elusiveness suggests the fragility of that hoped-for state. And it is through responsive reading, an immersion in the text, that we participate in, and are perhaps changed by, this complex understanding of hope and fear, illusion and disillusionment.

These, then, are some of the qualities of the novel that are unaccounted for by an allegorical reading. In order to move to parallels outside the world of the book, many of the rich and sometimes apparently quite contingent details of the text have to be ignored, as do narrative temporality and succession (and this includes the extensive use made of gaps in the narrative sequence).[14] The powerful physical depictions, the intimate experience of an individual's inner states, the unsuccessful attempts at interpretation, the posing (but not resolving) of delicate ethical dilemmas: all these have to be played down if we are to seek meanings in worlds elsewhere. Yet these are surely what give the work its uniqueness and its appeal, these are what engross and move readers (though most would be hard put to name the complex affective responses that are aroused). And all of these attributes, which reach us as events of reading, are brought into being by the shaping of language, the phrasing of syntax, the resonating of syllables, the allusions and suggestions—historical, cultural, even physical—that play continually through the text: a manifestation of linguistic power that is central to our enjoyment.

Life & Times of Michael K invites a different sort of allegorical reading. Since it, too, occurs in a setting that is outside actual history (though in this case not outside real geography), there is an immediate obstacle to taking it on its own terms. South Africa in an imaginary future (since 1994 we have had to read it as a future that fortunately did not happen) is therefore understood as an extension of South Africa at the time of writing, that is, the early 1980s. Once again, this allegorical interpretation responds to important features of the novel: the portrayal of a country ruled by means of military and police coercion, in which there are no unpatrolled spaces for the misfit, the opter-out, the maverick, and in which the liberal conscience —personified now by the medical officer—struggles (largely unsuccessfully) to find a way of palliating the violence of the state. And once again, I want to ask what else there is to the novel's power and singularity, and in particular what it is that grips and compels us as we read, producing an experience, disturbing and pleasurable at the same time, of new possibilities at the very limits of our habitual thoughts and feelings.

As in all Coetzee's fiction, the work is full of detail far in excess of any allegorical reading. Vivid physical particularity, complex emotions, evocations of the passage of time, moments where interpretation is thwarted, narrative gaps—these and many more features have their own effectiveness and resist integration into an account of the novel as a description of the apartheid state or a warning about its likely future. Equally, details of this kind play little part in a more universal allegorizing reading, such as the one proposed by the medical officer and mentioned above: Michael K as the signifier that escapes systematization, the force of *différance* that both subverts and makes possible the articulation of meaning. But I shall focus briefly on another aspect of what I see as the novel's unallegorizability: its invitation to the reader to apprehend, and follow in its twists and turns, a consciousness unaffected by many of the main currents of modernity, including modernity's emphasis on generalized moral norms, its preoccupation with the measuring and exploitation of time, and its sense of the importance of profit and progeny. (These aren't, of course, peculiar to modernity, but they take on a particular modern intensity.)

At first sight, it may seem paradoxical that Coetzee extends this invitation through a narrative style that not only avoids the first person (except for the section in the voice of the medical officer) but that makes only intermittent use of free indirect discourse, the technical device apparently most suited to conveying an individual's inner world while remaining in the third person (and one that Coetzee uses abundantly in other novels). Even rarer in *Michael K* is the mimicking of thought itself by syntactical elisions and interruptions, Joycean interior monologue. The consequence is that phrases like "he thought" are frequently resorted to, continually reminding us that we are outside Michael K's consciousness.[15] Yet this stylistic choice—together with the use of the past tense—allows Coetzee to sustain throughout the fiction the otherness of K's responses: although we learn in moving detail of his thought processes and emotions, we never feel that we have assimilated them to our own. The language in these accounts is not necessarily that which K would use in articulating his thoughts—indeed, we often suspect that what are represented as thoughts scarcely exist in an articulated form. All this is in strong contrast to the Magistrate in *Waiting for the Barbarians,* who speaks in the first person and the present tense and is an altogether more knowable and representative character; in his case, it is what happens to him that produces the novel's powerful singularity.

There is space here to look at only a couple of passages as examples of the representation of K's inner world. K is hiding in a cave above the Visagie farm, no longer able to water the pumpkin seeds he has planted there:

> He thought of the pumpkin leaves pushing through the earth. Tomorrow will be their last day, he thought: the day after that they will wilt, and the day after that they will die, while I am out here in the mountains. Perhaps if I started at sunrise and ran all day I would not be too late to save them, them and the other seeds that are going to die underground, though they do not know it, that are never going to see the light of day. There was a cord of tenderness that stretched from him to the patch of earth beside the dam and must be cut. It seemed to him that one could cut a cord like that only so many times before it would not grow again. (65–66)

The sentences of this paragraph lead from a simple thought about the distant pumpkin plants into an extraordinary conceptual and emotional realm, a realm that—at least for the duration of the sentences—we share, yet one that retains its foreignness. In their vocabulary, the two first-person sentences offered as a direct quotation of K's thoughts are plausible representations, although their rhythm of successive, paratactically ordered phrases is recognizably Coetzeean. The thoughts and associated feelings they convey are those of a remarkable consciousness, however: the spring of hope in the idea of running all day to save the seeds, the pang of pity in the notion of seeds unaware of their fate.

The following sentence, with its startlingly material conceit of the "cord of tenderness," seems more likely to be an external rendition of a complex of thought and feeling not articulated in words: it is presented in the third person, readable as a narrator's statement *about* K's state of mind. One has only to rewrite it in the first person to sense that it belongs to a different mental and verbal domain from the previous two sentences: one cannot easily imagine K thinking, or Coetzee writing, "There is a cord of tenderness that stretches from me to the patch of earth. . . ." Yet by the end of the sentence we seem to have swerved back to K's consciousness by means of free indirect discourse: the imperative of "must be cut" sounds more like an echo of K's thought than a comment by the narrator. And the final sentence, with its explicit "It seemed to him . . . ," encourages us to think that the cord *is* K's imaginative creation, now less an umbilical cord than the stem of a plant (like a pumpkin) that has to be carefully nurtured—although the continuing use of the third person means that we still can't be sure.

It would be crudely reductive to say that Coetzee here (and in the many related passages in the novel) celebrates or advocates an ecological sensitivity, though what he does do is convey as few other writers have done the intensity that the bond between human and plant life can acquire. He does this through a writing that demands the closest engagement, the living-through by means of language of a singular experience, moving undecidably between two consciousnesses.

Just as K's relation to the earth and to cultivation implies a resistance to modernity's drive to exploit natural resources—though a resistance that never becomes an alternative moral norm—so his behavior toward other people obeys no codes given in advance. Here's a characteristic meditation by K, prompted by the comment "People must help each other, that's what I believe," spoken by a stranger who has, unasked, given him food and lodging: "K allowed this utterance to sink into his mind. Do I believe in helping people? he wondered. He might help people, he might not help them, he did not know beforehand, anything was possible. He did not seem to have a belief, or did not seem to have a belief regarding help. Perhaps I am the stony ground, he thought" (48).

Once again, we are on terrain outside the familiar moral world; for K, the fundamental injunction of neighborliness (from which he has just bene-fited) is something of a conundrum, a riddle he cannot solve. And again, Coetzee uses directly represented thought and something that hovers be-tween free indirect discourse and narratorial reporting to engage us with K's mental process while registering the strangeness of this attitude. The rhythm of the clauses, the quasi-philosophical speculation ("a belief regard-ing help" sounds as though it has come from a philosophy textbook), are not K's, but they convey all the more powerfully the challenge to conventional morality he embodies. Finally, the echo of the parable no doubt heard as a child in Huis Norenius, the institution in which he was raised, brings us back to reported thought and a sentence K can be imagined articulating.

What are we to make of this challenge? That K is some kind of amoral being, more animal than human, or that he is perhaps still an infant at heart? Certainly not; the very fact of his open-minded speculation on this matter indicates a profound ethical awareness. Rather, I would argue, pas-sages like this provide a taste of what it might mean to resist the urge to apply preexisting norms and to make fixed moral judgments—which, as I've suggested, is one form of allegorizing reading—and to value instead the con-tingent, the processual, the provisional that keeps moral questions alive. It's not for nothing that both the passages we've looked at from the novel have sentences beginning "Perhaps." Allegory cannot handle perhapses.

THE argument I am making has two levels. First, I want to suggest that *all* engagements with literary works—in so far as they are engagements with *literary* works—benefit from what I have been calling a literal reading: a reading that defers the many interpretive moves that we are accustomed to making in our dealings with literature, whether historical, biographical, psychological, moral, or political. Still speaking rather generally, I would label all these modes of interpretation allegorical, in that they take the lit-eral meaning of the text to be a pathway to some other, more important, meaning. When carried out with subtlety and responsibility, such accounts can inform and enrich the experience of the text, but if they displace the literal reading they do damage to the literary work as a work of literature. It's important to add that I am not speaking here of all the estimable effort that has gone into enriching the reading of literary texts by illuminating relevant historical contexts: indeed, literal reading *fails* if the reader is not possessed of the necessary contextual information. Literal reading needs all the history it can get.

And by a literal reading, let me repeat, I mean a reading that occurs as an event, a living-through or performing of the text that responds simultaneously to what is said, the way in which it is said, and the inventiveness and singularity (if there is any) of the saying. There is nothing new about this kind of reading; it is the most basic, perhaps the most naive, way of interacting with a literary work. But this does not mean that it's the easiest way to talk or write about literature; on the contrary, there exists a significant gap between, on the one hand, what we do and what we enjoy and even what we learn when we read works of literature with the fullest engagement, and, on the other, what we feel is appropriate to say as commentators (casual or academic), or even what we are *able* to say in the vocabulary we have available to us. Allegorizing readings arise less, I would suggest, from the actual experience of the works than from the imperatives that drive literary commentary. The more sophisticated and complex our critical tools become, and the more varieties of commentary the academic community endorses, the less attention is given to the primary engagement with the literary work. Approaches that examine the process of reading and interpretation itself—using the techniques of stylistics, psychology, or cognitive science—also tend to operate at a remove from this experience, whatever their analytic value may be.

There is, however, an important qualification to be made to this account. If reading a work as literature means making the most of the event of reading, an event by which our habits and assumptions are tested and shifted (if only momentarily), then *the event of the allegorizing reading* may be part of the literary experience. In a similar way, the event of the historicizing or psychologizing reading may be an element in that experience, although the historical or the psychological facts arrived at are only secondary. In other words, one may be doing justice to the singularity and inventiveness of a literary work by responding to its invitation to allegorize, to its quality of what we might call allegoricity, because in so doing we are working through the operations of its meaning—irrespective of whether we arrive at some stable allegorical scheme. Allegory may thus be *staged* in literature, along with so many other aspects of the way we make sense of the world. The reader may become conscious of the power and allure of allegory, of the temptation to generalize or codify meaning, and at the same time gain a heightened awareness of the specificity and contingency of language and human experience as they resist such generalizations and codifications.

The second level of my argument has to do more specifically with Coetzee's writing, and with *Waiting for the Barbarians* and *Life & Times of Michael K* more particularly. If all literary works demand a literal reading, in the sense in which I am using the term, Coetzee's works yield more richly to this kind of reading than most. Many contrasts with other works would be possible, but let me just mention one of the few novels by a South African writer that can match Coetzee's in brilliance and importance: Zoë Wicomb's *David's Story.* This is a novel that involves us, through supple and focused writing, in a moving sequence of felt events taking us into unfamiliar territory—moments in the experience of a woman participating in a male-dominated liberation struggle, for example, or of a man reliving the endeavors of his forebears to found a nation. But its importance also lies in the contribution it makes to our understanding of South African history, not only by rehearsing some little-known facts but by conveying their significance through the immediacy of the writing and characterization. We are not only informed about but given a way of engaging with and emotionally relating to the nomadic existence of the Griqua people as they strive to forge an identity and a viable home, or to the sometimes brutal treatment of women in the ANC during the fight for freedom. Although the novel achieves what it achieves as literature, its importance is finally not only literary.

I'm not sure one could say the same of Coetzee's work, though such claims have often been made. The significance of *Age of Iron,* for instance, seems to me much less as a portrayal of the 1980s in South Africa than as an invitation to participate in, and be moved by, a very specific narrative: if we learn from it, what we learn is not about South Africa (or, to take the opposite kind of allegorical interpretation, about death and love and commitment), it's not a "what" at all, it's a how: how a person with a particular background might experience terminal illness, violent political oppression, the embrace of someone entirely other. *Disgrace,* to take another case, was immediately read as a depiction of, and bleak comment on, postapartheid South Africa; but this, to me, is an allegorical reading that must remain secondary to the singular evocation of the peculiar mental and emotional world of an individual undergoing a traumatic episode in his life, challenging us to loosen our own habitual frameworks and ways of reading and judging.[16] This is not to claim that the historical and political dimensions of these novels are somehow irrelevant; on the contrary, the intensely particularized representation of South Africa (or rather the Cape) in several of the novels, and in the memoirs, is a major ingredient in a literal reading, which involves a constant testing of, and by, the ethical dilemmas that arise from those particulars.

I am not against allegory, then, in spite of this essay's title; allegorical readings of many kinds have been and will continue to be of the greatest significance. But I am *for* reading as an event, for restraining the urge to leave the text, or rather the experience of the text, behind (an urge that becomes especially powerful when we have to produce words about it), for opening oneself to the text's forays beyond the doxa. If Coetzee's novels and memoirs exemplify anything, it is the value (but also the risk) of openness to the moment and to the future, of the perhaps and the wherever. Allegory, one might say, deals with the *already known,* whereas literature opens a space for the other. In presenting this argument, I take my lead from Coetzee's writing: not only from the rewards to be gained from reading his work in this way, but from the experiences of allegorizing that it invites us to participate in but also to judge—whether it be the mythography of Eugene Dawn, the interpretations sought by the Magistrate and the medical officer, the grand allegory of apartheid whose effects are depicted so bleakly in *Age of Iron,* or the accountability demanded by the university authorities in *Disgrace.* Coetzee ended his inaugural lecture as a professor at the University of Cape Town by asking by what privilege criticism claims to tell the truth of literature, the truth that literature cannot tell itself. Perhaps literary criticism, he suggested, cannot afford to say "why it wants the literary text to stand there in all its ignorance, side by side with the radiant truth of the text supplied by criticism, without the latter supplanting the former" ("Truth," 6). His novels demand, and deserve, responses that do not claim to tell their truths, but ones that participate in their inventive openings.

Notes

1. Dominic Head, in *J. M. Coetzee*, does full justice to allegorical readings of the fiction and refers in the course of his book to many other such readings. Sue Kossew also discusses the frequent appeal to allegory among Coetzee's commentators in her introduction to *Critical Essays* (5, 9–11). As its subtitle indicates, a different kind of allegory is proposed by Teresa Dovey in *The Novels of J. M. Coetzee: Lacanian Allegories*.

2. One instance is David Attwell, who quotes the medical officer's allegorical interpretation to Coetzee (*Doubling*, 204). Coetzee, instead of endorsing or rejecting this proposed interpretation, speaks of his reluctance to comment on his own novels. (Attwell, I should add, is fully aware of the novel's undermining of the medical officer's attempts to interpret K.)

3. Coetzee himself proffers two alternative views in referring in an interview to Vercueil as someone Mrs. Curren "recognizes as, or makes into, a herald of death" (*Doubling*, 340).

4. This is not an enterprise without precedents. For example, Brian Macaskill forcefully rejects allegorical readings of *In the Heart of the Country*, arguing that a poetics of the "middle voice" "calls such baneful readings into question by denying the facile transitivity under which allegorical exegetics marshals its master code into battle against idiolect, the notion of doing-writing" ("Charting J. M. Coetzee," 79). Chiari Briganti also questions allegorical readings of *In the Heart of the Country* ("Bored Spinster," 93). Peter McDonald proposes a reading of *Disgrace* that resists allegorical interpretation ("*Disgrace* Effects").

5. Of course, there would be something misguided about attempting a nonallegorical reading of some works—*Pilgrim's Progress* or *Animal Farm*, for instance—since they clearly have continuous allegorical interpretation as their raison d'être (though even in these cases I would argue that making such an attempt might produce some interesting and important insights). Coetzee's novels can hardly be said to fall into this category, however.

6. After its initial publication in the *Evergreen Review* in 1964, the essay was included in, and gave its title to, a 1966 collection of Sontag's essays.

7. The essay was first published in *Critical Inquiry* in 1978, and included in Davidson's *Inquiries into Truth and Interpretation*.

8. See also Jameson's summary of the postmodern revaluation and reinterpretation of allegory in *Postmodernism* (167–68).

9. For examples, see Dovey, "Allegory" and "*Waiting*"; Wade, "Allegorical Text"; Ashcroft, "Irony"; Korang, "Allegory."

10. The understanding of the literary I sketch here is more fully elaborated in *The Singularity of Literature*.

11. Coetzee's essay on Kafka's "The Burrow" is a superb analysis of how syntax can be used to involve the reader in the narrative as an event and to challenge conventional notions of time (*Doubling*, 210–32).

12. In their books on Coetzee, Dovey, Gallagher, and Head all refer to the allegori-

cal aspects of *Waiting for the Barbarians* and in doing so contribute valuably to our understanding of the novel's procedures.

13. For a full discussion of this and related issues, see Rosemary Jolly's account of the novel in *Colonization*, 122–35.

14. Coetzee both discusses and enacts the skipping of narrative material in "Realism," the first chapter of *Elizabeth Costello;* see esp. 16.

15. Benita Parry has criticized the repeated use of "he thought," "he found," "he said" as involving a "speaking for" the character ("Speech," 154). My argument is that they signal just the opposite: the authorial voice's inability or reluctance to speak for the character by means of free indirect discourse.

16. See the discussions of the novel by Peter McDonald (*"Disgrace* Effects") and Derek Attridge ("Age of Bronze"). Gareth Cornwell, although he contends that all Coetzee's fictions "are essentially allegorical rather than mimetic plots," speaks of these two modes as operating in *Disgrace* "in a relationship of negotiation or mutual interrogation" ("Realism," 320). I would argue that this holds true of all of Coetzee's novels.

Bibliography

Ashcroft, Bill. "Irony, Allegory and Empire: *Waiting for the Barbarians* and *In the Heart of the Country.*" In Kossew, *Critical Essays,* 100–16.

Attridge, Derek. "Age of Bronze, State of Grace: Music and Dogs in Coetzee's *Disgrace.*" *Novel* 34, no. 1 (2000): 98–121.

———. *The Singularity of Literature.* London: Routledge, 2004.

Benjamin, Walter. *The Origin of German Tragic Drama.* Translated by John Osborne. London: New Left Books, 1977.

Briganti, Chiari. "'A Bored Spinster with a Locked Diary': The Politics of Hysteria in *In the Heart of the Country.*" In Kossew, *Critical Essays,* 84–99.

Coetzee, J. M. *Age of Iron.* London: Secker and Warburg, 1990.

———. *Doubling the Point.* Edited by David Attwell. Cambridge, MA: Harvard University Press, 1992.

———. *Elizabeth Costello: Eight Lessons.* London: Secker and Warburg, 2003.

———. *Life & Times of Michael K.* London: Secker and Warburg, 1983.

———. *Truth in Autobiography.* Inaugural lecture. Cape Town: University of Cape Town, 1984.

———. *Waiting for the Barbarians.* London: Secker and Warburg, 1980.

Cornwell, Gareth. "Realism, Rape, and J. M. Coetzee's *Disgrace.*" *Critique* 43 (2002): 307–22.

Davidson, Donald. *Inquiries into Truth and Interpretation.* Oxford: Clarendon Press, 1984.

———. "What Metaphors Mean." In *On Metaphor,* edited by Sheldon Sacks, 29–45. Chicago: University of Chicago Press, 1979. First published in *Critical Inquiry* 5 (1978): 31–47.

de Man, Paul. *Allegories of Reading: Figural Language in Rousseau, Nietzsche, Rilke, and Proust*. New Haven: Yale University Press, 1979.

――――. "The Rhetoric of Temporality." In *Blindness and Insight: Essays in the Rhetoric of Contemporary Criticism*, 2nd ed., 187–228. London: Methuen, 1983.

Dovey, Teresa. "Allegory vs. Allegory: The Divorce of Different Modes of Allegorical Perception in Coetzee's *Waiting for the Barbarians*." *Journal of Literary Studies/Tydskrif vir Literatuurwetenskap* 4, no. 2 (June 1988): 133–43.

――――. *The Novels of J. M. Coetzee: Lacanian Allegories*. Craighall, South Africa: Ad. Donker, 1988.

――――. "*Waiting for the Barbarians*: Allegory of Allegories." In *Critical Perspectives on J. M. Coetzee*, edited by Graham Huggan and Stephen Watson, 138–51. London: Macmillan, 1996.

Frye, Northrop. *Anatomy of Criticism*. New York: Athenaeum, 1969.

Head, Dominic. *J. M. Coetzee*. Cambridge: Cambridge University Press, 1997.

Jameson, Fredric. *The Political Unconscious: Narrative as a Socially Symbolic Act*. Ithaca: Cornell University Press, 1981.

――――. *Postmodernism, or, The Cultural Logic of Late Capitalism*. Durham, NC: Duke University Press, 1991.

――――. "Third-World Literature in the Era of Multinational Capitalism." *Social Text* 15 (Fall 1986): 65–88.

Jolly, Rosemary. *Colonization, Violence, and Narration in White South African Writing: André Brink, Breyten Breytenbach, and J. M. Coetzee*. Athens: Ohio University Press, 1996.

Korang, Kwaku Larbi. "An Allegory of Re-reading: Post-colonialism, Resistance, and J. M. Coetzee's *Foe*." In Kossew, *Critical Essays*, 180–97.

Kossew, Sue. *Critical Essays on J. M. Coetzee*. New York: G. K. Hall, 1998.

Macaskill, Brian. "Charting J. M. Coetzee's Middle Voice: *In the Heart of the Country*." In Kossew, *Critical Essay*, 66–83.

McDonald, Peter D. "*Disgrace* Effects." In "J. M. Coetzee's *Disgrace*," edited by Derek Attridge and Peter D. McDonald. Special issue, *Interventions* 4, no. 3 (2002): 321–30.

Parry, Benita. "Speech and Silence in the Fictions of J. M. Coetzee." In *Writing South Africa: Literature, Apartheid, and Democracy, 1975–1990*, edited by Derek Attridge and Rosemary Jolly, 149–65. Cambridge: Cambridge University Press, 1998.

Slemon, Stephen. "Post-colonial Allegory and the Transformation of History." *Journal of Commonwealth Literature* 23 (1988): 157–68.

Sontag, Susan. "Against Interpretation." In *Twentieth Century Literary Criticism: A Reader*, edited by David Lodge, 652–60. London: Longman, 1972. First published in *Evergreen Review* (December 1964).

――――. *Against Interpretation and Other Essays*. New York: Farrar Straus and Giroux, 1966.

Wade, Jean-Philippe. "The Allegorical Text and History." *Journal of Literary Studies/Tydskrif vir Literatuurwetenskap* 6, no. 4 (December 1990): 275–88.

Wicomb, Zoë. *David's Story: A Novel*. New York: Feminist Press, 2000.

4

DEATH AND THE SPACE OF THE RESPONSE TO THE OTHER IN J. M. COETZEE'S *THE MASTER OF PETERSBURG*

Michael Marais

How DOES one begin to talk about the ethics of J. M. Coetzee's novelistic practice? It seems clear that any ethical claim about literary writing rests on a range of assumptions about the way in which the literary text relates to history. During the apartheid era in South Africa, for instance, a form of criticism developed that took for granted the status of history as an a priori system in its relation to the literary text. In its simplest and most normative form, this mode of historical criticism valued those literary texts that unambiguously addressed the substantive issue of racial oppression. Quite understandably, in this climate Coetzee's writing was found wanting —one remembers, for example, the acrimony, even dismay, with which the publication of *Foe* in 1986 was met. While the country was burning, quite literally in many places, the logic went, here was one of our most prominent authors writing about the writing of a somewhat pedestrian eighteenth-century English novelist. Nothing could have seemed further removed from the specificities and exigencies of life in the eighties in South Africa. Michael Chapman probably summed up the mood and sentiments of many South

African readers and critics when he dismissed the novel in the following terms: "In our knowledge of the human suffering on our own doorstep of thousands of detainees who are denied recourse to the rule of law, *Foe* does not so much speak to Africa as provide a kind of masturbatory release, in this country, for the Europeanising dreams of an intellectual coterie" ("Writing of Politics," 335).

It goes without saying that such assessments accuse Coetzee not only of bad politics but also of bad ethics. He is seen to have abnegated his social responsibility through failing to respond to the suffering of his fellow human beings in his time and context. On a fundamental level, according to this line of thinking, Coetzee is guilty of a lack of respect for the other person. Bad politics thus begin as bad ethics.

Coetzee's essays "The Novel Today" and "Into the Dark Chamber" may be read as a response to some of these accusations. In "The Novel Today," he distinguishes between a mode of writing that "supplements" history by "depending on the model of history" for "its principal structuration," and another which "rivals" history by "occupy[ing] an autonomous place." The latter, he argues, "operates in terms of its own procedures and issues" and, in the process, is able to "show up the mythic status of history" (2–3). In "Into the Dark Chamber," Coetzee again draws this contrast in his differentiation between writing that "follows" the state in representing violence, and that which endeavors to "establish" its "own authority," that is, "to imagine torture and death" on its "own terms" (364).

Although he does not elaborate on this somewhat ingenuous, undoubtedly polemical, distinction in either of these articles, he does do so in an essay on Desiderius Erasmus's *Praise of Folly*, in which he examines the possibility of attaining an uncommitted nonposition in "the political dynamic, a position not already-given, defined, limited and sanctioned by the game itself" (2). The focus of this essay is Erasmus's argument for a type of madness that is "a kind of *ek-stasis*, a being outside oneself, a being beside oneself, a state in which truth is known (and spoken) from a position that does not know itself to be the position of truth" (10). Significantly, the essay implies a congruity between the "position" of madness and the "position" of literature, both of which are ambivalently located "in-but-not-in" the political dynamic (2). Like Michael K in *Life & Times of Michael K* (1983), madness and literature "scandalously" and "outrageously" "take up residence in a system without becoming a term in it" (228)—that is, they hold out the possibility that the self can divest itself of a controlling subjectivity and thus be in history, the realm of subjective possibility, without occupying a position within it. Interestingly, then, in these three essays which respond, albeit indirectly, to critical reactions to his fictional writing, Coetzee "defends" the politics and ethics of his writing practice by questioning the assumption of history's causal relation to the literary text that is implicit in such critiques.

In this chapter, I argue that Coetzee's fiction self-consciously prioritizes the text's relation to an otherness beyond history and that, in this regard, his position is similar to that of Maurice Blanchot, who argues that literature is grounded in an alterity that is radically exterior to the world of subjective possibility and action ("Future of Art," 211–20). The novel to which I refer in developing this argument is *The Master of Petersburg* (1994), a text that employs the phrase "writing for the dead" (245) to suggest literary writing's relation to an alterity that exceeds history. If my argument is valid, the understanding of the text's relation to alterity that emerges from my analysis should have a bearing on the way in which we talk about the ethics of Coetzee's writing practice.

IN *The Master of Petersburg,* the opposition between supplementarity and a rivalry grounded in autonomy, of which Coetzee writes in "The Novel Today," is self-reflexively staged in the character Dostoevsky's responses not only to the exigencies of history, but also to the imperative of a more nebulous, though equally demanding, "force" that exceeds history and is figured by means of the trope of death. Initially, however, this writer figure's choices all seem to fall within the ambit of history, as is apparent in the parallel between Dostoevsky's meeting with Councillor Maximov, the state functionary (31–49), and his various meetings with Sergei Nechaev, the revolutionary (95–107, 117–22, 174–203). Ostensibly, the ethical choice presented by these encounters is a relatively straightforward one, that is, between endorsing state oppression and supporting revolutionary change. However, in a manner reminiscent of Michael K's decision against joining the guerrillas in *Life & Times of Michael K* and Mrs. Curren's decision not to immolate herself in protest against the apartheid government in *Age of Iron* (1990), Dostoevsky declines this choice.

The question, of course, is why he should do so. After his initial contact with the revolutionaries, Dostoevsky explains his reluctance to continue his association with them in terms of a desire to resist being "poisoned by vengefulness" and thus to maintain a degree of autonomy (111). The suggestion here is that he does not wish to occupy a rivalrous position in a binary opposition or, to use Coetzee's term, relation of "contestation" ("Jerusalem Speech," 98), which would predispose him to respond to others in generic terms and, by extension, predispose others to respond to him similarly. If, as Coetzee notes, history "erects itself" out of such oppositions and contestatory relations ("Novel Today," 2–3), Dostoevsky's reluctance would seem to indicate a refusal to supplement history and, by implication, a desire for a state of innocence beyond the corrosive influence of history.

Indeed, just such a wish is articulated when, after noting that Anna Sergeyevna sees his "lack of zeal" to meet with Nechaev as "apathy," Dostoevsky reflects as follows:

> To make her understand he would have to speak in a voice from under the waters, a boy's clear bell-voice pleading out of the deep dark. "Sing to me, dear father!" the voice would have to call, and she would have to hear. Somewhere within himself he would have to find not only that voice but the words, the true words. Here and now he does not have the words. Perhaps—he has an intimation—they may be waiting for him in one of the old ballads. But the ballad is in no book: it is somewhere in the breast of the Russian people, where he cannot reach it. Or perhaps in the breast of a child. (*Petersburg,* 110–11)

Dostoevsky's words at this point in the novel echo those of Mrs. Curren in *Age of Iron*. When Mr. Thabane, after showing her the effects of the state-sponsored violence in Guguletu, asks her the questions "What sort of crime is it that you see? What is its *name?*" (*Iron,* 90; italics mine), she replies, "These are terrible sights. . . . They are to be condemned. But I cannot denounce them in other people's words. I must find my own words, from myself. Otherwise it is not the truth . . . . To speak of this . . . you would need the tongue of a god" (91). Similarly, Dostoevsky's response to the historical imperative articulated by Nechaev—that is, to "write about" the Russian state's violence (*Petersburg,* 103) and "Make a start!" (181)—is to argue for a language that transcends the opposition between state and revolutionary out of which Russian history erects itself.

What we have here, then, is a desire not to *evade* history but to engage with it in a manner that does not supplement the relational structures that determine the form it assumes. What Dostoevsky wants is that which these oppositions exclude. In this regard, the filial metaphor in the first of the above citations, with its connotations of purity, love, and trust, is particularly telling. Seemingly, Dostoevsky is interested in the "thing itself," an immediate contact with the singularity of the other person that transcends any mediation by the binary discourses of history and that he associates with a state of innocence.

Ultimately, it would seem that what is staged in Coetzee's novel is not so much the protagonist's refusal to choose between positions within history as his desire for that which transcends the contamination of history or the "poison of vengefulness." So far, so simple. But Coetzee complicates this position irrevocably by making it quite clear that Dostoevsky is ineluctably situated *in* history. He is *in* the world and *of* the world. Coetzee emphasizes this point by playing on the historical Dostoevsky's literary response to revolutionary nihilism in *The Devils*. Here Dostoevsky uses the biblical story of the Gadarene swine—a tale of unclean devils that, having been exorcised from a sick or mad man by Christ, enter a herd of swine that then rushes headlong down a steep bank into the sea (Mark 5:2–20)— to generate a series of analogies that suggest that Russia is a sick or mad man possessed by devils and that the swine that the devils enter upon being exorcised are the revolutionaries (*Devils*, 647–48). In *The Master of Petersburg*, however, Coetzee applies the story of the Gadarene swine not only to Russia and the phenomenon of revolutionary nihilism but also to the character Dostoevsky himself. Thus, for instance, Coetzee depicts the latter as a "sick man" possessed by devils, the outward sign of this affliction being his epilepsy, a malady he refers to as "the emblematic sickness of the age" (*Petersburg*, 235). Coetzee's reworking of the story of the Gadarene swine clearly comments on the implication of the subject in the power dynamic or "sickness" of the political context in which it is located. Through applying the story to Dostoevsky, Coetzee suggests that it is not only the nihilists who have been "infected" by the "sickness" of Russia but also Dostoevsky, who is a part of Russia and therefore also "sick." As he himself comes to see, he is "required to live . . . a Russian life: a life inside Russia, or with Russia inside me" (221).

The irony that follows on Coetzee's emphasis on his writer figure's being-in-the-world is that, despite Dostoevsky's reluctance to assume an oppositional position within history, he *already* occupies such a position. After all, the decision not to assume a position is itself a position. It is a choice exercised by a subject in a world of possibility.

What does Coetzee's ironic presentation of Dostoevsky's desire for transcendence mean? Does it suggest that transcendence is impossible and, by implication, that history is therefore a total structure? I would argue that, while this presentation qualifies Dostoevsky's understanding of transcendence, it does not dispense with the notion of transcendence altogether. In place of Dostoevsky's assumption that it is possible to occupy an acosmic position, the novel posits a notion of transcendence in and through excession, that is, a form of transcendence that derives from the erosion of the position of the subject. It is here that the importance of the trope of death in the text emerges.

Dostoevsky's desire for transcendence is figured in the novel as a desire for death: he desires to reestablish contact, through language, with his dead son, Pavel, who, in Dostoevsky's dreams, is repeatedly depicted as occupying a watery realm (*Petersburg*, 17–18, 56, 58), the "deep dark" that is referred to in the passage, cited earlier, in which Dostoevsky articulates his wish to position himself outside history. Particularly in terms of language, this depiction of the realm of the dead is reminiscent of that which we find in the closing pages of *Foe*, where an anonymous first-person narrator enters a dark, watery underworld where s/he finds the corpse of Friday and attempts to speak to it: "But this is not a place of words. Each syllable, as it comes out, is caught and filled with water and diffused. This is a place where bodies are their own signs. It is the home of Friday" (*Foe*, 157). Like the first-person narrator in *Foe*, Dostoevsky, in *The Master of Petersburg*, discovers that the space of death is a space in which language has no place. When he swims toward Pavel and attempts to call him, he finds, "With each cry or call water enters his mouth; each syllable is replaced by a syllable of water" (*Petersburg*, 17).

An unavoidable implication of this portrayal of Dostoevsky's desire for transcendence as a desire for death is that the "true words" he so desires are unattainable. However, even as it indicates the impossibility of a language of transcendence, of speaking with the "tongue of a god" and thereby articulating signs that are directly and naturally linked to their referents, this depiction points to that which exceeds the order of representation. Dostoevsky cannot find the "true words" because death is precisely that which is unrepresentable, that which cannot be adequated with the already-known and which cannot be reduced, through comprehension, to the knowing subject.[1] Dostoevsky's encounter with death is an encounter with the limits of his powers of comprehension and therefore with the limits of his culture. In its irreducibility and absolute exteriority from language and culture, death points to the excess and incompletion of closure—to the remainder that always exceeds adequating consciousness. In other words, death indicates that the totality supposedly constituted by language, culture, and history is limited and that this apparent totality is continually breached by the limitlessness implied by its limits.

So, while the trope of death in *The Master of Petersburg* points to the impossibility of a language of transcendence, it *also* points to the fact that the world of representations (and, by implication, history) is not total. Although the subject is implicated in history, history is not immanent. The problem, and this is a corollary of my discussion thus far, is that that which exceeds history cannot be *chosen*. If the subject's encounter with death is an encounter with the limits of its powers of comprehension, death is that which cannot be grasped and controlled. It is beyond the subject's jurisdiction (Blanchot, "Original Experience," 240–41). Differently put, it is outside the world of action, the world of subjective possibility. Indeed, the space of death is a space in which possibility becomes impossible.

It would seem to follow that Dostoevsky's desire for death as a space of transcendence is futile. What are the implications of this conclusion for the apparent choice between supplementarity and rivalry, through autonomy, that is posited in *The Master of Petersburg*? Is Coetzee's only point that, while history is not total, still it cannot be transcended? That, in fact, there is no choice for the writer between supplementing history and rivaling it, as he suggests there is in "The Novel Today" and "Into the Dark Chamber"?

The answer to these questions lies, I think, in the affinity that Coetzee establishes between death and writing in *The Master of Petersburg*. This affinity emerges in his use of the myth of Orpheus and Eurydice as an analogue for writing. As the following passage in the opening chapter of the novel indicates, Dostoevsky's desire for the dead Pavel is, from the first, figured by means of this myth:

> He is there: he stands by the door, hardly breathing, concentrating his gaze on the chair in the corner, waiting for the darkness to thicken, to turn into another kind of darkness, a darkness of presence. Silently he forms his lips over his son's name, three times, four times.
>
> He is trying to cast a spell. But over whom: over a ghost or over himself? He thinks of Orpheus walking backwards step by step, whispering the dead woman's name, coaxing her out of the entrails of hell; of the wife in graveclothes with the blind, dead eyes following him, holding out limp hands before her like a sleepwalker. No flute, no lyre, just the word, the one word, over and over. (5)

Gradually, in the course of the novel, it becomes evident that the myth serves as a metaphor for that desire which inspires Dostoevsky to write. This is evident in the complex of associations invoked by Coetzee's use of the turtle/tortoise motif. In the dream in which Dostoevsky swims toward Pavel in the "deep dark" of the realm of the dead, he has assumed the form of a turtle (17–18; see also 235). Later in the novel, this image recurs in the description of Dostoevsky's posture at his writing desk: "Stiff shoulders humped over the writing table, and the ache of a heart slow to move. A tortoise heart" (152–53; see also 236). The application of this image first to an encounter with the dead and then to the act of writing seems to suggest some relation between writing and death. Indeed, this suggestion is strengthened by the fact that Coetzee's use of the turtle/tortoise motif in the context of a depiction of the space of death and then of writing once again invokes the Orpheus myth, since Orpheus, the artist, gains access to the underworld by playing music on his lyre, an instrument made from the shell of a tortoise.[2] Writing is inspired by a desire for that which is beyond representation: it originates in a desire for death. Thus, when Dostoevsky sits down to write in one of the concluding passages in the novel, it is to follow a "shade" into "the jaws of hell" (241), to pass "through the gates of death" (242). The writer-as-Orpheus is inspired to write by a desire for death-as-Eurydice.

In determining what comes of this desire, it is useful to examine Blanchot's meditation on literary inspiration in his essay "Orpheus' Gaze." In Blanchot's hands, the Orpheus myth becomes a reflection on the impasse in which the writer finds him/herself owing to the incommensurability of his/her desire for that which exceeds language, with the linguistic and literary means with which s/he must attempt (and ultimately fail) to realize that desire. Orpheus desires Eurydice, the darkest point of the "*other* dark" (177; italics in original). His work is to invest death, which is without form and substance, with form and substance in the light of day (177). This is to say that he must place himself under the jurisdiction of the "law" of the work of art (177, 180)—he must make use of the conventional forms of writing. Through obedience to the latter's logic of manifestation, which is signified in the myth by the gods' injunction that he avert his gaze, the writer-as-Orpheus is able to approach Eurydice (177, 180). By extension, the moment in which Orpheus looks at Eurydice signifies a desire that always exceeds the law of the work. Orpheus gazes on Eurydice because his actual desire is not to make the invisible visible but to see the invisible *as* invisible (178).

Blanchot's point here is that the writer's desire for the "other dark" not only inspires, but also destroys the work of art. In being true to his desire, the writer both creates and destroys the work. He *betrays* the work, himself, Eurydice, and the "other dark" (180). However, this could not be otherwise. Betrayal is a necessary corollary of the unpresentability of Eurydice's radical alterity and the resultant aporia in which the writer finds him/herself in writing.

Blanchot's discussion of inspiration in "Orpheus' Gaze" elucidates the profound sense of betrayal Dostoevsky feels following his Orphic "descent into representations" in the closing pages of *The Master of Petersburg* (241). In the terms of the child metaphor with which he figures his desire for a state of transcendence, Dostoevsky's writing does not reestablish, but rather betrays, the filial relation. The concrete image of that betrayal in the novel is, of course, the narrative that emanates from his Orphic descent, that is, a story about the seduction and perversion of a child (242–45, 247–49).

My argument is that the emphasis on betrayal with which *The Master of Petersburg* ends foregrounds the aporetic nature of writing. Betrayal is the corollary of the writer's excessive desire to reveal in writing that which revelation destroys. Read thus, Dostoevsky's sense of betrayal indicates, as opposed to represents, the other's excession of the text. It thereby points to the failure of the text, that is, the absence in the text of that which he desires. It is the trace of that absence; the trace of that which exceeds the apparent totality of the text. Differently put, Dostoevsky's sense of betrayal foregrounds the crucial and ironic disjunction between what he desires to write about and what he does in fact write.[3] As a result of this dichotomy, the words produced by his Orphic descent reveal only, and incessantly, their inadequate relation to that which they attempt to reveal. The disjunction, which makes what has been said refer to the unsayable, causes the text to become the locus of its own excess, since it constantly points to that which remains unsaid and, indeed, cannot be said.

Dostoevsky's sense of betrayal therefore indicates an irreducible tension between the apparent totality of the text and an infinity that lies beyond and so belies that totality. In referring to this remainder, this excess of closure, his sense of betrayal exposes the radical incompletion of his text. The consequent paradox is that, in failing, Dostoevsky's work works: through failing, it responds to that which is infinitely other than its form. And, in its incompletion, it establishes what Emmanuel Levinas terms an "unrelating relation" (*Totality and Infinity,* 295) with that which is outside text, world, and history and so asserts its affinity with an alterity that is other than history. The text thus reveals its origin in an absence, that is, in a desire for that which is not in history and which its sheer inability to represent imparts a sense of.

There is a further irony here. While it follows from my argument that Dostoevsky *does* succeed in arriving at an autonomous mode of writing, it also follows that he does so *despite himself.* In fact, he only succeeds through failing. Through failing to find the "right words," he establishes in writing a relation to an alterity which exceeds history and, in so doing, transcends history. By implication, the kind of transcendence that he "achieves" is not a result of an exercise of choice in the realm of subjective possibility, but of an encounter, in writing, with that which is beyond the sphere of subjective action and control.[4] The transcendence that he "attains" is not the result of an action in the world. It is precisely the result of his *inability* to adequate and thereby control that which he encounters in writing. As Blanchot puts it, in writing the writer loses the right to say I ("Where Now?" 194). It is in this sense that one is able to say that Dostoevsky succeeds, but does so despite himself.

What one ultimately finds staged in *The Master of Petersburg* is therefore not a choice but an irreducible tension between supplementarity and a rivalry premised on autonomy. There is no choice here because autonomy in literary writing is never the action of an I that is able. Autonomy *happens* because of the writing subject's encounter with that which falls beyond its jurisdiction. In fact, the disabling relation to alterity that the writer instantiates in the moment of writing renders literature radically ambiguous. Blanchot maintains that the writer who attempts "to express things in a language that designates things according to what they mean" ("Literature," 332), that is, to bring "things" into the "light of the world" (329), may find that his/her prose treacherously evokes the insubstantiality of the "night." Conversely, the writer who is concerned with "what things and beings would be if there were no world" (333), that is, with things "prior to the day" (329), may find that his/her writing betrays that concern. It is just such an ambiguity—that is, one concomitant on the writer's loss of control—that is enacted in Dostoevsky and Anna Sergeyevna's uncertainty about the outcome of their sexual commerce (*Petersburg,* 225–26). Will the product of their sexual activity (and, of course, sexual activity here serves as a figure for literary activity) be a devil or a savior? Will it supplement history by becoming one of the devils that possesses the "sick man" of Russia, or will it transcend this context and thereby gain the ability to "save" it? Dostoevsky *does not know,* because he loses control over what he creates. Like sex (230) and, indeed, death (118) and epileptic seizures (53, 54, 68–69, 71, 213), writing is a falling (234, 241, 249) that ecstatically divests him of a controlling subjectivity.

In contrast to the madness of vengefulness that is inspired by the subject's implication in history, the madness of literary inspiration derives from the self's possession by an otherness *outside* history. Inspiration is the individual's *possession* by a radical alterity that leaves him/her beside him/herself.

Dostoevsky's anxiety about the effect of his literary activity mirrors that of Coetzee. It reflects Coetzee's uncertainty about whether his writing will supplement the contestatory relations in South Africa or rival them. What is interesting about the novel's ontogenetic anxiety is that it testifies to the *intentionality* of Coetzee's writing project. Coetzee wishes to exploit what, for Blanchot, is the strangeness of literature, that is, the fact that it is in the world but not of the world. Coetzee *wants* his novel to rival history and to do so by occupying an "autonomous place." However, he is aware that autonomy, the text's relation to alterity by default, cannot be chosen. In writing about a writerly loss of control that enables the text to occupy an autonomous place, he is in fact attempting to gain autonomy through an assertion of control. Couched in the terms of his deliberation on *ekstasis* in his essay on Erasmian folly, Coetzee *knows* that he is depicting "a state in which truth is known (and spoken) from a position that does not know itself to be the position of truth" ("*Praise of Folly,*" 10), and that, in so doing, he puts himself "in the position of the subject supposed to know," the position he (foolishly) claims not to occupy (12). Through its ontogenetic anxiety, *The Master of Petersburg* signals its knowledge of the acute irony of such a project.

Indeed, in its consciousness of the irony inherent in knowingly writing about a position that cannot be occupied knowingly, the novel would seem to contradict itself or, more precisely, expose a contradiction in its argument. Does it follow that the text thereby suggests that there is no stance outside the totalizing political, no access to the kind of knowledge that might derive "from a position outside, a position that does not know itself" (Coetzee, "*Praise of Folly,*" 5)? If this is so, it should also follow that the irony through which the text signals this contradiction is that of the knowing *eiron*. This, however, is patently not the case. In pointing to a radical disjunction between the unknowing position that Coetzee attempts to thematize and the position of knowledge from which that attempt necessarily proceeds, the novel activates a form of irony that derives not from a stable relation between said and unsaid in which the latter is always already determined by the former in a way that consolidates the ironist's position of knowledge, but rather from the said's relation to that which *cannot* be said and which is therefore always disablingly beyond the compass of subjective possibility.[5]

The irony at work here thus not only admits that that which it attempts to thematize is necessarily compromised by the very act of thematization but also indicates that it is *unthematizable* and so outside the jurisdiction of the writing subject. Accordingly, this mode of irony perturbs rather than consolidates the writer's position of knowledge. At the same time, though, the irony self-reflexively renders itself ironic: it knows that the gesture that questions the writer's position of knowledge is, in itself, inevitably an attempt on the part of the knowing, writing subject at asserting control and therefore deeply ironic. By further extension, the novel's awareness of the irony of this enterprise is itself, once again, ironic. The movement of irony here discernible is consequently infinite. In doubling back on itself and rendering the previous attempt at asserting control ironic, each stage in this infinitely regressive process demonstrates the writer's loss of control in attempting to assert control through questioning control. And, in its ineluctably ateleological nature, the skeptical movement of this form of irony exemplifies the radical incompletion of the text. In other words, the endless movement of irony in the novel talks ceaselessly of that which always remains unsaid and is unsayable.

The only knowledge that derives from the work of irony and the ontogenetic anxiety that it enacts in *The Master of Petersburg* is therefore the profoundly skeptical awareness that, if Coetzee's work works—if it establishes an "unrelating relation" to alterity and thereby achieves a certain autonomy—it does so despite him, that is, despite the position of knowledge that he attempts to occupy in thematizing a writerly loss of control.

WHAT is the relevance of this discussion of the way in which *The Master of Petersburg* aligns itself with an alterity that exceeds history—and thus questions history's status as an a priori structure relative to literature—to a debate on the ethics of Coetzee's novelistic practice? If action is defined in Hegelian terms as negation, the relation that is established with alterity in the moment of writing points to that which exceeds the closure of the dialectic. It points to the excess that remains after negation and, accordingly, the impossibility of nothingness. Indeed, this relation performs the impossibility of nothingness by showing that the representation that it engenders is not total, and by insisting that if it were, it would leave nothing.

•

If totality is an impossibility, *there* always *is*. For this reason, Emmanuel Levinas, in his account of the *il y a,* the "there is," refers to the "plenitude of the void" and the "murmur of silence" (*Existence,* 63–64). And Coetzee, in *Age of Iron,* has Mrs. Curren, his writer figure, inquire why it is that, when "the rest should be silence," her "voice that is no voice" keeps going "on. On and on" (149).

My concluding argument, then, is that this preoccupation with the excess of closure in *The Master of Petersburg* destabilizes the Hegelian relation and, in doing so, opens the possibility of an alternative basis of sociality to those Hegelian and post-Hegelian descriptions of intersubjectivity that ground relations between humans in a dialectic of recognition. In other words, the novel's concern with excess indicates the possibility of a relationship with other existents that is grounded not in correlation, and accordingly in notions of reciprocity and symmetry, but in nonrelation, that is, the subject's *inability* to foreclose on the otherness of the other. Owing to this inability, the subject finds itself in relation to something that is nothing definable, that is, in Levinas's words, in "a relationship with the exterior . . . without this exteriority being able to be integrated into the same" ("Philosophy," 54). This "unrelating relation" between "separated beings" (Levinas, "*Totality,* 295) is the precondition for a recognition of and respect for difference. It is a relationship in which the other, with its singularity intact, absolves itself from the relationship. For Levinas, such an "unrelating relation" is the very condition of ethics.

It is just this possibility of an ethics that is premised on the failure of subjective possibility that is depicted on the presentational surface of Coetzee's novels. Elsewhere, I have argued that Coetzee's novels routinely portray characters who inexplicably and unaccountably become involved with other existents (2000), that is, develop a sense of responsibility for these beings and do so despite themselves. In *Age of Iron,* Mrs. Curren comes to realize that, if she is to love her daughter, she must love the vagrant, "John," that is, the unlovable: "I must love, first of all, the unlovable. I must love, for instance, this child. Not bright little Bheki, but this one. He is here for a reason. He is part of my salvation. I must love him. But I do not love him. Nor do I want to love him enough to love him *despite myself*" (125; italics mine). Contrary to the Levitical injunction, then, she must love her neighbor not as herself but despite herself. Similarly, Dostoevsky, in *The Master of Peters-burg,* must learn that, if he is to love Pavel, he must love the unlovable, Sergei Nechaev. This point is made by the sequence of scenes in which Dostoevsky attempts to call up Pavel's face in his mind, only to find that the image of Nechaev appears instead. In the first of these scenes, he tries to "dismiss the image" with the words "Go away!" (49). This action adversely affects his attempt to "summon up Pavel's face": "'Pavel!' he whispers, conjuring his son in vain" (49). When Pavel does eventually reappear in a vision, he is together with a bride who Dostoevsky thinks may be one of the women who has lured him to the nihilists' garret. Significantly, it later transpires that the woman in question is Nechaev in disguise (96). It is in this context that Dostoevsky finally asks himself the question, "Is that what he must learn: that in God's eyes there is no difference between the two of them, Pavel Isaev and Sergei Nechaev, sparrows of equal weight?" (238).

In *Foe,* one similarly finds that the protagonist, Susan Barton, notwith-standing her protestations that Friday is nothing to her, is quite plainly, in her actions, consumed by responsibility for him (147–49). She cares for him and does so despite herself. And, in *Disgrace,* David Lurie, who con-tinually asserts his autonomy, that is, his detachment from other beings, realizes with some surprise that he has *unaccountably* come to care for the dogs at the Animal Welfare League clinic in Grahamstown and for the sheep that Petrus intends to slaughter. Coetzee's use of the following agentless sen-tence in his description of the bond that emerges between David Lurie and the sheep is, I think, deeply significant:[6] "A bond seems to have come into existence between himself and the two Persians, he does not know how" (126).[7] On a syntactical level, one finds enacted in the language of this latter novel a form of responsibility that derives from the subject's loss of control.

My ultimate contention is that the basis for the kind of responsibil-ity that Coetzee depicts on the presentational surface of his novels is self-reflexively performed in his texts' preoccupation with the relation to alterity that is established in the act of writing, that is, the moment in which writ-ing ceases to be the action of a subject in the world and becomes some-thing rather different. In its performance of its ontogenesis, the text points to that which exceeds history as realm of subjective possibility and thus to the imbrication of being with otherness. And, in indicating this imbrication, the text suggests the ethical possibility of living with difference, that is, the possibility of a respect for the singularity of the other existent that derives from an erosion of subjective possibility, the subject's loss of control over the other.

Notes

1. See Blanchot, "Original Experience," 240–41.
2. See Baines, "Lyre."
3. See "Irony and Otherness," Johan Geertsema's impressive, pioneering study of the relation between irony and otherness. Geertsema devotes his final chapter to a discussion of Coetzee's *Age of Iron.*
4. See Blanchot, "Characteristics of the Work of Art," 231–32. See also Derek Attridge's insightful reading of Dostoevsky's "falling into writing" in ""Expecting the Unexpected."
5. See Geertsema, "Irony and Otherness."
6. I am indebted to Carrol Clarkson for pointing this out to me.
7. See Coetzee's discussion of the agentless sentence ("Agentless Sentence").

Bibliography

Attridge, Derek. "Expecting the Unexpected: Coetzee's *Master of Petersburg* and Some Recent Works by Derrida." In *Applying: to Derrida,* edited by John Brannigan, Ruth Robbins, and Julian Wolfreys, 21–40. London: Macmillan, 1996.

Baines, Anthony. "Lyre." In *The New Oxford Companion to Music,* edited by Denis Arnold, 2:1106. 2 vols. Oxford: Oxford University Press, 1983.

Blanchot, Maurice. "Characteristics of the Work of Art." In *The Space of Literature,* translated by Ann Smock, 211–20. Lincoln: University of Nebraska Press, 1982.

———. "The Future and the Question of Art." In *The Space of Literature,* 211–20.

———. "The Original Experience." In *The Space of Literature,* 234–47.

———. "Orpheus' Gaze." In *The Sirens' Song: Selected Essays by Maurice Blanchot,* edited by Gabriel Josipovici, translated by Sacha Rabinovitch, 177–81. Brighton: Harvester Press, 1982.

———. "Where Now? Who Now?" In *The Sirens' Song,* 192–98.

———. "Literature and the Right to Death." In *The Work of Fire,* translated by Charlotte Mandell, 300–43. Stanford: Stanford University Press, 1995.

Chapman, Michael. "The Writing of Politics and the Politics of Writing: On Reading Dovey on Reading Lacan on Reading Coetzee on Reading . . . (?)." Review of *The*

Novels of J. M. Coetzee: Lacanian Allegories, by Teresa Dovey. *Journal of Literary Studies* 4, no. 3 (1988): 327–41.

Coetzee, J. M. "The Agentless Sentence as Rhetorical Device." In *Doubling the Point,* 170–80.

———. *Age of Iron.* London: Secker and Warburg, 1990.

———. *Disgrace.* London: Secker and Warburg, 1999.

———. *Doubling the Point: Essays and Interviews.* Edited by David Attwell. Cambridge, MA: Harvard University Press, 1992.

———. "*Erasmus' Praise of Folly:* Rivalry and Madness." *Neophilologus* 76, no. 1 (1992): 1–18.

———. *Foe.* Johannesburg: Ravan, 1986.

———. "Into the Dark Chamber: The Writer and the South African State." In *Doubling the Point,* 361–68.

———. "Jerusalem Prize Acceptance Speech." In *Doubling the Point,* 96–99.

———. *Life & Times of Michael K.* Johannesburg: Ravan, 1983.

———. "The Novel Today." *Upstream* 6, no. 1 (1988): 2–5.

———. *The Master of Petersburg.* London: Secker and Warburg, 1994.

Dostoevsky, Fyodor. *The Devils.* Translated by David Magarshack. 2nd ed. Harmondsworth: Penguin, 1971.

Geertsema, Johan. "Irony and Otherness: A Study of Some Recent South African Narrative Fiction." PhD diss., University of Cape Town, 1999.

Levinas, Emmanuel. 1978. *Existence and Existents.* Translated by Alphonso Lingis. The Hague: Martinus Nijhoff.

———. 1987. "Philosophy and the Idea of Infinity." In *Collected Philosophical Papers,* translated by Alphonso Lingis, 47–59. Dordrecht: Martinus Nijhoff.

———. 1991. *Totality and Infinity: An Essay on Exteriority.* Translated by Alphonso Lingis. Dordrecht: Kluwer Academic Publishers.

Marais, Michael. "'Little Enough, Less Than Little: Nothing': Ethics, Engagement, and Change in the Fiction of J. M. Coetzee." *Modern Fiction Studies* 46, no. 1 (2000): 159–82.

5

A BELIEF IN FROGS

J. M. Coetzee's Enduring Faith in Fiction

Dominic Head

COMPLICITY IS a topic that is familiar in postcolonial criticism, where it may often identify the guilt of the colonizer, or of those who can be associated with this guilt on historical grounds. Complicity often then becomes a bridge to link a writer, or a literary work, with particular historical or political questions. For Coetzee, such a procedure inevitably evokes the broader anguish of the liberal whites of South Africa and, more specifically, of those who, like Coetzee, recognize that the label Afrikaner may be applied to them, as an external act of naming, even though they may not choose that affiliation for themselves.[1]

The association between writer, work, and political context in relation to the late-colonial situation of apartheid South Africa was inevitable. But one of the implicit assumptions of this essay is that, as apartheid recedes into history, such a chain of association becomes less compelling. It is true that all along Coetzee has betrayed a dynamic of resistance that challenges the dominance of the political over the literary; but it is equally true that his work up to and including *The Master of Petersburg* (1994) acknowledges the power of contemporary politics to delimit any fictional project.

Waiting for the Barbarians (1980) is representative of the kind of bleak intensity that results where the writer's impulse toward resistance—as a complex figure for creative independence—comes up against the felt obligation to respond to history. Coetzee has acknowledged that this novel is specifically about torture and its impact on the "man of conscience." In his essay on this topic he goes on to consider the justification for, and also the dangers in, the preoccupation with torture in the South African novel. Writers are drawn to the topic, argues Coetzee, first because the connection between torturer and tortured is an extreme, compelling metaphor for authoritarian oppression more generally; and, second, because there is no individual interaction more private and extreme than that which occurs in the torture chamber. Coetzee's implication is that the novelist feels a moral obligation to interrogate this hidden "vileness" but finds therein an archetypal situation of fictional creativity, ideal for the revelation of dark human mysteries.[2]

Despite the metaphorical association that might transform the ambivalent fascination with torture into a literary project, it is still grubbily mired in its actual context. Torture, or the possibility of it, was a fact of daily life for many people in South Africa in 1980, and so the representation of it strikes a chilling and literal chord.

This sense of historical recontainment can be peculiarly suffocating. It is not just that Coetzee feels obliged to write about political repression but that in seeking to do so on his own terms the gesture may be self-defeating. In connection with *Waiting for the Barbarians,* Coetzee outlines the basic dilemma in the treatment of torture in a context like apartheid South Africa, where the writer fails either by ignoring it or by "reproducing" it through representation. The writer becomes the unwitting agent of the repressive state, reproducing the fear upon which its power depends. Resolving this dilemma is the difficult task the writer faces, in seeking to imagine torture and death on his or her terms (*Doubling,* 364). We may feel that Coetzee resolves the problem very well in *Barbarians.* In those scenes where the Magistrate is tortured, Coetzee treads a fine line between prosecuting the character's moral journey and generating a stultifying fear of moral protest. Yet the whole is delimited at some level by the double bind that obtains in the treatment of violence in such a context.

The richness of Coetzee's works between 1974 and 1994 may come partly from the strategies he developed to contest, or at least ameliorate, the effects of the apartheid straitjacket. His complex and ambivalent use of allegory is a notable means by which history and literature are kept apart; the investigation of the confessional mode is another. Even in *Age of Iron* (1990), Coetzee's most realistic novel of the apartheid era, the threat to the white, liberal sensibility is steered skillfully away from the generation of reactionary terror: for Mrs. Curren, her emerging sense of personal insignificance is made manifest through an exploration and development of the confessional mode, a distinctly literary project that comes to dominate the book.

The representation of violence, however, remains fraught with difficulties, especially for the writer who is pushed to the limits of inventiveness to prevent literature collapsing into politics. For example, it is certainly risky for Coetzee, in *In the Heart of the Country* (1977), to depict the rape of a white woman by a black man in the exploration of postcolonial intellectual repression, not least because the fantasy about the black man as rapist is a recurring topos in the discourse of racism. *In the Heart of the Country* evades the problem through its elaborate narrative procedures: this is a ludic, postmodernist novel in which the certainty of event is made open to doubt and secondary to the investigation of how discourse constructs the self: "I make it all up in order that it shall make me up" is the instructive summary of this impulse offered by Magda, the narrator, or rather, monologist, of the novel (73).[3]

The multiple rape that lies at the heart of *Disgrace* (1999)—a novel that is more bluntly realistic than Coetzee's earlier novels—is more problematic. The actual event is not described, but the brutality of it and its effects are made quite clear. David Lurie's daughter, Lucy, seems to accept her father's analysis of the rapists, or some version of it, that "it was history speaking through them" (156). By refusing to lay charges, and by accepting the arrangement offered by her neighbor Petrus—to become an additional "wife" to him, in exchange for his protection (200)—she seems to capitulate to a protracted exercise in blackmail and extortion. Of course, the parallel between the sexually predatory Lurie and the rapists is obvious enough. But as the punitive sexual violence endured by Lucy seems bound up with Petrus's expansionist designs on Lucy's land, her defeat seems to epitomize a depressing postcolonial lesson. As Elizabeth Lowry puts it, "what *Disgrace* finally shows us is the promised victory of one expansionist force over another, with women as pawns, the objects of punitive violence" ("Like a

Dog," 14). Coetzee seems to have lost the desire to keep history at a distance; neither does he pursue distinctively literary modes—such as allegory or confession—in familiar ways.

In both *Age of Iron* and *The Master of Petersburg* Coetzee engages in an extended investigation of the potential of the confessional mode, seeking to extract from it a secular equivalent of absolution. In *Disgrace* Coetzee seeks a secular equivalent of absolution too, but now he has recourse to other means that are quite different from his rich investigations of the confessional mode in previous novels. Confession, in fact, becomes banal in *Disgrace.* This is clear in the episode in which Lurie is brought before the committee convened to consider the complaint brought by Melanie Isaacs, the student with whom Lurie has an affair. Ostensibly, this is an "inquiry," but it soon becomes clear that some members of the committee have prejudged the issue. Dr. Farodia Rassool is the punitive feminist who carries the burden of Coetzee's censure. Forgetting the committee's brief, she seeks to punish Lurie and forces him to make a "confession" of guilt (51–52). However, Lurie's willingness to accept the charges and his confession that he "became a servant of Eros" are not presented in the terms that Rassool requires, that is, a confession to the "abuse of a young woman" (53).

One is initially reminded of Colonel Joll's pursuit of truth/pain in *Waiting for the Barbarians,* where torture is deployed to generate the desired "truth." In that novel, the allegorical dimension, embracing the mutability of language as well as the imperial mind-set, affords a treatment of interrogation on more than one level. The more overtly realistic codes of *Disgrace,* by contrast, make this episode seem a flat renunciation of political correctness.

There is, of course, an important political dimension to this. Coetzee challenges the liberal sensibility that might have to accept the integrity of a "confession" made in terms that seem quite other to the normative codes of a situation. And, in the context of a contemporary South Africa experimenting with its Truth and Reconciliation Commission, this demonstration of a hearing in which justice is predetermined strikes a disturbing note.[4] In the same way that an uncompromising feminism might find it uncomfortable to confront the "otherness" of male desire, so did the TRC struggle to remain impartial at all times.[5] Complicity is a various phenomenon.

Yet the immediate political resonance of *Disgrace* is ominous and depressing. One reason for this is that Coetzee seems to be turning away from the allegorical structures of his earlier novels and the kind of multi-faceted layered meaning that critics have come to look for in his work. But if there is a shift of emphasis in *Disgrace,* a partial turning away from earlier concerns, what is Coetzee turning to? There is certainly a distinct shift in this novel from the early Cape Town chapters to the scenes centered on the daughter Lucy's smallholding and Lurie's journey of self-relinquishment. This is the heart of the book, in which a newly oriented gesture of resistance is discernible.

Before considering this, however, it may be fruitful to consider the significance of resistance in Coetzee's work. Indeed, he places great stress on resistance, and, in observing this, we may be encouraged to connect different levels of resistance: the resistance of the individual, faced with socially imposed obligations to act or think in a particular way; the resistance of the author, faced with interviewers' questions that appear to oblige him to sanction one reading or another; the resistance of the novels, and the characters within them, to yield their meaning.

Pursuing this line, we can connect particular textual operations with a larger vision. Thus, the simultaneous reliance on and distrust of allegory in Coetzee's work puts his readers through the experience of being enticed to overlay a work with a template of meaning before realizing the incompleteness or even complicity of such readings. We are encouraged to wonder, with Coetzee, about the nature of criticism: "what can it ever be, but either a betrayal (the usual case) or an overpowering (the rarer case) of its object? How often is there an equal marriage?" (*Doubling,* 61). Like the colonizer, armed with his own inflexible codes for understanding the world, the reader must balk at his or her own inclination to order, simplify, explain, in the face of the alterity of the text. And here we may well be justified in making a clear connection between recent enthusiasm for narrative ethics and the resisting Coetzee text.

Both impulses, it would seem, are accounted for in Derek Attridge's case for "responsible reading" that "attempts to do justice to the alterity, singularity, and inventiveness of the literary work." Attridge locates the ethical in the event of an appropriately inventive or responsible reading, which is also a response to "inventive *writing*." A responsible reading, for Attridge, does "not attempt to pigeonhole a work": "To read a work responsibly . . . is to read it without placing over it a grid of possible uses, as historical evidence, moral lesson, path to truth, political inspiration, or personal encouragement. It is to trust in the unpredictability of reading, its openness to the future" ("Ethics," 34).[6] This would seem to represent the critical equivalent of Coetzee's insistence on the autonomy of the writer and the novel, especially the felt need to establish a position of "rivalry" with history, when the only other option seems to be "supplementarity" (Coetzee, "Novel Today," 3). But insofar as Attridge is consciously constructing a version of critical reading—an ethical event—in which the inventiveness of the work is matched, or at least responded to, by the inventiveness of the critic, we may wonder if he points the way to the "equal marriage" between critic and work that Coetzee implies is virtually impossible.

Here is not the place to debate the degree to which such an equal marriage is desirable (or the extent to which it might indicate a loss of proper critical distance). But it is appropriate to add this qualification: that the idea of this equal marriage, when applied to a single author and the ideas about writing and criticism his fictional works seem to stimulate, can operate at only a very generalized level. The connection is vulnerable at every turn to the shifting emphases in successive works. Tracing some of these shifting emphases, however, can be instructive.

I defend the idea that the title character of *Life and Times of Michael K*, at one plane of significance, makes us think about the problem of textual meaning and, by extension, the danger of critical "betrayal" or "overpowering." The probing of the medical officer in the second section of the novel, whose desire is to make K "yield" his story, serves to overemphasize the sense in which the character's elusiveness is also an allegory of textual meaning (152). The important moment here is when the medical officer imagines pursuing K, calling out to him his interpretation that K's stay in the camp was an allegory of "how outrageously a meaning can take up residence in a system without becoming a term in it" (166). This is complex because different ideas of allegory are in play: the political allegory that K inhabits yet resists, the allegory of the deferral of meaning that is also undercut by the dogged earthiness of K, and the allegory of reading. In the connection with the latter, we must have a dual response to the medical officer, whose sense of urgency to interpret K gives him, on the one hand, the hue of an "overpowering" reader. Yet, on the other, his understanding that K has a meaning that is somehow beyond the "system" he seems to inhabit is a redeeming feature. In this sense he shows an incipient understanding that his apparent frustration is inappropriate: he is on a journey, it seems, to the site inhabited by Attridge's responsible reader.

Another passage, this time from *Disgrace,* could also lend itself to a reading that reveals the same different planes of signification: a representation of South Africa and a simultaneous metaphor for the processes of critical reading. This is the description in which we learn why Lurie decides to take responsibility for the incinerating of the dogs' corpses, after they have been killed humanely at the Animal Welfare League clinic. On the first occasion, he had simply delivered the corpses to the hospital for incineration:

> Rigor mortis had stiffened the corpses overnight. The dead legs caught in the bars of the trolley, and when the trolley came back from its trip to the furnace, the dog would as often as not come riding back too, blackened and grinning, smelling of singed fur, its plastic covering burnt away. After a while the workmen began to beat the bags with the backs of their shovels before loading them, to break the rigid limbs. It was then that he intervened and took over the job himself. . . .
>
> Why has he taken on this job? To lighten the burden on Bev Shaw? For that it would be enough to drop off the bags at the dump and drive away. For the sake of the dogs? But the dogs are dead; and what do dogs know of honour and dishonour anyway?
>
> For himself, then. For his idea of the world, a world in which men do not use shovels to beat corpses into a more convenient shape for processing.
>
> The dogs are brought to the clinic because they are unwanted: *because we are too menny.* That is where he enters their lives. (145–46; italics in original)

Because of the series of deliberations on textual meaning in relation to questions of power in Coetzee's oeuvre, one might be tempted to see in the use of "shovels to beat corpses into a more convenient shape for processing" a metaphor for the critical betrayal or mastery of a text, processed by the critic careless of the text's integrity. Where Lurie stands for a world in which men do not beat corpses in this way, does Coetzee not stand for a world in which critics do not do "violence" to works of literature? But this is a thought that should make us feel instantly uncomfortable. Of course, the depiction of a dead dog in literature can always be taken as a metaphor for something else; but in the context of *Disgrace,* most readers, I suspect, would find that suggestion sickeningly reductive or, at least, *unresponsive,* an unethical appropriation.

In a more responsive reaction to this section of *Disgrace,* Raimond Gaita highlights the shift from one explanation to another. Gaita is interested in the way that Lurie, trying to make sense of his reactions, is reported to feel "at first that he acts not for the dogs, but for the sake of a world in which this sort of thing is not done," for himself, that is. However, "It is soon evident to him that the horror of what is done is the horror of what is done to the dogs and that the world he hopes for is a world in which dogs are spared the dishonour of having their corpses beaten. . . . So he concludes that he acts for the dogs, . . . to save 'the honour of corpses'" (*Philosopher's Dog,* 90–91).

Gaita considers the rational position of those who would find this argument unconvincing, those for whom a corpse, even a human corpse, is deemed to be beyond honor or dishonor. Yet he also explains that he quotes Coetzee "in the hope that such people might find him persuasive even if they are not in the end persuaded," and because he wants "to reflect on what it means to be rightly persuaded by a writer of such grace and power" (93). This opens up the realm of literary alterity (from a moral philosopher's perspective), which can generate a kind of knowledge rooted in emotional engagement, and which is not subject to the norms of objective reason: "I grant readily and fully that the understanding of the heart will never lead to knowledge of the kind that can accumulate through the ages and become settled in the great encyclopaedias of our culture. But that does not mean that it is not a genuine form of understanding" (106).

Gaita also makes this telling observation about literary language (or "poetry" as he puts it): "The life that poetry sustains in language is life that is always threatened by our disposition to sentimentality, to cliché, to banality, to pathos and so on. It is, however, intrinsic to the lucidity we achieve when these are overcome that they are always overcome in the midst of life and never once and for all. It is also intrinsic to that lucidity that its achievement does not find its way into textbooks and encyclopaedias" (103). This is well said, if we take it as part of an extended response to *Disgrace,* because the risk of pathos and sentimentality is a risk that Coetzee deliberately courts, while simultaneously alerting us to its dangers. In the passage quoted earlier, the allusion to Little Father Time and the children's suicide in *Jude the Obscure*—"done because we are too menny"—is a clear signpost. This, perhaps the most arrestingly sentimental moment in Hardy, works in precisely the way Gaita describes: lucidity is gained when the social issues are grasped beneath the scene of heightened pathos. Neither does the process make us invulnerable to the pathos of life.

A shifting critical stance is demanded by Coetzee's changes of emphasis, it seems. But to follow closely the particular contours of Coetzee's recent engagements with ethical questions may also serve to reinforce the notion of an equal marriage between the critic and the writer in the ethical event of reading. In one sense, the critic might seem to lose autonomy in this cozy relationship and also a critical identity. This is implied, perhaps, in Attridge's insistence that the critical reader must "trust in the unpredictability of reading, its openness to the future." He goes on, however, to say, "from this reading, of course, a responsible instrumentality may follow, perhaps one with modified methods or goals" ("Ethics," 34).

It is that idea of "responsible instrumentality" that is the crucial element in this account of critical reading, for me, since it assigns a place for the critic's own intellectual context. Academics need a concept of "responsible instrumentality," in fact, to justify much of what they do. Even something as humdrum as making a selection of books for a course reading list requires this responsibility (since this is a minor act of canon formation and, potentially, an exercise in pigeonholing). If this kind of activity takes its place as an appropriate component of our responsible reading, without compromising our attempt to register the "resistance and irreducibility" of a literary work, we may arrive at an appropriately modified (and evolving) ethical overview of a field of study (34).

The evolving effect of resistance in Coetzee, perhaps since *The Master of Petersburg,* seems to be rooted in a movement to a new kind of spareness or "truth." The movement in *Youth* toward an unflinching honesty of expression, in which baser motives are rendered without apparent amelioration, is a parallel development to the drive in the fiction to force an engagement with particular philosophical issues, unambiguously drawn.

It is a revealing development, viewed with hindsight, that seems clearly linked to political circumstances. As apartheid recedes into history, the ideological squeeze on literature has become less pronounced, it seems: a space has emerged in which Coetzee has been able to pursue his more overtly literary and ethical concerns, less constrained by the particular violence of colonialism and the anxiety of personal complicity. Coetzee has come a long way from "The Narrative of Jacobus Coetzee," in his first book, *Dusklands* (1974), which fictionalizes—and seems at times to reproduce—the horrors of the colonial violence perpetrated by eighteenth-century explorers of the Cape. This first book, haunted by the idea of the pornographic, is a far cry from the fastidiousness of the character Elizabeth Costello concerning the moral dubiety of depicting violence in fiction, as we shall see.[7]

Elizabeth Costello (2003) is certainly a key work in this later phase, alongside *Disgrace* and *The Lives of Animals* (1999). These are works that concern themselves with the problem of how the aesthetic effects and ethical questions generated by literature bear on the relationship between human beings and the rest of nature.

I shall take *The Lives of Animals* first, for, despite the fact that the later *Elizabeth Costello* subsumes it, it still has a coherence in itself that has been "written out" of the longer work, where a more pronounced inconsistency in the central character suits the development of Coetzee's concerns. In *Lives* Coetzee makes us wonder whether we should share a "literal cast of mind" with Elizabeth Costello, who insists that "when Kafka writes about an ape," he is "talking in the first place about an ape" (32). The consideration of animals, perhaps, is not substitutable, a convenient vehicle, merely, used to foreground more general questions of professional ethics. Perhaps the problem of animal rights is bound inextricably together with questions pertaining to professional ethics and literary aesthetics in these works. And if this implies a challenge to given cultural and epistemological boundaries, these boundaries may have a bearing on the teaching and reception of literature, as well as on the utilitarian evaluation of animals, a notorious legacy of Enlightenment rationality.

Reading *The Lives of Animals,* we cannot know the extent to which Costello espouses the author's own views, although there is a temptation to wonder if Coetzee uses Costello to adumbrate ideas that would be difficult for him to address directly, in another format. For example, in an earlier essay Coetzee rehearses a challenge to the "species argument" that permits the killing and consumption of some animals, but not others, and wonders, "is it fair to remind ourselves of the Nazis, who divided humankind into two species, those whose deaths mattered more and those whose deaths mattered less?" ("Meat Country," 45). Costello's views do arrest our attention, but they are systematically—and forcefully—challenged by other characters in the narrative, though she is sometimes seen to occupy the intellectual as well as the moral high ground.

Costello (and so Coetzee) is well versed in moral philosophy and animal rights. Her conviction about animals is that they may well (in ethical philosopher Peter Singer's words) "possess both memory of the past and expectations about the future, . . . that they are self-aware, that they form intentions and act on them" (*Practical Ethics,* 115). This refutes "the doctrine that places the lives of members of our species above the lives of members of other species," and removes the justification for killing those nonhuman animals that possess the attributes of "persons" (117). Costello's familiarity with this kind of argument locates her intellectual position: that of a post-Christian challenge to the doctrines of "speciesism" (88–89). Coetzee seeks to make his readers uneasy about the self-interest implicit in humanist reason and rationality, but, in another unsettling maneuver, he takes us beyond a straightforward rational and literal engagement with the arguments.

Sympathy is crucial here, and one is reminded of Gaita's "understanding of the heart" in following Costello's emotional trajectory. Indeed, our reception of the principal characters is determined as much by the domestic drama as it is by the quality of the arguments. There is mutual hostility between Elizabeth and her daughter-in-law, Norma, but it is the embittered Norma's failure to extend hospitality to her aging mother-in-law that is emphasized. Thus, even where Norma might offer a credible intellectual challenge to Elizabeth's views, we are not inclined to let her carry the day. One of the most important observations is given to Norma, in fact: that "there is no position outside of reason where you can stand and lecture about reason and pass judgment on reason" (*Lives,* 48). This difficulty undermines Elizabeth's arguments to an extent; but Coetzee coaxes his readers to sympathize with Elizabeth rather than Norma, and so to experience the principle by which sympathy is privileged over reason.

Costello's intellectual objection to reason is formalized in the account of experiments on an ape in a cage, experiments designed to test his problem-solving skills when his food is placed increasingly further from his reach. Costello suggests that the thoughts of an ape in such an experiment might conceivably be focused on its relationship to its captors—"why is he starving me? . . . Why has he stopped liking me?"—rather than on the more mundane "how does one use the stick to reach the bananas?" Yet the ape is driven from "the purity of speculation" and toward "lower, practical, instrumental reason" (28–29).

As she develops this opposition, Costello pits "ethics and metaphysics" against "practical reason"; she privileges "fullness, embodiedness" over "thinking, cogitation" (33). She is interested in the faculty of the heart "that allows us to share at times the being of another," insisting that "there are no bounds to the sympathetic imagination" (34–35). (In the seminar presentation in "The Poets and the Animals" Costello seeks to demonstrate this through a reading of Ted Hughes's poems "The Jaguar" and "Second Glance at a Jaguar" [50–55].)

Without relinquishing the desire to promote the sympathetic capacity, a focus of *The Lives of Animals,* and of *Elizabeth Costello* beyond it, is to highlight the contradiction inherent in that desire. For the sympathetic faculty, which the literary effect can promote, is identified by dint of intellectual effort, much as Costello's war with reason has to be conducted through a process of careful reasoning. Costello (as, it seems, does Coetzee) implicitly accepts the paradox that she also laments. Her visit to Appleton College serves to demonstrate the inevitability of this contradiction and to imply that it is always a factor in our benign interventions in the nonhuman world. She demonstrates that it is the essence of our being to be caught between sympathy and reason, much as Coetzee's text puts his readers through the same contradictory experience.

There is a wisdom in seeking to come to terms with this contradiction, and this contrasts with the reaction of Costello's son. On the last day of her visit he asks her, "Do you really believe, Mother, that poetry classes are going to close down the slaughterhouses?" and the reader should feel the blunt inappropriateness of the question. Costello has argued that it is the business of literature and of literary analysis to foster and examine the human faculty for sympathy with another as an ethical imperative, even while the experience and the process might reveal crucial limitations and contradictions. The mechanistic, causal chain implied in the son's question is of a different order of thinking. It is, in the terms established by *The Lives of Animals,* an unethical question, of the same order as "how does one use the stick to reach the bananas?"

The ethical questions that *The Lives of Animals* asks us to consider are "what is the relationship between literature and the faculty of sympathy, and how does the intellectual life frustrate this faculty?" At the end of the book the son attempts to console his mother, overcome by the terror of her vision, where the reasoning element (which invites her to draw a comparison between the slaughterhouses and the Holocaust) links up disastrously with her empathic sense: she senses a stupefying crime being committed by meat eaters all around her, and this poisons her social relations (69). The book ends with a clear intimation of Elizabeth's mortality.

In the final analysis, rather than a partisan intervention in animal rights, *The Lives of Animals* is an attempt to grapple with paradox and contradiction. The justification for an ecological philosophy is called into question where Costello is struck by the irony that the knowledge and appreciation of ecosystems can be comprehended by human beings alone and so cannot lead to a state of at-oneness. The implication is clear: the capacity for sympathy, for a different kind of being-in-the-world, is simultaneously produced, yet frustrated by humanity's intellect (53–54).

In *Elizabeth Costello* we see an extension of the trends I have been discussing, most especially the drive toward a more literal spareness, coupled with an attempt to embrace paradox. There is also a much clearer sense of the author's critique of his creation than in *The Lives of Animals,* and so a felt distance between Coetzee and Costello. This is indicated in one of the most uncomfortable episodes in the novel, "The Humanities in Africa," where Costello finds herself in acrimonious debate with her sister, Blanche, "a classical scholar retrained as a medical missionary," who has "risen to be administrator of a hospital of no mean size in rural Zululand" (116). Blanche's stark message is that "textual scholarship" in the humanities lost its way "five centuries ago," when "the purpose of finding the True Word" in the Bible began to be diluted (122). A key scene in Elizabeth's attempt to confront Blanche's hostility, and to expose the lack of humanity in her religious zeal, is in their dispute in Zululand about the crucifixion as an artistic motif, following on from Elizabeth's concern at the plight of the local carver, Joseph, adopted by the hospital station. He has spent years carving the same wooden crucifix over and over again (135–36). Elizabeth puts the following points to Blanche: "Why does the model you, or if not you then the institution you represent—why does the specific model you set before Joseph and tell him to copy, to imitate, have to be what I can only call Gothic? Why a Christ dying in contortions rather than a living Christ? A man in his prime, in his early thirties: what do you have against showing him alive in all his living beauty?" (138).

It is an old objection, as the subsequent discussion makes clear (139–41). But we are not called upon to engage with religious history or art history: the impact of this moment has to do with simple and immediate questions about art, beauty, and the depiction of violence.

We might be tempted to sense Coetzee taking Costello's side in a scene such as this. It is interesting to note, however, the following published remark about violence and the crucifixion, from one of the interviews with David Attwell, which suggests a rather different view: "Violence, as soon as I sense its presence within me, becomes introverted as violence against myself. . . . I cannot but think: if all of us imagined violence as violence against ourselves, perhaps we would have peace. (Whether peace is what we most deeply want is another story.) Or, to explain myself in another way: I understand the Crucifixion as a refusal and an introversion of retributive violence, a refusal so deliberate, so conscious, and so powerful that it overwhelms any reinterpretation, Freudian, Marxian, or whatever, that we can give to it." Coetzee goes on to say: "I think you will find the contest of interpretations I have sketched here—the political versus the ethical—played out again and again in my novels" (*Doubling*, 337).

The ethics of treating violence is a prominent topic in *Elizabeth Costello*, and it is closely linked to the question of expression and reinterpretation.

Costello herself attacks the novelist Paul West for inventing too vividly, in his novel *The Very Rich Hours of Count von Stauffenberg*, the thoughts and actions of Hitler's henchmen as they carry out the executions of the July 1944 plotters (157–58). Her own experience of violence, when she was savagely beaten by a man at the age of nineteen (165–66), appears to give her some authority on the topic of evil. However, the reflection, that this is a male author imagining female victimhood, is a complicating factor.

The paradox that comes to dominate *The Lives of Animals*—that reason is required to establish the limits of reason and the nurturing of sympathy—has a parallel in *Elizabeth Costello* that takes us to the heart of Coetzee's predicament. Here the wistful hankering after spareness, directness, is given a directly confessional moment but is shown to be susceptible to appropriation, reinterpretation. At the end of the novel Costello is depicted petitioning "at the gate," required to account for the beliefs of her life before a board of judges. At her first hearing she fails, claiming not to have any beliefs. Recovering her faith for a second hearing, she makes a petition that is more in keeping with the earlier episodes. This statement of belief concerns a childhood memory of rural Victoria, on the River Dulgannon, where "tens of thousands of little frogs" would be woken from their "tombs" in the sun-baked mud following seasonal "torrential rains." Costello is apologetic for her lyrical impulse in recounting the memory:

> "Excuse my language. I am or have been a professional writer. Usually I take care to conceal the extravagances of the imagination. But today, for this occasion, I thought I would conceal nothing, bare all. The vivifying flood, the chorus of joyous belling, followed by the subsiding of the waters and the retreat to the grave, then drought seemingly without end, then fresh rains and the resurrection of the dead—it is a story I present transparently, without disguise.
>
> "Why? Because today I am before you not as a writer but as an old woman who was once a child, telling you what I remember of the Dulgannon mudflats of my childhood and of the frogs who live there, some as small as the tip of my little finger, creatures so insignificant and so remote from your loftier concerns that you would not hear of them otherwise. In my account, for whose many failings I beg your pardon, the life cycle of the frog may sound allegorical, but to the frogs themselves it is no allegory, it is the thing itself, the only thing.

"What do I believe? I believe in those little frogs. . . . It is because of the indifference of those little frogs to my belief . . . that I believe in them." (216–17)

This is a paean to nature, but it is also a writer's appeal for the power of fiction, on the basis of whatever claims can still be made for its spare immediacy and here given the religious intensity of a writer petitioning "at the gate." James Wood has claimed that this is "the moment at which this highly religious book finally declares itself—but only to appropriate religion in a pagan turn. . . . To enter the frog's life is like entering a fictional character's life. And this is a kind of religion, akin to the worship of a God who gives us nothing back" ("Frog's Life," 16).

Here we see the clearest and most important intellectual distinction between Coetzee and Costello. She is done with fiction, since she doubts its benefits (160) and its goodness (167). Her petition is rooted in the power of a witnessed natural event, the allegorical dimension of which she tries to suppress. Yet it is the allegorical dimension that resonates with her judges (218, 220) and, probably, with readers of the novel. However, the simple association of levels (if allegory it is)—the parallel between Costello's belief in the frogs and Coetzee's enduring belief in fiction—brings with it another paradox: the writer cannot escape the imposition of metaphorical levels on his or her expression, and this may produce a nightmarish sense of being misunderstood (as in Costello's parodically Kafkaesque experience "at the gate"). In this sense, the frustration of Costello is a way for Coetzee to explore and express the limits of fiction and of the writer's authority.

Coetzee is also suggesting something about the enduring power or value of fiction, however. The burrowing frogs on the Dulgannon, each one creating "a little tomb for itself" in the dry season, waiting for the rains that encourage the dead to waken (216), suggests an irresistible parallel. The dry season of apartheid, and its aftermath, which brought with it strictures about how to write—from the ANC as well as from the ruling Nationalist Party—may finally give way to the rains that might herald greater tolerance and freedom for the writer, a moment that is emerging, judging by the latest phase of his work. But the setting for Coetzee (like Costello) is now Australia, and not the Karoo, so, for both, in different ways, the redeeming rains will be too late.[8]

Notes

1. See Coetzee, *Doubling,* 342–43.
2. See "Dark Chamber," 363.
3. The rape itself is described differently five times in consecutive passages (104–7). This both emphasizes the sense of violence and ordeal, whilst also suggesting the possibility of fantasy, Magda as psychological victim.
4. Critics of the TRC have suggested that it might have had "a very partial and selective approach to the truth," and that "had it been more balanced, expert and authoritative, its impact would have been far greater." See Johnson, "Painful History" (9, 10).
5. Johnson locates particular atrocities where the final *TRC Report* is highly selective in the evidence it uses.
6. My essay was written before the publication of Attridge's *Singularity of Literature,* in which these ideas are given a more extended treatment.
7. The reception of *Disgrace* might seem to give the lie to this narrative, in which the writer is increasingly freed from external ideological pressures. Yet the complaints about the theme of black violence do not alter the fact that the opening scenes of *Disgrace* are written in a mode of unfettered direct realism—unusual for Coetzee—in which he explicitly attacks the kind of inflexible, rule-driven judgment that, ironically, was then directed at the work.
8. Coetzee quietly left South Africa for Australia, in the wake of the furor caused in South Africa by the treatment of black violence in *Disgrace.*

Bibliography

Attridge, Derek. "Ethics, Otherness, and Literary Form," *European English Messenger* 12, no. 1 (Spring 2003): 33–38.
———. *The Singularity of Literature.* London: Routledge, 2004.
Coetzee, J. M. *Disgrace.* London: Secker and Warburg, 1999.
———. *Doubling the Point: Essays and Interviews.* Edited by David Attwell. Cambridge, MA: Harvard University Press, 1992.
———. *Dusklands.* Johannesburg: Ravan Press, 1974.
———. *Elizabeth Costello: Eight Lessons.* London: Secker and Warburg, 2003.
———. *In the Heart of the Country.* 1977; Harmondsworth: Penguin, 1982.
———. "Into the Dark Chamber: The Writer and the South African State." In *Doubling the Point,* 361–68.
———. *Life & Times of Michael K.* Harmondsworth: Penguin, 1985.
———. *The Lives of Animals.* Edited by Amy Gutmann. Princeton, NJ: Princeton University Press, 1999.
———. "Meat Country." *Granta* 52 (Winter 1995): 41–52.
———. "The Novel Today." *Upstream* 6 (1988): 2–5.

Gaita, Raimond. *The Philosopher's Dog.* London: Routledge, 2003.

Johnson, R. W. "Why There Is No Easy Way to Dispose of Painful History." Review of *The Truth about the Truth Commission,* by Anthea Jeffery. *London Review of Books* 21, no. 20 (October 14, 1999): 9–11.

Lowry, Elizabeth. "Like a Dog." Review of *Disgrace* and *The Lives of Animals,* by J. M. Coetzee. *London Review of Books* 21, no. 20 (October 14, 1999): 12–14.

Singer, Peter. *Practical Ethics.* 2nd ed. Cambridge University Press, 1999.

Truth and Reconciliation Commission of South Africa Report. 5 vols. Cape Town: Truth and Reconciliation Commission, 1999.

Wood, James. "A Frog's Life." Review of *Elizabeth Costello,* by J. M. Coetzee. *London Review of Books* 25, no. 20 (October 23, 2003): 15–16.

6

J. M. COETZEE, ELIZABETH COSTELLO, AND THE LIMITS OF THE SYMPATHETIC IMAGINATION

Sam Durrant

> There is no limit to the extent to which we can think our way into the being of another. There are no bounds to the sympathetic imagination.
>
> —Elizabeth Costello in *The Lives of Animals*

AT THE heart of *The Lives of Animals* (1999) is a polemic against the "willed ignorance" of the suffering of others and an exhortation to "open your heart and listen to what your heart says" (37). Listening to one's heart, the voice of conscience, the other within, Costello implicitly argues, leads to an awareness of the other without and the reality of other lives. This movement from ignorance to attentiveness would seem, at least at first sight, to parallel the ethical trajectory of Coetzee's fiction. In *Waiting for the Barbarians* (1980), for instance, a government official's attempts to block his ears to the sounds of torture give way to an awareness of "the sighs and cries . . . echoing forever within the second sphere" (112). In *Age of Iron* (1990) the potentially self-absorbed letter of a privileged but terminally ill woman ends up testifying not simply to her own suffering but also to that taking place in the townships. And in *Disgrace* (1999), a literature professor ignores the well-being of the student he seduces and subsequently has sex with against her will,[1] but later finds himself attending to the suffering of animals.[2]

However, as I have tried to indicate in the noncongruence of my title and epigraph, Coetzee's position is ultimately irreducible to Costello's. Costello's assertion that "there are no bounds to the sympathetic imagination" is turned in upon itself in Coetzee's fiction, which one might describe as acts of sympathetic imagination that continually encounter their own bounds. While Costello has apparently rewritten *Ulysses* from the perspective of Molly Bloom, Coetzee has written a book about the impossibility of recovering the point of view of Friday from *Robinson Crusoe.* This is, of course, an asymmetrical comparison: the consciousness of a slave in an eighteenth-century fictional autobiography may well be more inaccessible than that of a woman in a multiperspectival modernist narrative. And Coetzee is able to think himself into the mind of a woman (*Heart of the Country* [1976], *Foe* [1986], *Age of Iron*), just as Costello has in other novels, according to her son, been able to think herself into the mind of a man (*Animals,* 22). However, almost all Coetzee's fiction is narrated, whether in the first person or third, from a position of social and/or racial privilege. In the one exception, *Life & Times of Michael K* (1983), K's thought processes are often inaccessible, even to K himself ("His was always a story with a hole in it" [110]), and the narrative is briefly forced to abandon his perspective for that of a doctor who understands K even less than K himself does.

Even a literature professor specializing in Romantic poetry, and thus perhaps the character most likely to share Costello's belief in the power of the imagination, finds there are certain limits to his capacity to think his way into other lives. In David Lurie's opera, Coetzee's mise-en-scène of an artwork, of how art works, Lurie is seemingly able to move beyond the position of Byron, whose love life has certain affinities with his own, and take up that of his abandoned mistress, Teresa. But in the more immediate circumstances of the main narrative he finds himself unable to imagine what his daughter went through at the hands of her rapists. Costello's self-confident assertion becomes an unanswered question, an expression of self-doubt: "he can, if he loses himself, be there, be the men, inhabit them, fill them with the ghost of himself. The question is, does he have it in him to be the woman?" (160).

Coetzee's fiction is thus always in tension with itself: while the author himself is able to imagine his way into the consciousness of a limited array of narratorial personae, these personae are themselves unable to imagine themselves into the lives of those less privileged than themselves. Or more accurately, they are unable to imagine certain structural experiences of unprivilege or oppression: torture, slavery, apartheid, rape. Their failure to think themselves into these other lives is not *willed* ignorance but persists despite or even precisely because of their will to overcome their ignorance, their desire to enter into the reality of other lives. This is most clear in the fiction of the early to mid-1980s. In *Waiting for the Barbarians, Life & Times of Michael K,* and *Foe,* Coetzee's figures of otherness—the barbarian girl, K, Friday—doggedly resist the attentions of their sympathizers. The obdurate surfaces of their bodies would seem to mark the absolute limit of the sympathetic imagination.[3]

In one sense, then, Coetzee's fiction unequivocally rehearses the failure of Costello's sympathetic imagination, the failure of the literary endeavor itself. And yet I want to argue that this failure is the precondition for a new kind of ethical and literary relation, a relation grounded precisely in the acknowledgment of one's ignorance of the other, on the recognition of the other's fundamental alterity. It is as if attentiveness to the difference of the other becomes possible only in the wake of the failure of the project of the sympathetic imagination, the failure to think one's way into the reality of other lives.

One might say that Coetzee's novels do not so much move *from* ignorance to attentiveness as *through* ignorance to attentiveness. While the ignorance of those who lived alongside the concentration camps or enjoyed the privileges of apartheid clearly involved a willed denial of other people's suffering and thus constituted the inverse of attentiveness, a certain mode of *unwilled* ignorance, in which it is precisely the will that is given up, would seem to provide a passage toward attentiveness. If, as Foucault has exhaustively demonstrated, knowledge is inextricably linked to the will to power, then a certain state of ignorance would seem to constitute the ground for a noncoercive relation to the other. While ignorance may simply indicate a profound indifference to other lives, it can also indicate the wisdom of "knowing not to know," a state of humility or self-doubt that undoes the logic of self-certainty that founds the Cartesian tradition and underwrites the enterprise of colonialism.

The Magistrate ends *Waiting for the Barbarians* "feeling stupid, like a man who lost his way long ago but presses on along a road that may lead no-where" (156). Two decades later, Coetzee's protagonists are none the wiser: David Lurie ends *Disgrace* pursuing a vocation that he describes as "stupid, daft, wrongheaded" (146). His work with animals and their corpses seems to be both a way of "living out [his disgrace] from day to day" (172) and an approximation of a state of grace.[4] With hindsight, it becomes clear that stupidity, morally exemplified in the innocence of Michael K, "whose mind was not quick" (*Michael K,* 4), has always constituted the ethical destination, or anti-*telos,* of Coetzee's fiction.[5] For Coetzee's world-weary, intellec-tual personae, the only way to achieve such a state is to engage in an anti-intellectual labor in which they are literally, if only momentarily, able to lose their minds. Repeated physical contact with the body of the other, with that which marks the limits of their own minds, would seem to induce a certain stupor, a suspension of the will, and a mysterious but overpowering tiredness. Both Lurie and the Magistrate submit to bouts of unconscious-ness stretched out alongside the body of the other and then begin to sleep-walk through their waking lives. The Magistrate "falls into oblivion . . . in the act of caressing" the barbarian girl's body (*Waiting,* 31). Unsure of his intentions, he "loses his way like a storyteller losing the thread of his story" (45), dimly aware that "something is in the course of happening to [him]" (43). Soon after sleeping alongside an old bitch called Katie, Lurie "feels his interest in the world draining from him drop by drop" (*Disgrace,* 107), aware only that "he does not understand what is happening to him" (143). Both find themselves "simply bewildered" (*Waiting,* 43) by a process that they do not understand and that does not bring understanding.

Costello's lecture preaches the necessity of awakening to the reality of other lives, a passage from willed ignorance to willed wakefulness that only comes about through an act of volition, a conscious decision to open the heart. Coetzee's novels, by contrast, describe a kind of fall into sleepfulness, a cessation of the will that leads to a dreamy or somnambulistic mode of attentiveness to other lives. And yet these trajectories may not be as far apart as they may appear. Costello's attentiveness to the lives of animals is more a compulsion than an act of the will, and it leads her to become so alienated from the lives of humans that she comes to ask herself "Am I dreaming? . . . What kind of house is this?" (69). Her question echoes that of the reader-narrator at the end of *Foe*, who, like Costello, encounters a world of corpses, and asks him/herself "what is this ship?" (*Foe*, 157). Both questions point to a demimonde of suffering that lies just beneath the surface of the "real" world. The passage in *Foe* begins with the narrator picking up a manuscript and diving overboard into a kind of textual unconscious; it thus offers itself as an allegory of what happens both when we dream and when we read. As an allegory of dreaming, it suggests that the material suffering of the other may only be accessible to us in the form of a dream, that true wakefulness, or attentiveness to other lives, may be possible only when we are dreaming. It is tempting to make a certain leap here and suggest that literature, fiction, is a mode of dreaming, simultaneously a descent into the otherness of the self and an encounter with others, and thus that it functions, in itself, as a mode of attentiveness. However, the liminal status of the final passage, or dive, in *Foe*, which can only take place after the death of both narrator (Susan) and author (Foe), suggests that the sympathetic imagination can encounter otherness only when the narrative has become other than itself, when it has forgotten its desire to discover the other's story. And even here, in *Foe's* impossible *hors-texte*, the empathetic leap of the imagination still falls short, landing not in the consciousness of Friday but alongside his corpse.

Coetzee's "dreamy" mode of attentiveness recalls Jacques Lacan's work on ethics, to which Coetzee gestures in interview: "some of Lacan's most inspired remarks have been about speaking from a position of doubt" (*Doubling*, 29–30). In a seminar entitled "On the Subject of Certainty," Lacan argues that a certain ignorance of the other constitutes the ethical basis of psychoanalysis. He famously argues that "the status of the unconscious is ethical" (33) precisely because the unconscious marks the limit of the analyst's knowledge. In contrast to Descartes, who stakes all on the certainty of his own thought (*cogito ergo sum*), Freud stakes everything on the certainty of a thought that is elsewhere. While Descartes makes his doubt the basis of his self-certainty: "*By virtue of the fact that I doubt, I am sure that I think,*" Freud, according to Lacan, understands his doubt as proof of another thinking:

> Freud, when he doubts—for they are his dreams, and it is he who, at the outset, doubts—is assured that a thought is there, which is unconscious, which means that it reveals itself as unconscious. As soon as he comes to deal with others, it is to this place that he summons the *I think* through which the subject will reveal himself. In short, he is sure that his thought is there alone with all his *I am,* if I may put it like this, provided, and this is the leap, someone thinks in his place. (36; italics in original)

At the heart of psychoanalysis, then, is a certain sympathetic leap of the imagination, but it is a leap in the dark toward the existence of a thought that "thinks in [the analyst's] place," takes the place of his own thought or places his own thought in abeyance. Despite the Freud who thought of himself as making scientific discoveries, this leap does not produce knowledge but rather undoes knowledge and undoes the pretensions of the analyst, whom Lacan ironically dubs the subject supposed to know.

The psychoanalytic term for this leap in the dark is "transference," what one might describe as the involuntary or unconscious leap of the sympathetic imagination. The space of the transference in the analytic session is analogous to the space of dreams within Coetzee's fiction. Both spaces constitute an elsewhere that suggests the possibility of another mode of encounter between self and other, an encounter that would take place outside the realm of reason and the will to power. As the Magistrate's dream-encounters with the barbarian girl make clear, this space may simply be governed by the desire of the subject and thus be an expression of fantasy —the fantasy of a secret accord with the other. But it may also be the place where, as Susan Barton suggests in her meditation on the significance of dreams, the subject forgets itself and "another voice, other voices, speak in our lives" (*Foe,* 30).

This other speech would not be the verbal exchange that takes place in the psychoanalytic session or the narrative proper but a nonverbal language of affect. Here is Kristeva's description of the transference: "[a] sad analytic silence hover[s] above a strange foreign discourse, which strictly speaking shatters verbal communication. . . . It is necessary that the analyst's interpretative speech . . . be affected by it in order to be analytical" (*Powers*, 30). In *Foe*, Friday's "foreign discourse"—the stream of the bubbles dislodged from his corpse—becomes the tears of the reader-dreamer: "Soft and cold, dark and unending, [the stream] beats against my eyelids, against the skin of my face" (157). In *Waiting for the Barbarians*, the Magistrate also awakes from his dreams of the barbarian girl bathed in tears (109). The other remains silent in this dream space but this silence has a certain "affectiveness." Such encounters do not yield knowledge of the other, but the dreams nevertheless constitute, paradoxically enough, a moment of awakening.

This is precisely the point of Lacan's reinterpretation of the dream in which a dead son appeals to his father with the haunting words "Can't you see I'm burning?" It turns out that the son is indeed burning in the room next to the one in which the father is sleeping: a candle has fallen over and set his corpse on fire. While Freud, in accordance with his understanding of dreams as wish fulfillment, comes to understand the dream as a prolongation of sleep and an avoidance of reality, Lacan argues that it is only in the dream that the father is truly alive to his son's death, truly awake to the reality of his suffering: "It is only in the dream that this truly unique encounter can occur" (*Fundamental Concepts*, 59). Lacan takes the dream as exemplary of the traumatic nature of the ethical relation: one can only hear the cry of the other when it is too late to come to the other's assistance. As Cathy Caruth puts it, "Awakening, in Lacan's reading of the dream, is itself the site of a trauma, the trauma of the necessity and impossibility of responding to another's death" (*Unclaimed Experience*, 100). The reality of the other's suffering is only accessible belatedly, as "a real that eludes us" (53), "a missed reality" (58).

In *Age of Iron*, Coetzee draws out the political implications of the father's dream. I can do no more than suggest the richness of this intertextual dialogue. In an age of iron (the insurrectionary violence of late-eighties South Africa), the cries of the burning go unheeded, as Mrs. Curren's domestic worker, Florence, relates: "I saw a woman on fire, burning, and when she screamed for help, the children laughed and threw more petrol on her" (45). Mrs. Curren herself is initially too focused on her own burning to attend to these cries: "The country smoulders, yet with the best will in the world,

I can only half-attend. My true attention is all inward, upon the thing, the word, the word for the thing inching through my body. An ignominious occupation, and in times like these ridiculous too, as a banker with his clothes on fire is a joke while a burning beggar is not. Yet I cannot help myself: 'Look at me,' I want to cry to Florence—'I too am burning'" (36). She becomes receptive to the call of the other not in a dream but in a nightmarish nocturnal visit to the Cape Flats. In an age of indifference, it would seem that dreams are not enough to produce attentiveness: one has to be hauled from one's bed and directed to the place of the other. And even then, the violence of a forced removal appears to her as an otherworldly spectacle, as if it were taking place on another plane of reality: "To speak of this . . . you would need the tongue of a god" (91). Apartheid has produced such a radical separation of realities that Mrs. Curren can experience the burning of the townships only as an encounter with a reality that continues to elude her powers of description.

Here then the sympathetic imagination encounters a certain verbal limit, an incapacity to describe the reality of other lives that is as much Coetzee's as Mrs. Curren's.[6] However, this moment of failure or missed encounter is quickly followed by a "real" encounter with the body of the other—real in the Lacanian sense that it irrevocably disrupts her sense of reality. As she stumbles about the township, Mrs. Curren encounters the corpse of Florence's son, Bheki. "Now my eyes are open and I can never close them again" (95). Like the Magistrate, she is no longer insulated from the world of the other: "something has fallen in upon me from the sky . . . this body, for which I am responsible, or so it seems" (*Waiting*, 43). The crucial political question becomes how to live out this responsibility, how to respond adequately to the call of the other.

Lacan emphasizes the helplessness of the subject, reading the father's dream as "the story of an impossible responsibility of consciousness in its own originating relation to others" (Caruth, *Unclaimed Experience*, 104). But in a reading that has implications for an understanding of Coetzee's own political position, Caruth reads this traumatic awakening to the impossibility of the ethical relation as the very possibility and necessity of bearing witness: "It is precisely the dead child, the child in its irreducible inaccessibility and otherness, who says to the father: wake up, leave me, survive to tell the story of my burning" (105). Mrs. Curren's cancer makes her responsibility slightly different from the father's: she must find a way of making her dying, rather than her survival, into a mode of bearing witness.[7]

Two responses present themselves: speech and silence. Although she cannot muster words in public to condemn "the crime being committed in front of [her] eyes," Mrs. Curren does have recourse to private words, to a letter that, if Vercueil is to be relied on, will survive her own death. However, it is not her own survival that she seeks in her account of her dying but the survival of her testimony to the dying of the others. She must find a way of writing that does not invite the traditional movement of identification, a way of bracketing her own suffering: she admonishes her daughter: "attend to the writing, not to me" (95); "Do not read in sympathy with me. Let your heart not beat in sympathy with mine" (96). A writing, then, at odds with itself, that writes against its own eliciting of the sympathetic imagination.

The alternative to the contradictions of verbal witness is the silent miming, or acting out, of the other's dying. After encountering Bheki's corpse she thinks: "If someone had dug a grave for me there and then, and pointed, I would *without a word* have climbed in and lain down and folded my hands on my breast" (96; italics mine). Silence, speechlessness, a melancholic identification with the corpse of the other, remains one mode of response, one way of being affected by the other. Mrs. Curren later considers the idea of setting light to her own body as a way of drawing attention to the burning of the other but fears that her act will be misunderstood. And finally she submits to a half-voluntary expulsion from her own home to sleep on the streets, in remembrance, it would seem, of the unhousing taking place in the townships.

In responding to the suggestiveness of *Age of Iron,* I have been inattentive to the claims of *The Lives of Animals.* In what remains I want to suggest that Costello's version of the sympathetic imagination is similarly caught between speech and silence, and that, like Mrs. Curren before her, the most 'telling' example she makes is that of her own body.

At first sight, Costello's valorization of the sympathetic imagination seems to rest on the Romantic valorization of imagination over reason. However, in her emphasis on embodiment and her warnings against the pitfalls of Platonic idealism or abstraction, her imagination would seem to be on guard against its own Romanticism. The question becomes: to what extent is her anti-idealist Romanticism Coetzee's? Or to put it another way: clearly both Costello and Coetzee seek a way of circumnavigating reason, but are they similarly alive to the difficulties of such a task?

While Coetzee's fiction seems to suggest that it is thought, consciousness itself, that needs to be bypassed, Costello at times sees it as sufficient to bypass a particular form of reason that she describes as "the specialism of a rather narrow self-regenerating intellectual tradition" (*Animals*, 25). She rightly suggests that Wolfgang Köhler's experiments with an ape called Sultan are only designed to test his capacity for "instrumental reason" (29), but her own suggestion that Sultan is more interested in questions of justice ("why is he starving me?" [28]) is a naked projection of her own concern for animal welfare and merely substitutes one form of reason (what she herself recognizes as "ethics and metaphysics") for another ("practical reason"). Nevertheless, her projection is so transparent as to be ironic or tongue-in-cheek: the passage does not ultimately tell us what it is like to be an ape but works simply to dislodge a particular tradition of enquiry into animal intelligence. And it may turn out that this work of dislodging, of keeping open the question of other lives, constitutes the "true" work of the sympathetic imagination.

In her lecture, Costello continues to tread a fine line between self-confident assertion and hesitation, between claiming a commonality or sameness and remaining open to an incalculable difference. For Costello, the grounds of our commonality is the fact of our embodiedness, our capacity to feel rather than our capacity for abstract thought. She invokes Thomas Nagel's essay "What Is It Like to Be a Bat?" and finds him "tragically limited" in his failure to answer his own question: "It will not help to try to imagine what it is like to have webbing on one's arms . . . [etc]. In so far as I can imagine this (which is not very far), it tells me only what it would be like for me to behave as a bat behaves. But that is not the question. I want to know what it is like for a bat to be a bat. Yet if I try to imagine this, I am restricted by the resources of my own mind, and those resources are inadequate to the task" (31).

Nagel's position seems to be in accord with a certain deconstructive respect for the alterity of the other and an admirable restraint against the pitfalls of projection. Costello's position also echoes aspects of deconstruction in her refusal of anthropocentrism, her contention that a bat's consciousness is no more alien than another human's. But in her attempt to establish a commonality, Costello must risk positing that which we have in common, a supposition as to the content of the bat's mind that must necessarily remain open to question, deconstructible: "To be a living bat is to be full of being, being fully a bat is like being fully human, which is also to be full of being. Bat-being in the first place, human-being in the second maybe; but those are secondary considerations. To be full of being is to live as a body-soul. One name for the experience of full being is joy" (33). In naming our common experience joy, Costello seems guilty of a certain arbitrariness or poetic license. Our commonality, one might object, may equally be grounded in other emotions or feelings, our capacity to feel pain, for instance, or fear.

However, Costello is careful to acknowledge this arbitrariness: *joy* is only one name among others for a feeling that is *without content,* or rather, a feeling that empties consciousness of its content. Consciousness of being is precisely the opposite of self-consciousness; in Costello's terms, it is a more a bodily sensation than a mental thought. One thinks of Michael K, losing himself in his project to disappear into the Karoo: "He wondered if he were living in what was known as bliss" (*Michael K,* 68). K's bliss is a moment of *ekstasis,* a state of being that literally means the state of standing outside oneself. Paradoxically, Costello's idea of the joy of embodiedness, of living within a body, is also the joy of living outside oneself, outside the borders of subjectivity: not disembodied but "dis-selved." Costello's ability to imagine herself into the mind of a bat rests not only on her capacity to lose or forget herself and the specifics of her own subjectivity but also on the *bat's* capacity to forget itself, its capacity to live in a state of self-forgetfulness. Woman and bat can only meet in a "no-man's land" where neither woman nor bat are themselves.

The interchangeable, empty nature of this common ground is emphasized by Costello's other rather cryptic argument that our ability to imagine our own death is somehow proof of our ability to think our way into the mind of a bat. Here the ground of our commonality is not our fear of death, nor even our capacity to feel anything at all, but rather our capacity to become unfeeling, insensate, empty of being. Here the project of the sympathetic imagination reaches another absolute limit, another no-man's land. However, Costello confidently asserts our capacity to imagine the impossible, to follow the Beckettian non sequitur: imagination dead imagine, in which the mind imagines passing beyond its own limitations: "We live the impossible: we live beyond our own death, look back on it, yet look back on it as only a dead self can. . . . What I know is what a corpse cannot know: that it is extinct, that it knows nothing and will never know anything any more. For an instant, before my whole structure of knowledge collapses in panic, I am alive inside that contradiction, dead and alive at the same time" (32).

The choice of a corpse for this bizarre thought experiment is not arbitrary. In his analysis of the sublime, Kant takes the mind's capacity to think beyond itself as evidence of its "supersensible vocation," of the triumph of human reason. Costello, by contrast, wishes to emphasize the fact of our embodiment, to assert humanity's "subsensible" destination, our affinity with other animals rather than with God, matter rather than ether. Her concept of the joy of being turns out to be resolutely antitranscendent: "To thinking, cogitation, I oppose fullness, embodiedness, the sensation of being —not a consciousness of yourself as a kind of ghostly reasoning machine thinking thoughts but on the contrary the sensation—a heavily affective sensation—of being a body with limbs that have extension in space, of being alive to the world" (33). As she goes on to demonstrate in her seminar on "The Poets and the Animals," literature, the realm of aesthetic judgment, which Kant saw as the vital bridge between pure and practical reason, seems in fact to present a passage out of reason. Mingling "breath and sense in a way that no one has explained and no one ever will" (53), it is valuable not for its uplifting passage to transcendence but for its anchoring of the human mind in the material world, what Geoffrey Hartman would term "descendence." Or at least this is what literature should do: the example she chooses is untrustworthy. In their ecologism, Ted Hughes's jaguar poems tend to lose sight of the individual animal, and Costello is forced to concede that "despite the vividness and earthiness of the poetry, there remains something Platonic [idealist, transcendent] about it" (53).

Perhaps Coetzee's fiction would have been a better example than Hughes's poetry, if not for its thinking of the reality of animal lives, then for its systematic reduction of the human to the level of the animal. Descendence is a good way of describing not only K's living out of the ecstasy of a thoughtless body but also the Magistrate's reduction to "a pile of blood, bone and meat that is unhappy" (85). *Disgrace,* in which the project of becoming animal is rendered most explicit, provides a road map of a Romanticism turned against itself. If he is to live "like a dog," David Lurie, lover of Wordsworth and Byron and would-be Byronic lover, must discard the egotistical sublime and learn a Keatsian negative capability. Sprawled out next to the bitch Katie on the concrete, Lurie mimes the grounds of a certain similarity or solidarity. However, his articulation of their similarity— "abandoned, are we," he murmurs, before he falls asleep—falls prey to anthropocentrism: as Lucy points out, Katie may be missing her children rather than her owner (78). As soon as the sympathetic imagination acquires a content, it forgets the difference of the other. To remember the other is to place the imagination in abeyance: it is only in his stupefying work with animals that he avoids imaginative projection and enacts a singularly *un*imaginative sympathy.

In accompanying dogs to their death and their corpses to the incinerator, Lurie seems to literalize or act out Costello's advice "to walk, flank to flank, beside the beast that is prodded down the chute to its executioner" (65). In so doing, he bypasses the need for the sympathetic imagination. However, what Lurie literalizes, we, of course, experience as fiction. We imaginatively accompany Lurie as he accompanies dogs to their death and their corpses to the incinerator, or the Magistrate as he submits to a regime of torture that may or may not bring him closer to the suffering of the barbarian girl, or Mrs. Curren as she gets turned out of her own house and ends up sleeping on the streets, "like" a vagrant (or a dog). Rather than enter into the consciousness of dogs, barbarians, or displaced squatter-camp residents, Coetzee's sympathetic imagination, if that is its name, draws us toward that which it can't imagine by turning a position of privilege into an *approximation* of an oppressed position.

In place of the traditional concept of the sympathetic imagination, in which the self attempts to mentally inhabit the position of the other, Coetzee's fiction works to other the self, to deprive the subject of its privileges until it is reduced to an approximation of the other. In place of the mental process of imaginative *pro*jection, Coetzee's subjects undergo a bodily experience of *ab*jection, in which the subject is violently expelled from the domain of language and society.[8] As Kristeva puts it, abjection "places the one haunted by it *literally* beside himself" (*Powers,* 3; italics mine). To place the subject beside itself is to bring it into bodily proximity with the other, with those bodies that have never been granted the privileges of the subject. True abjection, as experienced by Kristeva's patients, is a lonely, melancholy experience that can often lead to suicide. The task of the analyst, of the writer, is not to attempt to rescue the patient—an impossible task, perhaps —but to learn how to be with the patient in that lonely place of suffering. This is the possibility of the transference, the possibility of being affected by "a strange foreign discourse, which strictly speaking shatters verbal communication" (30). If literature works, then, it works not as verbal communication but as the shattering of words. It works only if it is able to forget itself, its own status as fiction. Only then can it bring the reader into relation with a world of bodies or bring our bodies into relation.

At stake is what the Jewish poet Abraham Stern, objecting to Costello's comparison of the treatment of Jews and animals, refers to as "the nature of likenesses" (*Lives*, 50). According to Lucy, reconciliation, or at least cohabitation, in postapartheid South Africa is dependent on the relinquishing of privilege, on learning to live "like a dog" (*Disgrace*, 205). The simile marks resemblance but also recognizes a certain limit: one can imitate the life of a dog but never actually lead a dog's life, never actually *be* a dog. However, in "The Doctrine of the Similar," Walter Benjamin suggests that "our gift for seeing similarity is nothing but a weak rudiment of the once powerful compulsion to become similar and also to behave mimetically" ("Doctrine," 698). Mimesis, which for Plato was the weak imitation of ideal forms, was "once" the literal movement of bodies toward each other. We might say that Coetzee's fiction, in its constant striving to bring bodies together, into relation, writes itself in remembrance of this dream of becoming-similar.

How are we to respond to literature's miming of an original compulsion to "behave mimetically"? Should we respond by returning literature to its origins, by taking literature literally? What kind of example is Coetzee's fiction; what kind of demands does it make? If, like Costello, we "have a literal cast of mind" (*Costello*, 32), shouldn't we follow Lucy's example—the example of the Magistrate or Mrs. Curren—and give up our rights and privileges?

I want to end by attending to *The Lives of Animals* not as lecture but as short story, as literature, in order to highlight the terrifying exemplarity of its protagonist. Inverting the end of *Gulliver's Travels,* to which Costello has already alluded, Costello finds her radically alienated from a human race that appears to her as monstrous in its rationality rather than its lack of it. It becomes clear that she is on the edge of a nervous breakdown. But it also becomes increasingly evident that she is losing her will to live, giving in to a certain will to die. As the BBC film wonderfully captures in the shots of her applying cold cream in the mirror, she is literally turning into a corpse, silently, involuntarily, miming the fate of animals, in the ultimate gesture of the sympathetic imagination.[9] If she cannot become an animal, then at least she can become, like them, a corpse.

However, the end of the narrative is darker still in its deliberate negation of Costello's example: as she gives way to tears on the way to the airport, her son takes her into his arms and, in this bodily proximity, "inhales the smell of cold cream, of cold flesh" (69). Flank to flank with his own mother, he recognizes the fact of her imminent death but sinisterly replaces her bodily act of identification with all the conventional banality of verbal sympathy: "There, there. It will soon be over."

In conclusion, *The Lives of Animals* relates to Coetzee's other work not as the theory that explains or contradicts the novelistic practice but as a story to other stories, as one example in a series of singular examples. Like his other work, it is both theory and practice combined, irreducible to a set of beliefs about the imagination.[10] And this resistance to abstraction is, of course, the point: it is in the putting-to-work of the theory, its inevitable difference from itself, that Coetzee's "message" resides. If Costello can only realize her identification with the lives of animals in her own death, then the novel must also go beyond its own limits, enact its own death, if it is to transcend—or rather descend—the limits of the sympathetic imagination.

Notes

1. Lucy Graham argues that Lurie's actions need to be clearly identified as rape ("Giving Him Up,'" 13). While it is important not to take Lurie at his word ("not rape, not quite that" [25]), it seems difficult to be categorical about an event to which we have only mediated access.

2. In comparing Elizabeth Costello's ideas on the sympathetic imagination, as articulated in *The Lives of Animals,* with Coetzee's novelistic practice, I have assumed

that Coetzee's practice remains more or less consistent, and I draw my examples from a number of the novels without being able to do justice to their singularity.

3. I work with these novels at length in "Bearing Witness to Apartheid." The current essay builds on some of the arguments advanced in the earlier essay, especially those concerning abjection and transference.

4. See Attridge "Age of Bronze."

5. I foreground this argument in an early version of this paper, "Becoming Stupid."

6. In an interview, Coetzee admits that "his thinking is thrown into confusion and helplessness by the fact of suffering in the world" (*Doubling*, 248).

7. This belief in the possibility and necessity of bearing witness rescues Coetzee from the "nihilism" that Lucy Graham, in an otherwise highly persuasive essay, suggests may be his "literary affiliation/background" ("Giving Him Up," 14).

8. See Durrant, "Bearing Witness," and Boehmer, "Not Saying Sorry," which also draws on the category of abjection in its reading of Lurie's rite of passage in *Disgrace.*

9. Many thanks to Teresa Dovey and Kai Erickson for pointing me toward Benjamin's concept of the mimetic faculty.

10. Of the responses to *The Lives of Animals* published in the same volume, only Peter Singer's recognizes this irreducibility by replying in the form of a story.

Bibliography

Attridge, Derek. "Age of Bronze, State of Grace: Music and Dogs in Coetzee's *Disgrace*." *Novel* 34, no. 1 (Fall 2000): 98–118.

Benjamin, Walter. "The Doctrine of the Similar." In *Selected Writings*, 4 vols., vol. 2, translated by Rodney Livingstone et al., edited by Michael W. Jennings, Howard Eiland, and Gary Smith, 694–98. Cambridge, MA: Belknap Press, 1999.

Boehmer, Elleke. "Not Saying Sorry, Not Speaking Pain: Gender Implications in *Disgrace*." In "J. M. Coetzee's *Disgrace*," edited by Derek Attridge and Peter D. McDonald. Special issue, *Interventions* 4, no. 3 (2002): 342–45.

Caruth, Cathy. *Unclaimed Experience: Trauma, Narrative, History.* Baltimore: Johns Hopkins University Press, 1996.

Coetzee, J. M. *Age of Iron.* Harmondsworth: Penguin, 1990.

———. *Disgrace.* London: Secker and Warburg, 1999.

———. *Doubling the Point: Essays and Interviews.* Edited by David Attwell. Cambridge, MA: Harvard University Press, 1992.

———. *Foe.* 1986. Harmondsworth: Penguin, 1987.

———. *In the Heart of the Country.* 1976. Harmondsworth: Penguin, 1982.

———. *Life & Times of Michael K.* 1983. Harmondsworth: Penguin, 1985.

———. *The Lives of Animals.* Edited by Amy Gutmann. Princeton, NJ: Princeton University Press, 1999.

———. *Waiting for the Barbarians.* 1980. Harmondsworth: Penguin, 1982.

Durrant, Samuel. "Bearing Witness to Apartheid: J. M. Coetzee's Inconsolable Works of Mourning." *Contemporary Literature* 40 (1999): 430–63.

———. "Becoming Stupid: The Limits of Empathy in J. M. Coetzee's Work." *Alter-Nation* 1 (Special Edition) (2002).

Graham, Lucy. "'Yes, I Am Giving Him Up': Sacrificial Responsibility and Likeness with Dogs in J. M. Coetzee's Recent Fiction." *Scrutiny2* 7, no. 1 (2002): 4–15.

Kristeva, Julia. *Powers of Horror: An Essay on Abjection.* Translated by Leon S. Roudiez. New York: Columbia University Press, 1982.

Lacan, Jacques. *The Four Fundamental Concepts of Psychoanalysis.* 1973. Edited by Jacques-Alain Miller. Translated by Alan Sheridan. London: Penguin, 1994.

7

SORRY, SORRIER, SORRIEST

The Gendering of Contrition in J. M. Coetzee's Disgrace

Elleke Boehmer

DISGRACE (1999) is notable in the Coetzee oeuvre for having drawn a remarkable level of national and international recognition: it may well have paved the way for the 2003 award to the writer of the Nobel Prize in Literature. One of the reasons for the attention the novel has received is that, against the 1990s background of the Truth and Reconciliation Commission (TRC) spectacle, it features a hero, David Lurie, who notoriously refuses to say he's sorry for an abuse of power. The teasing conjunction of nonconfession novel and postapartheid catharsis in particular has exercised critics, who tend to see the text, too, as a diagnostic reflection on the "new South Africa." While taking account of the country's continuing social and economic divisions, the novel addresses above all the topical question of what it is to come to terms *both* with past horrors *and* with a transformed society.

From the evidence of *Disgrace,* and the 1992 essay collection *Doubling the Point,* Coetzee appears to cast doubt on the possibility of achieving closure on a painful past, of ever—in a secular society and in language—adequately saying he's sorry, of being fully contrite. Instead, it seems to me, he proposes the far more painful process of enduring rather than transcending the degraded present, where the present is more often than not a rehearsal and prolongation of the past. In order to do so he works through, as I will later describe, a calibrated display of contrition, in which traditionally objectified bodies, of women and dogs, are made to act as the bearers or carriers, as Wole Soyinka puts it in relation to Yoruba culture, of a community's sin.[1]

Disgrace itself explicitly introduces the idea of "carrying" wrong, or scapegoating, in chapter 11. This, the very chapter in which the violent attack on the farm takes place, begins with a relatively peaceful morning walk during which David Lurie and his daughter, Lucy, converse amicably. Given that this is the cusp moment after which the configurations of relationship on Lucy's smallholding are disrupted to the core, and disgrace enters their lives (176), it is instructive to look again at what father and daughter have to say to each other. They talk, significantly, about desire as both a state of possession and as undesired infliction, in both cases as a burden, involuntarily imposed (89–90). Lurie cites the instance of the Kenilworth dog of Lucy's childhood, which was punished, without any result, for its sexual excitation. Expanding on but inflecting this concept of an unwanted burden (sexually induced), Lucy then refers to Lurie's expulsion from the academic community due to his refusal to confess as an instance of scapegoating (91). Lurie, however, rejects this with an elaborate statement about the untenability of scapegoating in a secular age:

> I don't think scapegoating is the best description. . . . Scapegoating worked in practice while it still had religious power behind it. You loaded the sins of the city on to the goat's back and drove it out, and the city was cleansed. It worked because everyone knew how to read the ritual, including the gods. Then the gods died, and all of a sudden you had to cleanse the city without divine help. Real actions were demanded instead of symbolism. The censor was born, in the Roman sense. Watchfulness became the watchword: the watchfulness of all over all. Purgation was replaced by the purge. (91)

Lurie's statement is crucial as it pulls together a number of the chief questions posed in the novel. How do we achieve moral cleansing in both an individual and a collective capacity in a secular age? What are the modern methods of purging? Is such cleansing, if it exists, ever anything more than rhetoric or a public performance, as demanded by a censoring authority, rather than from the heart, as especially the later Lurie would wish it to be?[2] In relation to the representation of both women and dogs in the novel, and the main protagonist's verbal protestations to the contrary, the answers to these questions seem to me, symbolically at least, to be fairly traditional.

This essay makes a contribution to the critical discussion surrounding the reconciliation of, and abjection to, historical responsibility in Coetzee by looking at the highly subjectivized, inevitably animalized, but also gendered process of coming to terms, of reduced secular atonement *and* of the *embodiment* of wrong in the novel. Interestingly, such atonement via submission and endurance is anticipated in the bodies of the barbarian woman and of Elizabeth Curren in the earlier novels, *Waiting for the Barbarians* (1980) and *Age of Iron* (1990), respectively. Here too the bodies involved are female: what Coetzee then adds to the equation in *Disgrace* are the carrier figures of dogs. Moreover, in *Disgrace,* I suggest, secular atonement is proposed as an *alternative to* the public and Christianized ritual of redemption through confession, of reconciliation through a possibly self-serving catharsis, or "real actions," which the TRC, for example, has offered.

Both David Lurie and his raped daughter, Lucy, eventually seek to accommodate a history of violence and violation through a traditionally feminine or at least emasculating physical abjection to, and new responsibility for, that history, rather than through a staged narrative. Instead of dramatizing the distanced past in confession, they keep on simply by keeping on, by a dogged bodily endurance, and, moreover, they have little choice in the matter of so doing. They survive by living in what is essentially the dangerous now of Walter Benjamin's understanding of history, in which the pain of the past must be continually revisited upon the present.[3] In further conceptualizing this process of coming to terms, I join with critics like Mike Marais in proposing that Coetzee sets up the difficult Levinasian ethic of being for the other, of feeling intensely the being of the conventionally sublimated other—or, in Lucy's case, of living as other.[4] It is a process of empathetic abjection that is at once deeply personal, when viewed subjectively, and yet impersonal, or at least impersonalizing. The ethic is centrally expounded in Coetzee's *The Lives of Animals* (1999) and subsequently in *Elizabeth Costello* (2003), which can be productively read as in many ways his own intertextual commentary on *Disgrace* (and vice versa).

As Coetzee implies via a quotation from Benjamin in a review essay on the German theorist's *Passagen-Werk,* it is through a "great love" alone, an unstinting, self-emptying love, that the recognition of the other and the other's pain is achieved.[5] *Disgrace* ends with the disgraced former academic and harassing Don Juan Lurie fully absorbed (in spite of himself) in his task of putting down stray dogs, what he calls Lösung (that is, the final solution) or sublimation (142). This mercy killing is, as he acknowledges, a gift of love—it is also a confrontation with a teasing, synaesthetic nonpresence, something that is at once numinous yet sensorily experienced as almost real, "the soft, short smell of the released soul" (219). Dogged endurance produces this expiation or release.

Controversially, therefore, the primary other in the alternative ethical schema explored in *Disgrace* is not human, not the historically degraded human, but the "wholly other" or the extreme alterity of the stray dog.[6] Being-for-the-other in effect involves—as I will explore more fully later— an elision of another conventional other, the silenced woman: most obviously Lucy but also the abused Melanie. As before in Coetzee's fiction, one can seemingly only witness to the suffering of human history, and in this case the specific suffering of apartheid (and of sexual abuse), by a paradoxical refusal to witness, to make a conscious assessment, by the action rather of relieving the suffering of dogs. As do *Foe* (1986), *Waiting for the Barbarians,* or *Age of Iron, Disgrace* again explores the extreme difficulty of what it is to speak on behalf of as well as to represent another (Attridge, "Age of Bronze," 102; Coetzee, *Doubling the Point,* 10). The self that has inflicted suffering is here broken down and transformed by a partially unintended participation in the suffering (of the carrier), and also by silently, bodily, bearing witness to it (as a surrogate carrier).

This essay will move on, therefore, to asking whether this abjection can be seen as a satisfactory response when it concerns not so much the perpetrator as the victim of a wrong, one who is already abjected. As Mr. Isaacs, the father of Lurie's sexual victim, Melanie, says, "The question is, what are we going to do now that we are sorry?" (172). Sorriness here complexly signifies both the state of offering an apology for wrong, and the pitiful-ness of abjection to, or as a result of, wrong. The novel arguably shifts the reader through the calibrated semantics of *sorry*, moving from the more prevalent sense of "offering a burden of apology" (*Concise OED*, meanings 1 and 3), through "feeling sympathy for" (*Concise OED*, meaning 2), to-ward the less common sense of pitifulness, being "in a sorry state" (*Concise OED*, meaning 4).

The debate in *Disgrace* about adequately responding to social disgrace and bodily violation is carried out, too (and perhaps most eloquently), at the formal level, via the novel's widely described diptych structure. In par-ticular two key questions emerge from the deliberate symmetries. Is Lurie's final abjected position as a "dog-man," his own name for himself, as one who serves or services dead dogs, an adequate form of atonement for the wrong—the near rape—he inflicted in the first half of the narrative? And is the perpetrator Lurie's refusal to verbalize and fully account for his ac-tions comparable to the victim Lucy's refusal to speak her rape? Are their silences in any way commensurate with one another, or are the parallels between them, their dual roles of literally "carrying" (Lurie of the dead dogs, Lucy of her pregnancy), a disturbing whitewash of the differences that in fact irreconcilably divide her situation from his?

In an interesting instance of historical foresight, Coetzee early on made a contribution to the ongoing discussion, in part forged by the TRC, about paying for the past in South Africa, and so about the ethical status and epistemological limitations of secular confession. In a 1985 essay, "Confes-sion and Double Thoughts," he followed a characteristic Derridean argu-ment by suggesting that, in the absence of a deity—"illumination from the outside"—as final arbiter, confession, of which the goal was ostensibly truth, in fact became an endlessly repeating series of substitute confessions. Within this series no one story could have a greater purchase on authentic-ity and self-revelation than any other: "self-consciousness works by its own laws, one of which is that behind each true, final position lurks another po-sition truer and more final" (253). The impossibility of truth telling in lan-guage is of course a dilemma with which Coetzee's fiction has long wrestled. From that dilemma the only release proposed is, as David Attwell has recog-nized in the editorial apparatus to *Doubling the Point*, "unawareness," the impossible replacement of things-for-consciousness, words, by things-in-themselves. The truth of suffering therefore is acknowledged through the refusal to represent it and instead to bear or act it on the body, in the body. Such redemptive ethical unawareness is, as Attwell further notes, the idealized endpoint of all Coetzee fictions: an authorial abnegation or nontextual truth telling, as in the evocation of the mute Friday in *Foe*. Taking a line from Coetzee's own reading of Dostoevsky—"true confession . . . comes from faith and grace"—Attwell experimentally terms this state of unawareness *grace:* a state imposed from without, not generated by the self (10–11, 243–50, 291). It is a word that evidently shadows a novel called *Disgrace*, yet one that Coetzee himself finally disavows as being a term predicated upon a Christian eschatology.

Even so, the question of how to deal in some meaningful way with—or make reparation for—the wrongs of the past remains. *Disgrace* is preoccupied throughout with dilemmas of retribution as well as redistribution, both of which essentially demand the acceptance of disgrace as a "state of being," as Lurie recognizes (172, 84). More than once he schematically conceives of the new South African society as a great circulatory system in which goods, which are always scarce and explicitly include women as booty (12, 16, 18), are ceaselessly redistributed, without much thought for reparative justice (98, 176). More obviously so perhaps than in any of Coetzee's previous novels, this acceptance of reduced lives, of disgrace on several levels— the loss of possessions, of self-esteem—is tied to the surrender of individualist, self-justifying reason. Lurie with his irony and Byronic self-justifications is of course the primary exponent of reason in the novel. Yet, simultaneous with his loss of the Byronic voice in the chamber opera he is composing, he begins to speak with increasing frequency across the narrative of responding from the heart. Reason therefore is given up in favor of an almost involuntary, because not self-aware (and so not self-substituting), love. This in a country that, as Coetzee has observed, has suffered from a failure of love. Rationality—the "unframed framer" or deity-substitute of the intellectual (*Doubling*, 97)—gives way to a self-emptying *respect* for the other, which in *Giving Offense* Coetzee describes as "a variety of love" (10, 15).[7] It is a very similar surrender or giving way to which the novelist Elizabeth Costello appeals in *The Lives of Animals* and in *Elizabeth Costello* as the basis on which to build her arguments for animal rights. Sympathy, Costello crucially and repeatedly says, is a central faculty not of the reason but of the self-dissolving heart.

Self-dissolution is something that Lurie, too, in time learns. "There are no bounds to the sympathetic imagination," Costello elucidates; and in *Disgrace* we find Lurie, who once saw his temperament as dry, cold as a snake, and above all "fixed, set" (2, 7, 16, 38), imagining himself into the yearning being of Byron's bereaved and aging lover Teresa. She is the only character in his chamber opera who now engages his heart (181). He also accompanies or "escorts" stray dogs to the incinerator, into death and beyond, in an attempt to preserve their bodily dignity (84). In other words, we see him taking the quality of sympathy beyond its conventional limits, the divides between the living and the dead, between humans and other animals, without being precisely sure why he is doing so. He achieves, in Elizabeth Costello's terms, an unconscious redemption from evil: his self becomes a site on which pity is staged.[8] Fundamentally, therefore, this evil is the evil of having objectified others through reason as entirely different from ourselves and therefore to be used as we see fit. As Lurie himself says, though at this stage still in a spirit of rational superiority, "if we are going to be kind, let it be out of simple generosity, not because we feel guilty or fear retribution" (74). In short, *Disgrace* along with Coetzee's published essays since 1999, proposes animals as the essential third term in the reconciliation of human self and human other, where reconciliation equates with the embodying of an elastic and generous kindness.[9]

As I have implied, the question of Lurie's achievement of kindness and redemption hinges on his reduction to the self-assumed role of "dog-man" (64). This derogatory term, which Petrus, Lucy's assistant and coproprietor, explicitly rejects (129, 151), is acquired by Lurie in incremental stages. During his time with Lucy, Lurie begins by handling dog meat (77), then agrees to help Bev Shaw in the animal refuge "out of the goodness of his heart," though he resists the description. He becomes by degrees almost literally the underling, the underdog, the "untouchable" or *harijan* as he himself says, the one who serves not just dogs but dead dogs, "untouchable" carrion, doing not only demeaning but useless work that no one else would do (146). He agrees with Lucy that he is (and they are) effectively reduced to the state of being no better than a dog, without status, without dignity (204): "let it all go to the dogs," he unconsciously but revealingly puns (121). Lurie thus works out ways of responding feelingly to history—without, however, consciously aiming to do so (61–62). The "escorting" job he finally takes upon himself, which no one else will do, he can significantly give no reason for doing. He is merely lessening what he sees as the "disgrace" of the dogs' deaths (143).

At the same time as the dogs, a second, related chain of equivalence between Lurie and animals is set up, which connects even more obviously with the concept of scapegoating. This relationship emerges with the implicit but powerful analogy between the diseased he-goat brought into the Animal Welfare League clinic and Lurie, burdened with concupiscence, the sin of the goat. As a teasing sign that, Lurie's asseverations to the contrary, scapegoating is not to be entirely abandoned as a cleansing practice, *Disgrace* cites, just before Lurie's conversation about the lust-burdened Kenilworth retriever, this iconic, and graphic, image of the suffering goat. Among this scene's significant resonances are Bev Shaw's observation that the goat has been savaged by dogs and the detail that its genitals in particular have been targeted: his wound is now suppurating. The traditional symbolic associations of the goat are signposted at least once, in the reference to the "obscene bulge" of the infected scrotum. Even though the he-goat in several ways represents masculinity under its conventionally positive aspects—he is "combative," "brave," "confident" (82–83)—Lurie significantly mentions that the goat, the scapegoat, is also a traditional object of sacrifice: goats, he observes, are used to death by steel and fire.

The goat's fruitless visit to the clinic represents the first time that Bev Shaw has occasion to speak to Lurie of escorting animals into death, which on this occasion she doesn't actually do: the goat is taken back to the township for slaughter by its old woman owner. Yet, with its proximity to the conversation about scapegoating between Lucy and Lurie, the scene connects not only Lurie and the goat but also, in an extended parallelogram of calibrated association, the Kenilworth retriever and, finally, Lucy. The retriever, the reader is soon to hear, "hates its own nature," unknowingly introjects its own punishment, and makes an ignoble, which is to say sorry, spectacle of itself. Lucy, though not herself a subject of desire will, immediately following Lurie's "lecture" about scapegoating, herself be attacked, not unlike the goat. She will have unwanted desire and sorriness in the sense of wretchedness inflicted on her and will thus be forced into the position of victim or sacrifice, a lamb for slaughter, much like Petrus's slaughter-sheep (123–27).

Does this tightly packed matrix of associations suggest that Lurie, at least, manages to work out a partial secular atonement by as it were emptying out his self-regard through inadvertent acts of self-lowering identification with dogs, a goat, and even his daughter? The primal scene in the toilet where Pollux and his accomplices beat him and lock him up while Lucy is being gang-raped, certainly figures in the novel as a culminating act of abjection.[10] Unable to aid either his daughter or the dogs, who are shot, Lurie is denied the roles both of father and of dog-man, roles he was recently learning to reclaim. Finally he is set alight, blackened, and burned, just like any dead stray dog, victim of sacrifice, or scapegoat. He is both bodily and ethically disgraced. Most serious of all, he has been passive before a second act of violation, where the first was the "almost rape" of Melanie Isaacs, with her sacrificial family name.

Significantly, it is from this point on that Lurie begins to work out that breakthrough into *feeling* the self of another rather than rationalizing its experiences in terms of his own needs. There are however at least two problematic aspects to this secular and ultimately male-led atonement as represented in the novel. The first is that for Coetzee Lurie is by definition not conscious of his salvation; he does not mastermind it. Although he has gained release from the self-love that is fundamental to the drama of confession, are we then convinced by this "third-term" atonement, by this abjective identification with the animal other? Learning to live from the heart through taking upon himself the burden of dealing with the disgrace of dogs, through scapegoating himself, living out day by day the humiliation of being without honor and status "like a dog" (205), does Lurie come to terms with the wrong he has committed? Who or what authorizes such atonement? These are but two of the questions without an answer that run throughout Coetzee's work.

The second and probably more serious difficulty (as it is one the narrative does not fully confront) has to do with the raped Lucy, too, taking on this doglike, or, more particularly, goatlike, status. This is the difficulty of a difference of *position,* that of object not subject, in relation to the novel's ethics of abjection. Lucy, too, accepts the roles of underling and underdog. The novel moves through its graduated chains of association of contrition and of scapegoat (imposed sacrifice, suffering, purgation), to attribute both the role of carrier and the state of sorriness directly to her. Like Lurie she achieves an eventual release from her personal and the political past through the unquestioning acceptance of her suffering. She insists that what the men did to her was not a historical act, not a symbolic gesture of revenge; this is partly why she will not speak of it or seek its redress. Yet—to put it bluntly—the suffering she thus resolves to endure bodily is *her* suffering, not another's, not a dog's.

The difficult question silently asked through the medium of the tightly patterned narrative is whether it is not outrageous to align this acceptance (for which there is no alternative, as Lucy makes plain) with Lurie's acts of unconscious expiation. For, whereas Lurie has been an agent of desire, Lucy has been the passive recipient of a form of violent desire, one she experienced as an intensely personal infliction of hatred (112, 133–34, 156). In her case the victim of historical violence—and, as a woman, a historical victim —is forced to take upon herself (even if she denies doing so) the consequences of that violence. She physically, if not verbally, accepts a burden of accountability for the wrongs of the past. While rejecting the abstraction of words like *atonement,* she lives with what has happened to her by practical survival, "immersing" herself in her life on the land (134). She takes on the role of the victim of a history of violence and deprivation: this, she suggests her attackers believe, is the price of staying on (158).

At that point in the narrative where this is recognized, Lucy significantly compares rape to a sacrificial killing: "pushing the knife in; exiting afterwards, leaving the body behind covered in blood." In effect, Lucy embeds in herself, her person, her body, the stereotypes not only of the wronged woman but also of the sacrificial victim of history, the lamb, the scapegoat. The narrative shows us, just as the men have shown her, to quote from the text, "what a woman is for." Unlike in Lurie's case, where pity involves projection, her sorriness, her pitifulness, is fully internalized or introjected, like the retriever's. That is, it is internalized until of course, like a classic scapegoat, she begins visibly to bear the burden of her pregnancy, of paying for the past, of bearing the sins of her fathers. Remembering back to the figure of the text's living (scape)goat, the pregnancy is, despite the romantic way in which it is pictured, yet another "obscene bulge."

Lucy therefore embodies not only the stereotype of the wronged, muted woman but of the abused and to-be-again-abused of history: she becomes, in a phrase, the figure of a double silence. Her dogged carrying on fits the terms of what secular atonement signifies in *Disgrace:* that is, abjectly living through the consequences of a violent action, making private accommodations with a legacy of horror. Thus Lucy, far more than Lurie, becomes *the* human body-in-pain of the text, that which Coetzee terms the ultimate "standard," the limit to "that which is not" (*Doubling,* 248). As a body she is the nonintrospective arbiter of what it is to live the truth of the new South Africa. She stages through her pitifulness, even if unwillingly and unwittingly, an apologia.

Yet in that Lucy is a woman, the implications of such action are worrying —especially considering that women have been described as circulating objects within the new South African system. Is this, as Lucy herself puts it, the price of staying on for a woman (black or white): the surrender without significant change to traditional forms of subjection, servility, and abnegation (158)? In highly traditional terms, do silent women-in-pain remain the ground on which a new society is brought into being? Lurie abjects selfhood and achieves a kind of unselfconscious redemption; Lucy has abnegation forced on her and has herself committed no wrong. Coetzee would want to see her embodiment as signifying a certain power, yet it is a power traduced by its fixity, its entrenchedness. She must make herself ready for more of such violation. For her, any sympathy for the other must mean to live in inevitable disgrace. For Lurie, by contrast, sympathy involves a limited yet still *willing* identification with another's suffering. Lurie in this sense remains a subject, even if a self-substituting one; Lucy's self-substitution involves becoming reconciled to the position of conventional object (159). Lurie's redemptive and self-redeeming care for the dogs places them in the position of the "carriers" of his former disgrace. Lucy becomes herself a carrier—most immediately of her disgraceful pregnancy. Throughout *Disgrace* animals are seen either waiting for slaughter or slaughtered. Lucy, too, "marked" after her rape, must like any scapegoat, be continually prepared to be sacrificed. Therefore, while a feminizing or animalizing atonement may represent a meaningful recompense for a man, for a woman, always-already a creature of dumb animality, it is a matter of no change; a continuation of subjection that it would be preposterous to propose as redemptive.

In an attempt to refract this situation differently, Mike Marais has tried to interpret Lucy's passivity as the text's way of signifying an occluded otherness (between human self and animal alterity)—an otherness that must be recognized if the dialectic of oppressor and oppressed is to be broken down ("Ethical Action"). Yet to argue this, it seems to me, is to bracket away (as does Levinas) the conventional and ungainsayable valencies of such passivity and thus to reinforce Lucy's secular scapegoat status. Against a background of the traditional gendered binary of oppressor and oppressed, how can this passivity be regenerative other than in the most obvious fashion? How —it remains crucial to ask—can we speak of atonement if it entails that women as ever assume the generic pose of suffering in silence or, as does Lucy, of gestating peacefully in her garden? Is reconciliation with a history of violence possible if the woman, the white Lucy, or indeed the black wife of Petrus, is, as ever, barefoot and pregnant, and biting her lip?

Notes

1. See, in particular, Soyinka, "Strong Breed," 113–46.

2. On the cultures of mutual surveillance of modernity, see Coetzee, *Giving Offense.*

3. Benjamin writes, "To articulate the past historically . . . means to seize hold of a memory as it flashes up at a moment of danger." His belief is that the past has a claim on us, requiring us to understand it as connected to each lived moment—in this lies redemption from history. See "Theses on the Philosophy of History," 255–56. For further discussion of Benjamin as well as Adorno in relation to Coetzee, see Durrant, "Bearing Witness."

4. See Levinas, *Ethics and Infinity;* Marais, "'Little Enough."

5. See Coetzee, "Shopping for Truth."

6. See Spivak, *Postcolonial Reason,* 169–97.

7. See also *Disgrace,* 219.

8. This relates to Coetzee's comment on *The Kreutzer Sonata* that, as a consequence of an already existing "truth-directedness," the self is a site in which a change takes place—change is not willed. See Coetzee, *Doubling the Point,* 250, 261.

9. See, for example, Coetzee, *Lives of Animals*, 105.

10. To Julia Kristeva the abject is a recognizably "feminine" state of at once "extreme subjectivity" *and* of the awareness of the absolute objectivity or unassimilable "nonunity" of the other, comparable to Levinas's insistence on the absolute demand of the other. See Kristeva, *Powers of Horror*, 9–10.

Bibliography

Attridge, Derek. "Age of Bronze, State of Grace: Music and Dogs in Coetzee's *Disgrace*." *Novel* 34, no. 1 (2000): 98–121.

Benjamin, Walter. "Theses on the Philosophy of History." In *Illuminations: Essays and Reflections,* edited by Hannah Arendt, translated by Harry Zohn. New York: Schocken Books, 1969.

Coetzee, J. M. "Confession and Double Thoughts." In *Doubling the Point,* 251–93.

———. *Disgrace.* London: Secker and Warburg, 1999.

———. *Doubling the Point.* Edited by David Attwell. Cambridge, MA: Harvard University Press, 1992.

———. *Elizabeth Costello.* London: Secker and Warburg, 2003.

———. *Giving Offense: Essays on Censorship.* Chicago: University of Chicago Press, 1996.

———. *The Lives of Animals.* London: Profile Books, 2000.

———. "The Man Who Went Shopping for Truth." *Guardian Review,* January 20, 2001, 1–3.

Durrant, Samuel. "Bearing Witness to Apartheid: J. M. Coetzee's Inconsolable Works of Mourning." *Contemporary Literature* 40, no. 3 (1999): 430–63.

Kristeva, Julia. *Powers of Horror: An Essay on Abjection.* Translated by Leon S. Roudiez. New York: Columbia University Press, 1982.

Levinas, Emmanuel. *Ethics and Infinity.* Translated by Richard A. Cohen. Pittsburgh: Duquesne University Press, 1985.

Marais, Michael. "'Little Enough, Less Than Little: Nothing': Ethics, Engagement, and Chance in the Fiction of J. M. Coetzee." *Modern Fiction Studies* 46, no. 1 (2000): 159–82.

———. "The Possibility of Ethical Action: J. M. Coetzee's *Disgrace*." *Scrutiny2* 5, no. 1 (2000): 57–63.

Soyinka, Wole. "The Strong Breed." In *Collected Plays.* 2 vols. Oxford: Oxford University Press, 1986.

Spivak, Gayatri. *A Critique of Postcolonial Reason: Toward a History of the Vanishing Present.* Cambridge, MA: Harvard University Press, 1999.

8

GOING TO THE DOGS

Humanity in J. M. Coetzee's Disgrace, The Lives of Animals, *and South Africa's Truth and Reconciliation Commission*

Rosemary Jolly

The Furor over Rape in Disgrace

WITH THE transition from apartheid rule to democratic government in 1994 came the hope, both within and outside South Africa, that "the time when humanity will be restored across the face of society" had come (Coetzee, "Dark Chamber," 35). Yet Coetzee's first postapartheid novel, *Disgrace* (1999), set in South Africa, is remarkably bleak. As Derek Attridge has remarked, *Disgrace*'s negative portrayal of the relations between communities, coming from an author widely read in South Africa and internationally, can be seen as a hindrance to, not a support of, the massive task of reconciliation and rebuilding that the country has undertaken. Touching on the central role of Coetzee's fiction in debates over the role of writers in contexts of extreme social injustice,[1] Attridge remarks that "even readers whose view of the artist's responsibility is less tied to notions of instrumentalism and political efficacy than these questions imply—and I include myself among these—may find the bleak image of the 'new South Africa' in this work hard to take, as I confess I do" ("Age of Bronze," 99–100).

Within the African National Congress, *Disgrace* was rejected outright as racist. The ANC, in its 1999 submission to the Human Rights Commission's investigation into racism in the media, names *Disgrace* as a novel that exploits racist stereotypes. This caused a furor of debate in the press. Mike Nicol, himself a novelist, cites the relevant passages both from the novel and the ANC submission. He quotes Lucy's response to Lurie, after she has decided to keep the baby following her rape and form an alliance with Petrus, to settle the land issue.

> Lucy is quoted as saying: "Yes, I agree, it is humiliating. But perhaps that is a good point to start from again. Perhaps that is what I must learn to accept. To start at ground level. With nothing. No cards, no weapons, no property, no rights, no dignity."
>
> If this does not represent a pragmatic, if sentimental, attempt at reconciliation, I [Nicol] don't know what does.

But the ANC submission interpreted these scenes somewhat differently (punctuation and word usage have not been changed):

> In the novel, J M Coetzee represents as brutally as he can, the white people's perception of the post-apartheid black man. . . . It is suggested that in these circumstances, it might be better that our white compatriots should emigrate because to be in post-apartheid South Africa is to be in 'their territory,' as a consequence of which the whites will lose their cards, their weapons, their property, their rights, their dignity. The white women will have to sleep with the barbaric black men.
>
> Accordingly, the alleged white "brain drain" must be reportedly regularly and given the necessary prominence. J M Coetzee makes the point that, five years after our liberation, white SA society continues to believe in a particular stereotype of the African. ("Blackboard Bungle")

In this instance, I would *not* put Attridge and the ANC in the same camp. The ANC has been negligent in its refusal to confront the extent of women's abuse in South Africa; and the ANC's desire to see fictional production conforming to a positive image of the new(ish) South Africa cannot but be read with the basest of political motives in mind. Focusing on the supposed racism of the novel, the ANC is able to ignore the extent to which *Disgrace* explores the systemic aspect of the rape epidemic in South Africa.[2]

Coetzee, from *Dusklands* (1974) to *Disgrace,* has consistently portrayed the role of discourses of engendered hegemony as key factors in a methodical brutality that is nonetheless sexualized for being racialized. Specifically, I wish to reflect on *Disgrace* as a text that demonstrates Coetzee's commitment to the principle that, in order effectively to understand social violence, our most intimately held notions of what it means to be human need to be thoroughly scrutinized. *Disgrace* examines the extent to which the related concepts of humanity and humanitarianism on the one hand and patriarchal culture on the other are essentially constitutive of one another. The novel interrogates what to be humane might mean without recourse to the species boundary between human and nonhuman animals, what acting as a humanitarian might mean without invoking public testimony and the law as watchdogs, and how our sense of ourselves as human is radically undermined by our addiction to a cult of the rational—what Coetzee's recent work identifies as an irrational fetishization of instrumentalism, a profoundly secular devotion to the god of efficiency.

Patriarchy, Colonialism, and Racism in the Species Divide: Human/Animal

Disgrace acknowledges and interrogates a history of reading what is supposedly bestial about the human through reference to nonhuman animals. This is a history that Kate Soper, among others, has traced in the traditions of Western representation more generally.[3] In such traditions, that which is female, corporeal, black, and/or otherwise antirational (and, therefore, antimale) is allied with that which is animal.[4] Indeed, I read the somewhat uneasy reception of Coetzee's latest fiction in part as a response to our wariness of the proximity in which Coetzee places humans and other animals in this novel.[5] What, we may well wonder, is Coetzee trying to say about the relation between human violence toward other humans, and humans' inhumane treatment of dogs? Especially in the wake of the Tanner[6] Lectures, we may well be tempted to speculate as to whether Coetzee, like Elizabeth Costello, the protagonist of *The Lives of Animals* (1999) and the subsequent *Elizabeth Costello* (2003), really believes that our treatment of animals as objects for consumption resembles the crime against humanity that is the Holocaust.[7] Further, are Pollux and Lucy's other, unnamed rapists, "dogs" for raping Lucy, even in the postapartheid South Africa of *Disgrace,* in which politics should dictate that as blacks, they are no longer "supposed to be dogs"? And if men—David Lurie included, say—are "dogs" who behave according to their "nature" as nonneutered animals, is the rape—or possibly, are the rapes—of the novel explained, if not excused, on those terms?

I approach *The Lives of Animals* and *Disgrace* as enquiries in their different ways into our obsession with reading human behavior against what we perceive to be nonhuman, animal behavior. In his fiction Coetzee investigates the fact that our representation of animals is the locus of a language through which human beings measure their ethical worth as humans. The ironies of this are, of course, not lost on a writer such as Coetzee. Think of the scene in *Waiting for the Barbarians* when the Magistrate is locked up. He reflects:

> When Warrant Officer Mandel and his man first brought me back here and lit the lamp and closed the door, I wondered how much pain a plump comfortable old man would be able to endure in the name of how his eccentric notions of how the Empire should conduct itself. But my torturers were not interested in degrees of pain. They were interested only in demonstrating to me what it meant to live in a body, as a body, a body which can entertain notions of justice only as long as it is whole and well, which very soon forgets them when its head is gripped and a pipe is pushed down its gullet and pints of salt water are poured into it till it coughs and retches and flails and voids itself. . . . They came to my cell to show me the meaning of humanity, and in the space of an hour they showed me a great deal. (115)

The obvious irony is that the animal supposed most capable of ethical thought, indeed, often considered as the only animal capable of ethical behavior—the human—exhibits the most wanton cruelty.

Yet a less obvious irony presents itself. The object of the abuse, contrary to becoming more human in light of this treatment, becomes, in a sense, more of an animal. No longer concerned with "throw[ing] high-sounding words in their [his torturers'] faces," the Magistrate "lie[s] in the reek of old vomit obsessed with the thought of water," not to wash himself, but because he has "had nothing to drink for two days." "What I am made to undergo is subjection to the most rudimentary needs of my body: to drink, to relieve itself, to find a posture in which it is least sore" (115).

What I am calling the less obvious irony, then, is Coetzee's undermining of the notion that he who suffers unjust torture can be described as humane, "civilized," within the conventions we have to describe those attributes. His struggle may well have ethical dimensions: but the victim's reduction to his bodily needs is more closely associated with a state we ascribe to nonhuman animals. His mind, his intellect, his "human" attributes are sublimated to his effort to survive as a living body.[8] This explains why victims, even if their suffering is in the service of ethical resistance, can come to be described, or will describe themselves, as animals. The language of animalism is invoked to express the reduction of the victim to her or his body and its abuses. This creates a non-sense that we need to explore further: perpetrators are animals because of their infliction of human rights violations (HRVs) on victims; but victims are also described as animals because they are reduced to this status through their abjection.

The Body as Other

It is because of this need to live an embodied existence that we, as humans, have historically associated ourselves with beasts. Living with our bodies, at least from Descartes on, is a state we associate with the other. This other is both the Lévinasian other and more than that. For the other onto whom the nonthinking, nonmoral body is projected is not a face per se but a profoundly embodied other whose corporeality exceeds the image of the face. To have a body in the Western tradition, both pre- and post-Enlightenment, is for the most part to acknowledge one's vulnerability. The body is predominantly the locus of desire, and thus sin, pre-Enlightenment;[9] post-Enlightenment, it signifies everything that is opposed to the rational. It is part of the pathology of the history of this tradition that the body is subconsciously read as the locus of vulnerability and that this vulnerability is registered in the projection of the offending body onto the other.

This tradition is the one in which Coetzee is, by training and by conscious self-acknowledgment, deeply immersed;[10] it is also a tradition that he attempts—and this, to my mind, is the substance of Coetzee's ethics— to both inhabit and envision from the outside, from an-other perspective. In this respect, the language of *Disgrace* exceeds the language of Levinas in its commitment to specific, embodied, others. For in Levinas, what distinguishes the human is its distinction from the "animal": the "being of animals is a struggle for life. A struggle for life without ethics. It is a question of might. . . . However, with the appearance of the human—and this is my entire philosophy—there is something more important than my life, and that is the life of the other" ("Paradox," 172).

Mike Marais has pointed out that, following Levinas and Blanchot's description of how language brings death into the world, it is the very act of representing the other that obliterates that other. For Levinas, the very act of representation is an act of containment, of mastery: "Intelligibility, characterized by clarity, is a total adequation of the thinker with what is thought, in the precise sense of a mastery exercised by the thinker upon what is thought in which the object's resistance as an exterior being vanishes" (*Totality*, 124; cited in Marais, "Possibility," 59). Yet Coetzee's art—and this is one of Marais's key points—has consistently involved attempts to traverse competing ethical imperatives. On the one hand, there is the imperative to represent the other, in order to represent the other's violation; but on the other hand, there is the imperative to represent the other so as to communicate to both the reader and the self—the writer—the unintelligibility of the other in the language of the self.[11] Thus, if Levinas's concern is to confront, without objectifying, the other, Coetzee's task is possibly more specific: that of rendering the corporeality of the other in terms that do not fall back on objectifying that corporeality through an identification of it with the traditionally objectifying discourse of the body as that which is animal, that which traditionally has no soul.

Coetzee's fiction has always existed in an uncomfortable space in the traditions of white South African writing because of its wariness of representing the other as intelligible. This is the source of the friction between Nadine Gordimer and Coetzee;[12] it can also be seen in the debates between Benita Parry and David Attwell over the nature of ethical responsibility in

Coetzee's work.[13] Yet I take Coetzee's wariness of liberal gestures of inclusion as more than attempts to avoid patronization of the other. If Coetzee's fiction concerns itself with those figures whose otherness escapes us to the extent that we exercise violence upon them without compunction, Coetzee does not see the solution to this as being to bring those who have been considered outside the human—and thus outside the fold of ethical concern—into that fold. This would be the liberal gesture par excellence, involving nominal, but not ethically meaningful, recognition of the other within the extant confines of the language of the self.[14] Instead, what is interrogated is the status of the self as an ethical being. How does the language of the self stand up to ethical scrutiny? Specifically, how does the refusal of the self as having a body, and the subsequent projection of that corporeality onto the other—be it female, black, animal, or even dead bodies—render our subject, "he/she who is humane," profoundly unintelligible *within* the parameters of our extant discourses of that which is human as opposed to that which is animal?

At the heart of the matter is a reevaluation of our long-standing anxiety over who is considered within the parameters of the human. Imperial anxiety over where to draw the line that defines the human as opposed to the animal pervades the sexualized and racialized discourses constructing black and female identity in the nineteenth century.[15] These discourses and their antecedents are not effectively contested, Coetzee proposes, by including women and blacks into an enlarged category of the human in a sort of putative metaphysical search-and-rescue operation. The anxiety I speak of, which we would like to think of as an aspect of time past, still haunts the discursive space between marginalized humans and nonhuman animals. This comprises the dis-ease with which the proximity between humans and animals in *Disgrace* is received; it also haunts our language when we attempt to think of the violence wreaked on humans by other humans. For if the human is opposed to the animal, how can the human perpetrator—no matter how violent he is—become animal? And how, as in the case of the Magistrate in the passage discussed earlier, do we represent the violence inflicted upon victims without undermining the humanity of the victim, deprived as the victim is of human rights, by expressing the victim's corporeal vulnerability in the language we have been accustomed to use for this purpose, namely the imagery of the bestial? Finally, how can we name violent humans animal, while at the same time measuring humaneness in terms of how an individual treats nonhuman animals?

The Non-sense of Animal Metaphors: Eliding the Difference between Perpetrators and Victims

The confusion of perpetrators and victims, in which both are described in the language of animalism, is no metaphysical matter. When we look at the transcripts of South Africa's Truth and Reconciliation Commission (Human Rights Violations transcripts, Amnesty transcripts, and Special Hearings), we see precisely this con-fusion. The first usage of such imagery is one we might expect, in which perpetrators are described as treating their victims as animals. Thus Wendy Orr, one of the commissioners of the TRC) says to Mrs. Biko and her family, "If we achieve anything in this process I do hope that we ensure that human beings are never again treated like animals and like non-people the way Stephen Biko was" (HRVTRANS, June 17–18, 1997, HEALTH SECTOR).[16] Both Desmond Tutu, chairperson of the TRC, and Dr. Mgojo, a fellow commissioner, refer to the perpetrators as those who have become animals because they are nonbelievers. Tutu responds to Ntati Moleke's testimony by telling him that those who tortured him are animals: "It is only the beasts or wild animals, which don't have the image of God, could treat a person like that" (HRVTRANS, October 8–10, 1996, WELKOM). Dr. Mgojo repeats this conceit, praising a victim-survivor, Mrs. Luthuli, saying that her faith has sustained her: "a non-believer is just like an animal," he says; and he urges the public attending the hearing "to recapture your humanity and stop behaving like animals" (HRVTRANS, November 4–6, 1996, EMPANGENI).

On the other hand, there are many occasions on which victim-survivors describe themselves being treated like animals; I shall enumerate just a few examples here. Mrs. September describes a police attack: "When they had finished shooting, some of them [the police] alighted from the Kaspir [armored vehicle] that was in front of the Matsolo house. I could see that they were pulling two people who I saw by the legs and they threw them into the Hippo [armored vehicle] just like animals" (HRVTRANS, February 10, 1997, CRADOCK). Mrs. Gcina explains to Desmond Tutu that the most difficult time in her life was when her parents were taken into custody under Section 29, and she and her eleven-year-old brother were left alone in the house, isolated even by friends and family due to their participation in the struggle: "We were treated like animals, my brother . . . and myself" (HRVTRANS, June 18, 1997, YOUTH HEARINGS PBURG). M. Maluleke testifies, "What hurts me most is I know that as black people we are like animals to policemen. Policemen, irrespective of colour, black or white treat us as objects like we are not human beings" (HRVTRANS, November 26–28, 1996, TEMBISA).

The next twist in tracing this discourse comes when both perpetrators and victim-survivors—the two opposing elements in the TRC—use the argument that because they, both victim-survivor and perpetrator, were as animals when the violation took place, another party should be held responsible. Perhaps the most notorious of these cases was discussed in the TRC. When Mr. Mabaso and his companions were shot in the Durban area by a number of men who came from the Richard's Bay area, a court case was held to determine responsibility. The perpetrators' defense was that they were "shooting at wild animals and actually killing wild animals" (AMTRANS, August 12–14, 1996, DURBAN). At the amnesty hearing Judge Wilson asks the legal advisers for confirmation of this defense. Mr. Purshotham confirms that in the original proceedings amnesty applicant Mr. Marais stated that he "believed black people were 'diere van die veld' (animals of the field) and that they had no souls and as far as he was concerned it wasn't murder to shoot them" (AMTRANS, August 12–14, 1996, DURBAN).[17] Here the victim-survivor argues for amnesty to be refused because he and his comrades were treated like wild animals; yet the amnesty applicant's original line of defense is that blacks are animals, therefore they can be shot. Here an element of racist discourse—blacks are animals—is used to explain, if not defend, the attack on the victims.

Note that the testimony from both sides—the TRC and the victim-survivors on the one hand and the perpetrators on the other—form a series of tautologies. The perpetrators are animals because they have abused humans to such a degree that these victimized humans have been reduced to, or become, nonhuman animals; the perpetrators have become animals in the process of victimizing humans; and the measure of the humanity of a subject is reflected substantially in terms of that particular human's treatment of nonhuman animals. Hence nonhuman animals are made to stand both as a marker of humankind's barbarity and a testament to humankind's innate humanity.

Note also the specific tautology involved in these defenses, which turns on questions of responsibility. If a man has acted "like an animal" toward other men, he is either responsible for the violence because he acted violently, as if he were an animal, or he is not responsible, because he has always been an animal. Correspondingly, in the latter case, the victims are to blame for their victimization because they have always been latent, if not actual, animals.

What these tautologies betray is the way in which a cult of instrumentalism disguises questions of ethical responsibility. The base logic of getting the job done is one in which they present themselves as agents in a larger discourse merely fulfilling the will of the church, nation, or state. Yet when the state, in the example I shall give, is called on to account for the violence committed in its name by the "animals" it has, in some sense, created, it refuses to do so; suddenly the perpetrators can no longer be termed animals, because the state needs to accrue agency to the individual as responsible citizen. In the case of the Caprivi Strip trainees,[18] legal defendants of the apartheid state argue that, because individual personnel used their military training in ways that the state argues it did not sanction and had no knowledge of, the supposedly wayward soldiers are responsible for their own actions; the apartheid state is not culpable.

Instrumentalizing Animals: TRC Victim-Survivors' Testimony

What this testimony highlights, in the context of Coetzee's work—besides the striking question of what one can or cannot tell from the manner in which humans incinerate dead dogs—is the similarity between the perverse uses of the primates to stand in for humans.[19] In his *Lives of Animals,* Coetzee has his narrator, Elizabeth Costello, relate the similarities between circumstances surrounding Kafka's Red Peter and actual events that took place on the island of Tenerife, where, according to Wolfgang Köhler, the

Prussian Academy of Sciences established a station devoted to "experimentation into the mental capacities of apes, particularly chimpanzees" (27). Costello focuses on Köhler's record of these events and especially on the fate of one Sultan, "the best of his pupils" (28). Sultan is forced to jump through a series of supposedly intelligence-oriented mental hoops. For example, his bananas are placed in more and more difficult places to reach, and Sultan is given the instruments to reach them; in one case, three crates that have to be put one on top of another by Sultan for him to reach the bananas. Costello gives her reading of this episode as one in which Sultan is driven toward instrumental reasoning:

> At every turn Sultan is driven to think the less interesting thought. From purity of speculation (Why do men behave like this?) he is relentlessly propelled toward lower, practical, instrumental reason (How does one use this to get that?) and thus toward acceptance of himself as primarily an organism with an appetite that needs to be satisfied. Although his entire history, from the time his mother was shot and he was captured, through his voyage in a cage to imprisonment on this island prison camp and the sadistic games that are played around food here, leads him to ask questions about justice and the place of this penal colony in it, a carefully plotted psychological regimen conducts him *away* from ethics and metaphysics toward the humbler reaches of practical reason. (28–29; italics in original)

The assumption here, Costello emphasizes, is that instrumental reason marks the limits of ape intelligence; a second, more interesting assumption from our point of view is that this is imagined to be the point at which Sultan most approaches *human* intelligence. That this instrumental reason is highly prized by human animals is clear; that human animals prize instrumental reason as an ethical activity in and of itself, without recourse to ethical assessment of the goals to which it is put, is the condition Coetzee challenges. He does so by pointing out that this cult of instrumental reason is neither logical nor ethical and that its consequence is violence.

On the one hand, then, the primates can never aspire to be human; on the other, Red Peter—especially given Elizabeth Costello's reading of the Kafka tale—Sultan, and the baboons used in the apartheid state–sponsored experiments—are made to "ape" human behavior; and they are simultaneously evaluated as lesser beings because this aping demonstrates their insufficiency as humans. In the case of Sultan, he is a slow learner because he has to learn how humans "think" through a putative demonstration of instrumentalist behavior; in the case of the Roodeplat baboons, they are like enough to humans to stand in for them; but this very capacity causes humans to kill the baboons. The other here is both like and not like that which is human. The other will be used in her capacity to mimic, be like, the human; but this use will be abuse to the extent that the other is not human.

Such moments suggest what we might have suspected all along, which is that what we say about animals says more about us than it does about the animals. Specifically, it says more about how we treat animals, human and nonhuman, than it does about the behavior, subjectivity, agency, or ethics of nonhuman animals. This does not mean, however, that we should discount the fact that not only do victim-survivors speak of themselves as being treated like animals, they occasionally refer to members of communities that were persecuted under apartheid as having *become* animals. What Elizabeth Costello makes evident in her explication of Sultan's "education" is that he is measured according to those standards that men hold themselves to, namely the standard of instrumental reason. It is not that Sultan can tell us what apes might think: it is that we are obsessed with replicating them in our own image. We turn him into an instrument, just as we teach him to view the world purely as an instrument for his own gratification. This is not about the education of the ape; it is about the training of Sultan to ape humans. What I take Coetzee to be saying in this context is that any ethical sense of community, one that would contest the profoundly human—but not humane—view of the human animal and its body as a potential object of use for instrumental self-gain, in an economy of consumer versus consumed, has been eliminated; we have trained generations of South Africans, both black and white, to ape humans, as Sultan has been trained to do.

Instrumentalizing Women: A Culture of Systemic Rape

This training bears much in common with David Lurie's understanding of what drives so-called education priorities in this day and age. It also is reflected in his attitude toward the sexual needs of his body and the ways in

which he goes about gratifying them. Coetzee's fiction has always manifested a care to trace the relations between ideologies that themselves exploit the false, ends-driven "work ethic" of instrumentalism. In many cases
he investigates the complicity of colonialism and patriarchy in the construction of hypermasculinities:[20] masculinities that view the other as a threat to
the self that can be mastered only through domination—a domination evidenced in both devastation of the land and the rape of women. Eugene
Dawn, Jacobus Coetzee, the Magistrate—even Magda in what we might
call her fantastical, masculine determination—and, of course, David Lurie
himself, all figure elements of hypermasculinity in their construction of
land and women as properties to be interrogated, owned, exploited.

Of Lurie's job we learn that

> he earns his living at the Cape Technical University, formerly Cape Town
> University College. Once a professor of modern languages, he has been,
> since Classics and Modern languages were closed down as part of the great
> rationalization, adjunct professor of communications. Like all rational-
> ized personnel, he is allowed to offer one special-field course a year, irre-
> spective of enrolment, because that is good for morale. This year he is
> teaching the Romantic poets. For the rest he teaches Communications 101,
> "Communication Skills", and Communications 201, "Advanced Com-
> munication Skills." (*Disgrace,* 3)

David Lurie recognizes the dangers of a putative education system that values humans as objects that can be trained into instruments, but he is not
so adept at realizing that, while he does recognize his body and its needs,
his manner of satisfying those needs replicates the model of consumption
he so avidly rejects as an intellectual in an education system that is, in actual fact, in the process of turning out instruments, not intellectuals. Indeed,
it has been so successful at doing this that many of the students subjected
to the training show signs of not desiring to be treated as anything other
than instruments. Yet Lurie's hypocrisy is evident in his treatment of the
sex worker he favors, Soraya. Soraya's training—since she is a consumable—
is effortless: "The first time Soraya received him she wore vermillion lip-
stick and heavy eyeshadow. Not liking the stickiness of the makeup, he
asked her to wipe it off. She obeyed, and has never worn it since. A ready

learner, compliant, pliant" (5). David is not willing to be reminded that this relationship—if one can call it that—is one based on supply and demand. He appears genuinely surprised when Soraya objects to his stalking her and phoning her at home. "You are harassing me in my own house. I demand you will never phone me here again, never," she responds.

After a typical Lurie-like correction of her speech, addressed to himself ("Demand. She means command"), Lurie reflects: "Her shrillness surprises him: there has been no intimation of it before." Then he explains her rejection of him as attributable to the proximity between mothers and animals: "But then, what should he expect when he intrudes into the vixen's nest, into the home of her cubs?" (10).

Melanie, the student who follows in the wake of Soraya from Lurie's point of view, is equally commodified. Her dark skin, "Chinese cheekbones" and "gold baubles on her belt [that] match the gold balls of her earrings" mark her as the exotic, desirable other. To his seduction of her, Melanie responds with a sense of her own commodification: if he gets sex from her, she should at least be released from her course requirements in return, especially since her malevolent boyfriend shows every sign of being able to take out her perceived disloyalty to him by attacking not only Lurie but Melanie herself. When Lurie takes her to task about absence from classes and missing a test, "she stares back at him in puzzlement, even shock" (34).

Lurie has indeed exacted a great price from Melanie, if one thinks one can describe her violation in those terms: he has raped her. She tells him several times on the occasion that he turns up at her apartment that she does not want to have sex with him; but he, titillated by the image of her in high heels and a wig he remembers from the rehearsal of her play, grabs her anyway:

"No, not now!" she says, struggling. "My cousin will be back."

But nothing will stop him. He carries her to the bedroom, brushes off the absurd slippers, kisses her feet, astonished by the feeling she evokes. Something to do with the apparition on the stage: the wig, the wiggling bottom, the crude talk. Strange love! Yet from the quiver of Aphrodite, goddess of the foaming waves, no doubt about that.

She does not resist. All she does is avert herself: avert her lips, avert her eyes. She lets him lay her out on the bed and undress her: she even helps him, raising her arms and then her hips. Little shivers of cold run through her as soon as she is bare, she slips under the quilted counterpane like a mole burrowing, and turns her back on him.

Not rape, not quite that, but undesired nonetheless, undesired to the core. As though she had decided to go slack, die within herself for the duration, like a rabbit when the jaws of the fox close on its neck. So that everything done to her might be done, as it were, far away. (25)

Accepting the inevitable should hardly be rendered as acquiescence. What we are dealing with here is an attempt by Lurie to associate a metaphysical ethic to what amounts to an attack on Melanie Isaacs, rationalized by her inability to force him away from her. If Wordsworth's view of the summit of Mont Blanc undermines his inner vision of what that moment would have been like, Lurie's image of Melanie, the actress, Lurie suggests, is strong enough to override any sense of the actual view of Melanie's resistance for Lurie: the triumph of the metaphysical is evidenced in rape.

This tendency to overlook the corporeal being of Melanie is replicated in some of the secondary criticism of the novel. Take, for example, Mike Marais' reading of this encounter as one that mirrors Blanchot's myth of the creation of the artwork as the descent of Orpheus into the underworld to undertake the impossible task of repossessing Eurydice: "Despite his observation that this invasion of Isaacs's privacy is 'Not rape, not quite that' (25), the Orphic terms in which the description is couched indicate that the scene must be read as Lurie's attempt to possess the Other, to assert control over her" ("Little Enough," 175). So far, I am in agreement with Marais. But I cannot agree with what he says next:

However, as the mythological allusions also suggest, she has always already escaped this attempted possession. This is the point of the references to death in the depiction of the scene. The Underworld in which Orpheus meets Eurydice and seeks to possess her is the realm of death in which power slips away and becomes impossible. Eurydice is dead and death is precisely that which cannot be controlled. It is not the *noema* of a *noesis,* an object of the will. In his encounter with Isaacs, then, Lurie is exposed to the radical ungraspability of death, its impossibility (Blanchot, "Reading" 7–9). (175)

I find this confusion of Eurydice and Melanie disturbing. It may be true that in the underworld power becomes impossible; but in this world, Melanie is alive, and Lurie's power over her living body is all too evident. If she mimics death to communicate her loss of power in the face of Lurie's attack on her, this loss of power should not be attributed to Lurie by a metaphysical sleight of hand. He is the subject who has rendered her the object of his will. If she exceeds his grasp it is because she is alive as he rapes her and remains so afterward; the rape has everything to do with his exercise of power, not his loss of it.

It is from this perspective that I disagree with those who view the rape of Lucy as Lucy's acceptance of punishment for the historical burden of apartheid. One element of Coetzee's novel that I respect is that he represents no alternatives that his female characters should have taken to avoid rape. This is frequently read as a form of masochism evident in the victimized women he depicts; if not in Melanie, then most certainly in Lucy, whose discussion of her own rape, meager as it is, is taken to represent her acquiescence, rather than her acceptance, of the attitudes of those who have raped her. Of her rape she has only this to say to David:

"I think they have done it before," she resumes, her voice steadier now. "At least the two older ones have. I think they are rapists first and foremost. Stealing things is just incidental. A side-line. I think they *do* rape."
   "You think they will come back?"
   "I think I am their territory. They have marked me. They will come back for me."
   "Then you can't possibly stay."
   "Why not?"
   "Because that would be an invitation to them to return."
   She broods a long while before she answers. "But isn't there another way of looking at it, David? What if . . . what if that is the price one has to pay for staying on? Perhaps that is how they look at it; perhaps that is how I should look at it too. They see me as owing something. They see themselves as debt collectors, tax collectors. Why should I be allowed to live here without paying? Perhaps that is what they tell themselves." (*Disgrace*, 158; italics in original)

It is true that in this passage we reach the limits of the sympathetic imagination: our sense of decency is offended by the notion that Lucy, who is guilty of nothing, should have to pay for the sins of the fathers. But note that Lucy has never subscribed to metaphysical moral values; her forte is refusing her father's habit of seeing the world through metaphysical glasses. This is why she refuses his bid to call her plot a farm; she is aware of the many narrative lines, from "modern girl" to sturdy *boerevrou* (lit., farmer's wife). In this context, then, *should* may well mean "this is the way I should see it if I wish to understand how the rapists work; this is how I should think to figure out how to survive."

The subsequent exchange between Lucy and David tells us that Lucy may well know more about the sins of the fathers than David could ever hope to know. David thinks that, if Lucy felt only hatred in their hands, it must mean that Lucy hates them. But Lucy refuses to complete the tautology. Instead, she puts her energy into attempting to understand what makes a man a rapist:

> "Hatred. . . . When it comes to men and sex, David, nothing surprises me any more. Maybe, for men, hating the woman makes sex more exciting. You are a man, you ought to know. When you have sex with someone strange—when you trap her, hold her down, get her under you, put all your weight on her, isn't it a bit like killing? Pushing the knife in; exiting afterwards, leaving the body behind covered in blood—doesn't it feel like murder, like getting away with murder?"
>
> *You are a man, you ought to know:* does one speak to one's father like that? Are she and he on the same side? (158–59; italics in original)

Well may Lurie ask the question. For Lucy's description of a man, say Lurie, having sex "with someone strange," say Melanie, does result in the obliteration of a woman's—Melanie's—subjectivity for the duration of the rape. Even in the case of sex with Soraya, Soraya turns out to live only when the owner of the pseudonym is unknown, dead to her sexual partner.

Yet Lurie has only inklings of his complicity in a sexual economy that preys on women. He views the rape purely as a consequence of racial difference, while Lucy sees it as an attempt to subjugate her as a woman living alone, easy prey for men who may seek to exact from her "a price" for her aping of a man's independence. While Melanie attempts to exploit her status as a product for consumption within a masculinist economy, Lucy understands this to be her ontological status. Not surprisingly, she has difficulty in getting David to comprehend this aspect of gendered victimization. Lucy refers to the rapists as "spur[ring] each other on":

> "That's probably why they do it together. Like dogs in a pack."
> "And the third one, the boy?"
> "He was there to learn."
>
> . . .
>
> "If they had been white you wouldn't talk about them in this way," he says. "If they had been white thugs from Despatch, for instance."
> "Wouldn't I?"
> "No, you wouldn't. I am not blaming you, that is not the point. But it is something new you are talking about. Slavery. They want you for their slave."
> "Not slavery. Subjection. Subjugation."
> He shakes his head. "It's too much, Lucy. Sell up. Sell the farm to Petrus and come away."
> "No." (159)

Here Lurie cannot believe that Lucy "chooses" to withstand the black predators. But Lucy is not talking about blacks, we find out. She is talking about men. Were she to leave the farm to Petrus, she would be giving up, as she puts it. She would merely be shifting from the protection of one man into the hands of another; her father's say, or the patronage of unknown relatives of his in Holland.

Lucy is no masochist. Her response to David forecloses, as much as is possible, on the reader who believes in her masochism: "You have not been listening to me. I am not the person you know. I am a dead person and I do not yet know what will bring me back to life. All I know is that I cannot go away" (161). We may be outraged at Lucy's situation, but we can accept it without acquiescing to the circumstances. Lucy acknowledges that her refusal to leave may result in her experiencing further violence. This is a clearheaded reading of the facts that results in her choosing to accept whatever protection Petrus may be able to offer her within their arranged marriage. Lucy's words make it clear that, for her, leaving would be tantamount to giving up—a spiritual death that would render her as inanimate as physical death, and no less corporeal.

After the rape she explains to an obdurate Lurie that what he proposes to her is not an option for self-preservation but yet another form of subjugation: "'You do not see this, and I do not know what more I can do to make you see. It is as if you have chosen deliberately to sit in a corner where the rays of the sun do not shine. I think of you as one of the three chimpanzees, the one with the paws over his eyes'" (161). Denial may be Lurie's initial course of defense, but we would not want to mimic him in this particular case; especially since Lurie's denial carries with it the taint of self-interested denial: Lurie does not want to see his own complicity with the rapists, as one who uses women.

Facing up—in Coetzee's fictional interpretation of Levinas—to the other has radical, and conceivably traumatic, consequences. Taking up the challenge of imagining the other, and the ethical demands attendant upon this act, requires us to be vulnerable to Elizabeth Costello's insight: what we want to say about human society remains outside the realm of the sayable. In other words, the language of humanity can occupy the place of the chimpanzee with the paws over his eyes. We can only sustain our extant conception of what constitutes the humane by turning our faces away from an atrocity that remains largely unspoken.

The war on women in South Africa occupies the same discursive space as the war on animals in Elizabeth Costello's discourse, in that we have, to date, failed to grasp the quotidian consequences of gender-based violence for a vast majority of women in South Africa and have thereby allied ourselves—through the complicity of silence—with the likes of Lurie. Note the description of Costello's alienation from the conventions that make a life of consumption without reflection possible—and her subsequent exhaustion at the prospect of alerting a largely uninterested populace as to the nature of their complicity in violence that they simply do not have either the will or the capacity to imagine. When her son, John, asks her what it is that will explain her interest in animal rights to him, she responds that what she wishes to say is not able to be spoken or heard in the language of everyday communality. This is the source of her alienation.

"What is it you can't say?"
"It's that I no longer know where I am. I seem to move about perfectly easily among people, to have perfectly normal relations with them. Is it

possible, I ask myself, that all of them are participating in a crime of stupefying proportions? Am I fantasizing it all?" (69)

Just as Costello is tempted to believe that the wholesale slaughter of non-human animals for consumption may be a fantasy of her own making, we may be tempted to read Coetzee's depiction of the wholesale attack on women as a parallel fantasy. It is perhaps not surprising, then, that many readers have focused on the influence of assumed racial identifications to explain the violent interactions between characters,[21] much as Lurie focuses on race in order to ignore the factor of gender—indeed, his own masculinity.

Disgrace is easily consumed as a novel exclusively about racial identifications, as an (ungendered) report on violence in the "new South Africa." Yet if we ignore the challenge *Disgrace* poses to us—to envision the epidemic of violence against women in South Africa in relation to international practices of patriarchy and ecological violence in the practice of redefining our humanity—we do so at our ethical peril. It may be tempting to allow ourselves to become Lurie, the one with his paws over his eyes. To do so, however, is to ignore the atrocities perpetuated by economies of instrumentalism and their inhuman and inhumane manifestations in definitions of the species divide; the category of the human; and who or what can be "proved" to be victimized subjects before the law.

Notes

1. For further discussion of the politics of Coetzee's reception see Attwell, *Coetzee;* Attridge and Jolly, *Writing South Africa;* Jolly, *Colonization;* Kossew, *Critical Essays.*

2. The statistics in South Africa concerning violence against women are extreme. For example, at least one woman in Gauteng is killed by her male partner every six days (Vetten and Dladla, "Women's Fear"); in a study of 1,394 men working for three Cape Town municipalities, approximately 44 percent admitted to abusing their female partners (Abrahams, Jewkes, and Laubsher, *Do Not Believe*); 39 percent of young women in South Africa between the ages of twelve and seventeen state that they have been forced to have sex; 33 percent said that they were afraid to say no to sex and 55 percent agreed with the statement, "there are times I don't want to have sex but I do because my boyfriend insists on having sex" (Lovelife, "Hot Prospects," 19). For further material on violence against women in South Africa see CIETafrica, "Beyond Victims"; Human Rights Watch, *Violence against Women;* Kottler, "Wives' Subjective

Definitions"; Leclerc-Madlala, "Crime in an Epidemic"; Stanton, Lochrenberg, and Mukasa, "Improved Justice"; Vetten and Bhana, "Violence."

3. Soper explains that animals, "used as a means of naming or thinking . . . seem to offer themselves as a register or narrative of human self-projections"; as "a manifest text or displaced commentary" that facilitates the evasion of "a more direct confrontation" with devalued or disallowed human characteristics (*What Is Nature?* 83).

4. Judith Plant, for example, claims that "there is no respect for the 'other' in patriarchal society. The other, the object of patriarchal rationality, is considered only insofar as it can benefit the subject" (*Healing*, 2). Edward Said reflects that, in this economy of the white, male subject, "the Oriental was linked thus to elements in Western society (delinquents, the insane, women, the poor [and, Merchant, Plant, Plumwood, and Soper would add, "nature"]) having in common an identity best described as lamentably alien (*Culture*, 207).

5. For an example of such dis-ease, see Fromm, "Coetzee's Postmodern Animals."

6. Coetzee no doubt enjoyed the irony of giving a lecture series on animal rights with this title.

7. The Tanner Lectures from *The Lives of Animals* are republished along with Elizabeth Costello's further fictional academic exploits in Coetzee's *Elizabeth Costello,* published in 2003.

8. In a rare comment on his own fiction, Coetzee remarks, "If I look back over my own fiction, I see a simple (simple-minded?) standard erected. That standard is the body. Whatever else, the body is not 'that which is not,' and the proof is the pain it feels" (*Doubling the Point,* 248).

9. For a reading of this tradition from Plato through Christianity to the early modern period, see Taylor, *Sources of the Self.*

10. When questioned by Eleanor Wachtel about what he might consider the canon to be, Coetzee responds in the first instance by reminding her of the limitations of his own tradition, stating that he is "someone of, finally, I think, Western culture, even though we're speaking in Africa" ("Sympathetic Imagination," 40).

11. The language of the self here refers not only to the limits of various discourses but to the actual limitations of a given language—in *Disgrace,* this is English. When Lucy gives Petrus and his wife a bedspread, Petrus thanks her, calling her his "benefactor." Lurie responds: "A distasteful word, it seems to him, double-edged, souring the moment. Yet can Petrus be blamed? The language he draws on with such aplomb is, if he only knew it, tired, friable, eaten from the inside as if by termites. Only the monosyllables can still be relied on, and not even all of them" (129).

12. Gordimer's review of *Life & Times of Michael K* is most telling in this regard.

13. See, for example, the debate between Attwell and Parry in Attridge and Jolly, *Writing South Africa,* 149–79.

14. We see this liberalism in its classic South African form in Alan Paton's *Cry, the Beloved Country,* the conservative lyricism of which can be traced to a tradition that includes William Plomer, a tradition that insists on rendering "black" and "animal" as allied in the writers' culturing of what they perceive to be natural. See Chapman, *Southern African Literatures,* 181–82.

15. On the relations between the female body, the body of the prostitute, and the radicalized other in nineteenth-century medical and scientific discourses, see Gilman, "Black Bodies."

16. Note that this and all subsequent references to the TRC Web site are cited in the format that is most useful in terms of locating the precise location of Web site material quoted in this book: the reference is the precise name of the file containing the testimony.

17. Mr. Purshotham is referring to the original trial against the perpetrators, citing that this particular testimony comes from page 157 of the original trial transcripts.

18. 208 Inkatha Freedom Party members who formed a hit squad for the party and who were also involved in apartheid-funded operations.

19. I am thinking here of Lurie's mission in the latter part of *Disgrace:* to ensure the respectful treatment of the dead dogs whose bodies are incinerated at the hospital grounds.

20. For examples of usage of the term *hypermasculinity* in international relations/development discourses, see Ling, "Cultural Chauvinism"; Milojevic, "Gender, Peace"; Replogle, "Feminism." For an understanding of the term specifically in the southern African context, see Morrell, "Of Boys and Men"; *Changing Men.*

21. For an example, see Fugard's notorious comments on *Disgrace* (Gorra, "After the Fall"). Note also that the ANC, in its 1999 submission to the Human Rights Commission's investigation into racism in the media, names *Disgrace* as a novel that exploits racist stereotypes (see above).

Bibliography

Abrahams, Naeemah, Rachel Jewkes, and Ria Laubsher. *"I Do Not Believe in Democracy in the Home": Men's Relationships with and Abuse of Women.* Tygerberg: CERSA (Women's Health) Medical Research Council, 1999.

Attridge, Derek. "Age of Bronze, State of Grace: Music and Dogs in Coetzee's *Disgrace." Novel* 34, no. 1 (2000): 98–121.

Attridge, Derek, and Rosemary Jolly, eds. *Writing South Africa: Literature, Apartheid, and Democracy 1970–1995.* Cambridge: Cambridge University Press, 1998.

Attwell, David. *J. M. Coetzee: South Africa and the Politics of Writing.* Berkeley: University of California Press; Cape Town: David Philip, 1993.

Blanchot, Maurice. "Reading Kafka." 1949. In *The Work of Fire,* translated by Charlotte Mandel, 1–11. Stanford: Stanford University Press, 1995.

Chapman, Michael. *Southern African Literatures.* London: Longman 1996.

CIETafrica. "Beyond Victims and Villains—The Culture of Sexual Violence in South Johannesburg." http://www.ciet.org/www/image/country/safrica_victims.html.

Coetzee, J. M. *Disgrace.* London: Secker and Warburg, 1999.

———. *Doubling the Point: Essays and Interviews.* Edited by David Attwell. Cambridge, MA: Harvard University Press, 1992.

———. "Into the Dark Chamber: The Novelist and South Africa." *New York Times Book Review,* January 12, 1986, 13, 35.

———. *The Lives of Animals.* Edited by Amy Gutmann. Princeton: Princeton University Press, 1999.

———. "The Sympathetic Imagination." Interview by Eleanor Wachtel. *Brick* 67 (2001): 37–47.

———. *Waiting for the Barbarians.* London: Secker and Warburg, 1980.

Fromm, Harold. "Coetzee's Postmodern Animals." Review of *The Lives of Animals* and *Disgrace,* by J. M. Coetzee. *Hudson Review* 53, no. 2 (2000): 336–44.

Gilman, Sander. "Black Bodies, White Bodies: Toward an Iconography of Female Sexuality in Late Nineteenth-Century Art, Medicine, and Literature." In *"Race," Writing, and Difference,* edited by Henry Louis Gates Jr., 223–61. Chicago: University of Chicago Press, 1986.

Goodwin, Christopher. "White Man without the Burden." *Sunday Times News Review,* January 16, 2000. http://www.sunday-times.co.uk/news/pages/sti/2000/01/16stirevnws01014.html.

Gordimer, Nadine. "The Idea of Gardening." Review of *Life & Times of Michael K,* by J. M. Coetzee. *New York Times Book Review,* April 18, 1984, 3–4.

Gorra, Michael. "After the Fall." Review of *Disgrace,* by J. M. Coetzee. *New York Times Book Review,* November 5, 2000, 36.

Human Rights Watch. *Violence against Women in South Africa.* New York: Human Rights Watch, 1995.

Jolly, Rosemary J. *Colonization, Violence, and Narration in White South African Writing: André Brink, Breyten Breytenbach, and J. M. Coetzee.* Athens: Ohio University Press; Johannesburg: University of the Witwatersrand Press, 1996.

Kossew, Sue, ed. *Critical Essays on J. M. Coetzee.* New York: G. K. Hall, 1998.

Kottler, Sharon. "Wives' Subjective Definitions of and Attitudes towards Wife Rape." MA diss., University of South Africa, 1998.

Leclerc-Madlala, Suzanne. "Crime in an Epidemic: The Case of Rape and AIDS." *ACTA Criminologica* 9, no. 2 (1996): 31–37.

Levinas, Emmanuel. "The Paradox of Morality: An Interview with Emmanuel Levinas." By Tamra Wright, Peter Hughes, and Alison Ainley. Translated by Andrew Benjamin and Tamra Wright. In *The Provocation of Levinas: Rethinking the Other,* edited by Robert Bernasconi and David Wood, 168–80. New York: Routledge, 1988.

———. *Totality and Infinity: An Essay on Exteriority.* Translated by Alphonso Lingis. Dordrecht: Kluwer Academic, 1991 (1961).

Ling, L. H. M. "Cultural Chauvinism and the Liberal International Order: 'West vs. Rest' in Asia's Financial Crisis." http://www.isanet.org/archive/ling2.html.

Lovelife. "Hot Prospects, Cold Facts." South Africa: Colorpress, 2000. http://www.lovelife.org.za/llwebsite/simple.asp?PageID=312.

Marais, Michael. "'Little Enough, Less than Little: Nothing': Ethics, Engagement, and Change in the Fiction of J. M. Coetzee." *Modern Fiction Studies* 46, no. 1 (2000): 159–82.

————. "The Possibility of Ethical Action: J. M. Coetzee's *Disgrace.*" *Scrutiny2* 5, no. 1 (2000): 57–63.

Merchant, Carolyn. *Earthcare: Women and the Environment.* London: Routledge, 1995.

Milojevic, Ivana. "Gender, Peace, and Terrestrial Futures: Alternatives to Terrorism and War." http://www.metafuture.org/articlesbycolleagues/IvanaMilojevic/Ivana_Milojevic_-_Gender_peace_and_terrestrial_futures.htm.

Morrell, Robert, ed. *Changing Men in Southern Africa.* Scottsville: University of Natal Press; London: Zed Books, 2001.

————. "Of Boys and Men: Masculinity and Gender in Southern African Studies." *Journal of Southern African Studies* 24, no. 4 (1998): 605–30.

Nicol, Mike. "It's a Blackboard Bungle." *Sunday Times,* April 22, 2001. http://www.suntimes.co.za/2001/04/22/insight/in02.htm.

Paton, Alan. *Cry, the Beloved Country.* New York: Scribners, 1948.

Plant, Judith, ed. *Healing the Wounds: The Promise of Ecofeminism.* Toronto: Between the Lines, 1989.

Plumwood, Val. *Environmental Culture: The Ecological Crisis of Reason.* London: Routledge, 2002.

————. *Feminism and the Mastery of Nature.* London: Routledge, 1994.

Replogle, Sherri. "Feminism and International Relations: From Deconstruction to Reconstruction." http://lilt.ilstu.edu/critique/Spring2001Docs/sreplogle.htm.

Russel, Diana. *Incestuous Abuse: Its Long-Term Effects.* Pretoria: Human Sciences Research Council, 1995.

Said, Edward. *Culture and Imperialism.* London: Vintage, 1994.

Soper, Kate. *What Is Nature? Culture, Politics, and the Non-human.* Oxford: Blackwell, 1995.

Stanton, Sharon, Margot Lochrenberg, and Veronica Mukasa. *Improved Justice for Survivors of Sexual Violence? Adult Survivors' Experiences of the Wynberg Sexual Offences Court and Associated Services.* Cape Town: University of Cape Town and Human Rights Commission, 1997.

Taylor, Charles. *Sources of the Self: The Making of the Modern Identity.* Cambridge: Harvard University Press, 1989.

Truth and Reconciliation Commission. CD-ROM of Web site http://www.truth.org.za. Copyright Steve Crawford and the Truth and Reconciliation Commission. November 1998. Official Web site moved to http://www.doj.gov.za/trc/index.html. (Not all testimony available on government Web site.)

Vetten, Lisa, and Joy Dladla. "Women's Fear and Survival in Inner-City Johannesburg." *Agenda* 45 (2000): 70–75.

Vetten, Lisa, and Khailash Bhana. *Violence, Vengeance and Gender: A Preliminary Investigation into the Links between Violence against Women and HIV/AIDS in South Africa.* Johannesburg: Centre for the Study of Violence and Reconciliation, 2001.

9

WHAT IS IT LIKE TO BE A NONRACIST?

Elizabeth Costello and J. M. Coetzee
on the Lives of Animals and Men

Michael Bell

Excuse me for talking in this way. I am trying to be frank.

—David Lurie in *Disgrace*

J. M. COETZEE has always been discomforting to read, but increasingly
the index of his significance has come to be the resistance he arouses, if not
the repression he reveals, in many of his readers. If his novel *Disgrace* (1999)
was meant actively to elicit such a response, it certainly succeeded. Some
hostile readers responded to it with a literalistic allegorizing compounded
perhaps by disapproval of its central character.[1] Although few such readers
would admit to simply identifying character and author, or to forgetting
that it is a work of imaginative literature, it is not clear that the implications
of these distinctions are fully understood. The response to Coetzee, and his
evident play with this response in the text, raises with unusual urgency the
nature of the literary in relation to the real. Of course, there is a vital connection between these domains, otherwise there would be no sense in the

difference, and without collapsing author and character one could find a significant guide to the spirit of Coetzee's novel by borrowing the central character, David Lurie's, remark: "Excuse me for talking in this way. I am trying to be frank" (*Disgrace,* 166). In Coetzee, the literary as such proves over and over again to be a radically discomforting, albeit indispensable, category for a certain kind of truth telling. T. S. Eliot's famous line got it slightly wrong. It is not, unfortunately, the case that "humankind cannot stand very much reality" (*Poems,* 118). As the other Eliot, a novelist, insisted, we can stand it only too well because we are so "well wadded with stupidity" (*Middlemarch,* 189). What many of us can't stand is truth. And that is the distinction at stake in the question of reality and fiction in Coetzee. Coetzee does his most significant thinking through the mode of literature: his discursive and critical essays, though good of their kind, are within a different mode of thought.

In this respect it is revealing that the novel should have close thematic interrelations with the generic hybrid published as *The Lives of Animals* (1999). Coetzee's oeuvre encompasses many works that, whatever their internal self-questioning, are clearly definable as either fiction or discursive essay. But here, with a mixture of formal ingenuity and apparently casual opportunism, Coetzee has devised a work that genuinely answers to each category and thereby succeeds in radically destabilizing both. In *Lives* the questions of response and of fictionality are overtly thematized yet still with the deceptive transparency that characterizes the metafictional self-questioning in almost all of his fiction. So much so that even this work, which raises these questions so frontally, has been read at a first-order level, as occurs even with the respondents whose lectures are included in the volume.[2] Of course, such a response is not wrong. Insofar as the fictional novelist Elizabeth Costello has put into the public domain a passionate conviction about the relations of human beings with animals, the work is a contribution, indeed a very telling one, to such debate. Nonetheless, as a fiction it has a significance beyond the topic of Costello's lecture and transforms the truth claims of her argument. At the same time, its force as a fiction also derives from its real-life situatedness.

It is necessary to emphasize this latter point since the lectures have since been republished in a volume collecting all the stories centered on the

Costello character, and, while it is useful to have all these pieces available in this way, the combined effect is disconcerting for an admirer of the original volume (*Elizabeth Costello*). The *Lives* lectures significantly change their character as they are detached from the rest of the lecture series in which they first appeared, and which in turn connected them to the historical occasion of their delivery. They become part of a horizontal axis of mutual reference between similar fictions rather than vertical penetrations of the interface between fiction and the world of extrafictional responsibilities. An evidently mystified reviewer of the Costello volume in the *Times Literary Supplement* saw it for the most part as an irritating and blandly circular self-communing of the author (Herford). The response is in some measure understandable and reinforces the significance of the generic liminality in *Lives*. Since the present essay was first written, the Elizabeth Costello character has returned even more remarkably in *Slow Man* (2005). Clearly this fictional alter ego has taken on a complex and continuing role in Coetzee's oeuvre, but for present purposes I wish to indicate two main implications of the formal complex created in *Lives* as it was originally published: it examines with bleak lucidity the relation of the morally convinced speaker both to her audience and to herself.

First, however, it is necessary to set out some of the governing structures of the fiction in which Costello's lecture is embedded. This may initially seem to be enquiring too curiously into an obvious device. One can readily see why a notoriously reticent, male author, often thought to be rather affectless, should construct a fiction in which views close to his own are expressed by a woman of forthright conviction and passionate intensity. As Coetzee has said in an interview: passion in discursive prose is like "reading the utterances of a madman," but a novel "allows the writer to *stage* his passion" (*Doubling,* 60–61; italics in original). No doubt Costello is a defensive or liberating device: a way of getting certain things said for which passionate intensity is of the essence and which Coetzee does not feel able to say in his own voice. But that leaves the propositional statement essentially the same within its fictional frame. There is something more at stake, something already hinted at in the reference to "passionate intensity," a quality for which Yeats's best alternative, or at least the alternative of the "best," was silence ("Second Coming," 211). Coetzee shares Yeats's unease yet cannot be silent: he faces the abyss that Yeats's rhetoric, in his historical moment, often enabled him to pass by. Coetzee's relation to Costello is suggested by a remark of Coetzee on the female central consciousness in *Age of Iron:* "There is no ethical imperative that I claim access to. Elizabeth is the one who believes in *should,* who believes in *believes in.* As for me, the book is written, it will be published, nothing can stop it. The deed is done, what power was available to me is exercised" (*Doubling,* 250; italics in original). *Lives* is a closely structured examination of why Coetzee himself cannot readily believe in "believes in."

Costello is not merely a defensive device like Rousseau's embedding of the deistic views of the Savoyard vicar in *Émile.* A closer parallel for Coetzee's deceptive hybrid of essay and fiction, and one with some closely related themes, is Thomas Mann's essay "Voyage with *Don Quixote,*" in which he recounts his supposed rereading of Cervantes while traveling to America in 1934.[3] Only if one realizes that the essay is essentially a fiction do the apparently adventitious circumstances of the voyage, such as the Jewish émigrés on the boat, become thematically pregnant and the author, while retaining his autobiographical "I," take on the significance of a fictional character. In Mann's case, if readers have not generally realized this, they have the excuse that the text observes all the appearance of literal autobiography and literary essay unproblematically combined. But Coetzee has created an evidently fictional character at the opposite extreme from his own social personality as if to foreground her status. The clue here is that Coetzee has in some measure fictionalized not so much himself as his function, and his relation to Costello should not be thought of as ironic if that implies substantive divergence from her views. For difference of views would distract from the more radical question: Coetzee places *en abyme* conviction as such, what it means to have one, how it can be communicated, and such questioning of conviction is the more telling if it is his own. At the same time, by placing Costello's argument in the *abyme* of his fiction, Coetzee reverses the thematic focus of the work. Within the narrative, the Jewish poet Abraham Stern is offended by Costello's use of the Shoah as an analogy for her case about animals; and Ian Hacking, in a sympathetic and penetrating review, confessed to sharing Stern's unease ("Fellow Animals"). But Hacking too is reading it here simply as a real lecture, as if he were on the same narrative plane as Stern. In Coetzee's fictional narrative, by contrast, the central theme is the Shoah itself with the animal theme as an analytic device for unsettling conventional ways of thinking it. The animal theme is a Trojan horse designed to deconstruct the nature of conviction in relation to all fundamental life issues, such as the Shoah or apartheid.[4]

While dramatizing the experience of conviction in Costello, Coetzee's narrative neither endorses nor dissents from her views. And it is similarly neutral on her interpretations of other authors. In drawing other writers into the powerful vortex of her lecture she radically traduces almost all of them and, if she were to be seen as a straightforward mouthpiece for Coetzee, then his readings would be at times questionable and at others disingenuous. For the innocent reader is nowhere tipped off that some of the authors most heavily criticized by Costello have expressed precisely the views she goes on to articulate against them. She unwittingly plagiarizes the very writers she excoriates. But as Costello's readings they are entirely in character. She misreads her authors because she leaps over their terms and discourse. Her antipathy to their way of thinking blinds her to what they are saying. This places her, if not Coetzee, in an ambiguous relation to these sources just as Coetzee elsewhere leaves it an open question whether D. H. Lawrence, a critic very like Costello, has misread Swift or has offered "a reading of genius" (*Doubling*, 309). Like Lawrence, Costello tends to override the internal niceties of irony in a literary work and go directly for its existential premises.

Costello's lecture raises questions of knowledge and communicability that are dramatically thematized in the surrounding narrative. In the first instance these questions are directed outward: what is our knowledge of the other and how can we communicate what we think we know? The animal theme focuses these themes within a specific history of debate and cultural change. The dominant assumptions respecting our continuity or otherness with regard to animals have shifted over the course of the twentieth century. Traditional definitions of the human were based on such unique capacities as reason, language, and tool making. Not only have these once confident boundaries become increasingly blurred, the general emphasis has shifted: we are less concerned for our distinction from animals and more for our commonality with them, including above all the capacity to feel pain. Costello feels this commonality with an immediate intensity overriding the slow shift in culture and the minute processes of argumentation in several disciplines. Her intuitive and apodictic leap, which makes her relation to other thinkers so hostile, is not just an objection to their discourse, we may infer, but to their making the matter open to question at all. If it is a matter of debate the pass is already sold. And her espousal of poetry against philosophical and scientific reason rather confuses the issue since her chosen philosopher and poets are actually close to each other and provide parallel vindications of her own argument. It is worth tracing some of the discriminations she overrides in these authors since the narrative as a whole is a literary, if not poetic, development of their combined insights.

She invokes Blake, Lawrence, and Ted Hughes to affirm the integrity of all animals' lives and to challenge Thomas Nagel's philosophical exposure of the anthropomorphic fallacy in his essay "What Is It Like to Be a Bat?" Actually, as Hacking pointed out, Nagel is not her opponent but her ally ("Fellow Animals," 22). Nagel argues against materialist reductions of consciousness and makes her point in advance. The phenomenon of consciousness in living beings is irreducible and, in denying that we can know what it is *like* to be a bat, Nagel assumes the creature has *some* mode of phenomenological subjectivity. This Thomas's doubt is benign, for if we cannot know the internal being of animals we equally cannot know that our intuitions of continuity with them are mistaken. Nagel's position of antianthropomorphic skepticism gives an absolute protection to the otherness of the nonhuman creature; a point made also by Wendy Doninger as if contra Nagel (*Lives,* 103). Costello misses the same point, more complexly perhaps, in her use of the poets. Mentioning Blake and Lawrence as predecessors, she concentrates mainly on Ted Hughes. In truth, by opting for Hughes rather than Lawrence she simplifies her own case and falls for a common misreading of Lawrence's animal poems. She supposes him to be claiming internal understanding of animal modes of being as if he were naively anthropomorphic in the way Nagel has analyzed. But the *pons asinorum* in reading his animal poems is the recognition that he does not naively assume he knows what it is like to be a fish, tortoise, or hummingbird (*Complete Poems,* 2:334–40, 356–63, 372). On the contrary, these poems typically depend on a bracketed anthropomorphism or, as Derrida might say, an anthropomorphism consciously "under erasure." The being of these creatures is unknowable and the poems typically show the concentrated exercise of sympathetic imagination that is required to confront experientially, rather than to recognize theoretically, their radical otherness. In a simple formula: there can be no otherness without relation and no relation without otherness. For Lawrence, therefore, the anthropomorphic gesture is the necessary condition for a more complex recognition. The other life form is in some unknowable measure both continuous with and different from the human, and what is ultimately at stake for him is an extension of *human* being rather than a claim to full internal knowledge, or imaginative possession, of the other life form in *itself*. Indeed, if the other form could be so known, it would no longer lend itself to this imaginative extension of human awareness. At the same time, the interdependence of otherness and relationship means indeed that otherness reinforces relation. The naive sense of encountering another mode of being that many readers take from Lawrence's animal poetry, therefore, is not wrong, but he achieves his extraordinary acts of sympathetic attention precisely through the awareness of radical otherness. In comparison, Hughes's poems on animals, however remarkable, are more open to the charge of naive anthropomorphism precisely because of their tendency to melodramatic, all-too-human, insistence on the inhuman; a point Costello goes on to acknowledge in commenting on the ultimately ideal, or Platonic, significance of Hughes's jaguar (*Lives,* 53–54).

Lawrence, then, anticipates Costello's affirmation of continuity with the animal precisely by accommodating the epistemological condition that she overrides and that Nagel articulates discursively. It is worth pausing on the case of Lawrence, however, and Costello's occlusion of him in relation to her theme. For Coetzee is a significant author for postcolonial criticism, which, insofar as it has become an orthodoxy, has tended to fetishize the notion of otherness and invest it with the anxieties of ideological correctness. Otherness was Lawrence's great theme, and postcolonial critics might usefully recognize him as a still significant precursor. His heuristic openness and indifference to correctness make him a valuable source of insights, including uncomfortable ones, rather than of doctrinal or ideological solutions. His peculiar importance as a writer lies in his constant ontological questioning of fundamental values, and the animal is a means to this throughout his works. Lawrence reminds us, among other things, that knowledge of the other is not necessarily a question of positive sympathy.

In the animal realm he once had to overcome his reluctance to kill a porcupine that had become a pest on his Taos farm. His essay "Reflections on the Death of a Porcupine" ponders the double relation of human to animal, our difference and continuity, in a language of bracketed anthropomorphism. Summoning the resolution to kill it, he walks behind the creature: "It waddled very slowly, with its white spiky spoon-tail steering flat, behind the round bear-like back. It had a lumbering, beetle's, squalid motion, unpleasant. I followed it into the darkness of the timber, and there, squat like a great tick, it began scrapily to creep up a pine-trunk" (460). To reflect on his response, or even to have a response, to the porcupine, Lawrence has to use the inescapably anthropomorphic medium of language. He signals this with a linguistic excess of tone and metaphor, and as he compares it in turn to a bear, a beetle, and a giant tick, we may recall Joyce's description of the midwives' dog in the "Proteus" episode of *Ulysses:* "The dog yelped running to them, reared up and pawed them, dropping on all fours, again reared up at them with mute bearish fawning. Unheeded he kept by them as they came towards the drier sand, a rag of wolf's tongue redpanting from his jaws. His speckled body ambled ahead of them and then loped off at a calf's gallop" (58). Joyce, whose modernism is as ever complementary to Lawrence's, plays, through Stephen Dedalus, with a variety of animal references to suggest the activity of the dog but even more to highlight the activity of language in the act of perceiving it. In Joyce, language itself rears up before us. Lawrence is equally aware of language as he seeks to enter into an internal relation with the nonhuman creature but stresses the aspect of sympathy; in Adam Smith's sense, that is, not of moral identification but of intuitive awareness.[5] Lawrence's first sentence, following the creature from behind, draws us into a physical reading of its actions, a sympathetic understanding through what the folk phrase calls its body language. In effect, our bodily perceptions perform a constant equivalent of the Turing test in obliging us to infer living identities that cannot be proven.[6]

Lawrence finds a discursively irresolvable conflict over killing the porcupine. On the one hand, there is a hierarchy of life by which one order of being dominates or devours another. At the same time, all individual creatures have an incommensurable vitality, a fullness of being in the "fourth dimension" ("Reflections," 358–63) that is an absolute value. As he puts it, "one truth does not displace another. Even apparently contradictory truths do not displace one another. Logic is far too coarse to make the subtle distinctions life demands" (357). Where Lawrence seeks to balance these incommensurable imperatives, Costello privileges the latter absolutely over the former. To do so, she first seeks to nail Nagel through her virtuoso parallel between two texts of respectively scientific and literary provenance: Wolfgang Köhler's *The Mentality of Apes* and Franz Kafka's "Report to an Academy," both dating from 1917. She recounts how Köhler, whose title might for us recall Lévy-Bruhl's *Primitive Mentality* (1923), sought to measure experimentally the intelligence of an ape called Sultan by accustoming him to being fed by a keeper who then places his food in progressively more difficult locations. Costello imagines a different thought process for Sultan in which, instead of puzzling out how to reach the bananas, he wonders why the keeper has suddenly withdrawn the kindly relationship. By a doubled and reversed anthropomorphizing, she imagines the ape having to work out what the human being is thinking or feeling. Objectively speaking, although she does not conceive it in this way, Costello exercises a bracketed anthropomorphizing. She can have no idea what the ape actually experienced, if such a formulation is even meaningful. Her need is simply to challenge Köhler's version. The significance of the captivity theme, however, is that Costello, just like Nagel and Lawrence, sees the similarity between human and animal life as lying in their fullness of their own being. Our modes of being may be incomprehensibly different but the fact and the fullness of it is a point of sympathy and connection: "To be a living bat is to be full of being; being fully a bat is like being fully human" (*Lives*, 45). The authentically Lawrencian ring of this affirmation makes one wonder if Costello, or Coetzee, is more aware of Lawrence than either wishes to let on.

The deeper connection with Lawrence, however, is that he sees no localized, special problem of otherness: all relations are radically other and his interest in the more overt instances—racial, sexual, or animal—is precisely to reveal the occluded otherness of human beings that habit, including habits of language and consciousness, disguises as knowledge. The real problem of otherness is our failure to experience it in the human beings closest to us. And in the human realm too, we not only have relative degrees of mutual comprehension, such comprehension may lead to an awareness of significant discontinuity. Sympathy under a negative sign is a primary motif for Lawrence, and it is evidently one for Costello too in the delivery of her lecture. Once again, her apparent misreading, or misuse, of her cited authors lends a further subtextual import to the social situation of her lecture.

Costello and the Audience

Costello's reading of Köhler is at variance with the impression made on most readers by his book. Far from simply isolating Sultan in the way she suggests, Köhler visits an established group of chimpanzees and ends his study with a long appendix on the sociality of chimps whose import is stated in the opening sentence: "It is hardly an exaggeration to say that a chimpanzee kept in solitude is not a real chimpanzee at all" (*Mentality,* 282). But captivity provides a sufficient parallel with the situation of Kafka's Red Peter, an ape who has been captured from Africa and attained a limited freedom by assuming human characteristics. Red Peter has developed the traditional capacity of the ape for imitation to the point where he has acquired speech and can deliver his lecture to an academic audience although his motive was not to become human but to escape captivity as an ape. Within the multiple suggestiveness of Kafka's fable, Red Peter overcomes the otherness of species, although he denies that he now has access to his earlier ape being any more than his human audience have to theirs. Costello exploits his doubleness by at once identifying with Sultan against Köhler's dehumanizing of him and at the same time seeing him as a figure of her own alienation. Even as Costello insists on his continuity with the human, therefore, Red Peter figures forth her discomfort in delivering her lecture to an audience of what she feels to be radically alien beings. Her alienness does not necessarily derive from being a writer, and a writer can represent a general condition. But as famous writer she is especially exposed: she may be required to articulate, and as it were perform, her personal convictions in public. Furthermore, it may be the fate of some writers, such as Lawrence, Kafka, Costello, and Coetzee, that their very function depends on being seriously at variance with their culture.

The point can be enforced by extending the chain of Costello's intertexts to include Max Scheler's *The Nature of Sympathy* (1st ed., 1913). In the second edition (1922), Scheler dismisses Köhler's claim for sympathy between the apes seeing it as merely emotional infection. He also quotes approvingly Bertrand Russell's *Principles of Social Reconstruction* (1916) and thereby touches on a *locus classicus* of intrahuman otherness.[7] Russell's book was the outcome on his side of a joint proposal for social renewal that he had briefly undertaken with D. H. Lawrence at the beginning of the Great War. Notoriously, Lawrence soon realized his fundamental difference from Russell and wrote to him proposing that they become "strangers" (September 14, 1915, *Letters*, 392). Russell's statements of social principle, as quoted by Scheler, would be for most people, perhaps even including Lawrence, well-meaning enough in their generality. Indeed, some of the last sentences of "Reflections on the Death of a Porcupine" are close to Russell in phrasing as well as analysis.[8] But Russell's abstraction was symptomatic for Lawrence of what he came to see as a fundamental incapacity for true fellow feeling. Russell, in his view, had developed elaborate mental substitutes for sympathetic connection. If Lawrence was the modern author with the most radical appreciation of the incommensurability of worldviews, or perhaps one should say world feelings, then he had a chiasmic counterpart in the philosopher Wittgenstein, for whom mutual understanding depended on a shared "form of life." Wittgenstein likewise made a formal break with Russell despite his even greater, and acknowledged, reasons for personal gratitude.[9] Both Lawrence and Wittgenstein shared language with Russell but inhabited it in different ways that the formal commonality threw into relief. Wittgenstein later remarked, "It is what human beings *say* that is true or false; and they agree in the *language* they use. That is not agreement in opinions but in form of life" (*Philosophical Investigations,* 88e; italics in original). But the mutual relation to Russell invites the opposite formula: human beings may agree in their opinions but disagree, if not in the language they use, then in their use of language. In other words, the same formal system of linguistic signs, particularly when operating at a high level of generality, may mask radical differences in forms of life. In such circumstances, the difference may be evident to one party and not the other. And by the same logic, it may be incommunicable in any terms that do not traduce it. Seen in this light, Costello has a rationale for blanking out Köhler's emphasis on simian sympathies, or Nagel's on fullness of being, because they have for her the same hollowness as Lawrence saw in the social concern of Russell.

Costello not only suffers an embattled isolation, she exacerbates it in order to face the challenge or to bring it fully into view. As her reflections on animals reflect her own estrangement from her surrounding human culture, she pursues the confinement theme into a deliberately discomforting realm: "Fullness of being is a state hard to sustain in confinement. Confinement to prison is the form of punishment that the west favours and does its best to impose on the rest of the world through the means of condemning other forms of punishment (beating, torture, mutilation, execution) as cruel and unnatural" (*Lives,* 46). This comment on liberal views of punishment is likely to disturb many readers. Is she, or Coetzee, arguing for the acceptance of these other punishments or making a more general diagnostic observation in the spirit of Nietzschean thought experiment? There is a comparable moment in Lawrence's essay on Richard Dana's *Two Years before the Mast* when Lawrence reads Dana's horrified description of a naval flogging directly against the authorial grain (*Studies,* 109–14). In endorsing the captain's action, Lawrence is partly responding with a novelist's dramatic and psychological sympathy with the captain's overriding need to preserve authority rather than with conventional moral sympathy for the victim. As he remarked in reviewing a banal memoir by a nice young man: "You have to have something vicious in you to be a creative writer" (*Phoenix,* 373). More significantly, he is seeking to catch in Dana's response a symptom of excessive idealism, and he refers approvingly elsewhere to Melville's sensible avoiding of a flogging. The true point, in other words, is not commentary on penal practice but that both Lawrence and Coetzee are pushing at the boundaries of the acceptable to test fundamental commonalities of value that are hard to bring fully into consciousness and that are not open to purely discursive justification. The Jewish poet Abraham Stern, affronted by what he takes to be Costello's merely rhetorical allusion to the Shoah, refuses "breaking bread" (*Lives,* 82) with her just as she declines doing so with his colleague Michael Leahy (66). Partly novel and partly philosophical dialogue, Coetzee's text follows both Fielding's *Tom Jones* and Plato's *Symposium* in drawing on the image of a social act of ingestion if only, in his case, to insist on the corollary of exclusion. Knowledge of the other, whether porcupine or human, may entail rejection.

In the latter part of his career, Lawrence felt, like Costello, a radical sense of estrangement from the norms of his culture, and he provides a close analogy for her embedded lecture in the opening of his Mexican novel, *The Plumed Serpent*. His earlier version, now published as *Quetzalcoatl*, is a more moderate treatment of the theme but it is as if he wished precisely to subject it, and the reader, to a testing extremity. The final version is generally, and I think rightly, regarded as a failure, with much solemn absurdity, and downright offensiveness, interspersed with brilliant passages. For present purposes, however, the interest lies in the readerly challenge Lawrence achieves through the heroine, Kate Leslie, who provides the principal arena of consciousness. If Costello is suspicious of bullfight ritual (*Lives*, 52), Lawrence begins with a bullfight in Mexico City at which the disemboweling of a horse arouses Kate Leslie's absolute disgust. As the bull's horn works slowly up and down in the horse's rear it suggests, as another variation of bracketed anthropomorphism, an obscene parody of human rather than equine sexuality. She is even more horrified that the crowd enjoys the spectacle and that her male companions fail to share her response. Kate's attitude to Mexico will change, but Lawrence is not ironizing her reaction. Indeed, by using her emotional viewpoint, and stressing her moral isolation, he throws an implicit metafictional challenge to the reader: a problem of evaluative commonality. If you do not respond to the event as Kate Leslie does, you cannot significantly enter the evaluative world of the fiction; although you can read the words and may have the illusion of doing so. Like her male companions, you may see and yet not see the same event (Bell, *Lawrence*, 187–98). Lawrence's Leslie and Coetzee's Costello are figures of authorial moral isolation; an effect reinforced by their both being gendered female in strongly masculinist cultures.

Costello's daughter-in-law, Norma, an unemployed philosophy PhD, is the character most outraged by the novelist's flouting of social and academic norms; a word play that is prepared earlier in the text (*Lives*, 60). Her son seeks to comfort his wife on the eve of his mother's departure with the thought that "in a few hours she'll be gone, then we can return to normal" (119). But as the elderly Elizabeth is driven to the airport by her son, John, she proves to be the one crying in the wilderness, a prospective wilderness of no monkeys. She confesses tearfully that the comparison of farm animals with Shoah victims is not rhetorical for her, or even a matter of strongly held conviction. She is in the grip of an emotional response that radically destabilizes both her own identity and her sense of social normality:

> "I no longer know where I am. I seem to move around perfectly easily among people, to have perfectly normal relations with them. Is it possible, I ask myself, that all of them are participants in a crime of stupefying proportions? Am I fantasizing it all? I must be mad! Yet every day I see the evidences. The very people I suspect produce the evidence, exhibit it, offer it to me. Corpses. Fragments of corpses that they have bought for money." (20–21)

Her extreme and unusual attitude makes her a significant emblem of any humane citizen living within an evil social culture. Her sincere and uncompromising oddness highlights a more general moral, political, and philosophical predicament. With what discourse or criteria do you mount a case against the implicit norms of your own culture? If the animal theme provides a completely naturalistic example within our cultural epoch of what we can see to be a universal question, it also has more specific resonances for the theme of conviction.

The older, more functional, attitude to animals is sometimes associated with Descartes, and the external dualism vis-à-vis the animal parallels an internal dualism of mind and body, and therefore by insinuation, of thinking and feeling. Coetzee and Lawrence see that the question is inescapably one of emotional response: not emotion instead of something called intellect or reason but the anti-Cartesian wholeness of Lawrence's definition of thought as "man in his wholeness wholly attending" ("Thought," *Complete Poems*, 2:673). Faced with the need to kill the porcupine, Lawrence was caught between the incommensurable recognitions of predatory hierarchy and fullness of being in living creatures. There is no Kantian universal imperative to guide him, and Lawrence's essay records a process of thinking, and feeling, his way to action. Through Costello, however, Coetzee problematizes even more sharply the nature of existential decisions that cannot be decided as a matter of reason. Costello replies to a questioner: "If principles are what you want to take away from this talk, I would have to respond, open your heart and listen to what your heart says" (*Lives*, 52–53).

Costello's problem is that her conviction must not just be understood by others as a possible "position"; it must be felt apodictically as a living truth to which there is no alternative. Indeed, the word *position,* after being used casually in the body of the narrative (25, 48, 60), is put under scrutiny at the end. When John drives his mother to the airport we recall the opening scene in which he met her with little physical warmth or touch. He now apologizes for his wife's hostility by saying, "I don't think she is in a position to sympathise" (68). In a context now charged with resonances of philosophical discussion, sympathy, and physicality, the word *position* lends itself to multiple implications. While John means merely that Norma is overrun with domestic obligations and resentful at her lack of an academic career, his phrase also suggests her adoption of an intellectual posture that excludes the act of sympathy. On that reading her position ceases to be simply circumstantial as internal resistance connives with external conditions. If thought is "man in his wholeness wholly attending," then philosophy can be a way of avoiding thought, and that leads to the second focus of the fiction: the relation to the self.

Costello and the Self

I have emphasized so far how Costello's situation as lecturer focuses her isolation, her difficulty in enforcing her own conviction on others. But her situation has an equally forceful inward reference with regard to her self-assurance. Her reply that you must "listen to what your heart says" echoes the words of Rousseau's Savoyard vicar, but Coetzee does not subscribe to the transparency of the Rousseauvian self.[10] If her espousal, with such anguished intensity, of a currently minority viewpoint makes us see her oddness through the eyes of others, it also, as her final confession reveals, makes her feel it too. The intuitive intensity of her belief, and of her belief in "believes in," ultimately threatens her belief in herself. It is extremely difficult to live outside of cultural norms, although the variety of norms available to most of us may disguise this fact. It is possible, for example, to gravitate from a provincial racist culture to a larger world in which such attitudes are abhorrent. But this, however desirable, is a change of norms. Such an individual can feel morally endorsed even while politically exposed. The issue here is more typically one of moral courage within a normative conviction. But Costello's response to the farming of animals puts the word *normal* under a more radical kind of epochal strain. Over the course of the twentieth century, public anti-Semitic discourse has become unacceptable but we still eat animals. The imbalance between these questions makes them not, as Abraham Stern thought, a cheap analogy but an analytic device. Although Costello may not be fully in command of the analogy, as her reference in a later Costello story indeed suggests (*Costello,* 156), Coetzee uses the asymmetrical cultural change to focus the question of how far any convictions are functions of norms.

Joseph Conrad memorably focused what we might call the *Lord Jim* problem: that we can never know for sure our own capacity for moral endurance under pressure. But the revelation that destroys Jim, disturbs Marlow, and provokes Captain Brierly to suicide, depends on their all clearly acknowledging the moral requirements for being "one of us."[11] Costello, however, embodies a different level of the question: who is "one of us" in the first place? The psychologist, Ruth Orkin, uses the phrase for the relation of humans and apes (*Lives,* 39), but it has most importantly an intra-human bearing. By the end of the twentieth century we know from several famous psychological experiments that individuals who in the abstract sincerely repudiate cruel or inhumane behavior will, in most cases, adopt it if they are placed even in a small and consciously artificial microculture in which it is endorsed as normal toward designated subgroups.[12] Modern history, of course, has conducted equivalent experiments, with notorious success, on whole populations. The degree to which the self is constructed from implicit norms, which may themselves shift and change, is in principle unknowable. By allowing Costello to use the Shoah to express her anguish about animals, Coetzee is using the animal theme to illuminate not just the psychology of the Shoah, or of apartheid, but of the historical judgments made about them. How many of those who sincerely subscribe to the antiracist culture of the late twentieth century would have done so at the beginning of it? How many are exercising independent moral responsibility and how many are animated, like the earlier perpetrators, by the mass emotions of their own day? This is not a question of sincerity, which is broadly knowable, but of authenticity, which is more elusive. Coetzee's narrative of minority and majority convictions does not destabilize moral norms as such but our internal relation to them and our consequent capacity to judge others. Never mind the bat, or the chimp, what is it like to be a racist? Not what *would* it be like for *me* to be one, but what *is* it like for the *other;* including the other that I might have been? And if we cannot say, how securely can we judge? Or, more subtly and crucially, what is it like to be a nonracist? On the available evidence, how many of us are actually in a position to know for sure that even we are one of us?

The predicament focused by Coetzee's narrative is that citizens of modernity, particularly when inhabiting political orders of some approximative democracy, have urgent obligations to exercise moral authority, but they have very uncertain right to claim it. As moral individuals and citizens, most of us can, and do, live with this, but a writer whose texts are of their nature public moral interventions can hardly avoid the implicit claim to authority inscribed in them. And where the political stakes are both urgent and painful, the predicament is the more intense. Coetzee's fiction constantly negotiates this question as an implicit and integral aspect of the narrative, and it would seem that, invited to give a public lecture, he has found a way of inscribing the same double awareness into its internal logic. Even to the extent perhaps of making the predicament itself the primary subject. Costello's simple and passionate conviction is genuinely admirable and therefore only the more seductive. In this respect, she is less like the author, for whom she partly deputizes, and more like some of his readers. We might all wish to live in a simpler world, and failing that we need the motivating focus of simple convictions, but Coetzee is bleakly aware of the noumenal core of the moral self.

The generic overlay of academic lecture, narrative fiction, and philosophical dialogue allows this internal tension to be embodied as different ways of inhabiting language. Although Costello appeals to poetry, her own language is not conventionally "poetic," and Coetzee's is even less so. His characteristic mode is a minimalist prose giving an immediate impression of transparency but with a luminous and enigmatic aura. In *Lives* the bare tautness of the language brings to the surface those dead metaphors that are the most likely locus of unexamined norms. The habitual premises of a culture are the hardest to scrutinize in being at once pervasive and banal, which may be why Costello, while espousing poetic against philosophical thought, remarks, "Like most writers, I have a literal cast of mind" (42).

Yet this very literalism is the means for a resonant rhyming of ideas and psychological formations. At the center of the work, after all, lies the clichéd analogy of the Jews in the Shoah being killed like cattle. In reversing and literalizing the analogy, Costello illuminates not just the state of mind in which the Shoah could occur but the difficulty of internalizing this history as moral self-knowledge.

Lives provides an analytic counterpart to *Disgrace* in which Coetzee's tautly minimalist technique pressures the most common terms to reveal unnoticed meanings. It may be because I am one of the apparently few who find the word "holocaust" distasteful as a reference to the attempted extermination of the European Jews, that I also find the conclusion of *Disgrace* has the force of a sudden kick in the stomach. Lurie's final remark about the dog ("I am giving him up") resists, as far as I can see, analytic articulation (*Disgrace,* 220). Obliquely invoking the Shoah, it speaks from the abyss of the self, combining both betrayal and abnegation within a transcendent, but not religious, implication of sacrifice. He does not know whether he is acting selfishly or generously at the level of motivation, but he is willing to do the right thing; the desire being focused precisely by the objective triviality of the occasion. Costello has something similar in mind when she speaks not of moral conviction but of saving her soul (*Lives,* 43). In *Lives,* we might take the college president's anticipation of "tomorrow's offering" (45) as a hint that Costello is not merely speaking for the animals but is putting herself in their place, effectively sacrificing herself as a dignified public persona. Following her earlier remarks on academic education (35), we may see an etiological reflection on her situation in her remark on Sultan: "only the experimenter's single-minded regimentation forces him to concentrate on it" (30). In seeking to induce particular qualities of thought, all educational institutions are sites of "concentration," if not *Konzentrationslager.* Concentration is necessary to thought, including artistic thought, and it is notably exemplified in many of Coetzee's own taut narratives. The mode of concentration is all and Coetzee is suspicious of ideological confinements, including, perhaps especially, those with unimpeachable motives. Taut in avoiding the merely taught, his lecture/story/ dialogue positions not just Costello but writer and reader too within a tight structure of generic enclosures with no evident exit from its moral concentration.

Notes

1. Responses to *Disgrace* are discussed in Attridge, *"Disgrace."*
2. Coetzee, Marjorie Garber, Peter Singer, Wendy Doninger, and Barbara Smuts. Garber raises the question of literary truth but does not know quite what to do with it. Singer is disturbed by the elusiveness of Coetzee without seeing its function. Doninger and Smuts make independent contributions to the questions raised while passing over the fictional dimension and effectively identifying Costello with Coetzee.
3. I discuss this in *Literature, Modernism, and Myth,* 161–81.
4. I prefer the word "Shoah," meaning "catastrophe," to "holocaust," the term for a Jewish religious sacrifice.
5. Adam Smith modified Francis Hutcheson's and David Hume's notions of "sympathy" as emotional *identification* to a more judgmental view of the impartial spectator as *understanding* subjective states, whether approving or disapproving. Hence, for example, his phrase "sympathetic resentment." See Smith, *Moral Sentiments,* 78.
6. Alan Turing proposed blind interaction with a machine and a human as a way of testing our capacity to distinguish between them, or of testing the distinction as such.
7. "I wish to show how the worship of money is both an effect and a cause of diminishing vitality, how our institutions might be changed so as to make the worship of money grow less and the general vitality grow more." From an extended quotation from Bertrand Russell in Scheler, *Nature of Sympathy,* 108. Coetzee admired Scheler's *Ressentiment* (1915). See *Doubling the Point,* 134.
8. Cf. "We are losing vitality, owing to money and money standards" ("Reflections," 363).
9. For some relevant comments on this fundamental difference see Monk, *Wittgenstein,* 53.
10. "Je ne voulais pas philosopher avec vous, mais vous aider à connaitre votre coeur" (Rousseau, *Émile,* 377).
11. "One of us" is Conrad's motif phrase in *Lord Jim* to identify a professional and moral community.
12. The Stanford experiment is the most notable instance. See Zimbardo, Maslach, and Haney, "Stanford Prison Experiment."
13. Marjorie Garber surely misses the point about "dead metaphor" here (*Lives,* 81).

Bibliography

Attridge, Derek. "J. M. Coetzee's *Disgrace:* Introduction." In "J. M. Coetzee's *Disgrace,*" edited by Derek Attridge and Peter D. McDonald. Special issue, *Interventions* 4, no. 3 (2002): 315–20.

Bell, Michael. *D. H. Lawrence: Language and Being.* Cambridge: Cambridge University Press, 1992.

———. *Literature, Modernism, and Myth: Belief and Responsibility in the Twentieth Century.* Cambridge: Cambridge University Press, 1997.

Coetzee, J. M. *Disgrace.* London: Secker and Warburg, 1999.

———. *Doubling the Point: Essays and Interviews.* Edited by David Attwell. Cambridge MA: Harvard University Press, 1992.

———. *Elizabeth Costello.* London: Secker and Warburg, 2003.

———. *The Lives of Animals.* Edited by Amy Gutmann. Princeton: Princeton University Press, 1999.

———. *Slow Man.* London: Secker and Warburg, 2005.

Eliot, George. *Middlemarch.* Edited by David Carroll. Oxford: Clarendon Press, 1986.

Eliot, T. S. *Complete Poems and Plays of T. S. Eliot.* New York: Harcourt Brace, 1930.

Hacking, Ian. "Our Fellow Animals." *New York Review of Books* 47, no. 11 (June 29, 2000): 20–26.

Herford, Oliver. "Tears for Dead Fish." *Times Literary Supplement,* September 5, 2003, 5–6.

Joyce, James. *Ulysses.* London: Bodley Head, 1960.

Köhler, Wolfgang. *The Mentality of Apes.* Translated by Ella Winter. London: Routledge and Kegan Paul, 1917, 1925; rev. ed., 1927.

Lawrence, D. H. *Complete Poems.* 2 vols. Edited by Vivian de Sola Pinto and Warren Roberts. New York: Viking, 1964.

———. *The Letters of D. H. Lawrence.* 8 vols. Edited by James T. Boulton. Vol. 2, edited by George Zytaruk and James T. Boulton. Cambridge: Cambridge University Press, 1991.

———. *Phoenix: The Posthumous Papers of D. H. Lawrence.* Edited Edward D. McDonald. London: Heinemann, 1936.

———. *The Plumed Serpent.* Edited by L. D. Clark. Cambridge: Cambridge University Press, 1987.

———. *Quetzalcoatl.* Edited by Louis Martz. New York: New Directions, 1995.

———. "Reflections on the Death of a Porcupine." In *Reflections on the Death of a Porcupine and Other Essays,* edited by Michael Herbert, 349–63. Cambridge: Cambridge University Press, 1988.

———. *Studies in Classic American Literature.* Phoenix ed. London: Heinemann, 1964.

Lévy-Bruhl, Lucien. *Primitive Mentality.* Translated by Lilian A. Clare. London: Allen and Unwin, 1923.

Monk, Ray. *Ludwig Wittgenstein: The Duty of Genius.* London: Vintage, 1990.

Nagel, Thomas. "What Is It Like to Be a Bat?" In *Mortal Questions,* 165–80. Cambridge: Cambridge University Press, 1979.

Rousseau, Jean-Jacques. *Émile, ou de l'Éducation.* Paris: Garnier-Flammarion, 1966.

Scheler, Max. *The Nature of Sympathy.* Translated by Peter Heath. London: Routledge and Kegan Paul, 1954.

Smith, Adam. *The Theory of Moral Sentiments.* Edited by D. D. Raphael and A. L. Macfie. Oxford: Oxford University Press, 1976.

Wittgenstein, Ludwig. *Philosophical Investigations.* Translated by G. E. M. Anscombe. Oxford: Blackwell, 1967.

Yeats, W. B. "The Second Coming." In *Collected Poems.* 2nd ed. London: Macmillan, 1950.

Zimbardo, Philip G., Christina Maslach, and Craig Haney. "Reflections on the Stanford Prison Experiment: Genesis, Transformations, Consequences." In *Obedience to Authority: Current Perspectives on the Milgram Paradigm,* edited by Thomas Blass, 193–237. Mahwah, NJ: Erlbaum, 2000.

10

A FEMINIST-VEGETARIAN DEFENSE
OF ELIZABETH COSTELLO

*A Rant from an Ethical Academic on
J. M. Coetzee's* The Lives of Animals

Laura Wright

In relationship to them [animals], all people are Nazis; for the animals,
it is an eternal Treblinka.

—Isaac Bashevis Singer, "The Writer"

The crime of the Third Reich, says the voice of accusation, was to treat
people like animals.

—Elizabeth Costello in *The Lives of Animals*

Rant: 1. *intr.* (or with *it*). To talk or declaim in an extravagant high-
flown manner; to use bombastic language. . . . 1747 in Doran *Mann &
Manners* (1876) I. xi. 250 "As an Actress . . . she does extremely well . . .
she rants a little too much whilst she is in woman's cloaths."

—*OED*

IN AN article on the Truth and Reconciliation Commission in which she
references J. M. Coetzee's *The Lives of Animals*, Jacqueline Rose says,

"intellectuals are always accused of talking too much, not acting enough" ("Apathy," 178). I choose to start with this quote for two reasons: first, Rose's statement speaks to the seeming disjunction between intellectualism and activism, between the spoken and the enacted that has been a predominant subject of critical debate concerning the fictional writings of J. M. Coetzee. Second, I want to explore the verb *to act,* meant in Rose's case, I am sure, in its kinetic sense, to respond physically (by taking action) to a set of given stimuli—apartheid, war with Iraq, or factory farming, for example. J. M. Coetzee is an outsider in the realm of white South Africa, as an English speaker with an Afrikaans surname and by virtue of his own self-placement, and his writing is continually characterized critically in terms of the *action* that it—and he, by extension—does not take: he does not express a political stance with regard to South Africa in his literature; he does not answer questions after public lectures; he does not write realistic fiction; and now, after a recent move to Adelaide, Australia, Coetzee, one of South Africa's most prominent writers, does not even live in South Africa.

Derek Attridge justifies the absence of explicit ethical action in Coetzee's work by claiming that "in both apartheid and post-apartheid society . . . such action is paradoxically undermined by its ideological premises"("Expecting," 59). Furthermore, Coetzee does not confess details about his personal life. In a recent interview with Eleanor Wachtel in *Brick*, Coetzee stipulated that Wachtel ask him no questions about "his own work, his life, or the political situation in South Africa" (Coetzee, "Sympathetic Imagination," 38). How then, one may wonder, will it be possible to interview him at all? What sorts of questions will he answer? Of course, the interview was all about language, about the choices one makes as a writer with regard to language, in Coetzee's case, a writer who grew up speaking "English at home, Afrikaans in [his] public life" (38) and who writes in English. Such a discussion is, in one sense, merely about language as a literal means of communication, not about Coetzee's life, his writing, or politics in South Africa. But then again, language, especially in the postcolonial, postapartheid context of Coetzee's work, always gives way to metaphor: in *Boyhood* (1997), for example, the protagonist, John, makes the unpopular choice of liking the Russians instead of the Americans because of his preference for the letter *r,* "particularly the capital R, the strongest of all the letters" (27). The literal, this aesthetic choice about language, has the symbolic power to place John outside of acceptable choices, and it is from this position as outsider that Coetzee's ethics arise and from which his authorial choices about language constantly shift from the aesthetic to the political and, in another sense, from a lived set of ethical principles to a body of fiction marked by its refusal to engage with certain expected ethical narratives.

There has been an abundance of criticism leveled at Coetzee for his refusal to realistically represent in his fiction South Africa's political situation as it unfolds before him. For example, Mike Marais describes the acrimony with which *Foe* (1986) was met: "While the country was burning, quite literally in many places, the logic went, here was one of our most prominent authors writing about the writing of a somewhat pedestrian eighteenth-century English novelist" ("Death," 83). But because one cannot read South African literature without reading apartheid, or as Stephen Clingman claims, "in Africa human cannot be separated from historical experience" (*Novels,* 3), Coetzee's novels never exclude this historical reality from which they are drawn; they simply deny that there is merely one way to tell any story, including the story of the history of apartheid in South Africa. The ethical action in much of Coetzee's fiction, therefore, is performative rather than didactic, and "acting" in *The Lives of Animals* is Coetzee's performance of a female subject position, the character of Elizabeth Costello. This act is Coetzee's mimetic exercise in embodiment and a critique of the limitations of imagined identification—with fictional characters, with animals, and with women.

In *The Lives of Animals,* Coetzee's Tanner Lectures delivered at Princeton in 1997, Coetzee addresses the ethics of meat eating and animal experimentation via the persona of fictional, feminist novelist Elizabeth Costello, a character who delivers two lectures, "disconcertingly like the Tanner Lectures" (Gutmann, introduction, 3) on animal rights at Appleton College. As an intellectual figure, Costello is also an activist who lives her ethics by virtue of her vegetarianism, claiming, "if I can think my way into the existence of a being who has never existed, then I can think my way into the existence of a bat or a chimpanzee or an oyster" (*Lives,* 35). Coetzee performs Costello, who acts when she refuses to eat meat just as she performs Plutarch in response to questions about the reasons for her vegetarianism:

"I, for my part, am astonished that you can put in your mouth the corpse of a dead animal, astonished that you do not find it nasty to chew hacked flesh and swallow the juices of death-wounds" (38). Furthermore, Coetzee acted as he stood before his audience at Princeton and performed Costello, embodied her position, imagined his way "into the existence of a being who never existed" (35), and posited an extremely problematic analogy, that factory farming is like the Holocaust.

Costello's analogy is so radical, in fact, her rhetoric so inflammatory and visceral, filled with phrases like "hacked flesh" and "death wounds," that the audience—her own within Coetzee's text and Coetzee's outside in the "real" world—recoils at what she herself refers to as the "cheap point-scoring" (22) of her argument. The audience, at least from a critical perspective, writes her out of the narrative. Ultimately and most vehemently, literary critics either repeatedly posit her fictionality, overdetermining the seemingly obvious fact that she is not Coetzee, or they conflate author and character, attributing the animal rights argument not to Costello but to Coetzee. The reason for the silencing of Costello is the critics' inability to recognize the performative aspects of Coetzee's text, attributable at least in part to Coetzee's tendency to disrupt conventional notions of genre. How do we categorize *The Lives of Animals*? Is this text a work of fiction or, because of the format in which it was delivered, is it Coetzee's argumentative truth presented in the guise of an analysis of the sympathetic imagination? And to make matters more complicated, how do we categorize *The Lives of Animals* within its new context as lessons three and four of the eight "lessons" that comprise Coetzee's penultimate novel to date—and the designation *novel* in this case is open to debate as well—*Elizabeth Costello*?[1]

Because Coetzee first presented the work and voiced the characters when he delivered his lectures at Princeton, *The Lives of Animals,* then and thereafter, constitutes something dramatic. It is a performance through which Coetzee enacts a rant: Elizabeth Costello's "excitable speech," in Judith Butler's sense, consists of "utterances made under duress, usually confessions that . . . do not reflect the balanced mental state of the utterer" (*Speech,* 15). Because the persona he speaks is a woman, this speech is feminized and negatively connotated; in the critical arenas of Appleton College and in critical academic discourse about *The Lives of Animals,* it becomes a rant characterized by sensible and feminine bodily reaction. But failure to grant Costello's voice alterity in this context is a failure of the sympathetic imagination, a failure, Costello argues, responsible for the way we treat animals.

Elizabeth Costello is a fictional character constructed by J. M. Coetzee, just as Coetzee is a fiction constructed by his critics. Despite the fact that Costello's voice may not be Coetzee's, neither is Costello's voice her own. The character of Elizabeth Costello, her argument that people treat animals the way the Nazis treated the Jews, and Coetzee's rendering of both of these variables establishes a third and perhaps more sentimental place from which to write against the primary binary opposition of animal/human. In terms of its dualistic connotations, sentimentality is excessive, female, emotional, and hard to attribute to Coetzee. As critics, we would much rather attribute it to Costello because it is easier to portray her reasoning as flawed, to find her excessive, just as the poet Abraham Stern does when he refuses to break bread with Costello, claiming, "the Jews died like cattle, therefore cattle die like Jews, you say. That is a trick of words that I will not accept" (*Lives,* 49). Yet it is precisely a "trick of words," the disruptive and nonnormative form that Coetzee employs, that makes *The Lives of Animals* so polemical, and it is a trick of gender that makes critics overdetermine the distance between Coetzee and Elizabeth Costello. Clearly, we cannot equate Costello and Coetzee, just as Stern cannot equate cattle and Jews, and Peter Singer, in his struggle to make sense of Costello's position, says in an essay that follows *The Lives of Animals,* "a comparison is not necessarily an equation."[2] But what strikes me is a pervasive need by many of Coetzee's critics who discuss *The Lives of Animals* to posit Costello's fictionality, at the very least to read her metaphorically. For example, according to Michael Bell, Costello provides Coetzee a way of getting things done; for Bell, "*Lives* is a closely structured examination of why Coetzee himself cannot readily believe in 'believes in'" ("What Is It Like," 175). Similarly, David Attwell claims that Costello is a surrogate for Coetzee, a reprisal; she is like Erasmus's fool. According to Attwell, Costello makes a case for the sympathetic imagination, a concept whose limits were critiqued by Sam Durrant's analysis of the ethics of stupidity and Dominic Head's examination of the irony in Costello's ability to reason "that reason is less valuable than sympathy" (Attwell, "Life and Times," 37; Durrant, "J. M. Coetzee, Elizabeth Costello";

Head, "Coetzee and the Animals"). Furthermore, the animal rights argument, as presented by Costello as presented by Coetzee, is also read metaphorically, according to Bell, as "a Trojan horse designed to deconstruct the nature of conviction in relation to all fundamental life issues, such as the Shoah or apartheid" ("What Is It Like," 176).

To claim that Coetzee is not Costello is to state the obvious for various reasons, not the least of which is that Costello is a fictional female character, and despite the playful temptation to make a case for Coetzee in drag, I will refrain except to say that given what we do know about South African history, it is probably safe to assume that Coetzee feels a certain and understandable degree of unease voicing his subject position, a South African masculinity complicated by the variable of whiteness. Judith Butler claims that "drag is a site of a certain ambivalence, one which reflects the more general situation of being implicated in the regimes of power by which one is constituted and hence being implicated in the very regime one opposes" (*Bodies*, 125). As a form of displacement and renegotiation of power, she claims that drag is not always a form of ridicule nor is it merely a way of passing as something that one is not. Furthermore, and perhaps most important to this study, drag is not exclusively the realm of male, homosexual performance. The performance of a gendered position other than that of the performer, however, is an attempt to understand the un-understandable aspects—or alterity—of the other, and as such it illustrates enactment of the sympathetic imagination. Therefore, *The Lives of Animals*, in my reading of it as a kind of performance, is essentially a lecture in drag, a performative dialogue clothed in the auspices of a fiction that examines the interaction and disjunction between two modes of discourse: the seemingly objective rhetoric of a philosophical lecture, and the subjective, lived experience of the polemical diatribe.

Being white and male in South Africa is to inhabit the subject position of colonizer and apartheid beneficiary, a position with which Coetzee is clearly at odds. Even his autobiographical pieces, *Boyhood* and *Youth* (2003), are narrated in the third person, a device that serves to alienate the author from a self he reluctantly claims as his own while simultaneously disrupting our notion of authorial and narratorial verisimilitude in the realm of autobiography. The third person–narrated *Disgrace* (1999), the novel that not incidentally followed the publication of *The Lives of Animals*, poses an interesting counterpoint because although both Coetzee and protagonist David Lurie are male and both teach university-level literature, critics do not concern themselves with setting up a distinction between these two; we seem to more readily accept that Coetzee and Lurie are distinct personas, and the "laws" that govern readings of fiction forbid us from doing something as reductive as conflating the positions of author and protagonist. But it seems more probable that such an option is never considered because Coetzee does not perform Lurie in the way that he performs Costello. According to Judith Butler, "the speech act is a bodily act, and . . . the force of the performative is never fully separable from bodily force" (*Speech*, 141). Therefore, the body of Coetzee the novelist who performs the lecture is never fully separable from the speech acts of Elizabeth Costello. In turn, it seems that a productive way of examining Elizabeth Costello is to posit her as the imagined body through which Coetzee enacts emotional speech, even as he examines the limitations of such sympathetic embodiment.

I reluctantly identify with Costello because as a vegan, animal rights activist, and literary scholar, I find myself drawn into her camp. I say that my identification is reluctant because I recognize the critical danger of such a stance. But it is from a perspective of identification that I want her to have a life of her own, so to speak, to occupy critical space as a creature who both speaks about and enacts her ethics, because that is my primary goal as an academic. I engage anecdotally for several reasons, not the least of which is my own desire to claim, despite the slippery slope of so doing, my ethical position, to place this personal aspect of my identity firmly within the realm of my academic practice. To confess my own ethical stance—and Coetzee has quite a bit to say about the problems the confessional stance engenders, "problems whose common factor seems to be a regression to infinity of self-awareness and self-doubt" ("Confession," 274)—is to attempt to answer seminal questions in my own work as an academic about the ways I try to align my intellectualism and my activism. First, I struggle, as we all must, to locate the place of the ethical in the study of literature and to question the tendency to identify with the supposed ethics of an author or a character within that author's fiction—and in Coetzee's work, such identification is problematized by the character of Elizabeth Costello, who expresses an ethical stance in some way for an author who refuses to do so. Second, I am trying in the most overt way to disrupt expectations and restrictions of ascribed forms of discourse—in this case the academic essay—by disrupting the objective with the personal, to provide a critique of philosophical objectivity.

Such disruption is precisely what Coetzee does in *The Lives of Animals;* as Amy Gutmann says in her introduction, "the form of Coetzee's lectures is far from the typical Tanner Lectures, which are generally philosophical essays. Coetzee's lectures are fictional in form: two lectures within two lectures, which contain a critique of a more typical philosophical approach to the topic of animal rights" (3). But perhaps the most significant reason for providing a less than wholly academic discourse on the subject of Elizabeth Costello is to restore her to the text as Coetzee's embodiment of the mediating voice, the performative voice that Coetzee inhabits when he speaks Elizabeth Costello, the voice that is neither Coetzee's nor Costello's, neither male nor female, neither fully rational nor emotional. This is the voice that not only problematizes the dichotomous logic responsible for the binary oppositions of colonial and patriarchal thought, including the animal/human dualism, but that also disrupts the privileging of the rational over the emotional by calling into question assumptions about author, narrator, protagonist, text, and audience. My argument, therefore, has less to do with Coetzee's text *The Lives of Animals* and more to do with the text of Coetzee's performance of Elizabeth Costello and the reaction of various audiences—Costello's, Coetzee's (at Princeton), and Coetzee's (the reader)—to that performance.

Claiming an ethical stance in an academic essay is frightening and tricky, as evidenced by a level-headed colleague who told me that the subtitle of this piece made me sound as if I were taking the moral high ground, saying essentially, "I'm more ethical than you are," and I realize that scrutinized for ethical content, my life would certainly fall short of ethical consistency. I realize the absolutism veganism implies, but I am also quick to recognize that an ethical shortcoming in one arena may be balanced by ethical over-achievement somewhere else. Furthermore, I hardly mean to imply that veganism is the only way to be ethical or that an animal rights agenda excludes other forms of ethical action. I also recognize the negative attributes associated with an animal rights agenda as summed up by activist literary figure Joy Williams's claim that "when people care too much about animals, it's suspected that somewhere, somehow, some person is being deprived of generic love and support and attention because of it" (*Nature*, 162). The point remains that whenever an individual, whether that individual is Costello, Coetzee, or me, performs an ethical decision in the form of a public stance, there is the potential for someone to claim that other ethical options have not been acted upon.

So the position I occupy in this essay and in life is a difficult one: do I get to claim a sort of moral high ground by virtue of my veganism, a more clearly defined form of dietary and lifestyle proscription than the vegetarianism practiced by Elizabeth Costello, who still carries a leather bag and wears leather shoes (but who nonetheless admits her conflicted nature, realizing that everywhere she looks, someone is offering her "fragments of corpses" [*Lives*, 69])? Or does such confession indeed send me into the infinite regression of which Coetzee speaks, forever in the kind of self-righteous competition parodied on *The Simpsons* when Lisa Simpson's vegetarianism is held in relief against that of a "fifth-degree vegan," who refuses to eat "anything that casts a shadow"? Furthermore, claiming an ethical stance with regard to animal rights, a cause that Williams feels is the most "extremist agenda, based utterly on non-self-fulfilment and non-self-interest" (*Nature*, 177), can make a person look like a kook indeed. Claiming that stance as a woman, and even more specifically as an old woman like Elizabeth Costello, is even riskier. One opens oneself up to all types of gender-based criticism, none of it very constructive. But here we are, Costello and I, and I defend the both of us.

Given the often antagonistic attributes associated with an animal rights position, it is little wonder that critics would want to distance Costello from Coetzee. While none of these distancing strategies is particularly negative—for example, the fool is not necessarily a doomed figure but instead, because of the impulsive nature of this archetype, takes risks and opens up the realm of possibility for either positive or negative consequences—they are in fact based on readings of Costello as woman. The distinction in and of itself need not be sexist; the reasons for that distinction, however, are undeniably tainted by Costello's status as both female and elderly, a "fleshy, white-haired lady" (*Lives*, 16). As such, she serves as the embodiment of all that is potentially least respected in academia, a space where a woman's intellectual desirability decreases exponentially as she ages, thereby marking the degeneration of her currency as surrogate daughter and imaginary lover within the academy. The result is the rather unself-conscious and resounding need for Coetzee's proponents to constantly deconstruct Coetzee and extract him from Costello without doing much in the way of analyzing the character of Costello herself. Instead, we theorize about the role Costello plays with regard to Coetzee's ideas about realism and are overwhelmed with the underlying "truth" in analyses of *The Lives of Animals* that Costello's voice is not Coetzee's, that Costello, as Austin Briggs claims, is a "made up novelist . . . who recast *Ulysses*—which recast *The Odyssey*—as *The House on Eccles Street,* in which she made up a character called Molly Bloom— whom, of course, Joyce made up" ("Who's Who," 11). Furthermore, and despite that we know that Coetzee is "a vegetarian who does not drink or smoke" (Susskind, "Émigré"), we also know that he does not voice his ethics in public; in fact he voices very little in public except his fiction, and he evades seemingly all attempts to get at the "truth" everyone else seems so eager to ascribe to his work.

For example, one can envision the squirming of both interviewer and interviewee when Coetzee said to Tony Morphet, "your questions again and again drive me into a position I don't want to occupy" (Coetzee, "Two Interviews," 464). Such antics cause Briggs to claim that Coetzee is "in conversation, the third most impossible person I have encountered in a fairly long life" (following Marisol and Ezra Pound; "Who's Who," 11). In a literary critical context, if we respect Coetzee's evasiveness, we must concede that *Lives* is not his argument about animal rights because Coetzee would not make such an argument; however, he would (we might be willing to admit) do some gender-bending linguistic acrobatics in order to tease out a discourse on the potential human ability—and therefore potential inability— for imagined identification. Michael Pollan, in his argument *against* animal rights, on the other hand, conflates Coetzee and Costello: "[W]ill history someday judge us as harshly as it judges the Germans who went about their ordinary lives in the shadow of Treblinka? Precisely that question was posed by J. M. Coetzee . . . in a lecture he delivered at Princeton; he answers in the affirmative. If animal rightists are right, 'a crime of stupefying proportions' (*in Coetzee's words*) is going on around us everyday" ("Unnatural Idea," II; italics mine). Similarly, animal rights proponent Charles Patterson attributes to Coetzee this passage from *The Lives of Animals* that he uses as the epigraph to the third chapter of his book *Eternal Treblinka:* "let me say openly: we are surrounded by an enterprise of degradation, cruelty, and killing" (51). Therefore, the "me" is assumed to be Coetzee, but readers know that this passage is spoken by Elizabeth Costello. If one reads for the animal rights argument, then, Costello's words become Coetzee's, but in the case of the critic or the animal rights philosopher one thing is very apparent: Elizabeth Costello is absent from the debate. Michael Pollan's claim that her words are "Coetzee's words" erases the character of Elizabeth Costello from the text, as does David Attwell's claim, mentioned earlier in this essay, that Costello is a surrogate for Coetzee. We are placed in another either/or dilemma—either this argument is Coetzee's or it is *not* Coetzee's —that denies Elizabeth Costello the power of signification within Coetzee's text.

As often as not, whenever there is a first-person narrator in Coetzee's fiction, that narrator is female, and much has been written about Coetzee's female narrators in the forms of Magda in *In the Heart of the Country* (1982), Susan Barton in *Foe* (1986), and Elizabeth Curren in *Age of Iron* (1990). Coetzee has been criticized by feminist critics who believe, as Kirsten Holst Petersen does, that his feminine narrative voice is "an assertion of appropriating male authorship" ("Dead End?" 251) and an inauthentic attempt at ventriloquism. Similarly, Josephine Dodd, who regards South African literature in general as "a pretty sexist affair," claims that in *Foe*, "as fast as Coetzee exposes the colonial intent . . . he reenacts it himself" ("Establishment," 327, 331). To complicate matters, often his female narrators, Magda and Susan Barton, for example, have been read—rather reductively—as allegorical.[3] While Coetzee is reluctant to claim that his voicing of the female has anything much to do with femininity per se, he is aware of what it may mean to inhabit the consciousness of the other sex. When Joanna Scott asked him what it meant for him to take on a female voice in the case of Magda in *In the Heart of the Country,* he answered, "A complicated question. One way of responding is to ask, is one, as a writer, at every level sexed? Is there not a level where one is, if not presexual, then anterior to sex? First anterior to sex, then becoming sexed? At that level, or in that transition between levels, does one actually 'take on' the voice of another sex? Doesn't one 'become' another sex?" (Coetzee, "Voice," 91). As an answer, this one seems particularly evasive and provocative. To suggest, as Coetzee does, that in a transition between sexes, one "becomes" another sex may imply a sort of interstitial hierarchy of the sexes; if one is first presexual and then female— as this answer would appear to imply—then does one perhaps finally arrive in the position of male? Or is it the other way around?

But, more importantly, Coetzee's response to Scott illustrates his ability to question, if not state a firm belief in, the notion that the writer must be able to embody and perform "another sex." Scott's question mirrors one the narrator asks of David Lurie in *Disgrace* as Lurie tries to empathize with his daughter Lucy's position after her rape: "Does he have it in him to be the woman?" (160). When his colleagues tell him they are not his enemies after he is called before them to explain the sexual license he has taken with his student Melanie, he says, "in this chorus of goodwill . . . I hear no female voice" (52), but it is the woman he must imagine granting forgiveness, and it is with women—and animals—he must identify if he is ever make reparations. He continues to hear "no female voice;" even as he apologizes to Melanie's mother and sister by dropping to his knees and touching his head to the floor, they are "astonished at the sight of him" and "fall silent" (173). If Lurie does "have it in him," the woman he can be is not Lucy but is instead Byron's Teresa in middle age, the woman whose story of betrayal David can imagine and enact through music. The opera he writes or will write is the dramatic performance of a bodily stance, a male-imagined and disgraced woman with whom Lurie clearly identifies.

In reading the character of Elizabeth Costello, the question arises, does Coetzee have it in him to be the woman, and more significantly, what does it mean to be the woman in the context of aged, feminist author, ex-colonial, and current vegetarian? Do we as critics have it in us to let Coetzee perform the woman, or do we call for Costello's position—or something like it—in Coetzee's own voice or in a voice that we can more easily and comfortably distinguish from Coetzee's? I know Coetzee is a vegetarian, and according to Attridge, in a description of two lunches, one with Derrida "who talks to [Attridge] about carnophallocentrism while eating with gusto a plate of steak tartare" ("Following Derrida") and a vegetarian lunch with Coetzee at Princeton before his Tanner Lectures, Coetzee lives that aspect of his ethical identity at least in his private life. Why mediate that position through a fictional woman? We cannot believe that Coetzee, "strictly observant of feminist rules," as Regina Janes claims, and "the first deliberately female-identified writer our tradition has produced" ("Writing," 107), is not deliberate in this enactment. Voicing a woman through fiction, Coetzee exposes the fallacious reasoning that there is any consistent notion of the "real," a claim that is further supported by the fact that Costello first rears her gray head in Coetzee's essay "What Is Realism?" Such a stance destabilizes binary oppositions and allows Coetzee a rant via Costello.

In *The Lives of Animals*, Coetzee foregrounds the content of Costello's lectures within the context of women's argumentative strategies—not only those of the empathetic Costello but also those of the philosophical Norma. These strategies are ultimately negotiated by Costello's somewhat patronizing son, John Bernard, who considers his mother's interest in animal rights a "hobby horse." What is therefore enacted by Coetzee is a debate that takes place primarily between two women, a debate reluctantly mediated by the auspiciously named John, who "has no opinions one way or the other" (17) about animal rights and who wonders why his mother cannot just stay home and care for her cats. Through John, the man who refuses to voice a position, Coetzee writes himself into the text while he simultaneously uses the power of women's rhetorical strategies about animal rights, a largely dismissed debate, to overwhelm and silence his own potential argument. In many ways, it is safe way out, this kind of performance, allowing us to pick apart not only Costello's problematic animal rights thesis but also to denounce the mode of that argument as sentimental or hyperbolic.

Furthermore, both Norma and Elizabeth's argumentative strategies constitute emotional "rants" when interpreted by John and his colleagues as well as (more often than not) by Coetzee's critics. Norma reacts bodily, "sighs" and "snorts" (32), during Costello's primary argument in "The Philosophers and the Animals" that to claim that "the meat industry is ultimately devoted to life . . . is to ask the dead of Treblinka to excuse their killers because their body fat was needed to make soap" (22). Furthermore, Costello's response to the treatment of animals is also bodily and therefore sentimental, as expressed through the self-righteous vegetarianism she practices to "save [her] soul"(43) and through her breakdown at the end of the narrative. But because Costello is voiced by Coetzee through his authorship of her speeches and through his literal voicing when he read them at Princeton, the gendering of her position is problematized. Terms like *rant, sentiment,* and *emotion* cease to find stability within a dualistic paradigm; that Costello is effectively written out of critical debate is illustrative of women's relative invisibility within the codification of philosophical argument. Costello presents an academically sanctioned argument, and as an oral presentation characterized by "acrimony, hostility, bitterness" (67), that argument serves to polarize her audience. Polarization, we want to tell her, is not the right strategy to employ in an argument, but such a claim returns us to some very binary thinking: either one provides a measured and well-reasoned philosophical commentary on the subject, or one is disqualified from the debate.

I want to give the character of Elizabeth Costello a feminist reading, even though it has always been hard for me to argue for feminism in Coetzee's texts, especially in *The Lives of Animals,* a text in which both Elizabeth and Norma are utterly intolerant of one another. As the narrator says, "Elizabeth does not like to see meat on the table, while Norma refuses to change the children's diet to accommodate what she calls 'your mother's delicate sensibilities'" (16). Furthermore, both women are silenced by John who tells his wife, "Norma, you're ranting" (68) and patronizingly placates Elizabeth's tears by telling her, "[T]here, there. It will soon be over" (69). Yet one of the strengths of Coetzee's text is that it does present the plight of the woman with strong ethical convictions: Elizabeth runs the risk of being silenced not only by other men, but also by other women, especially if her convictions are marginal to the dominant set of acceptable standards, and especially by women who have privileged rationality over feeling, as Norma has. As the narrator states, Norma "has never hesitated to tell [John] that his mother's . . . ethical relations with animals are jejune and sentimental" (17). Norma's willingness to embrace rationalist philosophy, to argue that "there is no position outside of reason where you can stand and lecture about reason and pass judgement on reason" (48), puts her at odds with Costello, who has concluded after "seven decades of life experience" that "reason is neither the being of the universe nor the being of God" (23). Furthermore, the language of female madness and gender-specific inferiority pervades this text, with Norma doing most of the name calling. She calls Elizabeth "confused" (36) and "naive" (47), her lectures "absurd" (67); she claims in response to John's assertion that his mother is sincere, "mad people are sincere" (67), and she asserts that Elizabeth's vegetarianism is mere food faddism, a "crazy scheme" (68). In conjunction, Elizabeth fights back, goading Norma by asking why the children are not eating with them, even though "she knows the answer" (16). Positioned as he is between the two women and despite his lack of stance (he says "I have no insight into my motives and I couldn't care less" [67]), John is hardly a neutral player. His male privilege is the cause of Norma's gender-specific "bitterness" (17) because he finds a job when she is unable to do so, just as he is the reason his mother dislikes Norma, a point inherent in his realization that "his mother would have chosen not to like any woman he married" (17). Symbolically larger than one husband or one son, John comes to stand for the male indifference that blocks women's interactions and affection for one another; the animal rights argument, in turn, becomes the metaphysical space within which both women beg John—and Coetzee's critics beg him—to signify within the narrative and to engage with the dialogue.

By relaying the animal rights argument through the female characters of Elizabeth and Norma, Coetzee effectively does several things, all of which have very much to do with femininity and feminism per se. Through the persona of Costello, Coetzee performs femininity and enacts embodiment in ways that counteract the masculinized notion of intellectual production Eugene Dawn, protagonist of "The Vietnam Project," describes in Coetzee's first work of fiction, *Dusklands* (1974), as "the capacity to breed out of our own head" (26), the negation of the body that is, according to Judith Butler, the domain of women, slaves, animals, and children. According to Butler, man, therefore, "is without childhood, is not a primate and so is relieved of the necessity of eating, defecating, living and dying; one who is not a slave, but always a property holder; one whose language remains originary and untranslatable . . . a figure of disembodiment" (*Bodies*, 49). The animal rights argument delivered by Costello is, at its core, about bodies after all, regardless of our human ability to prove or disprove the existence of intellect as distinct from or enmeshed with those bodies. Such a claim is in line with feminist performance theory of the kind exemplified by Butler, combining, as Elin Diamond claims, the "most pressing questions of theatrical representation: Who is speaking and who is listening? Whose body is in view and whose is not? What is being represented, how, and with what effects? Who or what is in control?" (*Mimesis,* ii). Through performance, Coetzee illustrates the potential plight of the female philosopher who uses empathy as well as logic in her argument. Especially in the realm of animal rights, a discourse always in danger of being trivialized or deemed sentimental in nature, the empathetic voice—male or female—may always run the risk of being feminized; if that voice is in fact a female voice, it runs the risk of being hystericalized as well. This voice is only treated in such a way, however, when underscored by John, the male player in this drama, whose apathy functions to silence the competing arguments of the two women in his life. In this context, the connections between animal rights and women's rights come to the forefront. Just as, according to Carol J. Adams, "animals are made absent through language that renames dead bodies before consumers participate in eating them" (*Sexual Politics,* 42), the more emotional rhetorical stance of Costello is negated in favor of rationality, and Costello herself becomes the absent referent in discussions about Coetzee's project.

The connections between animal rights and women's rights, indeed between animal rights and human rights, have been very explicitly stated by feminist scholars who seek to destabilize the binary thinking that designates animals as different from humans within the realm of rights. The underlying ecofeminist theory in works like Marjorie Spiegel's *The Dreaded Comparison: Human and Animal Slavery,* Lori Gruen's "Dismantling Oppression: An Analysis of the Connection Between Women and Animals," and Carol J. Adams's *The Sexual Politics of Meat: A Feminist-Vegetarian Critical Theory* is holistic in nature: humans learn to "other" humans in their othering of animals. Animal rights philosopher Charles Patterson supports the feminist claim that "the sexual subjugation of women, as practiced in all the known civilizations of the world, was modeled on the domestication of animals" (*Treblinka,* 12). To unlearn what I have termed this primary binary opposition, that of animal/human, is to begin to undo oppression from the ground up. But although women very often do the manual and emotional labor within the animal rights movement (Gruen, "Oppression," 81)—just as Bev Shaw is the person who euthanizes the animals in *Disgrace* while David disposes of their bodies—male philosophers like Tom Regan and Peter Singer, philosophers who privilege another either/or system of philosophical thought by advocating either an animal rights agenda based on natural rights theory or on utilitarianism, tend to get most of the credit.[4] It is therefore worth noting that in critical debate about *Lives*, the more rational aspects of the animal rights argument are attributed to Coetzee, while the excitable speech inherent in the rant is attributed to Costello.

Part of the rather obvious reason for the division of power and labor in the realm of animal rights is that philosophical rhetoric privileges reason over emotion. According to Josephine Donovan, Peter Singer's fear "that to associate the animal rights cause with 'womanish' sentiment is to trivialize it" ("Animal Rights," 167) is responsible for the contempt he expresses in the preface of *Animal Liberation* when he discusses a woman who claimed to love animals but proceeded to eat a ham sandwich and ask him about his pets. According to Gruen, the categories of woman and animal serve the same symbolic function in patriarchal society, a connection constructed as a means of oppression ("Oppression," 61). Furthermore, "by focusing on the role of reason in moral deliberation, these philosophers [Regan and Singer] perpetuate an unnecessary dichotomy between reason and emotion" (79). I do not mean to imply that things are stationary; with an emergent body of feminist/humanist/ecological theory,[5] women's voices are claiming a predominant place expressing a more inclusive and holistic stance. Furthermore, essayist and novelist Joy Williams's collection, *Ill Nature* opens up a space for the diatribe, the rant, a highly personal and at times angry philosophical exploration akin to Costello's and Norma's modes of discourse. Essentially, Williams reclaims *rant*, a term whose connotations are negative and feminine; in her essay, "Why I Write," Williams claims that her nonfictional style is "elusive and strident," meant "to annoy and trouble and polarize" (3). While polarization might seem counterintuitive to any stance that opposes dichotomous thinking, Williams consciously claims such a position just as Costello concedes, "reason is the being of a certain species of human thinking" (*Lives,* 23). By virtue of disrupting a model that allows for only two options, the rational and the emotional, authors like Williams and Coetzee validate the rant as one form of argument among various others.

That a male voice reads Costello's problematic thesis, that the slaughter of animals in contemporary cultures is analogous to the Holocaust, pushes an already precariously balanced argument over the rhetorical precipice.

The woman as conduit for such an argument marks such a comparison as excessive. Elizabeth Costello even admits to an excess of feeling, embracing the rhetoric that designates and negates her as hysterical, when she breaks down and cries to her son John at the end of the narrative: "I seem to move around perfectly easily among people, to have perfectly normal relations with them. Is it possible, I ask myself, that all of them are participants in a crime of stupefying proportions? Am I fantasizing it all? I must be mad!" (69). Yet Isaac Bashevis Singer made the same claim before Costello, and his statement from "The Writer," that "in relationship to [animals], all people are Nazis; for the animals, it is an eternal Treblinka" (271), forms the title of Charles Patterson's 2002 release of *Eternal Treblinka: Our Treatment of Animals and the Holocaust*. It would seem that since this book is being heralded as perhaps the most important animal rights text since Peter Singer's *Animal Liberation* (Akers, "Questions"), the contentious Holocaust comparison is one whose time has come. But a look at the history of the animal rights movement in the United States and an examination of the plight of Elizabeth Costello makes clear the frustration that women have long experienced in the formulation of the kind of ethical philosophy for which Patterson is receiving so much praise. Very often the female voice has been quieted, removed from the intellectual debate by the time that debate reaches a codified context, and what is considered radical when presented from a male perspective is often considered hysterical when it comes from a woman. The overarching complaint among the feminist animal rights theorists discussed in this essay is with the pervasive acceptance of normative dualism within natural rights and utilitarian schools of thought, a binary paradigm that privileges reason over emotion, rational philosophy over rant.

Gruen states that "one way to overcome the false dualism between reason and emotion is by moving out of the realm of abstraction and getting closer to the effects of our everyday actions" ("Oppression," 79). Perhaps, then, we are talking about matters of consistency. If in fact we do take inventory of our daily lives, we see the places where our speech—academic, excitable, didactic—and our actions are incongruous with one another. And perhaps the primary role of ethics in intellectual practice is to cultivate an awareness of those inconsistencies and look for ways to start simply with action and then to write about the results. Viewed from a linear perspective, South Africa, as elsewhere, testifies to the fact that addressing any problem at the tail end of history will do nothing to undo the damage caused by oppressive regiments; ending apartheid, for example, has not put an end to racial strife in South Africa. Although the Truth and Reconciliation Commission succeeded on one level in that it "rendered some lies about the past impossible to repeat," according to Michael Ignatieff, "South Africa remains what it is: a society where a person's chances in life are still determined by the colour of their skin" (Introduction to *Truth and Lies*, 20). Similarly, at a recent lecture at the University of Massachusetts, Amherst, South African author Sindiwe Magona stated her belief that in order for change to take place, the South African people must pay attention to township children. She said, "the measure of a society is how it treats its weakest." Such an assertion is essentially a preemptive and feminist strategy that rejects a linear notion of progress: Magona does not call for a return to a mythological pre-apartheid South Africa, nor does she seek the symbolic overthrow of apartheid institutions. She does seek to begin at a new place, however, to give voice to another voiceless other, the South African township child. The TRC, while it made the past impossible to deny according to Magona, did not deal with anything but "gross human rights violations." Because of the nature of the violations, therefore, "you are only then looking at the stars of oppression," not the small injustices that contribute to the legacy of Apartheid ("South Africa").

In *The Lives of Animals,* Coetzee examines the way we treat our weakest while he demonstrates the ethical conflicts and at times apparent impossibilities of holistic thinking that subvert notions of genre, dualism, and linearity. Conversely, in their unwillingness to allow Coetzee a performative and feminist enactment of an ethical stance, his critics have historically illustrated the limitations of the sympathetic imagination with regard to the character of Elizabeth Costello. But Coetzee's recent receipt of the Nobel Prize and the subsequent publication of *Elizabeth Costello* (2003) mark a historical literary moment during which this particular protagonist may get her theoretical due. Judith Shulevitz, in her review of the novel, questions the notion that Coetzee "seems to have found his alter ego" by examining the performative nature of Coetzee's project: "perhaps the way to look at

Costello is as just one player in a series of narratives that in their very sparseness achieve the dramatic tension of philosophical dialogue" ("Tour," 15). On October 22, 2003, I was present as Coetzee read the eighth lesson from *Elizabeth Costello*, "At the Gate," at the University of Massachusetts's annual Troy Lecture. In this narrative, Elizabeth Costello finds herself in a sort of Kafkaesque purgatory—and she realizes the literary references that abound, claiming, "the wall, the gate, the sentry, are straight out of Kafka" (*Costello*, 209). In order to pass through the gate, she must submit a statement of her beliefs to a panel of judges.

Coetzee's reading of the narrator's commentary and Costello's responses to her situation, her various and unsuccessful statements of belief, places his voice in dialogue with this, his contentious and complicated protagonist, and allows them both to discuss the layers of the performances in which they are involved. Coetzee, standing before his audience at UMass, asked Elizabeth Costello, "what would true stubbornness, true grit, consist of anyway but going through with the performance, no matter what?" (207) and she seemed to answer, "I do not give shows. . . . I am not an entertainer" (214). What emerges from Coetzee's conversation with Costello is the recognition of a kind of textual slippage, an uncomfortable acknowledgment of the parody at work, the mimetic nature of both writing and performance, "the gap between the actors and the parts they play, between the world it is given her to see and what the world stands for" (209). "At the Gate," and specifically Coetzee's performance of it, constitutes a kind of "meta," a meta-metafiction that should, by all logic, ring hollow at such a far remove from some agreed upon construct known as the truth. But, of course, it does not ring hollow at all, and the "real" that is cast back through the fiction becomes a reflection, the simulacrum, the thing beyond the gate that, "while bright, is not unimaginable at all" (196).

By enacting Elizabeth Costello in *The Lives of Animals*, Coetzee gets a rant and a sentimental voice presented through a rational argument, no matter how excessive any given audience may find that argument; he can illustrate the complexities of a lived ethical stance within the context of an intellectual presentation that runs up against literary and critical negotiations of the master narrative of philosophical debate. Costello's spoken animal rights argument within Coetzee's text is on the one hand about our treatment animals, both human and nonhuman, but it is also a rhetorical exercise of the sympathetic imagination and the role that imagining plays in breaking down binary distinctions. His performance of Elizabeth Costello restores the absent referent to the narrative, but her invisibility as an entity worthy of critical debate points to the resilience of those dualistic categories, the difficulty of ethical human change through identification with other lives including the lives of animals. As Joy Williams claims, "the animal people are calling for a moral attitude toward a great and mysterious mute nation. Their quest is quixotic; their reasoning assailable; their intentions, almost inarticulate. The implementation of their wisdom would seem madness. But the future world is not this one. Our treatment of animals and our attitude toward them are crucial not only to any pretensions we have to ethical behavior but to humankind's intellectual and moral evolution. Which is how the human animal is meant to evolve, isn't it?" (*Nature,* 177). The mediating and logical voice of John asks Elizabeth, "Do you really believe, Mother, that poetry classes are going to close down the slaughterhouses?" (*Lives,* 58). And one could ask Coetzee the same question of his own literature, a question that he is perhaps asking of himself and of us when he performs the character of Elizabeth Costello, the embodied presence that not only rants but also acts through the medium of fiction.

Notes

1. The eight lessons are "Realism," "The Novel in Africa," "The Lives of Animals: The Philosophers and the Animals," "The Lives of Animals: The Poets and the Animals," "The Humanities in Africa," "The Problem of Evil," "Eros," and "At the Gate."

2. Several "reflections" by various critics follow the two parts of *The Lives of Animals;* Singer's is on 85–91.

3. See, for example, Manus, "*Heart of the Country*"; Collingwood-Whittick, "Shadow of Last Things"; DuPlessis, "Bodies and Signs."

4. According to Lori Gruen's ecofeminist, animal rights critique in "Dismantling Oppression," "two of the most popular theories which call for animal liberation are the rights-based theory of Tom Regan and the utilitarian theory of Peter Singer. . . . According to Regan, at the very least all mentally normal mammals of a year or more are subjects-of-a-life and thus have inherent value that grounds their rights. Singer's view is based not on rights, but rather on the principle of equal consideration. According to Singer, all beings who are capable of feeling pain and pleasure are subjects of moral

consideration." Furthermore, Gruen claims that "while both of these theories argue for the inclusion of animals in the moral sphere, they rely on reason and abstraction in order to succeed," and therefore, "these philosophers perpetuate an unnecessary dichotomy between reason and emotion" (78–79).

5. See, for example, Peterson, *Being Human.*

Bibliography

Adams, Carol J. *The Sexual Politics of Meat: A Feminist-Vegetarian Critical Theory.* New York: Continuum, 1996.

Akers, Keith. "Asking the Big Questions." *Vegetarian Society of Colorado,* March 4, 2003. http://www.vsc.org/0502-Eternal-Treblinka.htm.

Attridge, Derek. "Expecting the Unexpected in Coetzee's *The Master of Petersburg* and Derrida's Recent Writings." In *Applying: to Derrida,* edited by John Brannigan, Ruth Robbins, and Julian Wolfreys, 21–40. New York: St. Martins, 1996.

———. "Following Derrida." *Tympanum* 4 (2000). http://www.usc.edu/dept/complit/tympanum/4/attridge.html.

———. "Knowledge and Narratives: Coetzee's Early Fiction." Paper presented at "J. M. Coetzee and the Ethics of Intellectual Practice: An International Conference," University of Warwick, Coventry, April 27, 2002.

Attwell, David. "The Life and Times of Elizabeth Costello." Paper presented at "J. M. Coetzee and the Ethics of Intellectual Practice"; ch. 1 of this volume.

Bell, Michael. "What Is It Like to Be a Non-Racist?" Paper presented at "J. M. Coetzee and the Ethics of Intellectual Practice"; ch. 9 of this volume.

Briggs, Austin. "Who's Who When Everybody's at Home: James Joyce/J. M. Coetzee/Elizabeth Costello." *James Joyce Literary Supplement* 16, no. 1 (2002): 11.

Butler, Judith. *Bodies That Matter: On the Discursive Limits of "Sex."* New York: Routledge, 1993.

———. *Excitable Speech: A Politics of the Performative.* New York: Routledge, 1997.

Clingman, Stephen. *The Novels of Nadine Gordimer: History from the Inside.* London: Allen and Unwin, 1986.

Coetzee, J. M. *Age of Iron.* 1990. London: Penguin, 1991.

———. *Boyhood.* New York: Penguin, 1997.

———. "Confession and Double Thoughts: Tolstoy, Rousseau, Dostoevsky." In *Doubling the Point: Essays and Interviews,* edited by David Attwell, 251–93. Cambridge: Harvard University Press, 1992.

———. *Disgrace.* New York: Penguin, 1999.

———. *Dusklands.* New York: Penguin, 1982.

———. *Elizabeth Costello.* New York: Viking, 2003.

———. *Foe.* 1986. Middlesex: Penguin, 1987.

———. *In the Heart of the Country.* 1977. Harmondsworth: Penguin, 1982.

————. *The Lives of Animals*. Princeton: Princeton University Press, 1999.

————. "The Sympathetic Imagination: A Conversation with J. M. Coetzee," by Eleanor Wachtel. *Brick: A Literary Journal* 67, no. 1 (2001): 37–47.

————. "Two Interviews with J. M. Coetzee, 1983 and 1987," by Tony Morphet. *Tri-Quarterly* 68/69 (1987): 454–64.

————. "Voice and Trajectory: An Interview with J. M. Coetzee," by Joanna Scott. *Salmagundi* 114–15 (1997): 82–102.

Collingwood-Whittick, Sheila. "In the Shadow of Last Things: The Voice of the Confessant in J. M. Coetzee's *Age of Iron.*" *Commonwealth Essays and Studies* 19, no. 1 (1996): 43–59.

Diamond, Elin. *Unmaking Mimesis: Essays on Feminism and Theater.* London: Routledge, 1997.

Dodd, Josephine. "The South African Literary Establishment and the Textual Production 'Woman': J. M. Coetzee and Lewis Nkosi." *Current Writing* 2, no. 1 (1990): 117–29.

Donovan, Josephine. "Animal Rights and Feminist Theory." In Gaard, *Ecofeminism,* 167–94.

DuPlessis, Michael. "Bodies and Signs: Inscriptions of Femininity in John Coetzee and Wilma Stockenstrom." *Journal of Literary Studies/Tydskrif vir Literatuurwetenskap* 4, no. 1 (1988): 118–28.

Durrant, Sam. "J. M. Coetzee, Elizabeth Costello, and the Limits of the Sympathetic Imagination." Paper presented at "J. M. Coetzee and the Ethics of Intellectual Practice"; ch. 6 of this volume.

Gaard, Greta. "Living Interconnections with Animals and Nature." In *Ecofeminism,* 1–12.

————, ed. *Ecofeminism: Women, Animals, and Nature.* Philadelphia: Temple University Press, 1993.

Gruen, Lori. "Dismantling Oppression: An Analysis of the Connection between Women and Animals." In Gaard, *Ecofeminism,* 60–90.

Gutmann, Amy. Introduction to Coetzee, *Lives of Animals.*

Head, Dominic. "Coetzee and the Animals: The Quest for Postcolonial Grace." Paper presented at "J. M. Coetzee and the Ethics of Intellectual Practice."

Ignatieff, Michael. Introduction to *Truth and Lies: Stories from the Truth and Reconciliation Commission in South Africa,* by Jillian Edelstein, 15–21. New York: New Press, 2001.

Janes, Regina. "'Writing without Authority': J. M. Coetzee and His Fictions." *Salmagundi* 114–15 (1997): 103–21.

Kossew, Sue. "'Women's Words': A Reading of J. M. Coetzee's Women Narrators." *Span* 37, no. 1 (1993): 12–23.

Magona, Sindiwe. "South Africa Now: What the Truth and Reconciliation Commission Left Out." Public lecture, University of Massachusetts, Amherst, April 11, 2002.

Manus, Vicki Briault. "*In the Heart of the Country:* A Voice in a Vacuum." *Commonwealth Essays and Studies* 19, no. 1 (1996): 60–70.

Marais, Michael. "Death and the Space of the Response to the Other in J. M. Coetzee's *The Master of Petersburg.*" Paper presented at "J. M. Coetzee and the Ethics of Intellectual Practice"; ch. 4 of this volume.

Patterson, Charles. *Eternal Treblinka: Our Treatment of Animals and the Holocaust.* New York: Lantern Books, 2002.

Petersen, Kirsten Holst. "An Elaborate Dead End? A Feminist Reading of Coetzee's *Foe.*" In *A Shaping of Connections: Commonwealth Literature Studies, Then and Now,* edited by Hena Maes-Jelinek, Kirsten Holst-Petersen, and Anna Rutherford, 243–52. Sydney: Dangaroo Press, 1989.

Peterson, Anna L. *Being Human: Ethics, Environment, and Our Place in the World.* Berkeley: University of California Press, 2001.

Pollan, Michael. "The Unnatural Idea of Animal Rights." *New York Times Magazine,* November 10, 2002, sec. 6, pp. 59–64, 100, 110–11.

Rose, Jacqueline. "Apathy and Accountability: South Africa's Truth and Reconciliation Commission." *Raritan* 21, no. 4 (2002): 175–95.

Shulevitz, Judith. "Author Tour." Review of *Elizabeth Costello,* by J. M. Coetzee. *New York Times Book Review,* October 26, 2003, 15–16.

Singer, Isaac Bashevis. *The Collected Stories of Isaac Bashevis Singer.* New York: Noonday Press, 1996.

Spiegel, Marjorie. *The Dreaded Comparison: Human and Animal Slavery.* Rev. ed. New York: Mirror Books, 1996.

Susskind, Anne. "The Émigré." *Bulletin with Newsweek,* April 9, 2001. http://bulletin.ninemsn.com.au/bulletin/eddesk.nsf/All/8BFC696B399A2924CA256ABD0048EDE4?open&ui=dom&template=domPrint.

Williams, Joy. *Ill Nature: Rants and Reflections on Humanity and Other Animals.* New York: Lyons Press, 2001.

11

TEXTUAL TRANSVESTISM

The Female Voices of J. M. Coetzee

Lucy Graham

> No, he tells himself, that is not where I come from, that is not it.
>
> —John in *Elizabeth Costello*

Elizabeth Costello (2003), which is made up of eight "lessons" and a post-script, has been the subject of a number of prominent reviews, including a recent appraisal in the *Times Literary Supplement,* which features a cartoon of Coetzee standing at a lectern in drag, as Elizabeth Costello (Wateridge, 5). Encapsulating the notion of Costello as a persona or an alter ego for the writer himself, the cartoon draws attention to the mode of "textual trans-vestism" that Coetzee has deployed in recent public lectures. Yet commenta-tors have disagreed as to the extent of Coetzee's investment in, or distance from, the character of Costello. David Lodge writes that "the question of how far we are meant to identify with [Costello] and her opinions per-sists, partly because of the teasing similarities between her and her creator" ("Disturbing," 6). In a review entitled "Alter Ego," the South African writer

Roy Robins claims that "occasionally Costello sounds like David Lurie. . . . But most of all, she sounds like Coetzee" (50). James Wood, writing for the *London Review of Books,* suggests that Coetzee's own confession lies behind Costello's words: "that Coetzee is passionately confessing, and that his entire book vibrates with confession" ("Frog's Life," 16). Two letters contesting that interpretation appeared the following week. In her letter, Mary Elkins from Stockport argues that Costello makes absurd claims that Coetzee would never entertain. Likewise, Mattias Brinkman from Minnesota maintains that Costello is not "preaching somebody's lesson," and that "the only thing [Coetzee] confesses to in the book is the elusiveness Wood won't allow him."

Critics who acknowledge Coetzee's "elusiveness" and the distance between Coetzee and Costello, however, may see Coetzee's use of Costello as mere evasiveness, as a distancing device, and some have expressed impatience with his apparent reluctance to take a stand himself. Oliver Herford writes that "Coetzee's studied withdrawal from the scene of his fiction becomes irritating and perhaps culpable" ("Tears," 6), and philosopher Peter Singer, in his response to Coetzee's *The Lives of Animals,*[1] claims, "Costello can blithely criticize the use of reason, or the need to have any clear principles and proscriptions, without Coetzee really committing himself to those claims. Maybe he really shares Norma's very proper doubts about them. Coetzee doesn't even have to worry too much about getting the structure of the lecture right. When he notices that it is starting to ramble, he just has Norma say that Costello is rambling!" (in *Lives,* 91). In a similar though less critical line of argument, Hermione Lee has proposed that Coetzee is "guarding his own beliefs inside [Costello's] 'beliefs' and arguments" ("Silence").

Commentators who assume that, in the case of Elizabeth Costello, Coetzee is confessing, and those who draw attention to his failure to confess, share an assumption that not only relies on a notion of the author as site of origin but also fails to take into account the splitting of selfhood that accompanies the writing enterprise. As I intend to argue, the question of origins—of who is anterior to whom—is figured and playfully challenged within the text of *Elizabeth Costello.* Furthermore, the *Costello* collection is not the first instance of Coetzee foregrounding a female voice. The "lessons" that make up *Elizabeth Costello* should be seen in the context of a tradition of female articulation in Coetzee's oeuvre. Like Costello, Magda in Coetzee's *In the Heart of the Country* (1977), Susan Barton in *Foe* (1986), and Elizabeth Curren in *Age of Iron* (1990) are women who write and reflect on the processes of writing. As this chapter demonstrates, the women in Coetzee's fiction play an important role in interrogating discourses of authority and origin.

"Not Where I Come From"

The first lesson of *Elizabeth Costello* (2003), entitled "Realism," concludes with a peculiar image of childbirth that is simultaneously misplaced, inverted, and negated. John, the son of Elizabeth Costello, looks into his mother's mouth, and down her throat, registering the sight with a mixture of fascination and discomfort:

> She lies slumped in her seat. Her head is sideways, her mouth open. She is snoring faintly. . . . He can see up her nostrils, into her mouth, down the back of her throat. And what he cannot see he can imagine: the gullet, pink and ugly, contracting as it swallows, like a python, drawing things down to the pear-shaped belly-sac. He draws away, tightens his own belt, sits up, facing forward. No, he tells himself, that is not where I come from, that is not it. (33–34)

The realism of this description belies a moment in the narrative that is self-reflexive on a number of levels. John's assertion that he does not come from his mother's mouth plays on an image of ventriloquism, on Costello as a mouthpiece for John Coetzee, a notion that is both uncannily recognized and rejected. Yet the play on "John" as articulating Coetzee's refusal is also challenged. If John is a stand-in for Coetzee, then his relationship with Costello disrupts the idea of characters and the text being parented by the author, since John is Costello's child, rather than her parent. The relationship of anteriority between Coetzee and Costello is thus called into question. On another level, the relationship between Costello and her son could also be read in terms of a Borgesian splitting of authorial identity, between the author, figured by Costello (Costello is a near anagram for

Coetzee), and the man, John.[2] In this reading, John, the man, could be re-fusing what J. M. Coetzee, the author and public figure, has made of him. Such a fracturing would complicate any attempt to trace origin back to the "one" who writes.

Costello made her first appearance (in Coetzee's fiction) in this essay, which was originally entitled "What Is Realism?" (delivered by Coetzee as the Ben Belitt Lecture in 1996 at Bennington College in Vermont). Here Coetzee introduced Costello as an elderly Australian-born author who has attained international fame, most notably on account of one of her early books, a rewriting of Joyce's *Ulysses*. In an impulse that calls to mind the emphasis on women's voices in Coetzee's fiction, Costello has supposedly rescripted this classic from the perspective of Molly Bloom. In Coetzee's story, Costello has herself been pressed to give a public address, and her lecture, which is also entitled "What Is Realism?" is enclosed within and mirrors Coetzee's lecture. Emphasizing the organs of speech, the overdeter-mined image that concludes Coetzee's piece reflects on the nature of the public lecture itself. The digestive tract, "contracting as it swallows, like a python" and culminating in "the pear-shaped belly-sac" of the stomach, is used to figure the lifeless "constriction" of identity that is related to the no-tion of forging origin in utterances.

Yet presumably the reproductive tract, the womb, though offstage, is acknowledged as a site of generation. John says of his mother, "Out of her very body I came, caterwauling" (28). Furthermore, in her lecture, Costello refers to her first book as her "first-born" (17), linking her to Coetzee's other female protagonists, who use images of birth to figure the literary process and to interrogate various types of discursive authority. Though Magda, the protagonist of *In the Heart of the Country*, suspects that she is barren, she nonetheless speculates on the possibility of giving birth to an "Antichrist of the desert" or "a litter of runty rat-like girls" (10). Her inability to bear children presents a subversion of the *vrou en moeder* (wife and mother) eu-logized in Afrikaner nationalist discourse, and her imagined children are direct parodies of the Afrikaner ideal. Her challenge to discursive authority also extends to that of her "father-tongue" (42). She writes, "Labouring under my father's weight I struggle to give birth to a world but seem to en-gender only death" (10). This laboring has a double meaning, joining and separating procreation and literary creativity. Thus Magda's "struggle to give birth" makes a connection between procreation and her desire to create "a language of the heart" to commune with the black laborers on her father's farm. Her attempt is abortive, however, as the oppressive language of her father, in which she seems to be trapped, ensures that she will "engender only death."

Foe, which rescripts the story of *Robinson Crusoe* from the perspective of a woman named Susan Barton,[3] draws on two gendered figures for literary creativity. The novel's dilemma is to negotiate a position of authorial power —*Foe* has been described, by Coetzee, as an "interrogation of authority" (*Doubling,* 247). Speaking of Susan Barton's position in an interview with Tony Morphet, he asked, "How can one question power from a position of power? One ought to question it from its antagonist position, namely the position of weakness" ("Almighty Pen"). Susan's position of weakness, it would seem, is directly related to her status as author*ess.* The solution she is granted in her search for authority is her attempt to appropriate literary power, in the form of the pen as phallus. Taking up the writing implement of the male author, (De)Foe, Susan writes, "the pen becomes mine as I write with it" (*Foe,* 66). In *Foe* authorship is also figured, via the image of childbirth, as a means of attaining immortality. Foe tells Susan the parable of a woman, condemned to die, who ensured the safety of her infant daughter and then said to her executioners, "Now you may do with me as you wish. For I have escaped your prison; all you have now is the husk of me." Foe goes on to say that the woman was referring to "the husk that the butterfly leaves behind when it is born," and confides that "there are more ways than one of living eternally" (125). This image of the mother's dead body as an empty husk from which the child-butterfly emerges resonates throughout Coetzee's next novel, *Age of Iron,* and is also echoed in the first story of the Costello collection.

Set in South Africa in the late 1980s, *Age of Iron* takes the form of a mother's letter to her daughter. The protagonist of the novel, Elizabeth Curren, is dying of cancer and argues for a story that she claims has little or no authority in the apartheid-era circumstances in which she finds herself. She likens herself to "one of those Chinese mothers who knows that their child will be taken away from them if it is a daughter, and done away with, because the need . . . is for sons with strong arms" (132). The daughter text, words from the womb, becomes a counter to discourses of power that ultimately demand male strength and authority. She claims, "I am just a shell, the shell my child has left behind" (69). Curren describes her soul as "a white moth, a ghost emerging from the mouth of the figure on the deathbed" (118). This moth, comparable to the butterfly in Foe's tale, may be read as a figure for the text itself, as Curren says: "the moth is simply what will brush your cheek ever so lightly as you put down the last page of this letter, before it flutters off on its next journey" (119). In a play on "the death of the author," such a trope does not rely on the notion of the powerful father-author and affords the text a life of its own. Elizabeth Costello, however, presents a more skeptical version of "living on" through literary creations.

In what appears to be a confession, Costello acknowledges in her lecture, "What Is Realism?" that her impulse, following the publication of her first book, was to telephone her publishers to find out whether deposit copies had been sent "to Scotland and the Bodleian and so forth, but above all to the British Museum" (16). Costello presents the following explanation for her telephone call: "What lay beyond my concern about deposit copies was the wish that, even if I myself should be knocked over by a bus the next day, this first-born of mine would have a home where it could snooze, if fate so decreed, for the next hundred years, and no one would come poking with a stick to see if it was still alive. That was one side of my telephone call: if I, this mortal shell, am going to die, let me at least live on through my creations" (17). Alluding to the imagery in Foe and Age of Iron, this passage evokes a sense of the writer as a dead "shell" and the text as a child. Costello, however, also appears to recognize the narcissism and pathos of the desire that may underlie the image. Her "ambition," she admits, was to have her place "on the shelves of the British Museum, rubbing shoulders with the other C's, the great ones" (16). Acknowledging the futility of a belief in literary immortalization, she dispels this as a humanist illusion: "But of course the British Museum or (now) the British Library is not going to live forever. It too will crumble and decay, and the books on its shelves turn to powder" (17).

Seen in the light of Costello's "ambition," the image of the text as child is not necessarily a challenge to authorship and authority. Furthermore, the "immortality" afforded in the view of the text as "offspring" belongs to the same humanist ideology that constructed the dominating figure of the author. In *Elizabeth Costello,* however, another way of figuring the literary process is explored. Rather than being a site of authority, the writer is presented as a "medium" between one sphere of existence and another. In an image first articulated by her son, Costello is rendered as a "mouthpiece," but not for Coetzee. In the first lesson of *Elizabeth Costello,* John describes his mother as a "mouthpiece for the divine" (31).

The Medium

Six of the *Elizabeth Costello* stories were published in earlier forms. The third and fourth lessons in the collection were delivered as the 1997–98 Tanner Lectures at Princeton University and were published in 1999 as *The Lives of Animals.* The teasing inclusion of academic-style footnotes in this earlier published version of the two lessons plays on expectations that lectures delivered in an academic context should be critical or theoretical forays, rather than works of fiction. The footnotes were not published in *Elizabeth Costello,* but one of these original footnotes, published in the Princeton edition of *The Lives of Animals,* presents an interesting dilemma. In her argument against some of the "piddling distinctions" of philosophy, Costello paraphrases the philosopher Michael Leahy, who questions whether a veal calf "misses its mother." The footnote to this paraphrasing reads:

> Leahy, *Against Liberation,* 218. Leahy elsewhere argues against a ban on the slaughtering of animals on the grounds that (a) it would bring about unemployment among abattoir workers, (b) it would entail an uncomfortable adjustment to our diet, and (c) the countryside would be less attractive without its customary flocks and herds fattening themselves as they wait to die (214). (66)

Clearly, the voice that brings about this paraphrasing is not sympathetic to Leahy's argument.[4] A certain amount of sarcasm, for instance, is noticeable in the third, and final, summary point. *The Lives of Animals* is narrated in the third person, and the author of the work is "J. M. Coetzee." So to whom may we attribute the tone of this footnote, if not to J. M. Coetzee? Given the apparent similarity of opinions between J. M. Coetzee and Costello, are we to conclude that a male author is using a fictional woman as a front for presenting his own beliefs and values? If so, is the gender difference between Coetzee and Costello part of a trick to effect distancing? I do not propose to answer these questions, but wish to suggest what, as figured in Coetzee's fiction, may be at stake in answering them.

In *Foe,* Susan Barton draws attention to such questions when she asks, in a letter to (De)Foe, "Who is speaking me?" Alluding to the girl who claims to be her daughter, but who is lifted from the plot of *Roxana* and therefore "fathered" by (De)Foe, Susan writes, "I thought I was myself and this girl a creature from another order speaking words you made up for her. But now I am full of doubt. I am doubt itself. Who is speaking me? Am I a phantom too? To what order do I belong? And you: who are you?" (133). Susan's question directs itself to the author, (De)Foe, but also gestures outside the text, to the author, who may be "speaking" Susan herself. Her doubt thus draws attention to the bond of power between the author and his creatures. Yet the inverse of asking who is speaking through the voice in the text would be to ask, who or what is speaking through the writer? Such a question could potentially perform a displacement of the author as the site of origin.

In the eighth lesson of *Elizabeth Costello,* entitled "At the Gate," which takes the form of a parody of a "Kafkaesque" nightmare of the afterlife, Costello is asked to make a statement of her beliefs. This confession is to be presented before a panel of judges. Borrowing the phrase "secretary of the invisible" from the poet and Nobel laureate Czeslaw Milosz, she writes in her statement, "I am a writer, and what I write is what I hear. I am a secretary of the invisible, one of many secretaries over the ages. That is my calling: dictation secretary. It is not for me to interrogate, to judge what is given to me. I merely write down the words and then test them, test their soundness, to make sure I have heard right" (199). Offering a secular version of the writer as "mouthpiece for the divine," as a "scribe" through whom "the word" is conducted, such a likeness emphasizes the utterances in the text rather than the one who writes. There is a direct parallel between Costello as intermediary for the invisible, and the position of the judges in her trial, who are themselves proxies for the law. As in Kafka's "Before the

Law," the notion of the law remains ultimately invisible or opaque. Yet, rather than postulating herself as a proxy for the law—that is for truth—Costello presents herself as an agent in the service of the fictive, of that which has no claim to truth. Costello continues: "I am open to all voices. Not just the voices of the murdered and the violated. . . . if it is their murderers and violators who choose to summon me instead, to use me and speak through me, I will not close my ears to them, I will not judge them" (204). She protests that inflexible beliefs would hamper her task, and claims, "I change beliefs as I change my habitation or my clothes, according to my needs" (195). Drawing attention to the mutable nature of selfhood, but retaining ambivalence, she protests, "We change from day to day, and we also stay the same." Even after she presents an exposition detailing her belief in the lives of the frogs of Dulgannon, who rise from the mud after the rain as if from death,5 she wonders whether she may be "skipping with laden head from one belief to the other, from frogs to stones to flying machines" (223).

The allusion to flying machines calls to mind the protagonist of *In the Heart of the Country*, who, toward the end of her narrative, apparently hears voices speaking in "a Spanish of pure meanings." According to Magda, these voices bear messages from the machines that fly far above her. She explains that their dictations seem "to reach my ears by night, or more often in the early morning just before dawn, and to seep into my understanding, like water" (127). As was the case with Costello, such a figuration performs a subversion of the omnipotence of the author. Furthermore, it offers a challenge to the hierarchical binaries of a master-slave dynamic and is not incommensurate with the poststructuralist notion of the writer as a scriptor who is spoken by tradition and discourse itself.6 In response to the voices, Magda composes a poem in what she imagines to be their language, which ends "LA MEDIA ENTRE." She elaborates: "The medium! Between! . . . Why will no one speak to me in the true language of the heart? The medium, the median—that is what I wanted to be! Neither master nor slave, neither parent nor child, but the bridge between, so that in me the contraries should be reconciled" (131). Magda's desired language is a form of pure communication unmediated by "the language of hierarchy and distance" (10), which she associates with her father. The pun on *medium* playfully figures the writer as a medium who records voices from another realm of being but also calls attention to the imperfect medium of writing itself, to the failure of "a language of the heart." On this level, Magda's carefully portrayed hysteria presents a relationship between the crisis of the hysteric and that of literary modernism in the early twentieth century, making *In the Heart of the Country* relevant to a reading of the discursive "affliction" expressed in the postscript to the Costello collection.

"Where Is Home?"

The postscript to *Elizabeth Costello* takes the form of a fictitious letter written by Elizabeth Chandos, the wife of Philip Chandos. Lord Chandos is himself an invented character whose voice is presented in an essay by the poet and librettist Hugo von Hofmannsthal. Entitled simply "A Letter" and published in a Berlin newspaper in 1902, Hofmannsthal's essay purports to be an epistle, dated 1603, from Lord Chandos to Francis Bacon, the Renaissance philosopher and father of inductive reasoning. In the letter, Chandos explains why he has given up writing, claiming that he has been affected by an incapacity that makes any judgment or abstract concept seem to break down "like rotten mushrooms in [his] mouth" (*Chandos Letter,* 10). The essay is often cited as an example of the so-called crisis of language, or *Sprachkrise,* expressed by certain German and Austrian thinkers around 1900, and it has been credited as precipitating literary modernism. In an introduction to Hofmannsthal's essay, Michael Hofmann claims,

> It is surely no accident that [Hofmannsthal's] letter has been set three centuries back, in the period of high humanism, and that it is addressed to Francis Bacon, a quintessential Renaissance man, one of the last representatives of a time when one man might still hope to understand the whole range of human endeavour. It is not extravagant to think *A Letter* is in part a lament about the rise of science and the end of a universal language. . . . Only after it can the literature of our century begin: difficult, allusive, fragmented, gamesome, private, or brazenly old-fashioned. (Hofmann, viii)

Composed a century after Hofmannsthal's *Lord Chandos Letter,* the letter from Lady Chandos to Francis Bacon doubles back on the literary tradition in which Coetzee finds himself. Chandos refers to the presence of his wife once in his letter, when he confesses, "I lead a life of almost unbelievable emptiness, and find it difficult to conceal from my wife the deadness that is inside me" (Hofmannsthal, 17). This is picked up in the Lady Chandos letter, as Elizabeth writes: "no husband can succeed in concealing from a loving wife distress of mind so extreme" (Coetzee, *Costello*, 227).

The retrieval of a woman's voice from within a modernist text has, of course, a fictional parallel in Elizabeth Costello's recovery of Molly Bloom as the protagonist of *The House on Eccles Street*. And, as was the case with *Foe*, in the Lady Chandos letter Coetzee has engaged with a seminal literary text, writing from the perspective of a woman. Though Coetzee's Chandos letter is less a challenge to a literary forefather than an homage to Hofmannsthal's essay, both *Foe* and the Lady Chandos letter disrupt relationships of antecedence. Through Susan Barton and her narrative, *Foe* supplants Defoe's position as originator of *Robinson Crusoe* in an illusionistic manner. When Susan wonders what sort of story Foe will create out of her tale, she has a suspicion that he will decide, in his version, to omit her altogether: "'Better had there been only Cruso and Friday,' you will murmur to yourself: Better without the woman" (72). In Susan's fear that (De)Foe will edit her out of the final tale of the island, she is fictionally preempting the story of Defoe's *Robinson Crusoe*. In this way, Susan's story, scripted by Coetzee, is rendered by artifice as anterior to Defoe's novel. The fact that Defoe appears in *Foe* as a fictional character emphasizes the multilayered relationship between illusionism and anti-illusionism in Coetzee's novel and forecasts the inversions of fictional and authorial identity that take place in "He and his man," Coetzee's further rewriting of Defoe, as delivered in his Nobel Prize lecture in December 2003.

The letter in which Elizabeth Chandos adds her plea to that of her husband does not display an impulse to supplant a literary forefather as originator but, employing illusionistic strategies, places Elizabeth Chandos in a position that is historically anterior to that of Coetzee. In fact, this fictional historical anteriority is doubled, as the text of the Lady Chandos letter casts itself back, not only to the date of Hofmannsthal's composition of *The Lord Chandos Letter* (1902), but also to a date three centuries before Hofmannsthal's act of writing (1602), which is purported to be the date on which Lord Chandos took up his pen. The naming of Elizabeth Chandos, however, which seems to be intertextually overdetermined, locates her as subsequent to her most immediate predecessors, namely Coetzee's other female voices. Her signature, "Elizabeth C," situates her within a tradition that includes Elizabeth Curren and Elizabeth Costello, women who share her forename and the letter that begins Coetzee's surname. In his scripting of Elizabeth Chandos's letter, Coetzee is evidently reflecting on his own roots in literary modernism. Yet why would he use a female voice to do so? Since Elizabeth Chandos supposedly adjoins her voice to that of her husband, is her letter merely a supplement to the Hofmannsthal letter? As I intend to demonstrate, in the extent to which Lady Chandos draws attention to the slippage of figurative language in particular, her letter highlights not only the shortfall of rationalizing language but also the limits of "likeness," the very category on which Elizabeth Costello's arguments for empathy had been based in *The Lives of Animals*. Moreover, Coetzee's Chandos letter may draw attention to the importance of women's voices in forging the strategies of the literary avant-garde.

Francis Bacon, to whom both Chandos letters are addressed, is best known as the theorist of modern scientific method. Believing that the scientist should observe nature and thus achieve power over it, Bacon was famous for advocating an empirical approach and for his dictum "Knowledge is power." He shunned theological arguments about the supernatural,[7] claiming that "Books (such as are worthy of the name of books) ought to have no patrons but truth and reason," and that "Books must follow sciences, not sciences books." In the extent to which he emphasizes truth and reason, Bacon's view privileges philosophy or science above poetry or literature. Such a dissociation goes back at least as far as Plato and is evoked in the two-part structure of *The Lives of Animals*—"The Philosophers and the Animals" and "The Poets and the Animals"—where Elizabeth Costello challenges the privileged status accorded to reason. Noting Bacon's function in *The Lord Chandos Letter*, Ritchie Robertson claims, "Bacon figures here as the proponent of the scientific world-view. Hofmannsthal has projected back into the seventeenth century the question that agitated him and his contemporaries: what place is there for poetry in an age of reason?" ("Language"). Whereas Elizabeth Costello describes herself, via Milosz, as "a secretary of the invisible," Bacon was famously described by one of his contemporaries as "the great secretary of nature."[8]

Yet the Lady Chandos letter reveals a fundamental reliance on figurative language, on "untruths," that may lie at the heart of a seemly transparent scientific language. Bacon's essays and aphorisms themselves are riddled with metaphors, as is the letter of Lord Chandos. Though Philip Chandos draws attention to the inadequacy of words as a medium and avoids the "perilous metaphorical flights of Plato" (Hofmannsthal, *Letter,* 11), he nonetheless uses likenesses to elaborate on his state. His incapacity to use language to express judgment and truth he likens to the spreading of "a corrosive rust" (10). Describing his previous plans to gain "understanding of form, of that deep, true, inner form . . . something as glorious as music and algebra," he writes that his former projects now seem to him "like sad mosquitoes in front of a drab wall, on which the sun of happier days no longer shines" (6). Elizabeth Chandos, however, constantly draws attention to the figurative language she is using, allowing "likenesses" to unravel. She refers to day-to-day moments of revelation, which are sited in her body and elude full elaboration in language. Describing the raptures she experiences through moments of intimacy with her husband, she writes:

> Soul and body he speaks to me, in a speaking without speech; into me, soul and body, he presses what are no longer words but flaming swords.
>
> We are not meant to live thus. *Flaming swords* I say my Philip presses into me, swords that are not words; but they are neither flaming swords nor words. It is like a contagion, saying one thing always for another (*like a contagion,* I say: barely did I hold myself back from saying, *a plague of rats,* for rats are everywhere about us these days). (Coetzee, *Costello* postscript, 228; italics in original)

Though Elizabeth addresses herself to one who builds judgments "as a mason builds a wall with bricks" (230), the notion of accessing foundational or original truths through language breaks down in the slippage of her metaphorical language, such that the notions of truth, origin, and home are called into doubt. She writes: "Only for extreme souls may it have been intended to live thus, where words give way beneath your feet like rotting boards (like *rotting boards* I say again, I cannot help myself, not if I am to bring home to you my distress and my husband's, *bring home* I say, where is home?)" (228; italics in original). Like Costello, Elizabeth Chandos presents a challenge to the master discourse of philosophical or scientific rationalism. But in order to examine the significance of her voice, it is important to understand Coetzee's interest in "a history of self-cancelling literature" (*Doubling,* 61) and to place Hofmannsthal's representation of "a fit of madness" (Coetzee, *Costello* postscript, 227) within the context of literary modernism.

As David Attwell has suggested, Coetzee's essay on Achterberg's "Ballade van de Gasfitter," which was published in the same year as *In the Heart of the Country,* reveals Coetzee's interest in "a poetics of failure" (*Doubling,* 86). In this essay, Coetzee reads Achterberg's poem as a self-reflexive meditation on the relation between poet and poem, with God as an absence, or literally as a "hole." Similarly, Magda in *In the Heart of the Country,* with reference to her anatomy, describes herself as "a zero, null, a vacuum" (2), as "a hole with a body draped around it" (41). Thus a certain psychoanalytic conception of feminine identity becomes a figure for the predicament of the modern subject whose being is profoundly marked by nothingness. If Coetzee's early fiction plays out modernist strategies in a self-conscious way, then Magda's voice performs an important role in bringing, as Attwell proposes, "a modernist legacy into a specially charged encounter with history in the form of colonialism and apartheid" ("Truth," 89). Yet *In the Heart of the Country* may also be read as a portrait of hysteria, and as such the novel presents a relationship between the hystericized narrative and the formal experiments of literary modernism.

Hysteria had tremendous implications, not only for the development of psychoanalysis but also for literature and the history of ideas in the twentieth century. Aligned with post-Enlightenment critiques of reason, it features in the antirationalist manifestos of André Breton and Louis Aragon, for instance, where it is acclaimed as "the greatest poetic discovery of the latter nineteenth century" and as "a supreme means of expression" ("Hysteria," 143–44). Moreover, as Claire Kahane points out in *Passions of the Voice,* the elements we accept as characteristic of the avant-garde would have not been possible without the discourse of the hysteric. According to Kahane, the hystericized narrative provided one of the strongest metaphors for the fragmentation of the individual subject in the early twentieth century: "By the end of the second decade of the twentieth century, hysteria was both self-consciously thematized as a trope of literary modernism as well as formalized as a poetics that could more adequately represent the dislocations of the modern subject. In this sense one can say that hysterical narrative voice has not only preceded literary modernism but made it possible" (*Passions*, xv).

Freud and Breuer's *Studies on Hysteria* was published in 1895 and had a definite and almost immediate impact on Hofmannsthal. Though Hofmannsthal abandoned poetry entirely from the time of writing *The Lord Chandos Letter*,[9] his first play, *Elektra* (1903), immediately followed the letter. In this version of the ancient tale by Sophocles, Elektra is a psychologically real character who clearly resembles the young women in Freud's *Studies on Hysteria* (written with Josef Breuer). Whereas many of Hofmannsthal's lyric poems tended toward impressionism, the stark and forceful language of *Elektra*, which was later to become an opera,[10] is much more reminiscent of Coetzee's own style. Like Hofmannsthal's Elektra, Coetzee's Lady Chandos, whose name, Elizabeth, has resonance with that of Elektra, should also be read within the context of the relationship between women's utterances and literary modernism. Foregrounding the voice of a woman, the Lady Chandos letter subtly pays homage not only to Hofmannsthal or even to Freud but to the speaking women whose bodies acted out a wordless language of desire and whose narratives were to have a major impact on twentieth-century literature and culture.

I have focused on some of the positional and discursive possibilities afforded by Coetzee's use of female voices. Clearly, such a textual strategy, which enables a challenge to discourses of authority and anteriority, is singular to fiction, or storytelling. Coetzee has suggested that, for the writer, the act of "becoming" another sex, in the medium of fiction, itself presents a challenge to notions of origin. When asked, with reference to *In the Heart of the Country*, what it meant for him to "take on a female voice," Coetzee responded, "Is one, as a writer, at every level, sexed? Is there not a level where one is, if not presexual, then anterior to sex? First anterior to sex, then becoming sexed? At that level, or in that transition between levels, does one actually 'take on' the voice of another sex? Doesn't one 'become' another sex? On the other hand, I must ask myself, who is this 'one' who is anterior to Magda?" ("Voice," 91). Elizabeth Costello is similarly quizzed on her textual transvestism, by an interviewer who asks whether she found it "easy" to write from the position of a man in one of her novels. She replies, "Easy? No. If it were easy it wouldn't be worth doing. It is the otherness that is the challenge" (*Costello*, 12). As Coetzee suggests, the writing self may not be reducible to a "sexed" identity. And as Costello proposes, the challenge of writing may be to imagine one's way into the existence of an other. Yet the challenge of otherness is clearly not reducible to gender difference. What would "taking on" the voice of an other mean, if that other were not merely of another sex but outside the writer's cultural inscription, or even outside language altogether? What is at stake in "becoming" such an other? Is there even an act of writing that is anterior to the cultural inscription and literary tradition in which a writer finds her- or himself?

In his fiction, there is a difference between Coetzee's use of white women narrators and his representation of women who are culturally other—such as the Namaqua women in *Dusklands* (1974), the barbarian girl in *Waiting for the Barbarians* (1980), and even the marginalized black women on the farm in *Disgrace* (1999). It has often been noted that while Coetzee has scripted the voices of women who share his own cultural inscription, characters who are "racially other" are marked by silence or extremely limited speech. Yet the first-person female voices in Coetzee's fiction depend, in discursive terms, on their relation to a more radical otherness. The success or failure of Magda's "language of the heart," for instance, hinges on her communion with the black workers on her father's farm. In *Foe*, Susan's quest for authorship is set against the backdrop of a more radical otherness, that of Friday, the mute colonial subject. Susan acknowledges that Friday's absent story makes her story of the island "hold its silence" (117). Similarly, Elizabeth Curren's text depends for its life on Vercueil, the homeless tramp who takes up residence in Elizabeth's house, since she has entrusted the delivery of her manuscript to him.

It marks a departure in Coetzee's use of white female protagonists that, in the figuration of authorship in the Costello stories, there is no such cultural other on whom the fulfillment of a particular discourse depends. Perhaps, given the eloquence of a character such as the Nigerian writer Emmanuel Egudu, who meets with Costello in *The Novel in Africa*, the debate should move on from a distinction between "the obsessional will to utterance in Coetzee's female and European narrators" and the "inaudibility" of his (post)colonial subjects (Parry, "Speech," 47–48). As we have seen, by representing the writer as an intermediary, as a "medium," Coetzee stages an abdication from a position of authorial power. Whether such a gesture also entails stepping down from a position of responsibility is a question that Coetzee has not been blind to. In "At the Gate," the last of the stories in the Costello collection, one of the judges at Costello's trial asks whether she has any opinions about children and "the Tasmanians." The question is an ethical one, as the judge reminds her: "Atrocities take place. . . . Violations of innocent children. The extermination of whole peoples" (*Costello*, 202). In response to what she interprets as a question about "historical guilt" (203), Costello states that the ancient Tasmanians are among the invisible for whom she is a secretary, though perhaps she does not qualify to be the scribe for such voices as they have not yet come to her. The story seems to suggest, however, that such questions are framed by putting the author on trial—either for what she/he does, or for what she/he fails to do. In the case of Coetzee's women, modes of literary criticism that depend on traditional notions of authorship and origin may not be best qualified to conduct such a trial.

Notes

1. First published by Princeton University Press in 1999, the two lectures that make up *The Lives of Animals* are reprinted as the third and fourth lessons of *Elizabeth Costello*.
2. See Borges, "Borges and I," 246–47.
3. In Defoe's *Roxana,* Susan is Roxana's secret name, as well as that of her daughter.
4. The original version of Leahy's argument against animal liberation runs thus: "I will mention only three areas of potential catastrophe. In the first place, a huge number of industries would be undermined, bringing the misery of unemployment to employees and their families where alternative jobs were not available. Many localities in Europe are dominated by livestock and poultry farming and vaster areas such as the states of Iowa, South Dakota and Texas are deeply involved. Argentina, Australia and New Zealand would have a considerable proportion of their national economies wiped out. Second, our social lives would need readjustment. If it is difficult to change habits like smoking or drinking, despite the best of intentions, then the switch to nut steaks and vegetable lasagne might be just as painful, and for those forced to it because of the unavailability of meat it would also be deeply resented. Most traditional French, Italian, British, American and even Oriental restaurants would cease to exist in their present

forms. Third, the idea of the European countryside, valuable to many as a source of beauty and national pride would also be transformed. Sheep would not safely graze nor would spring lambs nor calves; the average farmer could hardly be expected to stock them for old times' sake" (*Liberation*, 214).

5. Costello draws attention to the embodied being of these frogs, whose existence does not depend on whether she believes in them or not. On another level, the death and resurrection of these frogs may be a figure for the writer's own "double death," or doubling back on death, as Coetzee's use of Costello in "At the Gate" enables him to approach death in the medium of fiction.

6. Roland Barthes, who begins his famous essay with Balzac's description of a castrato dressed as a woman, describes the text as "a field without origin," "an innumerable tissue of quotations drawn from the innumerable centres of culture," claiming that "the writer can only imitate a gesture that is always anterior, never original" ("Death," 170).

7. This is not to say that Bacon did not believe in the existence of a God, for, as he said in "Of Atheism": "I had rather believe all the fables in the legends and the Talmud and the Alcoran, than that this universal frame is without a mind."

8. Izaak Walton referred to "the great secretary of Nature and all learning, Sir Francis Bacon" (*The Life of Mr. George Herbert*, 1670).

9. Similarly, Coetzee wrote and published poetry early in his career, from the 1950s until 1978. He abandoned this literary form shortly after *In the Heart of the Country* was published.

10. After watching a performance of the play, the composer Richard Strauss approached Hofmannsthal with a view to turning *Elektra* into an opera. They began collaborating in 1906, and the opera, which shocked many critics, premiered in Dresden in 1909.

Bibliography

Attwell, David. "The Naked Truth." *English in Africa* 22, no. 2 (1995): 89–98.

Barthes, Roland. "The Death of the Author." In *Modern Criticism and Theory*, edited by David Lodge, and Nigel Wood, 167–72. Harlow: Longman, 1991.

Borges, Jorge Luis. "Borges and I." In *Labyrinths: Selected Stories and Other Writings*. New York: New Directions, 1964.

Breton, André, and Louis Aragon. "The Fiftieth Anniversary of Hysteria." In *Surrealism against the Current: Tracts and Declarations*, edited by Michael Richardson and Krzysztof Fijalkowski, 143–44. London: Pluto Press, 2001.

Brinkman, Mattias. Letter to the editor. *London Review of Books* 25, no. 21 (November 6, 2003): 4.

Coetzee, J. M. *Age of Iron*. London: Penguin, 1980.

———. "The Almighty Pen." Interview by Tony Morphet. *Triquarterly* 69 (Spring/Summer 1987): 454–64.

————. *Doubling the Point: Essays and Interviews.* Edited by David Attwell. Cambridge, MA: Harvard University Press, 1992.

————. *Elizabeth Costello.* London: Secker and Warburg, 2003.

————. *Foe.* London: Penguin, 1986.

————. *In the Heart of the Country.* London: Penguin, 1982.

————. *The Lives of Animals.* Princeton: Princeton University Press, 1999.

————. *The Novel in Africa..* Occasional Papers. Berkeley: Doreen B. Townsend Center for the Humanities, University of California, 1999.

————. "Voice and Trajectory." Interview by Joanna Scott. *Salmagundi* (Spring/Summer 1997): 82–102.

Elkins, Mary. Letter to the editor. *London Review of Books* 25, no. 21 (November 6, 2003): 4.

Herford, Oliver. "Tears for Dead Fish." *Times Literary Supplement,* September 5, 2003, 6.

Hofmann, Michael. Introduction to *The Lord Chandos Letter,* by Hugo von Hofmannsthal. London: Syrens, 1995.

Hofmannsthal, Hugo von. *The Lord Chandos Letter.* Trans. Michael Hofmann. London: Syrens, 1995.

Kahane, Claire. *Passions of the Voice: Hysteria, Narrative, and the Figure of the Speaking Woman, 1850–1915.* Baltimore: John Hopkins University Press, 1995.

Leahy, Michael A. *Against Liberation: Putting Animals in Perspective.* London: Routledge, 1991.

Lee, Hermione. "The Rest Is Silence." *Guardian Review,* August 30, 2003.

Lodge, David. "Disturbing the Peace." *New York Review of Books,* November 20, 2003, 6.

Parry, Benita. "Speech and Silence in the Fictions of J. M. Coetzee." In *Critical Perspectives on J. M. Coetzee,* edited by Graham Huggan and Stephen Watson, 37–65. London: Macmillan, 1995.

Robertson, Ritchie. "Language and the Unsayable in German Thought and Poetry from Nietzsche to Celan." Paper presented at "Thinking and Speaking: A One Day Workshop on Aspects of Language," St. John's College, Oxford, January 11, 2003.

Robins, Roy. "Alter Ego." *New Statesman,* September 15, 2003, 50.

Wateridge, James. Cartoon for Herford, "Tears for Dead Fish," *TLS* 5.

Wood, James. "A Frog's Life." *London Review of Books* 25, no. 20 (October 23, 2003): 15–16.

CONTRIBUTORS

Derek Attridge is Professor of English at the University of York. He is the author or editor of a number of books on literary theory, poetics, James Joyce, and South African writing, including *Writing South Africa: Literature, Apartheid, and Democracy, 1970–1995* (Cambridge University Press, 1998) (coedited with Rosemary Jolly) and *J. M. Coetzee and the Ethics of Reading: Literature in the Event* (University of Chicago Press and University of KwaZulu-Natal Press, 2004).

David Attwell is Professor of Modern Literature at the University of York. He has published widely in anglophone African and postcolonial studies, including (with J. M. Coetzee) *Doubling the Point: Essays and Interviews* (Harvard University Press, 1992) and *J.M. Coetzee: South Africa and the Politics of Writing* (University of California Press, 1993). Recent publications include the South African contribution to the *Cambridge History of African and Caribbean Literature* (2004) and *Rewriting Modernity: Studies in Black South African Literary History* (University of KwaZulu-Natal Press, 2005).

Michael Bell is a Professor in English at the University of Warwick. He has published extensively in literary modernism and European fiction since the Enlightenment. His next book is *Open Secrets: Literature, Education and Authority from Jean Jacques Rousseau to J. M. Coetzee,* to be published by Oxford University Press in 2007.

Elleke Boehmer is Hildred Carlile Professor in Literatures in English and Director of Graduate Studies at Royal Holloway, University of London. Her most recent publications are *Stories of Women: Gender and Narrative in the Postcolonial Nation* (Manchester University Press, 2005) and the expanded tenth anniversary edition of *Colonial and Postcolonial Literature* (Oxford University Press, 2005). She is also a novelist and is currently working on a novel about haunting.

Sam Durrant is a lecturer in postcolonial literature at the University of Leeds. His research interests include trauma theory and memory as they pertain to the field of postcolonial studies. He has published on J. M. Coetzee, Wilson Harris, and Toni Morrison, and his monograph on these writers, *Postcolonial Narrative* *and the Work of Mourning*, was published by SUNY in 2003. He is currently working on a second book, titled *The Invention of Mourning in Postapartheid Literature.*

Lucy Graham is a lecturer in English, specializing in gender and postcolonial studies, at the University of Stellenbosch, South Africa, and a doctoral researcher at Lincoln College, Oxford. She has published widely on J. M. Coetzee and on contemporary South African literature in books and in journals such as the *Journal of Southern African Studies, Kunapipi,* and *Scrutiny2.*

Dominic Head is Professor of Modern English Literature at the University of Nottingham. He has published widely on twentieth-century and contemporary fiction. His books include *J. M. Coetzee* (Cambridge University Press, 1997), *Nadine Gordimer* (Cambridge University Press, 1994), and *The Cambridge Introduction to Modern British Fiction, 1950–2000* (Cambridge University Press, 2002). He is the editor of *The Cambridge Guide to Literature in English,* 3rd ed. (Cambridge University Press, 2006), and his next book, on Ian McEwan, is forthcoming from Manchester University Press.

Rosemary Jolly is Professor of Post-colonial Literatures at Queen's University, Canada. Her research interests are African literatures, postcolonial literature and theory, and gender. She has published *Colonization, Violence and Narration in White South African Writing: Breyten Breytenbach, Andre Brink, and J. M. Coetzee* (Ohio University Press and University of the Witwatersrand Press, 1996) and coedited *Writing South Africa* with Derek Attridge (Cambridge University Press, 1997). Her current projects include a manuscript on violence in South African narratives, including those of the Truth and Reconciliation Commission, and a project investigating narratives of those contending with the HIV/AIDS epidemic and gender-based violence in rural KwaZulu-Natal.

Michael Marais is Associate Professor in English at Rhodes University, Grahamstown, South Africa. He edits *English in Africa* and is interested in contemporary South African fiction. He has published widely on J. M. Coetzee and ethics.

Peter D. McDonald is a Fellow of St Hugh's College and a Lecturer at the University of Oxford. His research interests include literary modernism, the history of the book, and cultural production. He is the coeditor of a special issue on J. M. Coetzee's *Disgrace* in *Interventions* (with Derek Attridge) (2002); coeditor of *Mak-*

ing Meaning: "Printers of the Mind" and Other Essays by D. F. McKenzie (with Michael Suarez) (University of Massachusetts Press, 2002); and author of *British Literary Culture and Publishing Practice, 1880–1914* (Cambridge University Press, 1997).

Jane Poyner is a lecturer in postcolonial literature at the University of Exeter. She has published on J. M. Coetzee and postcolonial literature, and her monograph on Coetzee, *J. M. Coetzee and the Paradox of Postcolonial Authorship*, is forthcoming from Ashgate. She is currently working on a book about intellectual practice in contemporary South African fiction, *Writing under Pressure: The Ethics of Intellectual Practice in Apartheid and Postapartheid South Africa*.

Laura Wright is Assistant Professor of Postcolonial and World Literature at Western Carolina University. Her research interests include Southern and Western African literature, performance studies, and environmental literature. She has published in *The Journal of Commonwealth and Postcolonial Studies, The Journal of Dramatic Theory and Criticism, Mosaic*, and elsewhere. Her book *Writing "Out of all the Camps": J. M. Coetzee's Narratives of Displacement* was published by Routledge in 2006.

INDEX

abjection, 130–31, 137–39, 143–45, 152
absolution. *See* confession and absolution
Achebe, Chinua, 13
Achterberg, Gerrit, 230
Adams, Carol J., 208
African National Congress (ANC), 3–4, 8, 12, 78, 115, 149
Afrikaner National Party, 8, 115
Age of Iron (Coetzee), 15n.1; allegory in, 64, 78; bearing witness in, 125–26; belief in, 175; birth images in, 221–22; confession in, 102–103; contrition in, 137; cultural/racial others in, 232; death in, 64, 78, 125–26, 222; dreams in, 124–25; Dreyfus affair in, 6; excess of closure in, 96; historical choices in, 85; literal readings of, 78; public intellectuals in, 33; responsibility for others in, 96; silence in, 126; speaking truth in, 86; supplementarity/rivalry of history and literature in, 86; sympathetic imagination in, 118–19, 124–26, 130; women's voices in, 15, 175, 203, 219
allegory, 10–11, 63–82, 102–4; in *Age of Iron*, 64, 78; in *Disgrace*, 78–79, 80n.4, 81n.16, 106–8, 172; in *Elizabeth Costello*, 114–15; in *Foe*, 65, 122, 203; in *In the Heart of the Country*, 45, 80n.4, 203; in *Life & Times of Michael K*, 51, 64, 72–76, 105–106; postcolonialism and, 66; in *Waiting for the Barbarians*, 66, 68–72, 103
ANC. *See* African National Congress
animal rights, 109–10, 112, 141, 173, 200–2, 208–10. *See also* species boundaries; vegetarianism
apartheid regime: legacy of, 211; legislation, 17n.13, 18n.14; resistance literature and, 8–11, 21; self-censorship or complicity and, 11, 46, 48–49, 51, 53, 100–101, 103, 109. *See also* censors and censorship
Aragon, Louis, 230
Attridge, Derek, 10, 104–6, 108, 148–49, 194, 204
Attwell, David, 5–7, 9–10, 60n.7, 80n.2, 139–140, 153, 197, 203, 230

Bacon, Francis, 226, 228–29
"Ballade van de Gasfitter" (Achterberg), 230
Barthes, Roland, 13, 16n.2, 234n.5

Bauman, Zygmunt, 29
bearing witness, 125–26, 138
belief: in *Age of Iron*, 175; authority of fiction and, 14, 114–15, 132; Costello and, 114–15, 186, 212, 218, 222, 224–25; in *Life & Times of Michael K*, 75–76
Bell, Michael, 14, 197–198
Ben Belitt Lecture (Bennington College). *See* "What is Realism?"
Benda, Julien, 6–7, 28
Benjamin, Walter, 66, 131, 137–38, 146n.3
Biko, Stephen, 8, 68, 155
birth images, 219–22
black writing, 8–9, 60n.4
Blanchot, Maurice, 85, 91, 93–94
Boehmer, Elleke, 12–13
Borges, Jorge Luis, 219
Bourdieu, Pierre, 29, 32–33
Boyhood (Coetzee), 4, 32, 194–95, 198
Breton, André, 230
Breuer, Josef, 231
Breytenbach, Breyten, 8
Briganti, Chiari, 80n.4
Briggs, Austin, 202
Brinkman, Mattias, 218
"Burrow, The" (Kafka), 80n.11
Butler, Guy, 60n.4
Butler, Judith, 196, 198–99, 207

Carl Friedrich von Siemens Foundation Lecture, 34
Caruth, Cathy, 124, 125–26
Cavafy, Constantine, 15n.1
censors and censorship, 5, 8, 16n.2, 18n.16, 26–27, 35, 42–62
Chapman, Michael, 83–84
Clingman, Stephen, 52, 195
Coetzee, J. M.: on autobiography, 16n.2; on criticism and critics, 5, 22, 30–31, 52, 79, 104–5; early life and career of, 3, 44; genre, use of, by, 196; on intellectuals, 2, 5, 21–24; interviews with, 4, 21–24, 53, 59n.3, 60nn.4, 7, 80n.3, 104, 113, 122, 133n.6, 174, 194, 202, 221, 231; move to Australia by, 3, 17n.4, 24, 115, 116n.8; poetry and, 234n.8; private-public spheres, tensions in, 2–7, 10–12, 14, 21–23, 25–41, 52–53, 56, 58, 125, 137, 181, 194–195, 202;

in, 37, 140–41; violence in, 109, 112–14;
women's voices in, 14–15, 201, 206, 210,
219, 226–31. *See also* Costello, Elizabeth
(fictional character)
Elkins, Mary, 218
embodiedness, 152–55, 204; in *Disgrace,* 137,
145, 153; in *The Lives of Animals,* 111,
126–29, 195–96, 199–200, 207–8, 213
"Emerging from Censorship" (Coetzee),
42–43
Émile (Rousseau), 175, 186
engaged writing, 29, 55, 60. *See also* committed literature, movement for
Erasmus, Desiderius, 34–36, 60n.7, 84, 94
"Erasmus: Madness and Rivalry" (Coetzee),
28, 32–36, 84, 94

Felman, Shoshana, 39n.4
feminism, 203, 206
Fensham, F. C., 45, 48
fiction, authority of, 25, 34, 56, 59; belief in
"believes in" and, 14, 114–15, 132, 225;
truth telling and, 5, 14, 23, 63, 71, 79,
108–9, 135, 139–40, 173, 177, 190n.2, 202,
212, 225, 228–29. *See also* literature, as
supplement/rival to history
Fielding, Henry, 183
Fish, Stanley, 54–55, 57–58
Flaubert, Gustave, 32
Foe (Coetzee), 15n.1; allegory and, 65, 122,
203; birth images in, 221–22; censorship
and, 48; cultural/racial others in, 140, 232;
death in, 88, 122; dreams in, 122–24;
metafictional style of, 10, 221, 227; reception of, 83–84, 195; responsibility for others in, 97, 138, 140; sympathetic
imagination in, 120, 122–24; women's
voices in, 15, 203, 219, 227
Foucault, Michel, 28, 39n.4, 120
Freud, Sigmund, 122–23, 124, 231
Frye, Northrop, 65

Gaita, Raimond, 107–8, 110
Garber, Marjorie, 34, 190nn.2, 13
gender: atonement and, 137, 145–46; in *Disgrace,* 13, 159–61, 164–65, 199, 204, 208;
in *The Lives of Animals,* 196–98, 201–2,
205–9, 224; narrative voice and, 203–4,
231–33; rants and, 196–97, 206, 209; sympathetic imagination and, 198
Genet, Jean, 34
Girard, René, 39n.4
Giving Offense: Essays on Censorship (Coetzee),
2, 16n.2, 42, 140, 146n.2
Gonin, F. C., 48

Gordimer, Nadine, 4, 8–9, 13, 21, 27, 60nn.3–4,
153, 168n.12
grace, 140
Graham, Lucy, 14, 132n.1, 133n.7
Gramsci, Antonio, 1, 6, 28–29
Gruen, Lori, 208–0
Gulliver's Travels (Swift), 132
Gutmann, Amy, 200

Hacking, Ian, 175, 177
Hardy, Thomas, 108
Hartman, Geoffrey, 129
Head, Dominic, 10, 11, 197
Hegelian dialectic, 95–96
Herford, Oliver, 218
history: consciousness of, 31–32, 38; criticism
and, 83–84; literature as supplement/rival
to, 7, 27–28, 34, 52–53, 55–58, 84–89,
93–94, 94, 105; otherness beyond, 11, 85,
89, 92, 96–98
Hofmann, Michael, 226
Hofmannsthal, Hugo von, 226–29, 231
Holocaust comparisons: in *Disgrace,* 189; in
Elizabeth Costello, 150–51; in *The Lives of
Animals,* 110, 112, 131, 150–51, 175–76,
183–85, 187, 196–97, 209–10
Hughes, Ted, 111, 129, 177–78
Humanities in Africa, The (Coetzee), 34
humanity/humanism, 12, 148–71; in *Disgrace,*
141–42, 150–51, 153–54, 167; in *Elizabeth
Costello,* 113; in *The Lives of Animals,* 129,
150–51, 157–59, 166, 176–78, 180; species
boundaries and, 10, 150–59, 176–78,
180–81, 208; in Truth and Reconciliation
Commission hearings, 155–57; violence
against women and, 166–67; in *Waiting
for the Barbarians,* 151–52
Hutcheon, Linda, 10
hypermasculinities, 13, 160–61, 164–65
hysteria, 208, 210, 230–31

Ignatieff, Michael, 211
intellectuals: Coetzee on, 2, 5, 21–24; role of,
6–8, 13, 25–26, 28–29, 32–34, 38, 194,
199–200, 210–11; South African writing
and, 8–11; and truth, 5–7, 26, 34–35, 221.
See also Costello, Elizabeth
In the Heart of the Country (Coetzee), 15n.1; allegory in, 45, 80n.4, 203; birth images in,
220–21; censorship reports on, 45, 48, 50,
51; death in, 220–21; hysteria in, 230; literal
readings of, 80n.4; mediation in, 225–26;
narrative voice in, 14–15, 102, 219, 230; as a
philosophical drama, 36; universality of, 51;
violence against women in, 50, 102

"Into the Dark Chamber" (Coetzee), 48–49, 56, 84, 89
irony, 92, 94–95, 151–52

Jameson, Fredric, 65, 66
Janes, Regina, 204
Jolly, Rosemary, 12–13
Joyce, James, 119, 179, 202, 220
Jude the Obscure (Hardy), 108

Kafka, Franz, 80n.11, 109, 157–58, 180–81, 212, 224–25
Kahane, Claire, 230
Kant, Immanuel, 129
knowledge, 107, 120–23, 176
Köhler, Wolfgang, 127, 157–59, 180–81
Kristeva, Julia, 123–24, 130–31, 147n.10

Lacan, Jacques, 37, 39n.4, 122–25
Lawrence, D. H., 176, 177–85
Lazarus, Neil, 9–10
Leahy, Michael, 183, 223
Lee, Hermione, 218
Levinas, Emmanuel, 92, 96, 137, 147n.10, 152, 153
Life & Times of Michael K (Coetzee), 15n.1; allegory in, 51, 64, 72–76, 105–6; belief in, 75–76; censorship reports on, 45, 48, 50, 51; ecological sensitivity in, 74–75; embodiedness in, 128; historical choices in, 85; narrative voice in, 73–76, 119; nonposition in, 83–84; sympathetic imagination in, 120, 121, 129; textual meaning in, 105–106; universality of, 51
Lighton, Reginald, 45–50
literal readings, 10, 65–68, 76–79, 104–105; of *Age of Iron*, 78; of "The Burrow" (Kafka), 80n.11; of *Disgrace*, 78–79, 80n.4; of *In the Heart of the Country*, 80n.4; of *Life & Times of Michael K*, 64, 72–76; of *Waiting for the Barbarians*, 66, 68–72
literature: definitions of, 54–55, 57; as dreaming, 122; and an otherness beyond history, 11, 85, 89, 92, 96–98; as privileged aesthetic space, 7–8, 49–53, 58; singularity of, 67; as supplement/rival to history, 7, 27–28, 34, 52–53, 55–58, 84–89, 93–94, 94, 105; universality and, 50–51, 57–58; writing, act of, and, 25, 39n.4, 43, 49, 64, 90–95, 97, 98n.4, 218–219
Lives of Animals, The (Coetzee): abjection in, 138; death in, 128–29, 132; ecological sensitivity in, 109, 112; embodiedness in, 111, 126–29, 195–96, 199–200, 207–8; gender in, 14–15, 196–98, 201–2, 205–9, 224; Holocaust comparisons in, 110, 112, 131, 150–51,

175–76, 183–85, 187, 196–97, 209–10; humanity in, 129, 150–51, 157–59, 166, 176–78, 180; mimesis in, 131–32; performativity in, 34, 195–96, 198–200, 207–8; rants in, 14, 196–97, 205–6; reason in, 110–12, 114, 126–27, 140–41, 158–59, 206, 208, 228; reflections on, 36, 133n.10, 190n.2, 197, 218; republication of, 2, 173–74, 223; style and structure of, 173–176, 188, 196; sympathetic imagination in, 36, 110–11, 118, 121–22, 126–29, 131–32, 140–41, 166–67, 177–78, 180–82, 186, 196–99, 211, 213. *See also* Costello, Elizabeth (fictional character); *Elizabeth Costello*
Lodge, David, 217
Lord Chandos Letter, The (Hofmannsthal), 226–29, 231
Lord Jim (Conrad), 187
Louw, Anna, 45, 50, 51, 53
Lowry, Elizabeth, 102

Macaskill, Brian, 80n.4
madness, 34–36, 84, 93, 206
Magona, Sindiwe, 211
Mann, Thomas, 175
Marais, Michael, 11, 137, 146, 153, 162, 195
Master of Petersburg, The (Coetzee), 16n.1, 83–99; confession in, 103; death in, 11, 85, 88–91; excess of closure in, 96; irony and, 92, 94–95; metafictional style in, 10; Orpheus myth in, 90–91; public intellectuals in, 33; responsibility for others in, 97; supplementarity/rivalry of history and literature in, 11, 85–89, 93–94; writing in, 90–93
McDonald, Peter D., 5, 7–8, 80n.4
Merwe Scholtz, H. van der, 45
Mgojo, Khoza M., 155
Michael, John, 29
Milosz, Czeslaw, 224
mimesis, 131–32, 212
Morphet, Tony, 202, 221
movement for committed literature. *See* committed literature, movement for
Mulhern, Francis, 56–57

Nagel, Thomas, 127, 177–78, 180
narrative voice: in *Age of Iron*, 15, 175, 203, 219; in *Boyhood*, 4, 198; in *Disgrace*, 198–99; in *Foe*, 15, 203, 219, 227; in *In the Heart of the Country*, 14–15, 102, 219, 230; hysteria and, 208, 210, 230–31; in *Life & Times of Michael K*, 73–76, 119; in *Waiting for the Barbarians*, 70, 74; women's voices as, 14–15, 203, 210, 217–35; in *Youth*, 4, 198
Nature of Sympathy, The (Scheler), 181–82
Ndebele, Njabulo, 9

WITHDRAWN